No Easy Answers

Lawnce mulled it all over for a moment. Too many things didn't make sense. Why had that boy wanted so badly to risk his skin in a duel with the desperado?

Gainey smirked as he saw Lawnce puzzling. "I want to congratulate you, Lawnce. You didn't have the balls it took to face Maximo so you had your boy do it for you. I heard how it happened. You got Maximo all oiled up inside and then sent your boy after him with his rat pistol. And damned if he can't shoot straight with it after all!"

Lawnce felt his lip twitching under his mustache. He threw Gainey's engraved Colt into the corner, unbuckled his gun belt and threw his pistol on top of Gainey's. "I always wondered how hard a man your size would fall."

Books by Mike Blakely

Vendetta Gold
The Glory Trail

Published by HarperPaperbacks

ATTENTION: ORGANIZATIONS AND CORPORATIONS

Most HarperPaperbacks are available at special quantity discounts for bulk purchases for sales promotions, premiums, or fund-raising. For information, please call or write:
Special Markets Department, HarperCollins*Publishers*,
10 East 53rd Street, New York, N.Y. 10022.
Telephone: (212) 207-7528. Fax: (212) 207-7222.

THE GLORY TRAIL

MIKE BLAKELY

HarperPaperbacks
A Division of HarperCollinsPublishers

This is a work of fiction. The characters, incidents, and dialogues are products of the author's imagination and are not to be construed as real. Any resemblance to actual events or persons, living or dead, is entirely coincidental.

HarperPaperbacks   *A Division of* HarperCollins*Publishers*
10 East 53rd Street, New York, N.Y. 10022

Cover illustration by Harry Schaare

First printing: January 1990
Special edition printing: April 1996

Printed in the United States of America

HarperPaperbacks and colophon are trademarks of HarperCollins*Publishers*

10 9 8 7 6 5 4 3 2 1

To the memory of my brother, James Perry Blakely

Acknowledgments

I wish to thank Joe Vallely and Ed Breslin for gambling on the dark horses.

Also Doc, Patricia Dawn, Odell, and Jim B. Blakely for telling old stories.

1

In his thirty-nine years Lawnce McCrary had rubbed more tobacco into his eyes than some men could chew in a lifetime. Of course, he had chewed more than some men could chop, but chewing tobacco and chopping it made sense. Rubbing it in one's eyes, on the other hand, went against all the world's notions of natural behavior. But fatigue was tilting him in the saddle now, and the trail was getting rougher, switching back on itself, slanting down to the Rio Grande. He knew only one way to stay awake on this last leg of his ride and that was to rub the tobacco in under his eyelids.

By the time he dropped below the rim of the canyon, the tobacco was stinging like turpentine on a rope burn. Its fire leapt in the ranger's eyeballs and lashed back into his skull. It streaked through his shoulders and down his arms, tightening his grip on the reins. It shot down through his legs and locked his boot heels against the stirrups.

Lawnce lost Mexico behind the burning tears, but the mustang knew the trail. He squinted and listened to the creaking of saddle leather and the odd rhythm of Little Satan's hooves as they searched for footing, and finally he began to hear the rush of the Rio Grande. Though the tobacco had burned the idea of sleep out of his head, Lawnce still entertained contemplations of drink—water at the river and whiskey in Candelilla—and by the time his eyes had cooled enough to open, they found the blurred glisten of the border winding through a canyon pass.

At the threshold to Texas, Little Satan plunged his parched muzzle in to the bits. Lawnce swung low to dip his straw sombrero beneath the surface. He let a draft of sandy river water slip past the chaw in his jowls, then poured the rest over his head. He wrung the water from his mustache quills and shook his uneven crop of hair like a camp dog shaking off a pail of scalding water. The hot tobacco and the cool water had tempered his wits. He was now alert as ever.

Lawnce sat in the saddle a moment, thinking how pleasant it was to hear a horse sucking water after a long, dry ride. Then, beyond a bend upstream, something caught his eye. He had to blink hard to bring into focus the sizable group of figures under the cottonwoods on the Texas side. The Doubletree cowhands were there with their boss, One-Eyed Butch Gainey. Lawnce saw the squat mustangs of the cowboys standing next to Gainey's big Kentucky mare. He saw the massive humped shoulders of Gainey in the shade. When one cowpoke tossed a rawhide lariat over a tree limb, Lawnce knew the laws of Texas, and somebody's neck, were about to get stretched.

The little black mustang heaved in and became stiff-legged when Lawnce slid his Spencer rifle from the saddle scabbard. The ranger liked to boast that Little Satan held his breath to provide a steadier shot. In truth, the horse knew from experience how much noise a .52-caliber rifle could make and that such a blast usually followed the procedure of removing the Spencer from its boot. His lungs, as well as the rest of him, were frozen in horrific anticipation.

Lawnce believed in caliber for sidearms, too, and carried a big iron on his left hip, butt forward, in the crossdraw position. It was an old .46-caliber Remington re-

volver converted from cap-and-ball to take metal cartridges. He could have replaced both weapons with more
modern ones—a Colt revolver and a Winchester rifle that
would both use the same .44-40 cartridges—but in neither
case could he approve of the step down in caliber. Bore
meant more than accuracy, velocity, and rapidity of fire
to Lawnce McCrary.

"When they look at the hole in my muzzle, they take
a buck ague," he would say to critics of his obsolete arms.
"It makes 'em workable as a lassoed calf. That way I don't
have to waste powder and lead shootin' 'em. I like a bore
big enough to shoot pear-apples for bullets."

Spurs in his flanks started Little Satan's breath again.
Lawnce urged him across the river, where the legacies of
Spain and England clashed, over to Texas, and up under
the cottonwoods.

"Where in hell did you come from?" demanded One-
Eyed Butch Gainey in surprise, one paw propped on a
pearl handle. He had so much tobacco in his cheek that
he looked like a bull with a bad case of the lumpy jaw.
He was fat and getting old. His ears seemed to rest on his
shoulders, and his dark Stetson hid whatever his eye
might have betrayed. That cold orb, when it rarely caught
the light, looked like a pistol slug, gray-black and set deep
in the splotched, ruddy face.

Any civilized man would have worn a patch over the
empty socket. But Gainey enjoyed the intimidating effect
the sunken wound had on folks when he tipped his hat
back, so he left it uncovered.

Lawnce walked Little Satan up next to Gainey's Kentucky racehorse and, cocking its side hammer, cradled
his Spencer across his left arm. "Slack that gutline," he
ordered.

A Mexican boy no older than fourteen stood on the toes
of his moccasins to keep the reata from choking off his

air. He gagged piteously as two gaunt cowboys held the rope taut. The boy's eyes looked desperately to the ranger.

"Slack it!" Lawnce said.

"Oh, hell, Lawnce," One-Eyed Butch said, "he ain't nothing but a greaser. Anyhow, we don't mean to kill him."

"Rope kills sure as guns," Lawnce said. "Except it goes on instead of off. Let him down."

The Mexican boy began to sway on his toes, and blood flushed his features above the rawhide noose around his neck. Gainey chuckled, scratched, and shook his head.

"I'm just trying to do your job, McCrary. This little bean-eater is bound to know something about Maximo and his rustlers, and I aim to find out what it is. Any other ranger would be holding the rope for me."

"For all I know, you're a rustler much as Maximo," Lawnce said. He reached behind him and slapped his palm against the flap of his saddlebag. "And I got me a book called *The Revised Statutes of Texas* in my saddle pocket that outlaws the general public from shakin' out loops for human beans. If that boy don't draw fresh air quicker than hell can scorch a guinea feather, I aim to start enforcin' the Revised Statutes."

Gainey spit tobacco and stuck his thumbs under his gun belt. His hands disappeared under the roll of his stomach. The strangling Mexican boy was still swinging behind him. "Now, Lawnce," he said, "I know you had just enough schoolin' to read that law book of yours, but I think you missed a few cipherin' lessons." Gainey was smiling, but his mouth hung open the way it always did, reminding Lawnce of the mouth on a fat catfish gasping in the sun on a riverbank. "You see," he continued, "we got the odds against you about seven to one, and some of these boys can blast the balls off a pronghorn goat on a dead run."

Lawnce shrugged. The threats didn't move him in the least. He had a knack for figuring every man's weakness and had already found Gainey's in his Kentucky mare, which he treasured more than life for all humanity. The ranger shifted in his saddle and casually let the muzzle of his rifle drop about a foot. "If that boy's heels don't touch Texas quick," he said, "ol' Top Dollar's run her last race."

The smirk left Gainey's tobacco-stained lips as he saw the barrel of the big Spencer rifle pointing at his prized thoroughbred's neck. He knew Ranger McCrary would not hesitate to shoot a horse—not even a Kentucky race-horse in mustang country. Lawnce had lived with Comanches as a boy and still held to their views as far as horses were concerned. The Indians worshiped the horse as a species but gave no concern whatever to the suffering of an individual animal.

"Let the greaser down," Gainey grumbled.

As he hit the ground gasping, tears poured from the Mexican boy's eyes. Lawnce ordered one of the Double-tree hands to put the boy on Little Satan behind him. He backed his mustang out of the cottonwoods and then blazed a new trail through the Spanish dagger and creosote bush, up the canyon for the village of Candelilla.

Butch Gainey was heard a mile up and down the Rio Grande valley cussing the day of Lawnce McCrary's birth.

If August Dannenberg had known his boss was nearby that afternoon, he might not have made such deliberate plans, but he thought Lawnce was somewhere across the river on Maximo's trail. He grinned as he inspected the inside of the McCrary Livery Stables. The burlap feed bags had holes gnawed in every corner. Grain had spilled in tiny avalanches across the rawhide lumber flooring. It was time for a rat shoot!

August hustled across the barn to the tack room. Over the little cot where he spent his nights, his gun belt and holster and .32-caliber Smith & Wesson revolver hung on a wooden peg. He propped open a window for light and worked the belt and homemade holster over with saddle soap.

The gun was just a secondhand pocket pistol August had won off a Mexican cowboy in a bronc-riding contest. But the holster bespoke innovation. August fancied it made him something of a gunslinger. Calfskin lined the sleeve of the holster, making a slick draw easy, and the holster tilted forward on the belt to facilitate a smooth circular upswing of the barrel.

He dusted his hat, shook the hay stalks out of his clothing, and before buckling the shooting iron around his waist, tucked in his shirt, a threadbare plaid with long handles. He wiped the manure from his boots on a stack of empty burlap bags.

He wanted to look good. Between purchasing his cartridges and shooting the rats, he had an image to mold down on the Rio Grande.

There were half a dozen good horses belonging to Lawnce McCrary in his stable, but August singled out the old livery mule. It was a rule imposed by Lawnce that August ride the mule, bareback, when he traveled anywhere alone.

"No need temptin' the Injuns with good horseflesh and fancy leather," Lawnce had warned.

"But the treaty," August had argued. "They promised not to steal no stock."

"Injuns ain't no more good for keepin' treaties than gringos, kid. If you don't want the Injuns to strop your rump against a cactus, just do what I tell you. Ride the mule and maybe you'll grow to make a fine man."

The problem was, August, at eighteen years of age, considered himself already grown. And as for becoming a man, he was getting more desperate to prove he was up to that, too—with guns or girls or maybe even both. But for the time being, he stuck to Lawnce's rules. He rode the mule, whose name was Quatro.

Quatro was a beast of some notoriety on the Big Bend, though not a handsome specimen by any means. Lawnce had a contract to provide the overland stage company with mules, and he had fallen into the habit of branding all the mules he bought for the company with his own sign—a single character known as the Lonesome J. The name of the brand came from his nickname—Lonesome John McCrary. Of course, across the tongues of frontiersmen, the handle meandered into a thing that sounded like Lawnce-um John. Economy of speech had abbreviated it to Lawnce.

Occasionally Lawnce would buy a mule in Chihuahua that already wore the Lonesome J. Indians were constantly stealing the mules from the stage stations and running them off to sell in Mexico, where Lawnce would buy them again. Whenever he found a mule already wearing the Lonesome J, he always went ahead and branded it again. The overland stage company owned quite a few mules that had double J's burned into their hides. A few had triples. But Quatro was the only mule who had survived four brandings. After branding him the fourth time, Lawnce had named him for the Spanish number four and retired him to McCrary Livery.

It was this ugly beast with the four J's that August mounted and rode up the street to the Candelilla General Mercantile Store. He crumpled the crown of his hat into his hand as he entered. "Howdy, Mr. Grimes," he said to the man behind the counter.

Grimes noticed the gun belt slung around August's angular hips. "Must be time to shoot the rats again, huh, Augie?"

"Yes, sir."

"How many cartridges you want this time? A dozen?"

"Better give me eighteen or so, Mr. Grimes. I can pay as soon as Lawnce gets his ranger pay with the mail."

"Eighteen cartridges! Goodness, boy! The rats must be takin' over the livery business! And don't worry about the bill. Your credit's good here."

"Thank you, sir," August said.

Grimes made a big show of counting .32-caliber shells over the counter in half-dozens. "This time be sure to warn ol' Lawnce before the shootin' starts," he advised. "You know how jumpy he gets around gunplay. Even with that popgun of yours."

August turned red around the ears and hitched his belt up over one hip. He should have become accustomed to the storekeeper's gibes long ago. Grimes had taught him his letters and arithmetic and let him borrow a few books, but August had never liked the constant teasing. "Lawnce ain't in town," he said. "He's been out two days after rustlers. Somebody run off a hundred head of Doubletree yearlin's."

" 'Somebody,' your hat," Grimes said. "Everybody knows that Maximo and his boys rustled them beeves. Every time Maximo leaves Texas, so does a herd of Doubletree cattle. That ain't no coincidence and Lawnce knows it. Any other ranger would have arranged Maximo a necktie sociable by now."

August was scraping cartridges from the sales counter into his pocket. "Well, Lawnce says the Revised Statutes don't allow no lynchin's, even for Mexicans."

"I ain't complainin'!" Grimes said. "Ol' Lawnce keeps things pretty quiet around here. Damnedest thing is that treaty. You ain't never lived outside of this town, Augie, and you don't realize that there ain't another town in Texas that's got wild Indians fightin' with 'em instead of against 'em. At least not Apaches. Maybe some Delawares and Tonkaways. The only trouble we ever get around here seems to be Maximo shootin' one of Gainey's hired guns every now and then. And, hell, we've got to have some entertainment of a evenin'!" Grimes laughed and pounded his counter.

"Yes, sir," August said, turning toward the door. "Thanks for the cartridges."

"Sure thing, Augie. I'll tell my customers you're gonna shoot rats again so they won't think you're cookin' popcorn in there!" Grimes laughed and pounded the counter some more as August grinned in embarrassment and left.

Just before he slung himself across Quatro's bony withers, he spotted a tempting stalk of grass sticking out from under the boardwalk in front of Grimes's store. August had studied grass most of his life and knew the value of a sweet stem when his mouth felt woolly. He even believed he could identify different grasses by flavor alone. It helped him understand horses better, he thought, but few other folks appreciated his talent for tasting the subtle variances in grass species.

Lawnce didn't even like to hear about it. "If you keep braggin' about grazin' that way, some fool cow waddie'll round you up and earmark you," he would say. "Just think how ignorant you'll look with a swallowfork cut in your ear. And you'll git damn lucky if they don't make mountain oysters out of your balls while they got you throwed and hog-tied."

August reached down and pulled at the seed tassels of the sprout, easing the moist inner stalk out with a squeak. He stuck it between his teeth. A straw sticking out of August's mouth seemed as much a part of his face as his nose.

He tucked his shirt back into his pants and put a fresh crease in his crumpled hat. He tried to imagine what he would look like through another's eyes. The little pane of glass in the store window had so much dust on it that August might just as well have tried grooming by his reflection in a damp mud fence. There wasn't a looking glass in town except behind the bar at the Pitchfork Saloon, a place Lawnce didn't allow him to frequent. So he adjusted the tilt of his hat by looking at his shadow on the street and swung his stride across the bare back of the old mule.

2

Chepita Ybarra smiled into the sky when she heard the guttural squawk of her friend the heron. The long-legged bird unfolded her neck and stretched her feet downward as she landed in the shallows of an eddy.

Chepita thought she was like the heron in some ways. She spent much of her time with her feet in the Rio Grande, like Señora Heron. She possessed patience, like the motionless bird waiting for a minnow to swim within reach of her lancet bill. She admired the willowy grace of the heron, and she was also slender, if not as long-limbed as the bird.

But Chepita could only envy the ability of Señor Heron to spread her great bluish wings and soar away to calmer waters. There was no Mexico or Texas or trouble the bird could not escape on the wing. She smiled as the heron struck like a snake at the water.

Spreading a cotton shirt over a rock in the river, Chepita wondered where the señora would fly next. Birds were the leaves of her calendar and the hands of her clock. Her day began with the brash song of the mockingbird. She walked to the river with the roadrunners and moved almost as quickly as they, though she was more graceful and dovelike. The end of her summer came on the wings of early teal who paddled among the reeds and cattails of the river, and her spring arrived each year to the tune of the scissortail's chatter.

The birds were her solace and her only friends. No one

came near Chepita except to give her a pile of dirty clothes. Most of the time the wives gave her the laundry without looking at her or speaking to her, as if she were a fixture or a piece of furniture. They wouldn't let their husbands bring the wash, afraid Chepita's beauty would tempt them, for men were weak. The wives could not even count on their husbands' fear of Maximo de Guerra to keep them away from Chepita.

A man had put his hands on Chepita one day, and Maximo had beaten him to the ground with an iron poker. After that, other men tended to look away from her, to prevent her beauty from bringing out their lascivious nature. It wasn't easy for them to look away. They could imagine the pleasures Maximo experienced in her arms. But they could also imagine the agonies he could inflict with a poker. So they looked away from Chepita and resented her for her unapproachable beauty almost as much as their wives resented her for tempting them. She often thought how odd it was to be shunned simply because she was Maximo's woman. He was a hero to the Mexican people along the river. She was regarded as a common whore.

The river was pleasant, though, and away from the streets of the village. There was some shade there, patches of willow and cottonwood. She could watch her birds and dream of the peaceful valleys they crossed on the wing. It pleased her to spend her days there even if her back ached from beating clothes against the rocks. By evening she, too, felt cleansed as she carried her basket back to town on her head. She bore the load with the same effortless grace the tufted quail used in carrying the frail teardrop plumes that arched from their heads.

Chepita saw the heron bolt suddenly for the sky. Something had displeased the bird, so she had left for more peaceful shallows. She honked and squawked with every stroke of her great wings. Chepita watched expectantly, hoping to witness the bird's most amusing behavior. The heron did not disappoint her. With one last croak, she shot a stream of whitish excrement out from under her tail feathers, as if to sum up her opinion of the trodden earth.

Chepita, already tickled, looked toward Candelilla and saw who had worried Señora Heron. It was August. She smiled a little wider and rolled her eyes at the spectacle. It was time to shoot the rats again and time for August's ridiculous routine. He came riding to the river, as he did before every rat shoot, with his hat cocked at an outlandish angle, a straw sticking out of his mouth, and his little pistol bouncing on his thigh. He looked so peculiar riding bareback on his old mule that Chepita wanted to laugh out loud, but she couldn't bear to hurt his feelings.

She was standing in the shallows when August rode by. Her skirts were tucked up above her knees, and he could see her calves glistening with river water. He felt a hopeless, aching sensation that had become all too familiar to him. He rode near her as if he had somewhere important to go, tipped his hat, then circled back toward town.

Chepita nodded politely, then giggled uncontrollably as August rode out of earshot. How could he be so shy with girls, she wondered, yet choke down the wildest of broncos in the livery corral without fear? She wanted to invite him to talk with her at the river, but she wouldn't risk that. Maximo would drag the stable boy through a cactus patch if he saw them together. She let him ride back toward Candelilla without any further encouragement.

The mule-and-pistol show always left August feeling foolish, and he tended to blame Quatro. "You dang ugly old son of a jack," he said, giving the mule a vicious kick with his boot heels as he rode back toward town. He

looked over his shoulder, but instead of a last glimpse of
the lithe figure of Chepita he saw, to his utter disgust, dust
rising over the flats across the river and the mirage-like
figures of many riders.

Maximo. A stable boy's weapon would look like a popgun compared to his brace of nickel-plated Colts. His fa-
bled black sombrero, banded with silver medallions,
would make August's headgear look like a flop hat. And
of course Quatro would hardly fare favorably next to the
Spanish stallion Maximo would surely be riding. The
tooled saddle, the silver bridle, the flowing mustache—
they would all mock the desperate air August tried so
hard to exude.

He cussed his mule and bounced toward Candelilla.

Chepita called Maximo's name when she saw the riders
approaching. She gathered laundry into her basket. His
arrival meant her work was done for the day. She
watched as Maximo led the dozen riders, standing in his
stirrups and jerking at the reins. Coyote-lean and snake-
quick, he splashed into the Rio Grande and let his horse
walk to the Texas side, muzzling the water's surface. He
was small, but he could move with the strength and fury
of a mountain lion when he was in a bad humor. And with
Maximo, moods could come and go like flies.

"*Venga,* Chaparita!" he shouted to the laundry girl as
she ran to him. Like Lawnce McCrary, he was two days
in the saddle. But Maximo was in his physical prime,
twenty-eight years old and indefatigable. Chepita rose as
effortlessly as Señora Heron when he lifted her onto his
saddle skirt with one arm. He ordered a vaquero to carry
her laundry basket. The rider picked it up at a full run.

Chepita wrapped her arms around Maximo's waist as
they trotted toward Candelilla. "Thank God you are safe,"
she said. "How many cattle did you get?"

"Noventa y tres," Maximo said. "But five of them died running south the first night. Don Lawnce was close behind."

"Do we have enough now?" she asked. "When will we return to Mexico?"

Maximo's mood darkened instantly. "We will not go back until Maximo has revenge. Cattle are nothing. El Ojo must pay with his life."

Chepita rested her cheek against Maximo's shoulder. It was sweet to see him safe again but bitter to hear the words of hatred that crossed his lips.

3

By the time Little Satan loped into Candelilla, the Mexican boy was bouncing on the saddle skirt and laughing despite the noose burns around his neck. Lawnce asked in broken Spanish which shack he called home, and the boy pointed the way.

"Put some turpentine on that rope burn," he said as the boy slid down from Little Satan. Turpentine answered all of Lawnce's medicinal needs. Around his neck he wore a bandanna, which he soaked regularly in turpentine to ward off colds and fevers. He often smelled of turpentine and almost always of sweat.

At McCrary Livery the ranger grumbled at August's absence. "What in thunder do I pay that youngun for anyhow?" he asked himself as he filled a feed bag, though he hadn't paid August in months. After tending to Little Satan he trudged next door to the cantina called Las Quince Letras for a long-awaited swallow of tanglefoot firewater.

"*Cómo está*, Santos?" he said as he parted the rickety doors.

"*Bien,*" Santos said, getting up. He immediately went to the back door of the cantina and ordered his wife to cook something for Lawnce. Then he set up the first pint of whiskey on the bar. "Did you get close to the cattle thieves?" he asked.

"Found five head run to death, but that's all the closer I got."

Santos chuckled. "You will never catch that Maximo. He has too much help."

"I don't have to catch him. All I need is enough evidence to arrest him."

"You will never get any evidence against Maximo," Santos said. "He has too much help." He laughed and left to check on the progress of Lawnce's meal.

The first pint of whiskey was half gone by the time Santos brought in the steak, beans, and tortillas. Lawnce finished the bottle while he ate. He ordered another before he left. He more or less owned an interest in the cantina and didn't have to pay by the drink or the bottle. He kept the shelves stocked with store-bought liquor from Chihuahua and San Antonio and got his meals and August's in return, plus a small share of the profit.

"Tell the boy to come get his food," Santos said as Lawnce got up.

"He'll come when he gets hungry," Lawnce said. He shoved the second flask under his belt and pushed his hat down low over his eyes before stepping into the sunlight. He wove down the street, his eyelids fighting fatigue and whiskey. At McCrary Livery, he scaled the ladder to his bedroom, the loft. Collapsing on a wagon sheet spread across the hay, Lawnce wrestled the stopper from his pint and took a swig. He stared at the inside of his straw sombrero for a mere moment before becoming oblivious to everything beyond his livery stable.

4

"**W**hoa," August said to Quatro. He saw a rider coming hard from Candelilla. He looked for recognizable features, but decided he knew neither the man nor the horse. The horseman galloped past and headed for Maximo's band.

August saw that the fellow was not from Texas and was no cowboy. He rode a centerfire saddle—a single-cinch rig from west of the Rockies—and didn't carry a reata on it. The clothes were store-bought, the boots polished. Blue gun metal reflected afternoon sunlight. August knew there would be trouble and Chepita would be near. Lawnce would want a witness. He pulled the reins around, dug his heels into Quatro's ribs, and followed as quickly as the old mule would leave hoofprints.

Maximo saw the rider coming and ordered Chepita to the ground. His men fanned out, flanking him. To his right was young Fermin, wiry and still game after two days of riding, one handle of Chepita's laundry basket looped over his saddle horn. Beyond Fermin was the blank stare of Tristan, the tracker, and, to his right, three other banditos—Natividad, Apolonio, and Guzman.

To Maximo's left was Jesse Diaz, his second-in-command. Across his right shoulder he wore a pigskin bandolier ribbed with cartridges. Cheto, Susano, Abundio, and Luis waited to Jesse's left.

Chepita stood behind the guards as Maximo's stallion stomped nervously in its tracks. The gunman approached rapidly, but August still loped along well to the rear.

The pale, lanky rider in store-bought clothes jerked his horse to a slide and dismounted in one motion like a calf roper. Sand swirled around him as he swatted his horse on the rump. The animal trotted a short distance away.

"You're Maximo," the gunman said, sliding his holster around his hip and over his watch pocket.

"*Sí.*"

"I'm here to see you shot."

Maximo bared straight teeth that appeared white as pearls under his black mustache. He tucked his thumbs into the pockets of his beaded vest. "And who will do this shooting for you, *niño?*"

The Mexican riders laughed.

"I aim to kill you myself, of course," replied the gunman.

The Mexicans laughed louder.

From the jolting back of the livery mule, August saw Maximo swing his leg over his saddle horn and hit the ground without removing his thumbs from his vest pockets. One of the men led his horse away. He waved the others off, and they backed up to make an arena for gunfire. Chepita stood safely behind them. August took care not to ride through the line of fire behind the stranger, though he didn't expect Maximo would let a bullet get past the gunman without it going through him first.

The desperado leader looked at the pale features of the gunman facing him. "Why don't you go away?" he asked. "No one in the north of Mexico or the west of Texas is faster with guns than Maximo de Guerra. Save yourself, *niño*. Go away." Maximo saw the stable boy coming but disregarded him as harmless.

"I don't hail from this godforsaken west of Texas. I'm of California. And no stinkin' Mexican, from the north or otherwise, can outdraw me. I'd sooner kill a Mexican than squash a gray-back tick."

The teeth vanished behind the desperado's mustache. "Before you die, *niño,* perhaps you will say why you want to kill Maximo."

August trotted his mule near enough to hear the gunman's words.

"You ain't worth a nickel to me alive," the Californian said.

Maximo nodded. He had suspected that much. This was the Californian he had heard was coming to kill him. *"Bueno.* If we are going to fight a duel, where is your second?"

"My second what?" the gunman asked, disgusted.

"In a duel you must have a second. A man to stand with you, to see it is done properly."

"Hell, I didn't come to fight no fancy duel. I come to kill you and that's all."

"If you murder Maximo that way, these vaqueros will be forced to shoot you," Maximo said, glancing at his men. He pointed at Jesse. "Jesse Diaz is Maximo's second. Who will be yours?"

The Californian hadn't counted on Mexicans running things in Texas, but he could see that Maximo was used to it. He glanced to one side and caught a glimpse of August on the mule.

"That boy, there. He's American. He'll stand up with me."

Maximo and the Mexican riders laughed, and August felt humiliated. He made the mistake of glancing toward Chepita and found her looking at him, making his humiliation run even deeper. He suddenly wished he hadn't followed.

"No, he will not stand with you," Maximo said. "No one will stand with you when you stand against Maximo de Guerra."

August said nothing.

The Californian was getting irritated. "Then let my pistol be my second."

Maximo sighed. *"Bueno.* How will we fight this duel?"

"I heard you knowed how. Just grab hold of that shiny pistol on your belt."

The desperado looked as if he had a bad taste in his mouth. "Maximo is tired of fighting the same way every time. We will think of a new way." With his left hand, he pulled a long knife from the red sash around his waist. "Perhaps we will fight with knives in a dark cave," he said, twisting the blade in the air. "The one who loses will have the cave for a tomb." He put the knife away and jerked his thumb toward the bluffs up the river. "Come, there is a cave this way."

The Californian did not move. "Bullshit. I fight with my forty-five."

"Ah, you are *puro pistolero,*" Maximo said. "We must think of a new way to duel with *pistolas,* then." He snapped his fingers. "You ride over there," he said, pointing his left hand to the north. "Maximo will ride this way," pointing his right hand southward. "We will ride toward each other and shoot!" He clapped his hands together in front of his chest.

The stranger's pale features were turning red with anger. "Like hell!" he shouted. "We'll do it the usual way!"

"Which way?"

"Like this!"

The pale gunman jerked at a pistol in his holster. Maximo shot him before he could get the hammer cocked. The Californian died before he hit the ground.

The shot made Quatro flinch, and August instinctively grabbed the mane in case the mule intended to bolt or pitch. When Maximo glanced toward the mule, August avoided looking at his eyes. The desperado took his time replacing the spent cartridge, then holstered his Colt revolver.

It was nothing for Maximo to shoot a man standing thirty feet from him. He could look down the barrels of his guns and blast doves from the sky for supper. In a contest of marksmanship, no one bested him. He shot equally well with either hand. He could twirl the trigger guards around his fingers and, smiling, shoot behind his back. But that was all show. In a gunfight, Maximo drew one pistol—the right one—shot once, and did not miss.

He whistled through his teeth, and Luis brought his horse. Abundio took the reins of the Californian's mount and shook the centerfire saddle by the horn to see how it sat with just one cinch.

August lingered as the Mexican riders filed by. Then he saw Chepita approaching from behind. Once his eyes were fixed on her, they would not move. She was the only one to look at the dead man. She approached the body. Strangely, sadly, she bent to touch the gunman's shoulder. She removed the Californian's hat and looked to his eyes for life. Then she touched his pale face.

Maximo looked over his shoulder after he mounted. He saw Chepita stooping over the dead man like a nun. The stable boy was watching her. Such an image did not fit the woman of a desperado.

"Get away!" Maximo yelled. He spurred his mustang and charged toward Chepita as she rose. He meant to hoist her again onto the rump of his horse, but the animal shied at the body on the ground and leapt. The shoulder of the horse struck Chepita and sent her staggering, then rolling backwards.

"Hold on!" shouted August, springing from Quatro. "You don't treat a lady like that!" On impulse, he rushed between Chepita and the desperado.

Maximo checked his mount with a tight bit. He pushed

his spangled sombrero back to make sure his eyes saw correctly. "Maximo treats his women as he wants and stable boys do not molest him!"

"Nope. It ain't right!" said August. He felt surprised at his own brashness in facing the deadliest man in northern Mexico, if not also in western Texas.

Chepita stood up, trying to get her skirts in order and the dust out of her hair. "Don't fight," she pleaded. "I am not hurt. It was an accident!"

"There will be no fight," Maximo said. "There is only a muchacho with *una poca pistolita.*" He laughed at the ridiculous pocket pistol in the homemade holster.

August found jeering Mexican bandits gathering all around him on horseback. He stood his ground and spoke to Maximo. "There will be fightin' unless you apologize to this girl," he demanded.

"No!" Chepita reached forward and touched August's arm. "It is not necessary!" Jesse Diaz pulled her away instantly, and she struggled to get free of his grasp.

The señorita's fingers on his arm had given August unbelievable pluck. "Apologize now, or get ready to shoot!" he ordered as he spit the chewed straw out of his mouth.

Maximo rolled his eyes to the heavens. *"Chinga'o!"* he cursed. "How many times must Maximo shoot a gringo before he gets to drink the tequila?" The bandits guffawed. "If you want to die so young, muchacho, wait in front of your stable when the sun goes down. If you want to live longer, you must let Maximo handle his own women. Adios!"

"Hold on!" August said. But the desperado helped Chepita mount behind him and rode for town.

The gang of bandits followed. Chepita looked over her shoulder. "Please don't fight!" she called out.

August was left there with Quatro and the dead Californian. He had done some thinking about the way some men risked their lives and had concluded that risking life, like conceiving it, was a thing best done in the throes of some passion. That was why cattle and dogs bred in heat, when the time was right. That was why antlered bucks who otherwise browsed peaceably together, locked horns to destroy one another over an estrous doe, when the season demanded it. But August's time for passionate risk had just blown away in a swirl of west Texas sand. Now his temper would cool; he would brood over the consequences of gunfighting. He couldn't duel with a clear head; his nerves would falter.

But that was what Maximo would want. August made himself recall how the desperado had knocked down the girl for grieving over a dead stranger.

"I'll be there," he said to himself. "Sundown."

The livery hand finally mounted his mule and rode toward Candelilla. He would need to notify old Gavino Carranza, Candelilla's full-time drunk and part-time grave digger. Gavino would want to get the body of the Californian in the ground before the desert sun caused it to bloat and stink. Old Gavino drank so much that he seemed almost ready to retch at any given moment. A stinking corpse wouldn't help.

5

August sometimes saw Gavino haul the bodies to the cemetery across the backs of mules, and he sometimes heard how Maximo killed them. But he had never before seen the shooting himself.

The images would not leave his head. He saw Maximo's gun erupting with smoke, the pale gunman dying on his feet, and Chepita stooping to touch the body. He imagined himself there, the beautiful señorita reaching toward him. Even in death, one would cherish that embrace.

The sun had dropped behind the row of buildings across the street, and shadows crept into the livery stable. August stood in the feed room long enough to let his eyes adjust. To pass the time, he made lunges at his revolver with his right hand. He thought about the quickness of Maximo's draw. His own gun was quicker, he told himself—lighter and smoother out of the calfskin.

Finally August's eyes could focus on the corners and rafters. He could clearly see cobwebs hanging from the joists like Spanish moss from an old oak. He walked quietly to a stack of feed bags piled against the wall. With his left hand he grabbed the corner of a bag in the middle of the stack. He readied himself and toppled the entire column to the floor.

Three rats scurried for cover. August sent two of them rolling with head shots. Another rat scuttled across a rafter. He picked it off almost by sound alone. Rodents began to swarm and August Dannenberg fanned his piece like a tent show shootist.

Lawnce sprang up out of bed so quickly that he bumped his head on the rafters through his sombrero. His bottle slid across the loft floor. A stray bullet from below found a crack in the flooring and shattered the pint. Whiskey soaked into bluestem hay. The ranger's lip twitched under his mustache. He made a single leap through the trapdoor and hit the ground as the last shots rang out in the feed room. He came up with his Remington drawn, the hammer cocked, barrel swinging into position.

"Lawnce! It's just me!" August shouted. "Don't shoot!"

Lawnce stood saucer-eyed and panting, trying to reason despite two sleepless days in the saddle and two pints of whiskey in his stomach. In a moment he recognized his hired hand and understood. He did not approve.

"Kid! What in thunder you mean firin' off that pepperbox of yours in my sleep?" He eased the tension from his pistol hammer and jammed the Remington back into its holster.

"Sorry, Lawnce," August said. "The rats. I was . . . I was . . . I thought you were still in Mexico."

"Damn me if I don't wish I was! It's a mite safer down yonder with the bandits and the wild Injuns!"

"I'm sorry. I didn't know you were back. It won't happen again."

Lawnce propped his hands on his hips and frowned. "Well, no real harm done. Just the crown of my hat caved in. And my scalp underneath it." He rubbed the bump on his head. "And my skull."

August decided to change the subject. "Sorry I woke you up, but since you're awake, you might want to know there was a shootin' today."

"You mean a real shootin'?"

"Maximo killed a fella. I was there. I saw it happen."

"Who'd he put out of misery this time?" Lawnce turned a tin feed bucket upside down for a seat. He had twisted his knee jumping down from the loft.

"A hired gun. I heard him say so. Butch Gainey hired him, I'll bet."

"You hear him say that, too?"

"No, but Gainey hires all those gunmen, everybody says."

Lawnce rubbed his knee. "The Revised Statutes of Texas don't allow for no hearsay, August. Just tell what went on."

August related the story in every detail up to the Californian's death, except for some vagueness about why he had ridden near the river in the first place. Lawnce pulled his copy of *The Revised Statutes of Texas* from his saddlebags and thumbed through the weathered tome as he listened.

"Sounds like self-defense to me," he said, putting his finger on a certain paragraph, then shutting the book with a thud. "I better parley with Maximo about it, anyhow. Besides, somebody shot out my pint and I can't sleep without it. I'll go talk to Maximo and get a bottle, too."

"There's something else," August said.

Lawnce turned to listen, but August couldn't begin.

"Well, don't just stand there; unload it on me."

"I'm supposed to fight Maximo at sundown."

"Huh?"

"Maximo wants to fight me at sundown."

"What kind of fight? Cockfight? Not a fistfight, I hope."

"A gunfight."

Lawnce broke into a rare, wheezing form of laughter. He coughed four times, then caught his breath. "Goatsuckin' horn-frogs! Kid, you ain't no more gonna shoot it out with Maximo than I'm gonna run for a Republican seat on the Congress."

"I have to. I challenged him."

Lawnce knew how his hired hand had taken to the idea of a grown man always backing up words with actions. "Now hold on," he said, "just tell me what all this here's about."

August told the part about Chepita getting knocked down.

"You mean to tell me," Lawnce said, "that this whole fracas is over a Mexican washerwoman? You ain't dotin' on that little señorita, is you?"

"I kind of like her."

"Well, kid, I kind of like dancin' music, but every time I get too close to the fiddle player I get poked in the eye by the bow." Lawnce turned toward the double doors of the livery barn. "Anyhow, you ain't fightin' with Maximo."

"Why not?"

" 'Cause hired help is too hard to find in this town, that's why. Maximo's rough as a cob and you ain't nothin' but a tallow-face kid. I don't aim to watch you die."

"I'll be outside this barn at sunset. If Maximo shows up, we'll fight, all right."

The ranger turned. "Oh, you will, will you? Well, remember that duelin' is against the Revised Statutes and I'll jail you. At least I would if I had me a jail. But I'll chain you to the water trough just like I did all them other outlaws till I can git you into Presidio. Then the courts'll have your neck. I seen a young feller about your age found guilty of duelin' one day in San Antone. Want to know what they done to him?"

"What?"

Lawnce grabbed a corner of the dirty bandanna around his neck and pulled it upward while hanging his tongue out and making gurgling noises.

"Hung him?"

"Jerked him to Jesus!"

August thought for a moment. "Well, there ain't no law against standin' out in the street at sundown, is there?"

" 'Course there ain't and you know it!"

"And there ain't nothin' in the Statutes against defending yourself, is there?"

"No, there ain't," Lawnce said, "and there ain't no law against standin' in front of bullets neither—which is exactly what you're gonna do if you stand out in that street and face Maximo at sundown or midnight or any other hour! That's another thing: don't never shoot nobody at sundown, August. Maximo would just get you to his east and make you look at the sun. Blind you. Not like he needed to, fast as he is."

"I can beat him," August said in a deliberate tone Lawnce had never heard from him before. "You've seen me shoot rats. I'm fast and I don't miss."

Lawnce stepped forward, clamped his sinewy fist hard around August's arm, and breathed whiskey in his face. "Now look here, kid. Before you go carvin' notches in your puny plow handle for every roodent you kill, you better know somethin'. I've lived in barns ever since I was your size and I've seen a million rats. Never once have I seen one totin' a weapon. *Rats don't shoot back!*"

The two glared at each other. Neither would yield. August jerked his arm away. "I won't back down."

Lawnce shook his head. "I tell you what I'll do, then. I'll just go have me a little talk with ol' Maximo and see whether or not I can't save your blasted hide!"

The ranger's spurs jingled toward Las Quince Letras.

August sulked for a while, then went to picking up dead rats. He would hang them on the back fence of the livery corral, at the edge of town.

Of course, just about everything in Candelilla was on the edge of town. There was one main drag running southeast to northwest, parallel with the river. From the southeast, the Pitchfork Saloon was the first business establishment on the street. Then came various stores, a blacksmith shop and wagon works, Las Quince Letras, and McCrary Livery. Only Mr. Grimes's store was located off the main street, around a corner to the left.

The rest of Candelilla was a tangle of alleys, trails, livestock pens, cactus patches, adobe houses, and the brush jacales the poorer Mexicans lived in. The jacales were made by digging trenches where the walls were wanted, setting posts upright in the trenches, and chinking between the posts with mud. The mule drovers lived in them, and the hay cutters and goat herders and the farmers and the *zanjeros* who dug the crude irrigation canals down on the floodplain of the Rio Grande. There was a good cluster of jacales on the river side of the town. But they all seemed to be on the edge.

Sometimes the whole mess of dried mud and matchstick lumber seemed to close in on August as if it would smother him in dust. That was when he would kick open the loft doors, hang precariously out in the air with a straw between his teeth, and gaze at the barren Chinati Mountain peaks to the southeast or the Sierra Vieja to the opposite. It helped remind him that there was something beyond the adobes and mud-plastered jacales of Candelilla. It made him hopeful of someday seeing more of the world.

That was why he hung the rats on the corral fence—to escape Candelilla on a hunting trip. The Mescaleros would have heard the rat shoot and would come around in the night to collect the dead rodents. They would cook them whole, then peel off the charred hides to enjoy the delicacy of roasted grain-fed rat.

If August left them enough rats, maybe they would take him hunting again. Lawnce's treaty with the Indians forbade Candelillans from infringing on Indian hunting rights, but sometimes the Indians acted as hunting guides for nimrods like August. He arranged the rats nicely on the top rail, hung by the tails. It was a sorry existence, he thought, when a man had to purchase his adventures with dead rats.

6

Lawnce figured he'd find Maximo in the cantina. He borrowed two little earthen cups from Santos and carried them in one hand, clutched a bottle of tequila in the other, and had a fresh pint of red-eye stuck under his belt. The ranger sat in a chair at Maximo's table where he could see daylight through the swinging cantina doors. He blew the dust from his cup and filled it with whiskey, then shoved the other wobbly cup and the bottle of tequila at Maximo.

The subject of the shooting came up, and Maximo claimed self-defense. The subject of the stable boy came next, and Maximo laughed.

"Maximo does not waste his time shooting young boys with toy *pistolas*!" he declared.

Lawnce felt relieved but decided to let the liquor continue to flow. If he could keep Maximo drinking until dark, August would have less chance of getting his head shot out from under his crumpled hat. Lawnce kept an eye on the door and made sure Maximo had plenty of conversation to drink over.

"Well, Maximo," he said, "I reckon we're gonna have us a gully-washer this evenin'. I seen a rattlesnake track leadin' uphill today, and the red ants was buildin' their anthills up."

The desperado let a little tequila trickle into his cup. "These are good methods to foretell the rain, Don Lawnce," he said knowingly, "but there is a better way that Maximo will tell you about. Today the snails along *el río* were climbing high on the branches of the chaparral. These little creatures, they know how high the water will rise, and so they are more intelligent than people that way."

"Hot damn!" blurted the ranger. "I ain't never noticed them little critters! How you reckon they know?"

Maximo shrugged.

It wasn't the first time the two had sat together in the cantina, drinking and matching wits. Though rivals, the two men liked each other. Lawnce knew Maximo stole cattle from the Doubletree Ranch on a regular basis, and he intended to catch him at it and arrest him someday. Along other stretches of the border, Maximo would have been hanged by rangers long before. But Lawnce felt Mexicans were entitled to as much due process as lawyers or senators. He was half Mexican himself.

The libations continued to pour from the bottles until Lawnce decided to take up some business with his drinking companion. "Maximo," he said, "I've took notice of somethin' that maybe you can explain to me. How come every time you disappear from Texas so do about a hunnerd head of Butch Gainey's wormy ol' mossy-backed longhorns?"

The bandit's face turned sour. "Maximo takes nothing that does not belong to him."

Lawnce almost sprayed whiskey across the floor. "Listen, *mi amigo,* we're gonna think different when I finally catch you ridin' herd in back of Doubletree cows on Mexican dirt without a bill of sale!"

Lawnce could read a sign like an Indian and knew how to find even men who left no tracks. That Maximo had so far escaped his hounding was due only to the desperado's heroic reputation throughout the border country. Every Spanish speaker along the Big Bend would risk the curse of a one-eyed devil to cover Maximo's trail for him.

The desperado was known for tossing out coins like so
many tortillas. Once he had pried a silver medallion from
his sombrero to pay a crone for a night's lodging, adding
to the fame of his garish hat.

Maximo avoided the crux of the argument with
Lawnce. "No one in the west of Texas or the north of Mexico catches Maximo with horses!" he boasted. "Maximo
rides only *los caballos* that fly!" He made a motion with
his hand to show how fast he could ride.

"Flyin' horses! Great Gideon, there's a new one! Little
Satan can't quite fly, Maximo, but I'll tell you one thing—
damned if he can't beat birds!"

Maximo stomped his boots on the dirt floor and
laughed loudly. He repeated Lawnce's remarks in Spanish to the bandit riders sitting in the corner; they also
roared with laughter. Fermin punctuated the quotation
with a pistol shot through the roof that made the ranger
bounce his knees off the bottom of the table and reach
for his pistol grip. Santos calmly wiped away the dirt that
fell from the ceiling onto his bar. Tristan did not laugh
at all, but stared blankly ahead. He couldn't see humor
the way he could see a sign in the sand.

Lawnce propped his elbow on the table to steady the
bottle against the rim of his cup. "I wonder of a evenin'
sometime, Maximo, when I don't have more pressin' matters on my mind, what in thunder started this here feudin'
twixt you and ol' Butch Gainey. Just this afternoon, I
caught him holdin' a kangaroo court over a cottonwood
limb with a little ol' Mexican youngun at the chokin' end
of a rawhide lariat. Said the boy might know somethin'
about your whereabouts. Did you ever stop to think about
that kind of sufferin' on account of yourself?"

The desperado glared down the length of his index finger at Lawnce. "Do not blame Maximo for the actions of

a coward." He paused to swallow tequila from the rough earthen mug. "What became of the boy?" he asked.

"Well, I had to stand up for the Revised Statutes," Lawnce said. "So I told ol' One-Eyed Butch that if he didn't adjourn court, I'd shoot him right where it hurts." Lawnce poured another draft of whiskey and yawned.

Maximo waited for Lawnce to explain. "And where would you shoot him, Don Lawnce?" he finally had to ask.

"Right in the horse!"

Jesse Diaz cringed at the thought. He understood enough English to eavesdrop from the next table.

"Anyhow," Lawnce continued, propping his feet up on a stool. "I got the youngun out of there and dropped him over on the other side of town."

Maximo extended his earthen vessel toward the ranger. *"Gracias*, Don Lawnce, to you and your book of laws from Maximo and his people. *Salud!"*

Their cups touched with the grinding sound a boot heel made when smashing a scorpion against a rock.

"So tell me, Maximo," Lawnce said, pausing to yawn again, "what was it that got you and One-Eyed Butch so far afoul of one another?" The ranger didn't really expect Maximo to tell what his feud with Gainey was about. He had asked before and never gotten a straight answer. He leaned his handmade chair against the adobe wall and closed his eyes to contemplate the whiskey warmth he felt inside.

The chambers of Las Quince Letras had grown dimmer as the twilight came on. August would be completely out of danger soon.

All indications of affability vanished from Maximo's face at the mention of his beef with Gainey. He stared into the flame of the cantina's sooty lantern and sat silent for some time.

"El Ojo kills in a way *muy horrible*," he finally said.

"Maximo kills only with the gun, *muy rápido*." He slapped his hand against his pistol grip. "Be warned, Don Lawnce, you love your book of laws. But never let your laws stand between Maximo and El Ojo. He will die by the hand of Maximo de Guerra. And so, too, will any *tejano rinche* who stands in the way."

The desperado turned to Lawnce McCrary and found him asleep with his head against the wall, one shoulder quivering the way a dog's feet twitch when he's dreaming of chasing rabbits. Maximo suddenly felt drowsy himself. He finished drinking his cup of mescal, found his sombrero, and stepped out into the paleness of dusk, leaving his gang of bandits behind.

7

August had paced back and forth across the street for an hour. He never knew twilight could linger so. Every time he heard the creaking doors of the cantina swing open, he lost all bodily functions other than vision. His heart, his lungs, and his other innards suspended operations until he saw someone other than Maximo step from the adobe cantina.

As the dying rays of light filtered around him, August took a seat on the edge of the water trough where the muzzles of a thousand mules had smoothed the cypress planks. He felt relieved and yet cheated. His moment of glory seemed never to come.

The sky had started rumbling to the west at sunset. Clouds darker than the shadowy bluffs were rolling in, flashing yellow with periodic casts of sheet lightning. The moon rose, near full, a rainbow-like halo surrounding it. This the Mexicans called *casa de la luna*—house of the moon. It, too, meant rain. August saw just one star inside the house of the moon. This indicated one day of rain to superstitious border folk.

Just when he decided to repair to his cot in the tack room, the swinging doors creaked once more. August saw the unmistakable outline of Maximo step into twilight. The lantern flame reflected against the silver medallions around his sombrero as he walked toward the livery barn. August's bodily functions worked now to excess. His heart felt like a trip-hammer. His lungs pumped like a smithy's bellows. He rose from his seat and straddled a wagon rut.

He did not know the first rule in the protocol of pistol dueling, so he simply watched his adversary's every move and stood ready to shoot for his life. Maximo was famous for his knowledge and love of the formal pistol duel and the Code Duello—a vanishing tradition. August figured the Mexican would tell him what to do when the time came. He almost didn't trust his eyes when they saw Maximo turn up a side street and disappear behind a corner.

For a moment August considered letting him walk away. Then he decided he would no longer be ignored. He trotted to the corner and called Maximo's name.

"Who is there?" Maximo asked.

"August Dannenberg."

"Maximo does not remember such a name." He turned away.

The stable hand took Maximo's move as a sign of cowardice, and his confidence mounted. "Hold on! We're supposed to fight at sundown."

Maximo stopped. He turned around and looked at August in the waning light of the evening. "Ah, *sí*, muchacho," he said as the afternoon's events came back to him. "Maximo has decided to spare your life today. Go back to your rats and your horseflies." Again he turned away.

August followed him down the street. "Listen, Maximo! You will have to face me today whether you want to or not!"

Maximo wheeled around on the heel of one boot with a quickness that almost made August reach for his pistol. *"Cállate la boca!"* His shout echoed sharply across the narrow side street. "Go away! Maximo does not wish to shoot another gringo today!" He turned away one last time, stepped under the thatched porch of a small adobe, and prepared to open the door. It was Chepita's house. She lived in relative luxury. Her place was made of adobe bricks instead of mud-plastered pickets. She had an inside fireplace and a flagstone floor. Maximo reached for the latch on her door.

August couldn't stand to think of him alone in that little hovel with Chepita. He remembered how Maximo had treated her earlier. Only one other thing occurred to him as a method of getting the Mexican to fight. "You're a yellow-striped coward and a woman-beater!" the stable hand shouted.

The way the desperado stopped chilled August's insides. The trip-hammer and the bellows went to work again. Maximo took two steps away from the adobe before facing August.

A bolt of lightning struck something close. The blast made August flinch. He decided not to draw until Maximo did. He thought of rats scurrying across the barn floor. He remembered Chepita reeling and falling in the dirt. He watched the bandit's gun hand and felt he would snap like a clock spring wound too tight.

Maximo concentrated on the eyes under August's wrinkled hat brim. The door of the adobe opened; lantern light flooded across him, blinding him. He had to reach for his pistol. He pointed it toward August, but looked into the open doorway and motioned for Chepita to step back as he fired.

August knew he was beaten. Maximo's draw had come so quick that he saw it as a blur in the coal-oil light. But the flame from the doorway glinted against the nickel plating on the Colt and gave him a target to shoot at. He saw the blast from Maximo's muzzle as his own pistol swung upward. He felt his hat fly away from his head before he pulled his trigger.

Maximo felt the small slug of August's rat gun shatter

the bones of his pistol hand. He tried to make the fingers work, but they would not. He reached for his left-hand pistol.

The sound of Chepita screaming caused August to thumb back the hammer and jerk the trigger again. The bullet hit Maximo's right shoulder. August fired again as Maximo's second pistol continued to rise. The slug hit the Mexican in the ribs and caused him to shoot between August's feet. August fired methodically a fourth time, aiming now for the sombrero. Maximo staggered back and shot into the sky.

Above the clinking of tequila bottles and the swearing of Spanish voices, Maximo's men heard the boom of the Colt. They knew thunder from gunfire. They paused and listened. More reports followed, four of them from a small-bore weapon, punctuated by Maximo's final shot at the stars. They sprang for the door, knocking tequila bottles and rawhide-bottomed chairs across the floor.

Lawnce McCrary continued to snore at the ceiling. Santos shook him by the shoulder, but the ranger only slipped out of his chair and curled up on the dirt floor.

Chepita threw herself over the sprawled body of Maximo, as if to protect him from further gunfire. To August she looked like an angel come to collect his soul. But he would rather she embrace him than his dead enemy. The flickering coal-oil flame made the shadows of her hair dance across her face like magic. When he stepped forward, she rose to stand in his way.

"I killed him like I said I would," August claimed. "I did it for you. You won't have to fear any more—"

Chepita jolted him with a solid swat across his face. Her arms were strong from scrubbing clothes, and her hands were rough. The blow stunned August as if he had been struck over the head with a shovel.

"You have killed him!" she screamed. Tears beaded the corners of her eyes, and her shoulders began to shudder.

"He beat you!" August said, holding a hand over his right cheek. "I saw him knock you down."

"You fool! He would never mean to hurt me. I loved him and you have killed him." Chepita recognized the sincere expression of bewilderment on August's face. She felt sick with guilt. She had flirted with him only that afternoon. She deserved more blame than he.

"But I—I did it for you."

Chepita heard the jingle of Fermin's spurs approaching from a distance. She knew Maximo's men would kill August when they found what had happened. She didn't care to carry the guilt of another death.

"There is something else you must do for me," she said quickly, wiping a tear away.

"What?"

"You must leave me. Go now. If you want to prove you love me, you must never let me see your face again."

August read the desperation in Chepita's eyes. He could not fail her again. If Chepita wanted him to run—well, that was one thing he thought he could do. He stole a last glance at the way her hair swirled around her face. He stumbled away from the jingling spurs and running footsteps he heard coming up the street. His carefree life of ease had ended. Things would never be the same. Big raindrops began to splatter on his bare head.

Fermin reached the body first. He asked half a dozen questions of Chepita without waiting for the answer to any of them. When the rest of the bandit gang arrived, they milled about in confusion. Chepita sobbed.

Finally Jesse Diaz took charge. He asked who had done the shooting. Chepita shook her head and said she didn't know for sure, it was almost dark when the fight started. Jesse asked where the murderer had run. Chepita claimed he had escaped behind the house. Apolonio looked for evidence and found a hat with a bullet hole lying thirty paces away. They all recognized the crumpled felt brim. Jesse ordered two men to run for McCrary Livery and drag back the gringo boy.

The order went unheeded. The body of Maximo had stirred. A hand moved feebly, and life wheezed from his throat. Chepita's hopes soared like Señora Heron in flight from the *río*. She told the bandits to gather around. Gently they lifted the body of their leader and carried him into the adobe. Thunder echoed like resounding blasts of gunfire.

8

The framework of August Dannenberg's life had collapsed and splintered into kindling wood. He stumbled blindly through a misshapen neighborhood of thatched jacales and adobes, disturbing chickens and dogs as he ran. Every shadow gave chase, and the rain spouts sticking out of the adobe rooftops looked like huge gun barrels swinging around on him. He took the claps of thunder, all around him now, for rifle reports of the enemy hard on his heels.

He dodged one way, then another, lost his bearings, almost throttled himself on a twisted rawhide clothesline. Finally he collapsed beside a hog pen's picket fence made of driftwood sticks collected at the river. He tried to formulate some course of action, but had never had to plan anything more important than a rat shoot in a hurry.

An uncomfortable weight settled on August's back and held him down. It was a feeling not completely alien to him. He had felt the sensation before and knew it as guilt.

August hadn't done many things in his life to feel guilty about, but he remembered one incident that had made him feel exactly as he felt now. It had happened on one of the hunts the Mescaleros took him on in exchange for rats. His guide, a brave known as Blood, could imitate the sound of a pronghorn fawn to lure curious does within rifle range. When Blood succeeded in calling a doe in close that morning, August had jerked his trigger too hard, causing his bullet to fly low, breaking both forelegs of the doe.

The crippled antelope began bleating as if a coyote had her by the neck, and the sound made August fire again, hoping to drown out the squall and put the doe out of her misery. But his second shot had missed altogether and the animal somehow reared up on her hind legs and ran upright like a trained circus dog, her broken forelimbs flailing pitifully before her.

At that moment August had heard Blood chuckle—a rare form of expression for a Mescalero brave. But his own feeling was one of utter remorse, and it was that feeling he experienced now, with his face in the dirt beside the hog pen. Only this time his guilt was not over a bad shot; his shooting had been perfect. The guilt he felt now was caused by his hasty decision to shoot a man. It was one thing to shoot a rat on a whim, but quite another to take a human life. His stomach roiled and he wondered if this was how Gavino Carranza felt when digging a grave for a putrid corpse.

Maximo had knocked Chepita down with his horse. Was that reason enough to shoot him? August didn't know anymore. He had expected Chepita to thank him for killing Maximo. In fact, he thought killing Maximo would automatically make Chepita his woman. The entire idea suddenly seemed preposterous.

A dead man gripped his conscience. The back side of the hand he thought to win had struck him senseless. His guardian lay sleeping off a drunk in a cantina. His enemy's gang would find and kill him any minute. He had placed little value on the prospect of life without Chepita; yet now that his life was in danger he cherished it more than ever, even though he knew he would never see her again.

He didn't know where to run. He had never ridden outside of Presidio County. How would he find his way? Who would be his guide? Where could he hide? The rain splashed drops of pig-sty mud on him. August desperately clenched his hands around the crooked pickets in front of his face.

Those staves had come from the Rio Grande. They had fallen from timber growing somewhere upstream and floated to Candelilla. August had never seen trees thick enough to shadow so much as an acre, but he knew timber meant forests for hiding in. He could follow that ribbon of life to the sheltering woods lining the banks somewhere far upstream. The river would guide him, the timber conceal him. Those driftwood pickets were all the hope he could find.

He pulled himself up and moved cautiously toward McCrary Livery. He expected to find Mexicans waiting for him, but he saw none. He moved quickly and silently into the dark of the stables. He knew the layout of the barn the way an armadillo knew the locations of its burrows under a moonless sky. He carried saddle, blanket, and bridle to the corral.

August caught one of Lawnce's surest mounts, a gray gelding. The ranger owed him several months' wages; pay hadn't come from the Ranger Service or the overland mail for most of the summer; Indians or outlaws had stolen every strongbox from the stagecoaches. August could take the gray gelding for wages. His boss would understand, wouldn't he? What would the Revised Statutes say about the way August had goaded Maximo into shooting?

The rain was hitting hard on the barn shingles when August hit the leather. He didn't wear spurs, but the gray knew what boot heels against his flanks meant. Gusts were kicking sand into the air, and rain was bringing it back down. August felt the grit in the drops that hit him in the eyes. But the weather would soon beat the dust down and wash it in rivulets to the canyon. The clouds had shrouded the house of the moon and opened a rain spigot above Candelilla.

By the glare of lightning bolts, the fugitive cast a mournful gaze toward the home of his lost sweetheart and rode hard upstream. Her words wrenched his innards into knots: "Never let me see your face again." That sentence seemed crueler than anything Lawnce McCrary's law book could prescribe.

He rode the gelding harder than any horse he had ever straddled, and he had sat a few. He knew he couldn't ride at such a pace forever. The gelding had good bottom, but would have to blow soon or die running. August would have to get a fresh horse somehow, and not so much as a nickel jingled against the cartridges left in his pocket.

Lightning painted silver sparks on the river to his left. The flashes of light made August ride a little easier. They turned what looked like Comanche lances back into the stalks of century plants and made the blades of Spanish dagger no longer look like shivs ready to gore him. There was always the chance of getting struck by lightning, but August preferred the dangers of the storm to those waiting for him in Candelilla.

Hunger began to gnaw at him. Lawnce had never spoiled the boy with luxuries, but plenty of hot eats were always provided. August thought about the tortillas, frijoles, and peppers he ate in the kitchen of Las Quince Letras. The strips of beef skirt grilled over mesquite embers. The morsels of antelope steak dipped in wild honey. Those days had passed. Now he would have to provide his own rations.

Fort Quitman was somewhere upstream. Normally a day-and-a-half ride, August had heard. He thought he might make it by sunup, the way he was pushing the gelding. Perhaps there he could trade the gray for a green-broke mustang and get enough to boot for a few meals and a new hat. But only if the gray had something left at daybreak. He decided to ease up some. He trusted the gray, but the dark and the storm made hard riding in the canyon country dangerous.

The storm! August finally stopped cussing it. The thought struck him like a lightning bolt. Not even Maximo's tracker, Tristan, could follow a sign washed thin by such a pour. He let the gray slow, but just to a lope. Cooling too quick in the chilling rain could ruin him.

Frigid blasts whipped the hair of August's bare head, and volleys of hailstones raked him like a scourge. But the storm without scarcely rivaled the storm within. There were hurricanes in his head and twisters in his stomach. Gun thunder echoed among the whirling tempests of guilt until August could scarcely hear another sound.

9

Chepita held articles of clean laundry against Maximo's wounds to stanch the flow of blood. The shoulder wound bled the most. Blood came out in spurts until she pressed a homespun shirt against it. The hole in Maximo's ribs didn't bleed as much, but the bullet and pieces of shattered bone had cut the organs, which now swelled and protruded through the place in his back where the bullet had torn through. She would have to pick the bone fragments out and cut away the loose flesh before she bound the wound.

The injured hand did not concern her at the moment, and the head would have to heal to itself—it was hard enough. The .32 slug from the livery boy's revolver had clipped a silver medallion stitched onto the hatband, and the thick felt had also taken some of the impact. And the boy had aimed too high. The crown of the sombrero stood above the wearer's head. The shot had pitched upward, creased the scalp, and glanced off the skull.

Chepita had to stop the blood first; then she would prepare to fight whatever infections might occur. "Fermin," she said to the young bandit pacing restlessly behind her, "go to your horse and get some hair from the tail." She turned to Natividad. "Make a fire and boil some water."

Fermin left and Natividad began arranging mesquite roots in the corner fireplace.

The homespun shirt Chepita held against Maximo's chest was now dark with blood. She looked to Jesse. "I need some other things."

"What?" asked Jesse.

"A glass like they drink beer from. The dough that they use to make their biscuits. And some flour."

Jesse nodded. He knew those supplies could only come from the Pitchfork Saloon. But Jigger Shanks, the Pitchfork owner, didn't like Mexicans coming in his place. He liked Mexicans okay; in fact, he had married one. But when one entered his saloon, shooting almost always followed, especially when any of the Doubletree boys were on hand. Jesse didn't let the Doubletree crew scare him, though. "Yes, I will get it, even if I have to use my pistol," he promised.

Chepita was not impressed with his show of bravery. She did not like Jesse or trust him, but she felt he was the only one of the bandits who could enter the Pitchfork for the supplies and come out alive.

As the water boiled, she continued to hold the shirt against Maximo's chest wound. She knelt beside his bed and made the sign of the cross with her free hand. She prayed to the Savior, the Virgin Mary, to every saint in the City Celestial; she uttered every heavenly entreaty in her repertoire, first for Maximo's life, then for his soul.

Fermin's spurs announced his return with the horse hair. Natividad had a good fire going, so Chepita told him to put the hairs in the boiling water to soften them, then to rip and boil some white cotton shirts to use as bandages.

Jesse Diaz finally returned with a handful of flour and the sourdough, which he carried in a beer mug with the glass handle broken off—the only vessel Jigger Shanks would let him get away with. Chepita told him to put it aside for the moment.

She doctored by lantern light as the men stood around her. Some of them began to grumble about letting the gringo boy escape. "You cannot go after him now,"

Chepita said. "Maximo is barely alive. He needs you here to protect him. El Ojo will come if you leave him unprotected. Anyway, the storm out there will wash away the boy's tracks. How can you find him? He is gone. Forget about him. Think about Maximo."

"I will stay here with four men," Jesse said. "We will guard Maximo while Natividad and the others ride after the boy."

Natividad liked the idea. Even though he would have to ride all night in a thunderstorm, it meant a move up in rank for him to lead a search party. Chepita couldn't overrule Jesse's plans—he had more authority over such matters than she. Jesse was second-in-command and Chepita was just a desperado's mistress.

There had been a night, about a year back, when Maximo had heard Chepita scream from her adobe. Entering, he had found her blouse torn away from her shoulders and her skirts approaching the same condition in Jesse's hands. Maximo had taken the iron poker from the fireplace and beaten Jesse. A duel was expected to result, but Jesse never demanded one. Instead, he seemed repentant. As if to compensate for the indiscretion with Chepita, he began risking regular scouting missions onto the ranges of Butch Gainey's cattle company. He brought back regular intelligence concerning the location of Doubletree stock that might be rustled. He had not reentered Chepita's one-room adobe until tonight.

Chepita would rather Jesse lead the search party than Natividad. She didn't want Jesse in her house. She felt vulnerable with him there and Maximo in no condition to protect her. She wondered if Jesse would send the other bandits away after Natividad's party left. She wondered if she would be left alone with him. She forced the worries from her mind and concentrated on saving Maximo's life.

Jesse's order stood, and all but five of the bandit gang stuck their heads through the openings in their woolen ponchos and ventured out into the storm.

When Chepita finally released the blood-soaked shirt from Maximo's chest, she praised heaven for stanching the flow. The boiled horse hairs became sutures. She used them to pull the torn flesh together. Luckily, as a laundress, she owned a needle. The wounds, when cleaned, looked rather small and took just a stitch or two, except where the shot to Maximo's ribs had torn through the small of his back. The bullet that had struck his chest was still in him and would have to stay there.

Guzman had been boiling the stems of a creosote bush. When Chepita finished the stitching, she placed the boiled stems on bandages and bound the wounds with them. She delicately cleaned the wounds on Maximo's head and hand and wrapped them also. Then she knelt for more prayer.

When the rain ended, just before dawn, Chepita asked for the Pitchfork supplies. She mixed the flour and sourdough with water to make a runny paste in the broken stein. She went outside to scald a rock beside her door.

The glow of sunup lined the cloud banks to the east. It made Chepita wonder how far the stable boy had ridden. But she no longer thought of him as a stable boy. She pictured him spurring a horse across the rimrock, every bit the desperado he had wanted to be. Natividad's men would have to ride hard to catch him, even if they could figure his path. She was going to miss the way he rode his mule to the river on rat-shooting days.

The *curandera* turned her mug of paste upside down on the rock she had cleaned. She used the paste to make a seal between glass and stone. She ordered Guzman to guard it, lest it get knocked over or raided by a dog, pig, or chicken. Jesse and the other men came out of the dank

10

Fort Quitman greeted August about sunrise. The rain had stopped, and the clouds were breaking up. His gray gelding stumbled from exhaustion, almost pitching the weary rider from his saddle. A small collection of jacales stood around the adobe walls of the U.S. Army border post. August rode to the gate of the fort where a Negro corporal was standing guard. He hadn't seen many blacks in his life, so he gave the buffalo soldier a good once-over.

"Pardon," August said. "Where could I do some horse tradin'?"

The soldier looked hard at the gray gelding. "It appears like you rode all the value out of that animal. Maybe you should rest him a day 'fore you trade with him."

August explained that he needed a fresh horse immediately. The soldier sent for the captain. The officer had a shortage of good horseflesh and could see quality in the gray through the sweat lather. He paid August in cash from the post's commissary funds and directed him to a place where he could get a bait of grub and a five dollar green-broke mustang.

"What happened to your hat?" the captain asked.

"It was blowed off last night," August replied.

"Yes, some wind with that storm." The captain said he thought he could fix August up with a new hat. He had shot a border bandit out from under it just a week earlier, but it was a regular American hat. He also gave August a wool serape the bandit had carried. "It'll get cold where you're going," he said.

August looked at him cockeyed.

"I figured you're riding hard to catch the Ferrar herd heading up to Colorado," the captain explained.

"Oh—yes, sir. You figured me right. Where you reckon they are now?"

"They're probably the other side of El Paso by now. But you'll catch them in a day or two with a fresh horse. They were short on hands when they left here, so I know you'll be welcome if you can ride up to snuff of a top hand. Ferrar had trouble finding hands on account of the Indian trouble." The captain handed the used hat and serape to August. "That Mexican wasn't wearing that serape when we shot him, so there's not even any blood on it."

"Where's the Indian trouble?" August asked, pulling at a succulent stem of green grass he'd found sprouting against the wall of the fort.

"Where? My God, son, it's all over. Haven't you heard? Comanches are on the warpath along the Pecos. That's why Ferrar's pushing his herd up the Rio Grande. Cheyennes and Arapahos have jumped the reservation and are raiding toward Colorado where he's heading. Why, even the Utes are acting up."

"The Utes?" August had never heard of them.

"Hard to believe, isn't it? They haven't caused trouble in years. Settlers squatted on some of their reservation land up there on the White River in Colorado. The Utes got upset about it and went to war. An officer and several men were killed. Last I heard, they were heading south to their old range in northern New Mexico Territory, swearing they'd kill white-eyes to the finish.

"Anyhow, Ferrar had trouble finding hands with all the Indian trouble. I'm sure you'll be welcome if you can ride. Ferrar doesn't use any but top hands."

August slipped his apple-horn saddle, his blanket, and his bridle off the gray and turned the horse over to the black corporal to walk some. The news about the herd heading up the trail lifted his spirits. He could travel upstream with it, earn a few dollars and grub. And he would have some protection in case Maximo's men caught up, for cowboys looked out after their own. He thanked the captain and carried his tack down the road to the horse trader's shack.

A coyote-dun mustang mare cost August five dollars. He spent another four bits on dinner at the stage station. He consumed a pan of beans, a half-dozen eggs, a cake of shortbread, and unrecorded quantities of coffee. He then bought some jerked beef and dried apples for the ride. Also, a plug of tobacco.

August saddled his mustang and let her hump up a bit while he found a grass stalk to chew and cut a mesquite switch with thorns. The bronco pitched a minute or two before deciding to run when August applied the quirt. He didn't mind how fast the mare ran as long as she headed upriver.

11

Butch Gainey scratched himself as he rolled out of his four-poster bed. Shafts of sunlight made the particles of floating dust between him and the window look like minuscule snowflakes. He cleared his throat and scattered the little blizzard as he spit into a cuspidor beside his bed.

After dressing in yesterday's clothes, the rancher flung open his bedroom door of solid sawmill lumber and stomped out onto the front gallery of his fortified ranch house. "Coffee!" he yelled.

A ranch hand immediately jumped up from the floor of the gallery. "Mornin', boss," he said.

"Damn it, Dood, if I wanted somebody to sleep outside my door, I'd git me a lapdog. What in hell are you doin' there?"

Dood was Doodlebug Tatum, an Arkansas fugitive, outlaw, and cowboy. Tatum never stood where a seat was available and never sat when he might recline. Often his place of repose was a comfortable patch of loose dirt in which he wallowed and kicked sand like a doodlebug, hence his nickname. Unable to find a horizontal Arkansas livelihood, Tatum had taken to doing things perpendicular to the law and wound up a fugitive in Gainey's outfit of hard cases.

A bandy-legged little Mexican cook rushed along the gallery with a tin cup full of coffee. Gainey took the cup without looking at him.

"I got big news for you, boss," Dood said as he shook the kinks out of his leg bones.

"It better be big enough to keep your ass out of the saddle. I don't shell out greenbacks to cow waddies to have them bed down at my front door till after sunup. What's this news all about?" Gainey blew across the top of his coffee cup and took a sip.

"Well, last night, down at the Pitchfork in Candelilla," Dood began, "I was just sittin' there and—"

Gainey spewed coffee across the cowboy's shoulder and bounced the tin cup across the gallery floor. "Damn it, Tanno!" he yelled at his cook. The cook's name was Cayetano Pastor; Gainey had shortened it to Tanno. "Bring me a cup of *hot* coffee and put some whiskey in it for a change." He turned to Dood. "Wasn't enough whiskey in that cup to float a grayback."

"Will a grayback float?" Dood asked, suddenly intrigued.

Cayetano could be heard rattling the coffee pot in the kitchen.

"Dood," Gainey said, "I don't really give a damn what you did in the Pitchfork last night, but I want to hear about it just so I'll have a good reason to kick your butt when I find out how much of my time you're about to waste."

"Oh, this ain't no waste of time, boss. This is—"

"Just tell it to me!"

"Yes, sir. Well, I was just sittin' there when in runs this Mexican. And it's ol' Jesse Diaz."

Butch Gainey perked up. Mexicans didn't enter the Pitchfork Saloon any more than gringos drank at Las Quince Letras. Only Lawnce McCrary frequented both establishments. "What happened?" Gainey said.

Cayetano skulked up to Gainey's corpulent frame and handed over the second cup of coffee, more heartily fortified than the first. Then he stood there as if to seek approval.

"Well, of course we tried to run him off," Dood said, "but he pulled his guns out and said he didn't want no trouble. He got Jigger to give him some sort of flour or somethin' out of the kitchen, and then he wanted a glass drinkin' mug. So Jigger give him an ol' broke one and Jesse said that would do. It was the damnedest thing, because he didn't want no money or no gold watches—just flour and a broke mug. It sort of tickled me and—"

"Damn you, Dood," Gainey said, "I have got to go out to the shitter and crap, so if you ever get around to makin' your point, you can just yell it through the crescent moon!" Gainey took his cup of coffee, pushed Cayetano aside, and walked around the hitching rail running the length of the gallery.

Gainey's fort consisted of a four-room adobe house with a high-walled courtyard. The walls stood three feet thick all around and had heavy wooden gates opening to the east, south, and west. The house itself stood on the north side. The gates could be barred on the inside with beams. Two windows and two doors opened from the house into the protection of the courtyard. Around the rest of the house and the courtyard wall, only loopholes opened for shooting at Apaches and Mexican rustlers.

One door of the house came from Gainey's bedroom, the other from Cayetano's kitchen. They both opened onto the gallery, which faced south to catch the sun in winter and the wind in summer. Along the inside of the east courtyard wall narrow adobe steps led to the roof of the house. The thick adobe walls extending above the roof acted as breastworks to protect the Doubletree gunmen under siege. A wooden scaffold ran along the inside of the courtyard wall so guards could patrol the entire perimeter of the ranch house.

Northeasters seldom blew in the Big Bend country, so Gainey had located his barn in that direction with the outhouse beyond it.

One-eyed Butch plodded through the east courtyard gate with Dood in tow and turned toward the privy. Dood continued the story as he stepped in the big man's boot prints. Cayetano followed as far as the gate, trying to listen to Dood's story, but he didn't intend to follow all the way to the outhouse to hear it.

"Well," Dood said, "we all had a good laugh at ol' Jesse comin' around to steal flour and broken stuff, so I got all swelled up and told him if he didn't tell us what he wanted it for, we were gonna play mumblety-peg on his hide. He didn't argue none. In fact, he looked right at me and said he needed that flour for doctorin' because there'd been a shootin'."

Gainey stopped with a hand on the outhouse door handle. "Who?" he asked.

"Jesse Diaz!" Dood said.

"I mean who got shot, you piss-ant!" Gainey roared.

"Maximo," Dood said.

Gainey's mouth gaped like a freight hole. He slammed his fist against the outhouse door in a gesture of triumph. Coffee sloshed onto sand. "You mean my California gunslinger got him?"

"Nope, Maximo got your gunslinger," Dood said, squirming with enthusiasm.

"Then who killed Maximo? Don't tell me that half-breed Lawnce McCrary finally decided to do some rangerin'!"

"Nope!"

"Damn it, Dood, don't play a game with me! Who the hell shot Maximo?"

"You won't believe it!"

"You won't believe what I'm gonna do to you if you don't tell me!"

"It was McCrary's hired hand, the Dannenberg boy!"

Gainey gawked at the cowboy for a second or two. He saw Dood's grinning face bobbing like a roadrunner's head. "No!" he said. "It don't figure."

"Soon as I heard, I rode straight out here and camped on your doorstep. Only thing is, I don't know if Maximo is all the way dead yet."

"Well, why the hell didn't you wake me up to tell me, you—" A sparkle of good fortune twinkled in Gainey's eye, and he slapped Dood on the shoulder and grinned. He took off his gun belt, slung it over his shoulder, and squeezed into the outhouse.

"Saddle up ol' Top Dollar, Dood," he said from inside the privy. "And saddle you a fresh horse, too, and holler in some of the boys. We'll ride in to Candelilla and you can tell me the whole damn story all over again!"

As Dood ran toward the barn, he heard Butch Gainey laughing and stomping behind the crescent moon, sounding most pleased that someone had done for free what he would have paid the Californian hundreds of dollars for doing. What a glorious day it was going to be if Maximo was truly dead.

Cayetano Pastor backed into the courtyard. He had heard enough to know that Maximo was shot. He made the sign of the cross and prayed.

12

The rosary was draped over Chepita's slender fingers. Half-dreams of gun smoke and blood drifted across the canvas of her sleep. She saw Maximo dying, August Dannenberg riding. She saw herself alone in a desert with no familiar river at her feet. The heron flew low overhead, but Chepita could not follow.

A hinge creaked and the beads rattled in her hand as she awoke. She moved cautiously between the door and Maximo's pallet. A stream of light blinded her until a shadow cast by a man big enough to fill the doorway blotted out the sun.

Chepita saw the glint of sunlight on mother-of-pearl. Where was Jesse? Where was Maximo's guard? As Gainey's bloated hand reached toward the holster she drew her body in front of Maximo, prepared and almost anxious to end the tragedy begun the night before.

But the hand that clasped the pearl butt was made of bone, gristle, and rawhide. Lawnce McCrary put the gun against One-Eyed Butch's head. Nerves shook Gainey to the marrow when he heard the hammer catch on his own .45.

"Don't take the nervous rigors, now, Butch. Just keep yourself calm so you don't jostle my trigger finger. I got drunk last night, and I'm a little shaky anyhow. And maybe you better think up a respectful alibi while you're at it."

"I'm just calling on an ailing acquaintance," Butch said in a pant. He looked over his shoulder and saw his men sitting meekly under the cover of the ranger's own battle-scarred revolver.

"Tell them boys to vamoose."

Gainey gave the order, and his men gladly rode on.

"Back out of this door and walk easy to my livery," Lawnce ordered. He stopped to speak to Chepita before pulling the door shut. *"Vengo hablar contigo alla en día."* The Spanish, though imperfect, made clear his intention to return. Chepita nodded.

At McCrary Livery, Gainey answered questions at gunpoint. He admitted hiring the Californian, but only to work on the ranch, not for a killing. It was a weak lie, but Gainey uttered it without batting his one eye. To some of the other questions, the rancher found himself in the rare position of benefiting by the truth.

"Who peppered Maximo last night?"

"I heard your hired boy did it."

"How come him to do that?"

"Can't say as I know."

"Jesse Diaz and some of Maximo's boys rode out of here like liquored Injuns a while ago. Where was they goin'?"

"To hell, for all I care. I reckon they're after your boy."

Lawnce was still putting the pieces of Maximo's shooting together. His conscience didn't rest easy with him because he had slept through the entire episode, drunk. He tended to think Gainey had some hand in it.

"Butch," he said, "I figure there ain't a soul in this here county that don't hate your stinkin' fat guts. But ol' Maximo carves your name on his bullets. I ain't much for pokin' my nose in other folks' business, but I want to know what you done to him to git him so riled."

"Hell, I don't know," Gainey said. "I never saw the damn runt before he showed up and started stealing my cattle under your nose. A couple of years back I hadn't ever heard the name of Maximo de Guerra."

No one had. Everyone knew that Maximo had made up his name. It was a good name for a border bandit. Where he had come from or what his real name was, nobody could say. But from the moment he had shown up around Candelilla some two years before, he had been idolized by the Mexican population because of his personal war on the ever unpopular One-Eyed Butch Gainey.

Lawnce mulled it all over for a moment. Too many things didn't make sense. Why did Maximo badger Gainey so? That question had never excited him too much in the past, but now August seemed to have been dragged into it. Why had that boy wanted so badly to risk his skin in a duel with the desperado? Was it all for the love of a border harlot or had Butch persuaded him to do it? And why had Jesse left his boss unguarded to chase after a boy whose tracks the storm had blown into Mexico?

Gainey smirked as he saw Lawnce puzzling. "I want to congratulate you, Lawnce. You didn't have the balls it took to face Maximo, so you just had your boy do it for you. I heard how it happened. You got Maximo all oiled up inside and then sent your boy after him with his rat pistol. And damned if he can't shoot straight with it after all!"

Lawnce felt his lip twitching under his mustache. He threw Gainey's engraved Colt into the corner, unbuckled his gun belt and threw his pistol on top of Gainey's. "I always wondered how hard a man your size would fall." He spit on both palms, rubbed his hands together, and turned them into fists.

Gainey removed his hat and glared at the ranger with his one evil eye. He tossed the hat in Lawnce's face and made a dodge for the pistols. Lawnce moved in on him like a mockingbird pestering a fat old dog. He put his boot in Gainey's path and sent him tripping into a horse stall.

Gainey got up, slipped on a manure pile, and went back down.

Lawnce laughed even when Gainey came barreling out of the stall looking like a runaway locomotive. He pinned the ranger against the opposite wall and swung his fist out to smash Lawnce's face. The blow was powerful, but slow. It broke the wall boards as Lawnce ducked. He worked One-Eyed Butch's belly over good before the rancher could load up his swinging arm again.

Gainey backed off to catch his air, and Lawnce planted a quick jab right between his eye sockets. The rancher went over backwards and didn't feel the need to come back up.

Lawnce punched the loads from the pearl-handled Colt one by one while Gainey shook the cowbells out of his head. He clamped a sinewy fist around Butch's neck and shoved the pistol barrel into the rancher's nostril so he could look down the sights and see the hammer ready to spring.

"I reckon you know my weakness good as anybody," the ranger said. "It's called the Revised Statutes. If it wasn't for them I'd've hoisted you over these rafters a long time before now. But them statutes won't save your skin if I find out you badgered that boy of mine into a killin'. I'll come down on you like a red-eyed lion on a orphan baby, and I'll make you a damn sight deader than Maximo is right now."

Then he pulled the trigger just to watch Gainey quake when the hammer fell on an empty cylinder.

Chepita solved more puzzles for Lawnce than Gainey did. She trusted the ranger and told him everything she knew—about the muleback visits August made her on rat-shooting days, the confrontation between the stable hand

and the bandit the day before, the gunfight by lantern's glow. She accepted the blame.

The ranger could see that August had fired his pistol for glory in the eyes of a Mexican beauty, not because of any badgering Gainey might have done. But he just barely regretted having thrashed Gainey in the livery stable. That had been a foolish exercise, Lawnce now realized, but when he was galled he sometimes didn't stop to think things through.

His regrets fell more along the lines of having neglected to raise August up to go courting with young ladies in the normal fashion—at Saturday night dances and rides on hay wagons and such. But Lawnce had never had much practice in those matters himself. And he had never really noticed that August was of courting age. Now he would likely never see the boy again. He knew one thing for certain about August: he wouldn't lie to avoid a whipping, and if he promised his senorita he would stay away forever for her sake, then Candelilla would never feel his footsteps again.

There was one thing Chepita could not clear up. Jesse and four men had been positioned outside her house to guard Maximo. Some time after sunup, however, she had heard them ride away. Shortly after that, Gainey had arrived.

After looking over the feverish near-corpse of Maximo, Lawnce thanked Chepita for her information and said adios. As he left the dank adobe he stopped to inspect a broken beer mug turned upside down on a rock and filled with something that looked like biscuit dough. Hoofbeats turned his senses to other matters.

Jesse Diaz trotted his horse around the matchwood lumber of main street's buildings and led his followers between the jacales to Chepita's house. There he found Lawnce McCrary staring at him.

"Where'd y'all git off to?" Lawnce asked.

"Buscando por su muchacho."

"I don't reckon you caught much sign of him, after that blow we had last night."

"No, Don Lawnce," Jesse said with an apologetic grin.

"I don't recall makin' a posse out of y'all anyhow. You best let the law take care of this thing."

Jesse frowned.

"There was a feller skulkin' around here a while ago," Lawnce said. "A big ol' ugly feller by the name of El Ojo."

"Señor Gainey?"

"Oh, 'Mr. Gainey,' it is? I run him back to his ranch. But I wouldn't give odds that he won't come back. And we don't want nothin' to become of poor ol' Maximo in there, do we, Jesse?"

"No, Don Lawnce."

"No, I didn't think so," Lawnce said. "Y'all put a guard on him." He pierced the ambitious bandit with an unwavering stare until Jesse looked away and rode down the street.

13

August rode the dun mare so hard that by the time he made El Paso she was tired enough to appear saddle broken. He showed a horse trader how well she handled and then sold her for a dollar more than he had paid for her. He switched his saddle and tack to another green-broke mustang mare that he bought from the horse trader and stayed on the trail.

He intended to ride until nightfall, but fatigue soon began to pull him out of the saddle. His head drooped and his knees buckled. His new mare had a rough trot, and the bouncing threatened to pitch his limp body out of the seat. Finally August stopped and reached into his saddle pocket for the plug of tobacco he had bought near Fort Quitman.

Lawnce had told him of desperate riders who carried tobacco to brew a tea of it under their eyelids—a tea that burned sleep out of the eyes. He had even seen Lawnce use it once when, after spending all night catching a Mexican who had gotten drunk and stolen his neighbor's horse, he had to deliver a herd of mules to Fort Davis without stopping to sleep. Lawnce had crumbled the leaf into small particles, turned his face to the sky, and sprinkled the tobacco in his eyes. Then he had rubbed it in under his eyelids.

When August tried it, the initial results disappointed him. The tobacco crumbs felt like any other foreign particles in his eyes and merely irritated, the way the grit from a sandstorm would. But then the tears began to form to wash the tobacco away. The moisture released the leaf's magic potion for wakefulness.

When he first felt the stinging, August blinked involuntarily. The blinking action seemed to wring more of the potion from the tobacco, and it felt as if a flame had leapt into his eyeballs. His eyelids worked like fans. Every time they shuttered, the flames grew hotter. August tried then to keep his eyes open, but reflexes made them keep blinking, fanning the heat under his lids. He shook his head like a dog stung on the nose by a scorpion, but the burning continued. It grew. August got worried that he might be blinded, and his voice said something unintelligible even to himself. His eyes wanted to close again, but he willed them to stay open. He was wide awake and frightened that drowsiness would make his eyes close and burn again, so he made them remain open. That was how the tobacco worked.

August finally allowed himself to sleep some that night, on the ground out in the open air. But the next day he was back in the saddle, looking north for the dust cloud of the Ferrar herd. He found it toward sundown.

"Nighthawkin's the only work I got for you," Ferrar said.

"That suits me," August replied. He favored tending horses to punching cows, even if it meant lower pay and standing guard over the *caballada* all night.

"I might have to let you go this side of Santa Fe," Ferrar said. "I promised some boys there they could work the herd into Granada. If they show up, I won't need you after that."

"That's all right."

"You've heard of the Injun trouble up north, haven't you? We might see Cheyennes or Comanches with paint on."

"I've heard."

"One more thing," Ferrar said. "We've got nothin' but green mustangs for you to work on."

Three cowboys had peeled back from their flank positions with the herd to see who it was the boss was jawing with. The longhorns were in a mill in the river valley and ready to bed down for the night. The cook had let down the tailgate of his chuck wagon and was cussing every cowboy who came within a lariat's length. Rousing the cook to fury was the cowboys' primary diversion. But the trail hands were about to have even better entertainment.

"If I can handle this wall-eyed mare, I can ride anything you got," August boasted. "She looks pretty poorly now, but you should have seen her pitch this morning."

The night herders now held the herd together as most of the wranglers came in for chow. They gathered around and snickered a little when August started bragging.

"I'm afraid you'll have to prove it," Ferrar said. He turned to one of the cowboys. "Bob, rope the zebra dun out of the *caballada* and bring him over here."

August could smell beans frying and dried apples stewing. "Zebra dun?" he said. "I'd ride a she-grizzly for a bait of those fixin's."

The dun stallion had dark zebra stripes on his withers and legs. Four cowboys choked him with a lariat while August approached with his saddle and bridle.

"We tried to geld him three times, but he killed eight good cowhands so we give up on the idea," said one of the cowboys. "Tried to brand him once, but he broke the iron down to grapeshot."

August recognized a bit of exaggeration, but he didn't see a brand on the zebra dun.

A Mexican trail hand managed to get a bandanna over the stallion's eyes. The animal stopped fighting at once and stood trembling and sucking air through his nostrils. The dun was wise to the bridle; he kept his teeth clamped tight to keep the metal out of his mouth. "Cover his nose," August said. A cowboy cut off the dun's air by covering his nostrils, and the bronco had to part his teeth for the bit. August slipped the bridle on over the bandanna and then went to work with the blanket and saddle.

"I'll bet you five dollars he'll land on his ass," one cowboy said to another as August slung the saddle on.

"I'll bet his head," the other said, and shook the first one's hand to seal the wager.

The bronc held a deep breath when August first pulled the cinch strap. He waited for the dun to exhale and then cinched in four more inches of girth leather. He also pulled the flank strap taut so it would hurt every time the stallion pitched.

"You've rode some bad ones afore, ain't you?" said the hand who had bet on August's head. The choke rope was taken off, and two men held the dun's head down by the ears so August could mount. The blindfolded mustang trembled like a mountain in avalanche as August let his weight settle into the seat.

"No *quiere* no spurs?" the Mexican cowboy asked.

"It ain't gittin' him goin' that I'm worried about," the bronc-peeler said, "it's makin' him stop."

August nodded at the men holding the ears. "Watch him," one advised, "he'll sunfish and caterpillar on you all at the same time." August simply nodded again.

The vaquero yanked the blindfold away as they gave the dun his head. The stallion started the show by bunching up his hooves and making a half-dozen cyclone revolutions in one spot. "He's a dad-burn twister!" a cowhand yelled. August held tight on the reins to keep the dun's head up.

The stallion charged forward in two great leaps, then planted his front hooves up to the fetlocks and ducked his head. August leaned back so far that he knocked his hat off on the dun's rump and held his stirrups level with the withers to stay in the saddle. Then the stallion reared and leaped, pawing. "He's climbin' the sky," a young drover hollered. August had to hold the reins almost behind his back to keep the bit tight. The boys were all shouting and waving their hats.

Next, the zebra dun took to swapping ends. He'd bounce on all fours for two or three jumps, then swing his powerful neck one way and whip his hindquarters around opposite until August couldn't find his bearings no matter how low the sun sank in the west. The muscles in his hands began to burn from clenching the reins, but he dared not ease up.

"He'll sunfish, now!" a cowboy warned. Sure enough, the striped tornado sprang upward and kicked all four legs to the left. August thought the brute would roll over and fall on him, but somehow he landed flat-footed. The horse sunfished twice more, but still August refused to bail out.

Finally the zebra dun bolted in a dead run, and the cowboys filled the prairie air with cheers, except for a couple of the top hands who didn't like being shown up. Away from the clamor, August could ease up on the bit. He spoke to the stallion with soothing words between gasps for breath. The dun, too, panted like a woolly dog in July and began to slow down to a lope, venturing an occasional kick. August gave the dun his first lessons with reins until sundown, then rode back for chuck.

Mel Ferrar greeted his newest trail hand as half a dozen admiring cowboys came to relieve the exhausted dun of riding gear. "I didn't intend for you to ride him," the grinning trail boss said. "I just wanted to see if you had sand enough to mount him. You just busted the meanest bronco in the badlands."

"He did kick a bit," August said as the boys escorted him to the chuck wagon.

The beef, beans, biscuits, and stewed apples filled August up and made him feel so sleepy that he didn't know if he could get off the ground to take his plate back to the chuck wagon. But he had to. He was a night wrangler, and his shift was about to begin. He gave his plate to the cook, borrowed a rope, and walked to the remuda.

August had had his fill of broncs for one day, so he roped a gentle-looking claybank mare and easily saddled her by himself. The twilight had faded and the moon had yet to rise. He couldn't find the stirrup for a moment because the claybank was much taller than the mustangs he had been riding. But he soon got his foot situated and swung into the saddle.

The horses were content to graze or sleep on their feet. The zebra dun rolled every now and then as if to get the feel of the saddle off his back. August could hear the night herders singing to the cattle, and the songs almost put him to sleep. As much as he hated to, he had to rub more tobacco into his eyes to stay awake. It was either that or suffer the embarrassment of falling off his horse. He was so tired he felt that if he fell from the saddle he probably wouldn't move until Ferrar came over in the morning to fire him.

The tobacco worked its magic again and August felt more clear-headed. That was no pleasure either. He began thinking about Chepita and the gun duel with Maximo. He started to worry again about Maximo's men finding him. The horses behaved perfectly, but their good behavior gave the nighthawk no relief from his thoughts. He almost wished for a rattlesnake to crawl in among them and start a rousing stampede that would take his mind away from Candelilla. More than that, he wished for dawn so he could sleep.

When morning finally came, August was so tired that he couldn't even be interested in breakfast. He threw his saddle on the ground, covered himself with the serape he had acquired at Fort Quitman, and went to sleep before he could even rest his head against his saddle.

14

The heavenly hosts had watched over the broken beer mug for two days and three nights and nurtured the growth Chepita needed to mend Maximo's wounds. She knew the molds growing on the biscuit dough could fight infection as if by magic.

She put water on to boil. The wounds, red-streaked with the outstretched fingers of blood poisoning, were cleaned and prepared to accept dollops of God's gift cure for the pestilence. Chepita recited her prayers as she applied the gooey mold, then bandaged the wounds again.

The holy magic worked miracles. Within hours, the swelling receded and the brown tone returned to Maximo's skin around the bullet holes. In a day the injured tissue began to mend. In another day he stirred and called out in delirium, waking Chepita from her pallet beside him.

"Gracias a Dios!" she said.

Maximo raised his head and stared around to all the corners of the ceiling. "Where is he?"

"Who?" Chepita said.

"The gringo boy."

Chepita held a gourd of fresh water to Maximo's lips. "He is far away. Don't worry. He will never return."

"He must be found."

Chepita felt astonished. Maximo would not even look into her eyes. He didn't even have enough gratitude in him to thank God or his healer. Instead he thought only of a boy enemy.

"Why?" she asked.

The bandit stared incredulously at her. "To kill him, of course." He rested his head again and closed his eyes.

Chepita felt her heart ache to hear more words of vengeance on the lips of the man she loved so. He could have become a righteous man, but the kindness in him was overwhelmed by a hatred he had carried since boyhood. With all his energy he worked toward the ultimate and violent death of one Butch Gainey. And now he had another wrong to avenge. Chepita could no longer bear to think of men killing one another.

15

The Ferrar herd had taken on August Dannenberg at the threshold to one of the driest rides in the West. The Jornada del Muerto—the journey of the dead—stretched north of the Ferrar campsite. Ferrar let his cattle graze and water there at the camp an extra day, for there would be no water to speak of for over a hundred miles.

The Rio Grande made a bend to the west, pushed that way by the Caballo Mountains. Unwilling to follow the longer route along the bulge, explorers and soldiers and settlers and cattlemen for over three hundred years had taken the shorter path to the east of the Caballos while the river flowed around the western flanks of the range.

There was some discussion while August slept as to what he should be called. "His name is August Dannenberg," Ferrar said.

The top hand of the outfit was a cowboy named Bob Skull. "August?" he said. "That's a season of the year. Might as well call him January."

"I think we ought to call him Dun or Dunnie," another said. "Because he rode the dun yesterday."

"Let's call him Dan. Dan Dannenberg."

They arrived at no consensus, but when one of them woke August for supper, he said, "Wake up Danny. Time for chuck."

August was groggy but hungry. A couple of the boys tried to talk to him while he got his food, but he had trouble keeping his mind on what they were saying. A cup of coffee perked him up for a little while, but then he felt drowsy again. He decided he needed more sleep. It was still an hour before sundown. The cook had gotten supper ready earlier than usual because the herd hadn't moved that day.

August wanted to take a nap, but he didn't want the cowboys to have to wake him again. Then he remembered that Lawnce had once shown him a way to take a light nap and wake himself up from it, too. He stretched out on his blanket, flat on his back. He put his elbows on the ground but pointed his forearms toward the sky, balancing them so that it took only the slightest bit of energy to keep them from falling across his body. According to Lawnce, a man could sustain a light sleep in that attitude; if he slipped into a heavy slumber, his forearms would fall down on him and wake him up.

He was already having incoherent dreams when he felt his arms falling. He woke up even before his hands could fall against his stomach. It surprised him how well the technique worked, and he indeed felt rested. Judging by the sun, he had slept for half an hour. Feeling refreshed, he picked up his saddle and went to the wagon to get another cup of coffee.

The hands were around the remuda, picking their mounts. Ferrar had decided to start the cattle along the Jornada at dusk, and the cowboys were getting ready. When August finished his coffee he joined them. "Which ones need work?" he asked.

Bob Skull always got to pick his mount first and had roped the claybank mare August had ridden the night before. He looked at August distastefully as he led the claybank from the remuda, but then stopped to regard the horses while the other hands roped their mounts.

"See that bay with the white feet?" Bob said. "That's

Socks. He's got bad habits." With that, he led the claybank to the wagon where his saddle was.

August got one of the cowboys to rope Socks for him. He had no trouble getting the saddle and bridle on the horse, but when he tried to mount, he found out about one of Socks's bad habits. As soon as he put his left boot in the stirrup in preparation to mount, Socks bolted and jerked him off his feet. Luckily, August held on to the reins so the horse didn't get away and his foot slipped out so he didn't get dragged.

The hands laughed, which was to be expected. "Let me hold him for you, Danny," one of them said.

"Nope," August said. "He's got to learn."

He pulled the reins tight enough to bother Socks with the bit and held them down on the saddle horn. Then he vaulted into the saddle without using the stirrup. Socks tried to bolt again, but he was caught unaware and was still bothered by the bit. When August was situated, Socks just stood there meekly. "There, now," August said.

Most of the cowboys were saddled up and moving toward the herd. August decided to ride behind the remuda and get ready to move the horses up the Jornada. But when he nudged Socks and pulled the reins to the right, the horse disobeyed and turned quickly to the left, toward the chuck wagon. August tried to turn him, but Socks trotted purposefully toward the wagon, then broke into a lope. The bridle didn't persuade him in the least.

"Go, Socks!" Bob Skull yelled. The cowboys began to whoop, and the cook, when he saw Socks coming, ran clear of the wagon. Socks was galloping now and August could do nothing to stop him. He headed straight for the wagon, turned sideways just as he reached it, and slammed his left side, and August's left knee, against the tailgate. Then he rubbed as hard as he could, all along the side of the wagon, scraping August's left shin on the wagon wheels.

The cook had gotten the mules about half hitched to the wagon, and they began to kick and make a mess of the harnesses. As soon as August could get his left leg unpinned from the wagon, he jumped down on the right side of Socks and jerked him away from the wagon. He slapped Socks hard across his dinner-plate jaw, but the horse behaved like a gentleman now that the rider was off his back.

August led the horse to the Mexican cowboy who had blindfolded the zebra dun for him the day before. "I'll take them spurs now," he said, still shaking with anger. While the vaquero unbuckled his spurs, August took a stalk of grass from his hatband and stuck it in his mouth.

When he leapt back onto the saddle, August raked Socks fiercely with the spurs as soon as he turned for the wagon. He gouged the horse and fanned his rump with his hat until Socks began to pitch. Every time Socks disobeyed the reins, August applied the spurs. The horse would buck a few licks, then oblige the rider until his sides quit hurting, then bolt for the wagon again. Finally he was too exhausted to fight. August patted him on the neck and talked to him as he began to push the remuda northward along with the cattle herd.

The Jornada del Muerto held little allure for August Dannenberg. It meant riding away from the smell of the Rio Grande. The trail hands had no trouble keeping the herd moving all night, but their joviality grew as distant as the laugh of the river. The Jornada had a reputation for Apache attacks, and the hands had been spooked by all the talk of Indian trouble they would likely run into on the trail.

August didn't give a second thought to the possibility of an Indian attack. He had seen Indians often in Can-

delilla and had hunted with them. He didn't fear them the
way the other drovers did. But he was as low as the rest
of them for his own reasons. The memories of his last
night in Candelilla tormented him. The cowboys kept the
herd moving at a good rate through the night, but it was
a dull ordeal for August.

The glory trail he had expected to mount after his fight
with Maximo had not materialized. In dreams he had
clearly seen himself galloping across the desert, firing at
his pursuers, dropping them one by one from their saddles, with Chepita clinging to him, her arms embracing
him, her voice extolling him. . . .

After dawn, Ferrar stopped for an hour to let the cowboys fill up on coffee. Then he gave the order to continue.
The day became blazing hot, and August was glad he
didn't have to herd the horses directly behind the cattle
where the dust was so bad. He grew tired, but rode all day
without having to use any more of his tobacco.

By dusk the cowboys and the cattle were worn out, but
Ferrar made them keep moving. Indian attacks no longer
concerned them. It didn't seem possible that Indians
could survive in that desert. Some time before midnight,
the herd reached Laguna del Muerto. The summer had
been a wet one and the drovers found water there, but
not enough of it to satisfy the cattle. The first beeves stampeded into the little water hole, and the cowboys had to
move them out quickly so there would be some water left
for the weaker ones. When August finally let the horses
move in, the water was thick as soup.

Ferrar allowed the men to sleep about four hours before the cook kicked them out of their blankets for breakfast. To everyone's surprise, August roped the zebra dun
to ride for the day. "He's tired," August explained as he
saddled the blindfolded dun. "It's a good time to work

him." He wanted a difficult horse to ride to keep his mind off Chepita and Candelilla.

On the third night, the cattle stampeded into the Rio Grande north of the Caballos. They had not stopped moving since leaving Laguna del Muerto. It felt good to August to dip his head in the Rio Grande again and rinse the tobacco juice from his eyes. He had been riding so long that he couldn't figure out how many days it had been since he left Candelilla. He stayed awake with the horses that night while most of the drovers slept, but he spent the next two days sleeping and working with the horses as the stock recuperated from the ordeal of the Jornada.

North of the Jornada, the drive took on a more reasonable routine. By night August kept the remuda bunched up under a star-speckled blanket of desert sky. Early every morning, after eating breakfast in the dark, he would rope one of the wildest horses from the remuda and put on a show for the boys. This made him immensely popular. Ferrar expected the cowboys to use all the mounts in the *caballada,* and some of the bad ones were growing noticeably more docile because of August's work.

The cowboys hadn't taunted him as much as they would have any other new hand—not after seeing him break the zebra dun. Bob Skull was the only exception. "Hey, January," he said one evening. "What do you use for bullets in that popgun? Rabbit shits?"

The next morning August shot the eye out of a rattlesnake that had coiled up between Bob's legs overnight. The gibing ended there.

One morning a cowboy called Randy Joe came to August for advice. He was a flank rider and a pretty good roper and had ambitions of becoming top hand. The cowboys looked on in amazement as Randy Joe roped the zebra dun and saddled him, with August's help. He was thrown twice, but stayed on the third time and didn't risk a dismount all day, not even to relieve himself.

After that, Bob Skull, Randy Joe, and some of the braver punchers kept the zebra dun saddled about every other day. That allowed August to work more with Socks and some of the other broncs.

After taking his morning pitch, August would stake his bronc, help the cook hitch the mules, and sleep for a few hours on the ground as the herd continued north. The cattle moved slowly, so he had no trouble catching up by nightfall. Before rejoining the herd he always spent an hour or so by himself on the riverbank. When he was alone with no work to occupy his mind, he could think of nothing but Chepita. He spoke in tender words, pretending the river would deliver them downstream to her.

At times, alone on the river, he thought he heard Fermin's spurs jingle or smelled the aroma of Tristan's everpresent *cigarro* rolled in corn husk. Stranger still, when he saw the sun glint on some shiny object, he always thought of Maximo's hatband of silver medallions. His head turned habitually to look downriver as if a convulsive twitch pulled it that way every half-minute. It did comfort him to know that all the cowboys in the Ferrar outfit were heavily armed, expecting Indian trouble. If Maximo's men did come to get him, they would have to make a fight of it.

The river fostered a slender ribbon of greenery, the way it did at Candelilla, but the Ferrar herders had to ride a few miles away to avoid the villages that cropped up on its banks. They watered the cattle at the river and bedded them down there. There was usually enough driftwood to keep a fire going, and one of August's jobs was to help the cook drag it into camp.

An occasional bend in the river provided a flat floodplain where descendants of conquistadores and Pueblo

Indians irrigated crops. Corn, beans, peas, and other staples grew there unless washed away by floods. But August had seen such oases of agriculture along his own stretch of the river. It all looked too much like home to comfort him. He rode day after day without seeing the tall timber he had expected to find upriver.

Mel Ferrar recognized a forlorn despair in his night wrangler. The boy preferred to ride alone and didn't talk much around camp unless spoken to first. Ferrar also noticed that August had a peculiar habit of studying the driftwood along the banks of the Rio Grande. He spent the moments he had to himself sitting by the water as if he wanted the current to carry him back downstream.

Mountains towered in the west and east, far away. They seemed to follow the herd for days at the plodding pace of the longhorns. The mountains harbored scrubby green growth, but it didn't look like tall timber to August.

Albuquerque offered the first hope. There were mountains there. Real mountains, big mountains, with towering ponderosa pines growing thick on their shoulders. The two crescent ridges to the east of the old Spanish town were called the Sandia Mountains. *Sandía* meant watermelon. At dusk August noticed how the sun bathed the Alpine faces in the reddish hue of that fruit. The two Sandia crescents looked like heroic slices of watermelon with dark stands of pine representing seeds. From the foothills of the Sandias, he could see the whitewashed adobe belfry of a Catholic church a century and a half old.

"Boss," Bob Skull said as they gathered under the giant wedges of watermelon, "the boys would like to go to town for a while tonight."

"That town ain't like San Antone or Fort Worth," Ferrar said. "That town is slow and you boys are fast. I won't let you loose on it. Save your wages for Granada."

August didn't think much about abandoning the herd for the forested slopes of the Sandias. He sensed his sheltering forests stood somewhere farther upstream. Perhaps as far up as the river's headwaters, however distant that might be. Somewhere up there lofty pines spilled down mountain slopes to the riverbanks. Storm winds ripped their branches away and dropped them into the Rio Grande. Floodwaters carried them all the way to Candelilla where border denizens gathered them for firewood and fence pickets.

Funny thing about that river. No matter how far August rode from his old surroundings, the river remained familiar. It bound him like a tether to Candelilla and to Chepita and to the pleasant, dreary life he had destroyed. The river whispered sympathetically from its riffles and eddies. It bled for him: a vein of living water.

South of Santa Fe more Ferrar cowboys joined the herd to take over August's chores, but the boss offered to let the nighthawk ride on to Granada. He declined. Granada was situated far from the Rio Grande. The herd would turn east to follow the Santa Fe Trail around the Sangre de Cristo Mountains. August wanted to continue northward into Santa Fe and beyond. Ferrar provided him with some hardtack and coffee for the trail plus eighteen dollars for eighteen days of work.

"You'll need a horse," Ferrar said. "I should make you keep that nag you rode in on, but you've done so much work with the remuda, I'm going to give you your choice. I suspect you'll pick old Socks. He seems to take to you."

"No," August said. "I want that big claybank mare."

Ferrar laughed. "You know horses! I shouldn't have given you the choice." When he had settled up with August, Ferrar shook his hand. "What is it about that river that interests you so?" he asked before turning back to the herd.

"I reckon it's the tall timber."

August had never imagined so many people gathered in a spot as small as Santa Fe. Sheep, maybe, but not people. The old city beat all the frontier boy had heard about New York and St. Louis put together. He had once seen three hundred people at a horse race and had attended a hanging in Presidio that had attracted almost a thousand. But Santa Fe teemed with more human activity than a triple hanging and a horse race in two heats.

In Santa Fe a body could buy anything ever invented. August browsed in stores selling things he didn't even recognize. He inquired about one item. "What's that?" he asked the storekeeper.

"Coffee grinder. Do you want to buy something or just ask questions?"

In camp August had always ground his coffee beans against a rock with the butt of a pistol grip or the handle of a knife, the way Lawnce had shown him. And Santos used a metate at Las Quince Letras.

He lost count at twenty-five stores. He saw a bakery, too, and two haberdasheries and one shop where a fellow managed to earn a living by making boots and nothing else. Of course, there was a grogshop on every block.

August spent part of his wages on a used .44-caliber, octagonal-barreled Winchester rifle and ammunition for it. He figured on doing some hunting up the river. He looked forward to doing it on his own, without having to wait for Mescaleros to invite him in trade for dead rats. He also purchased an extra blanket and a small Dutch oven.

"I'd like to swap you out of that pocket pistol," the

trader said. "I could use that to wing me some shoplifters."

"No, thanks," August said.

He treated himself to a couple of good meals with real
yeast bread, and pie for dessert. In the cafés and stores
he heard more talk about Utes on the warpath up north.
"We didn't see one Ute feather," said a freighter who had
come down the Taos Trail. "But I could feel them there
in the timber and sometimes the mules would snort. And
I dreamed of Indians two nights in a row north of Taos.
They're all around up there, and they'll scalp somebody
for sure before they go back to the reservation."

After dark, August sat under the gallery of the govern-
ment palace and watched the Spanish girls walk around
the plaza with their chaperons. Young men circled the
public square in an outer path that moved in the opposite
direction. The glances of young men and young women
met; they exchanged nods and smiles. In such a way en-
gagements were declared, marriages arranged. August
imagined his own path crossing Chepita's in that strange
and romantic scene. There was something to it, he
thought. It would have been convenient to have someone
else arrange it all for him. He had tried to make his own
arrangements and fouled his life up forever.

Late that night the Texas fugitive rode down to the
Santa Fe River, one of the Rio Grande's fingers, to bed
down on the ground. He was glad he had purchased the
extra blanket. Early autumn nights at Santa Fe's altitude
felt like Candelilla in the wake of a norther.

He couldn't sleep. He was used to staying up nights,
after eighteen days of nighthawking, so he stared at the
stars for a while and fancied a bright one as the twinkle
of Chepita's eyes. He would never see her again, he reminded himself. Only the river bound them now. The
trickle of the water finally lulled him to sleep.

16

Lawnce could easily have followed August's trail. He knew the right questions to ask and the logical places to start. No fugitive other than Maximo de Guerra had eluded Lawnce, and he only because every Mexican under the sun covered for him.

In August's case, Lawnce already had a clue. The Mescaleros had told him of a certain army captain at Fort Quitman they had seen riding the ranger's old gray gelding.

But Lawnce didn't know if finding August would be the best move for anybody but himself. He sat under the thatched gallery of Las Quince Letras and puzzled over what he should do. He missed the boy he had coddled as a babe, and to think of August having to leave Candelilla between suns gave him no small amount of shame.

It had been eighteen years since the typhus epidemic in San Antonio had killed August's parents. "Folks were dyin' like sheep with the rot," Lawnce would say when telling of that plague. A lawyer was giving Lawnce room and board to care for horses and buggies, allowing him to live in the carriage house. One day at the height of the epidemic, the lawyer came back from court with a baby wrapped in a gunnysack. Someone had stashed the infant in his buggy. A note pinned to the sack said the child's name was August Dannenberg and his German parents had died of typhus. Probably the landlord of the baby's parents had rid himself of the burden by depositing it in the lawyer's buggy. The lawyer gave Lawnce a dollar to locate a home for the foundling.

Lawnce was unable to turn up any relatives who would look after the baby, and everyone else feared the little immigrant would pass on the disease, so Lawnce himself had taken the boy in, being no stranger to papooses.

After the epidemic had run its course, Lawnce hired on to buy mules for the overland mail. He left August with a German family while he founded Candelilla and treated with the Indians. Then he sent for "the kid," as he commonly called August. He couldn't rightly call him "son," and the name "August," to him, sounded too seasoned for a mere spring cub. There was no formal adoption, but everyone around Candelilla knew August was Lawnce's charge.

He got Grimes to school the kid and Santos to feed him, but Lawnce himself had assumed the responsibility of making him into a respectable man, and now he felt he had failed. He had been too quick with orders and too slow with good advice. It hurt him considerably not being able to recall the way the boy spoke or the way he walked or the way he looked with a straw in his mouth. He came to the painful conclusion that the whole affair was nobody's fault but his very own.

It was the time for the tunas to ripen on the prickly-pear cactus, and Lawnce had a basket of the pear-apples beside his chair. He peeled one as he mulled his problems over. First, he sliced the ends away from the oblong fruit. His leathery fingers turned the little clusters of stickers like a pair of bull-hide chaps. He made an incision down the length of the purplish skin of the fruit and then began to peel it off the way he had seen the whores at the Pitchfork Saloon remove their corsets after nightfall. He chomped on pieces of the pungent cactus fruit until a singular spectacle sapped his attention.

Under heavy guard, Maximo turned the dogleg of the side street opposite Las Quince Letras. His frame lacked its usual rigidity, but his eyes shone with more darkness than ever. He spotted Lawnce and changed his course to confront the ranger.

Lawnce felt charitable enough to meet the mending desperado halfway in the street. *"Cómo está?"* he inquired.

"Poco bien," Maximo said. "Where is the boy hiding?"

"I didn't think it likely I'd see *you* skulkin' down the street today, Maximo. But blame if you ain't here and all stood up straighter than a bodark fencepost!"

Maximo made no reply to the niceties. *"Dónde?"*

Lawnce let the grin slide out from under his mustache as he looked into the eyes of the desperado. "This trouble is liable to put you and me in different camps. I wish we could git around that."

"Don Lawnce, you are the only gringo Maximo knows as a friend . . ."

"Well, I ain't but half gringo, and I never called it my best portion, at that."

Maximo held his hand out weakly to interrupt. "Yes, but you do Maximo no honor if you do not say where the boy is hiding."

Lawnce shrugged. *"Quién sabe?"*

"Tú sabe. You know how to find the boy. It is said that you can find the souls of dead sinners. It is a gift with you."

Lawnce coughed out a single guffaw. "There you go tellin' them windies again. You know there's plenty of things I can't find and some I don't want to. I ain't been able to find the skunk that keeps stealin' those Doubletree cattle, now, have I? And the kid's trail is one thing I won't even stoop down to look for."

Maximo trembled with anger. "He cannot hide forever." He turned, holding the shoulders of his guards, and hobbled away. His insides were still sore, but he would soon be back on a saddle.

Lawnce had thought about arresting Maximo for the attempted murder of August Dannenberg, but decided he probably lacked the evidence demanded by the Revised Statutes. He was really not up to doing war with every *bandito* on the border anyway and thought he would probably have to if he arrested Maximo.

He knew one thing for certain: any attempt he made to find August would bring death down on the boy's shoulders. Maximo had a simple-minded tracker in his ranks named Tristan who could follow a cold trail at midnight.

Lawnce returned to his shady spot under the cantina gallery. He owed his life to the desperado, and—though he had probably returned the favor the morning he caught Gainey sneaking into Chepita's house—he couldn't get used to the idea of squaring off against Maximo.

It was just north of Chihuahua, over two years before, that Lawnce and Maximo had first met. Lawnce and two guards from the overland stage service were riding south, leading a mule loaded with a few thousand dollars in gold. Just when he was beginning to think they might get through to buy the mules without a scrape, the bandits struck.

The first volley killed the two guards and spooked the gold-laden mule. Lawnce caught the mule among the crags of a bald limestone knob and stayed there all afternoon, holding the bandits off with his Spencer. But his ammunition dwindled, and he knew he would be lucky to last till nightfall.

Then a remarkable thing happened. A rival force of bandits arrived and chased away Lawnce's attackers.

They were led by a reckless horseman wearing a silver-studded sombrero.

Lawnce could easily remember the first sentence he heard Maximo speak: "I am looking for a man with one eye."

Lawnce knew three one-eyed men. One of them had stepped in front of a cannon during a salute to San Jacinto Day. But he turned out not to be the one Maximo was looking for; he had lost an arm along with the eye, and Maximo was looking for a man missing only an eye. Another one-eyed acquaintance of Lawnce's was a Delaware Indian scout with the U.S. Cavalry who had lost an eye in a fight with Apaches. But Maximo was looking for a one-eyed gringo, a big man with a reddish face. That description matched Butch Gainey. Lawnce told his rescuer that Gainey ranched about ten miles east of Candelilla.

He offered Maximo a hundred dollars in gold for saving him from the first gang of bandits. Maximo gladly took it and escorted the mule buyer into Chihuahua. About six months later he showed up in Candelilla with his gang. Then Doubletree cattle began to disappear.

Maximo was a bandit. But every man in northern Mexico who was not a bandit was dictated to by one. Maximo simply would not be tyrannized. Most of the rival warlords, the hacendados, offered protection for a price to the villages in their realms. But Maximo provided his services as a favor and profited more than his enemies because he had something the other hacendados lacked—charisma.

It was regarded as a privilege to fund Maximo's campaigns, to house his bandits, to feed them, arm them, and hide them. It was considered an honor to touch the silver medallions on his sombrero for luck. His dash and charm earned him more than money; they earned him almost absolute loyalty.

He and his men also sold protection to trains of copper and silver wagons as they moved from the mines to Texas along the Chihuahua Road. There was good money in protecting the bull trains—more silver than Maximo could give away. Enough to establish a fine ranch somewhere. But for some reason Maximo preferred to stay in Candelilla, living with a mistress under a dried mud ceiling, snatching scattered herds of near-worthless cattle from a one-eyed rancher.

Lawnce peeled another pear-apple and brooded over the problem of Maximo until he heard a clatter approaching from the southeast. The mail hack was coming under escort of two cavalrymen. Something good might come of the day after all, he thought, for he was expecting several months' back pay and a new stock of firewater for the cantina.

As the hack got closer, Lawnce noticed a second person riding beside the driver. The sight made him squint and tip his hat back. It was a woman. A white woman.

The hack stopped in front of the Pitchfork Saloon. When the woman spoke to the driver, he pointed in Lawnce's direction. She wore a wide straw hat and practical store-bought garb. She looked uncommonly clean. Instead of waiting for the driver to come around and help her down, she jumped from the hack on her own account, brushing a loose strand of cinnamon hair over her ear.

Her figure was full and angular, sturdy, the kind of shape Lawnce associated with successful childbearing. He sized her up the way a stockman would look over a brood mare. He figured he outweighed her by fifty pounds, but she looked so able that he decided he wouldn't want to tangle with her, at least not in a tussle. She grabbed a single bag and walked toward the cantina.

Lawnce liked that; she knew how to travel light. She was attractive enough, but an authoritative air overwhelmed her good looks. Lawnce knew at once she had come for a reason, and he was thankful for whatever the reason was.

"I am looking for Ranger John McCrary." She spoke distinctly in a brassy voice. Her lips were dry and cracked, but rather red nonetheless. Lawnce figured her for about his own age, though she looked several years younger. She was from some big city back east where the houses and buildings had saved her features from the elements.

"The critter stands before you, ma'am. What can I do for you?"

She said nothing for a few seconds, but looked up and down Lawnce's slovenly frame. She had blue eyes, which he had seldom seen on a woman in the border country. Her sharp features—an angular chin, thin cheekbones, and a small nose that tilted upward—fit the way she liked to get to the point.

"You are the ranger?"

"Yes, ma'am. How can I help you?"

"Is there somewhere we can talk? Your office, perhaps?"

"Wait right there, ma'am." Lawnce ducked into Las Quince Letras and emerged with a rawhide-bound chair, which he dragged with his own into the widening shade against the east side of the cantina. He sat in the chair nearer the street and invited the lady to join him. She pressed her lips together hard, but took her seat without complaint, dropping her bag beside her.

"Well," Lawnce said, "it's a right pleasantful day. A little hot yet, but there's a good breeze out of the south." He could feel the wind cooling the back of his neck.

"I didn't come here to discuss the weather, Mr. McCrary."

"You just said you wanted to talk, ma'am. Didn't say what about."

Her lips bent into an impatient smirk that quickly became an involuntary smile. Buckteeth pushed against her lower lip. "Yes, of course. I shall try to be more specific. My name is Penelope Blankenship. I have two reasons for coming here. First, and more important, I'm looking for a man."

"Well, Miss Penelope, if a man's all you're after, I'd be happy to oblige a pretty lady like yourself." Lawnce grinned and winked to make it known he meant nothing offensive by the remark.

"I accept your compliment, sir," she said with a mere hint of blush in her cheeks. "And please call me Nelly."

"And you can holler Lawnce when you want me, Miss Nelly. Or John. John's my front name, but everybody calls me Lawnce."

"Yes, of course, Mr. McCrary—John. But actually, I'm looking for a particular man."

"Oh, that wouldn't be none of me then, Miss Nelly. I ain't particular about nothin' much but horseflesh."

Nelly suddenly put her sleeve to her nostrils. "Mr. Mc-Crary, may I sit in that chair?"

"Whatever makes you more comfortable."

"Is that better, ma'am?" Lawnce asked, checking on the new arrangement.

"Yes, much."

"How come?"

Nelly looked compassionately at the ranger. "Well, you were upwind."

Lawnce was almost crushed with embarrassment, but he sniffed his shirt and shrugged as if he didn't give a damn.

"The man I'm looking for is named Ryder—T. P. Ryder

or Thomas Payton Ryder or Reverend Professor Thomas Payton Ryder. Have you heard of him?"

" 'Fraid I ain't heard of nary of 'em."

"I was told in Presidio that you are the best manhunter in the Big Bend, so I thought I would ask for your help in finding Professor Ryder."

Lawnce let his reputation draw him up a little straighter in his seat. "What's this Ryder wanted for?"

"He's not a fugitive, Mr. McCrary—John. He is a dear friend and a former professor at Harvard. He came west to study tribes of Indians and disappeared several years ago without a trace."

"How come it's your job to find him?"

"It's not my job, sir, it's my avocation. My job is the second reason for my coming here. I have a contract with *Fulton's* magazine of Boston to provide feature stories from the West. They have agreed to pay my expenses abroad, which gives me the opportunity to search for Professor Ryder during my travels."

Nelly found a stare of bewilderment confronting her.

"I don't exactly follow you, Miss Nelly."

"I search for Professor Ryder in my spare time. My job is to write magazine stories, which I send back to Boston."

Lawnce nodded vacantly. "What story brings you here?"

"I heard of a sensational murder in this town, so I came to get the facts about it and ask your advice about finding Professor Ryder."

"Wasn't no murder hereabouts. Just a puny little gunfight. Nobody even got kilt."

Nelly reached into her bag for a writing case and had the pen dipped in the inkwell before Lawnce could finish his sentence. "I understood a very important leader among the Mexican community was shot," she insisted.

"Who? Maximo? Important? Don't fret none over him.
It ain't the first time he's got shot at."

"Who did the shooting?"

"Oh, that don't make much difference now, ma'am. The
kid that done it's plum out of the country and ain't likely
to ever come back. There ain't been no charges pressed
or nothin'."

"And what actions did you take to prevent the assailant
from escaping?"

"Ma'am?"

"What did you do to catch the . . . the gunman who shot
Mr. Maximo?"

"Couldn't do much of anything about it. I was so tanked
up at the time you could have shot me in the head and
I wouldn't have died till I sobered up."

Miss Blankenship stopped scribbling and looked
sternly at the ranger. "You don't like reporters asking
about police matters, do you Mr. McCrary?"

Lawnce curled his mustache handle for a moment and
looked beyond the brim of his straw sombrero. "Can't say
as I know, Miss Nelly. This here is the first time it's ever
happened to me. But so far, I'm findin' it plumb agree-
able, considerin' the reporter's good looks and all."

Nelly smiled and brushed her hair behind her ear
again. "Yes, thank you, Mr. McCrary, but I need the facts
on the shooting, or some other story to send to my magazine. If I don't find a story, I will have to move on, and
I would much rather stay here for some time to learn all
I can from you on the subject of tracing missing persons."

A white woman was too much of a curiosity in the Big
Bend. Lawnce didn't intend to let the one seated upwind
of him slip off before he had had a chance to study her
some.

"Oh, Miss Nelly," he said, "this here country is packed
full of yarns and windies, and I aim to help you every step

I can. I just don't jabber too good on a empty stomach. But if you'll have some supper with me this evenin', I'll tell you the whole story about the shootin' and tell you all I know about huntin' lost human beans to boot."

Nelly pondered the proposal. "Will you bathe first?"

"You mean warsh?"

"Yes."

"Well, the full moon ain't riz, and I generally don't warsh up till it does. But I reckon I can go it a few days early for your sake, ma'am."

"Don't you enjoy bathing?"

"No, ma'am, can't say as I do. The damned ol' Comanch' ruined it for me. They caught me when I was a youngun and they taken and throwed me into every blamed water hole they come to, and always before sunup of a mornin', no matter how cold it was. After I quit being a Injun, I swore off warshin' except on the full moon. I wouldn't warsh none then, neither, but I'd git so gamey I'd be liable to draw bears and painters on myself or spook the stock."

Nelly scrawled a note about Lawnce's history among the Comanche. "How did you come to be captured by the Indians?" she asked.

"Wasn't difficult," he answered.

"No, I suppose not. But I would like to hear the details. Were you captured from one of the American settlements?"

"Nope," Lawnce said. "Texan."

"I see. But that would be considered American, would it not?"

"I never even been to the states, ma'am, not even since they joined with Texas."

"You mean after Texas joined the states, of course."

Lawnce shrugged. "That's how some folks look at it. But you tell me, Miss Nelly. If a bunch a little ones join one big one—who joined who?"

Who joined *whom*, Nelly thought, but didn't endeavor to correct the ranger's grammar. "An interesting point of view, Mr. McCrary. At any rate, I think your personal experiences with the savages might make an interesting story, if they are true."

"Now, Miss Nelly, if you knowed me any better you'd caution yourself for talkin' that way. Lawnce McCrary ain't never told nothin' but the gospel."

Nelly observed him with some skepticism, but couldn't detect a wrinkle of falseness, and she had a keen eye for liars. "If the truth is as important to you as it is to me, Mr. McCrary, you will prove an invaluable source."

"*Muy buena,*" Lawnce said, slapping his knee. "So, how about that supper?"

"I would be pleased, sir. If you will direct me to the hotel, you may call on me there at seven."

"Ma'am, we ain't got no hotel in Candelilla. There's feather beds at the Pitchfork, but the ladies that sleep on 'em generally have company in there with 'em. I believe the safest place for you to camp is over at my livery. There's a good cot there, and you can latch the door and all. The kid that shot up Maximo used to bunk there."

Nelly agreed to quarter in the tack room if only to research the gunman who had shot the local leader of the Mexican community. Lawnce carried her bag and showed her into the livery. Before he left her, he spent a few minutes searching a cabinet of rough-hewn planks attached to the wall. He tossed out broken bits of bridle leather and odd pieces of hardware and finally found what he was looking for—a chunk of lye soap.

"I'll call on you about sundown, Miss Nelly, and see to it that you get as square a feed as a bloated heifer in a alfalfa patch."

17

The sun still commanded a high station when Lawnce rode Little Satan down to the river. He unsaddled the mustang and tied the reins to a willow switch. At the riverbank, he tugged at his boots for a few minutes until they came off. He put his hunk of soap in one sock and then looked up and down the river before shedding the rest of his clothes. He waded in under a willow branch with his gun belt over his shoulder and his clothes under his arm.

The water was only waist deep. He hooked his holster carefully over the limb, within easy reach. Holding the soap-stuffed sock in his teeth, he began rinsing his clothes in the river, working the dirt out of every garment, applying lather to the grimiest parts. By the time he had hung every stitch to dry, the sun was low enough to shine under the upper boughs and directly onto his clothes to dry them. A hot breeze from the south also helped.

After looking carefully around him again, Lawnce held his breath and ducked briefly under the water's surface. The perch kept nibbling at his backside like horseflies pestering an old stallion. He worked up some lather in his sock and scrubbed his hair with it, leaving his watchful eyes open despite the stinging suds. He washed his face, paying particular attention to his mustache, and then ducked under again to rinse.

The dusty layer of sky above the horizon began to filter the sun's light to orange. Lawnce was scrubbing his armpits with his sock when he heard Little Satan grumble.

Without splashing, he rinsed one hand in the river and then wrapped it around his pistol grip. In a few seconds he heard the rustle of skirts and saw Nelly's straw hat come over the rim of the riverbank.

"Good afternoon, Mr. McCrary—John. I was advised by Mr. Santos at the cantina to bathe in the river rather than in the tub at the Pitchfork Saloon. I see you take your own baths here." She sat down on a smooth driftwood log, a large log of ponderosa pine that had floated down from somewhere far upstream. She removed her hat and began unhooking the buttons on her shoes.

"Ma'am, it appears you've found me in a bashful way." He sank down until the water reached his Adam's apple.

"Oh, please, John. I believe in the sanctity of nudity."

"Huh?"

"Nakedness is innocence, sir." Nelly was rolling her stockings down her legs.

"That's sort of a squaw's way of thinkin'." Lawnce rose a little higher in the water and continued scrubbing.

"I knew you would understand." Nelly glanced at Lawnce and noticed his mode of bathing. "Is that your sock?"

"Yes, ma'am."

"Why do you wash yourself with a sock?"

"Well, if you put your soap in a sock, like a chicken in a gunnysack, you're not liable to lose it. And if you use your sock to warsh with, you won't never need no warshcloth, which would just be extra baggage. And you can save time by warshin' your socks and yourself all at once."

Nelly nodded approvingly. "An admirable economy of labor." She stood and began removing the hairpins from her tresses. They fell about her shoulders like the tails of a dozen palominos.

"Miss Nelly," Lawnce said as she unfastened the first

button of her blouse, "maybe you ought to turn around and let me clear out before you get any more nekkid." He piled his drying clothes on one arm and draped his gun belt around his neck.

"Nonsense, John. We are adults."

"That's what concerns me, ma'am."

By now Nelly was down to her whalebone corset. A mischievous smile curled one corner of her mouth. "Please don't feel embarrassed on my account." She was fumbling with the laces of the corset behind her back.

"Now, Nelly, I'm bein' honest with you when I tell you I'm fixin' to come on out in the open air."

"Then this is my opportunity to see what value you place upon honesty."

With mischievous delight, she watched the sunlight glistening on Lawnce's wet shoulders, highlighting the ripples of his musculature. Because he had Mexican blood, his skin was not pallid underneath his clothing like the bodies of some men Nelly had seen undressed. That had been the first thing to catch her attention upon finding him in the river. That and the strong, rough hands she had studied when they met. She was not attracted to men with hands softer than her own.

Nelly gasped when Lawnce splashed nervously up to the riverbank, strategically positioning his clothes.

"That is a horrid scar there below your ribs," she said.

"Is that all you seen?" Lawnce asked, trying to decide on the quickest way to clothe himself.

"How did it happen?" Nelly was still struggling with the laces of her corset. She refused to relieve Lawnce by casting her gaze elsewhere.

"Well, ma'am," Lawnce said, absentmindedly putting his shirt on over the holster across his shoulders, "it was back in 'sixty-four on the Llano Estacado. I was scoutin' for horse-thievin' Injuns when I came across a buffalo bull and decided to have me a little fun and rope the brute." He removed the shirt and buckled the gun belt around his naked waist to get it out of the way.

"I shook out a loop and dropped it over his woolly ol' head and took my dallies and throwed him on the ground. Then I got more thoughtful and figured I better not plug the critter 'cause the gunfire would bring Injuns down on me." Lawnce removed the gun belt and slung it back across his shoulders so he could get his pants on.

"But I couldn't stand to let him go with my gut line, or cut it neither, so while my horse kept the reata choked on him, I pulled my long ol' butcher knife out to cut the rascal's throat, but not before he jumped up and punched a hole in me with that horn of his." Lawnce put his right foot through the left leg of his trousers.

Nelly pulled her hair over one shoulder and approached Lawnce. He held his pants in front of him defensively. She touched the scar below his rib cage, making him flinch like a wild stud poked with a sharp stick. She turned her back to the ranger.

"Help me with these laces," she said.

18

Nelly Blankenship had filled several pages with notes on the life of Lawnce McCrary. They sat together on the porch of the cantina as the ranger kept the journalist highly entertained with his personal history.

". . . so I came to elbow my way into a sort of partnership in Las Quince Letras."

"What does that mean—Las Quince Letras?"

"Means 'the fifteen letters,'" Lawnce said. "What's that first letter you see up there on the sign?" He pointed to some faded red characters barely visible on the whitewashed wall.

"*L*," Nelly answered, squinting.

"That's number one. Now, what's the second letter?"

"*A.*"

"That there's letter number two. If you count heads on 'em all, you'll find fifteen Mexican alphabets on that sign, and that's why this here place is called Las Quince Letras."

Nelly smiled and jotted down the story behind the cantina's name.

"My stars," Lawnce said, looking at the compact shadow cast by a hitching post. "I've bunched my whole life into one mornin.' I guess you got more goods on me now than Carter's got oats."

"Including some information the magazine dare not publish for fear of invoking the wrath of those who enforce the obscenity laws," Nelly said with a seductive arch of one eyebrow.

Lawnce blushed across his forehead where his sombrero kept the sun from tanning his face. "Nelly, you are the forwardest woman I ever heard tell of!" He put his left leg across his right knee and thumped the rowel of his spur. "Not just your loose talkin', but comin' out on the border country by yourself and all. When I lived in San Antone, I knowed a newspaperman or two and they was all just that—menfolks. I never thought they'd allow a gal in that line of work."

"I grew up in a girls' orphanage in Boston," Nelly explained. "I was the biggest and toughest girl in the place, and I could do whatever I wished among the others. When I entered this man's world, I saw no reason to change for the sake of femininity."

"There you go. Now, suppose you tell me a little bit more about yourself," Lawnce suggested. "You're up on me in that respect."

"Before I do," she replied, "I want to tell you the history of Professor Thomas Payton Ryder. My own life truly began only after I made his acquaintance."

Lawnce felt jealous, but he shrugged and told her to get on with the story.

"T. P. Ryder was born to wealthy parents in Concord, Massachusetts, where he acquired the accepted social graces, excelled in all athletics, and was particularly proficient at his lessons. When he was sixteen years of age, his parents enrolled him in the private school where Henry David Thoreau taught. There he became a protégé to some of the greatest American thinkers—Emerson, Channing, and Hawthorne, in addition to Thoreau. He was a particular favorite of Emerson."

"Emerson who?" Lawnce asked.

"Ralph Waldo Emerson, the essayist and lecturer."

"Never heard of him."

"No, I don't suppose you would have. Well, to continue:
I am told that young Thomas Payton Ryder was one of
the most eligible bachelors in old Massachusetts. He was
even hardier than most young men of his age—robust,
with a commanding voice. He courted the most beautiful
society belles, but betrothed himself to none.

"After graduating with honors from Harvard, he traveled to Göttingen, Germany, to study theology. He took
an interest in the arts there and, after being approbated
to preach, became apprentice to a master sculptor in Flor-
ence. Then he traveled throughout the Continent and
learned to speak Italian and French in addition to his German. He later spent two years at a Portuguese mission
on the east coast of Africa, where he converted many of
the natives to Christianity."

Nelly saw that Lawnce was struggling to stay with the
story. "I say, John, is this all coming quite clear to you?"

"The man made a parson?"

"Yes, I suppose you could call him a parson. Reverend,
actually."

"Reverend's good by me. Go on."

"Well, Reverend Ryder returned to Massachusetts, but
soon, yielding again to wanderlust, booked passage on a
clipper ship bound for the Orient where, along the route,
he studied the habits and customs of island peoples and
the great civilizations of China.

"I was still living in the orphanage in Boston when Reverend Ryder returned from his travels abroad and became professor of anthropology at Harvard."

"What become of your folks?" Lawnce was still more
interested in Nelly's story than in Thomas Payton
Ryder's. He was particularly interested in her parentage.
He believed breeding was as important in humans as it
was in horses.

"I am told that my father was killed on a whaling ship before I was born and my mother died when a fish bone became lodged in her throat. I don't remember her. I was too young."

Lawnce was glad to hear that Nelly's father had died an active death, but the fish bone worried him. A robust woman should have been able to cough it up. Ever since he and Nelly had gotten naked together down at the riverbank, he had entertained himself by imagining what their offspring would look like if they were to start producing a herd of them. He didn't want to have any children who weren't strong enough to cough up a fish bone. He wanted his kids as healthy as Comanches.

"I recollect my folks, some," Lawnce said, thinking of his own bloodline. "But I done told you all that. Get on with your story."

Nelly supposed he meant the story of T. P. Ryder. "As a clergyman," she continued, "Reverend Ryder took an interest in the children at the orphanage. We girls worked behind the fish market at that time, cleaning the daily catch. Some of us were taken advantage of by . . . fishermen. But when Reverend Ryder saw the conditions under which we labored, he invested thousands of dollars of his own family's wealth to improve our lives. From that time on we received lessons in the afternoon and we only had to work half-days.

"One morning at the fish market, the reverend professor caught a man who had taken a girl against her will. He took the man below the decks of a scow and caned the filthy brute nigh to death.

"Sometimes Reverend Ryder would tutor us himself. He personally taught me how to read when I was fifteen."

Lawnce thumped his rowel so hard it spun like a whirligig. "You didn't know how to read?" he asked.

"I wasn't born reading."

"How long did it take you to learn?"

"The reverend had developed a system of teaching letters by means of which he could have almost any pupil reading simple passages in a matter of weeks. Why is that important to you?"

"Ain't important," Lawnce said. "I just figured a gal that writes readin' ought to have learned to read writin'."

"Yes, but I did learn. That is my point. I have just told you that Reverend Ryder personally taught me to read."

"But not till you was near growed. If you'd waited much longer you wouldn't have been able to learn it."

Nelly scoffed. "That is a ridiculous myth, John. The human mind retains a capacity for learning for the duration of life under normal circumstances."

"That ain't how it works for dogs," Lawnce replied. "You have to start learnin' them when they're pups or they don't learn nothin' at all."

"Dumb animals have no reasoning capability and are not to be placed in the same category with humans. At least not as far as learning is concerned." Nelly waited for Lawnce's rebuttal, but he was tired of arguing about it.

"Well, get on with the story about the reverend," he finally said.

"Anyway," Nelly continued, "I took an interest in all my studies, and Professor Ryder noticed. He began to spend more time teaching me, and when I was seventeen, he arranged an internship for me at the *Boston Globe* while I studied literature and journalism. Professor Ryder was my personal counselor and tutor."

Lawnce wrinkled his eyebrows suspiciously.

"He was rather like an uncle to me," Nelly explained for the sake of Ryder's reputation more than her own, "and I think I was like a baby sister to him. Of course, there was no romantic relationship between the two of us. I was an awkward adolescent; Professor Ryder was a bachelor of renown who courted the most beautiful ladies on the eastern seaboard. I was rather plain; he was huge and handsome and maintained his form through a daily regimen of swimming and walking. He took particular pride in his appearance. He wore the finest silk suits, tailored to perfection, and *daily* visited his barber, who trimmed his beard and shaped his marvelous head of auburn hair, which he had worn rather long and flowing ever since his travels in foreign lands had taken him beyond the reach of shears. Vanity, it seems, was his only vice." Nelly paused and stared blankly into the noon sky. "I suppose his hair could be graying by now. He will be fifty soon."

Lawnce understood only a slice of Nelly's terminology, but he could tell the image of the reverend professor was in her mind. "He ought to have got him a good horse."

"Why do you say that?"

"So he wouldn't have to do all that swimmin' and walkin'."

Nelly didn't try to explain calisthenics to the ranger.

"So how come the reverend to go Injun huntin'?" Lawnce asked.

"He came west to *study* Indians, John, not to hunt them."

The ranger bent his features into a quizzical expression. "I reckon he'll need all them smarts of his to figure out a Injun. I don't mean to upset you none, Nelly, but you ought to admit that maybe Reverend Ryder has studied the business end of a scalpin' knife by now."

"I have considered all the possibilities." Nelly pulled a folded scrap of paper from her satchel and handed it to Lawnce. "Here is his letter of resignation from Harvard. It explains his reasons for coming west."

Lawnce reluctantly accepted the message and turned

it over and around several times. "I never did learn to read handwritin'. Looks like somethin' a turkey scratched in the dirt to me. Would you read it for me?"

She reclaimed the document and cleared her throat. "'My Esteemed Colleagues,' et cetera, et cetera. 'On this, the eve of my fortieth year, I pause to reflect on my accomplishments and triumphs. I have traversed the wide meridians of the globe by forested land and stormy sea. I have loosened heathens from the bonds of idolatry and fetishism and set them aloft on the wings of Christianity. I have studied and taught the peoples of the earth from the Barbary Coast to the Sandwich Isles.

"'Yet, in my soul I hear the horn of a final hunt. It beckons me westward to the plains and mountains of our own great land. Verily, I have trod the soil of foreign continents and ignored my own. I must proceed forthwith, for no other shall equal our own times in our own West. Men of letters must go among the savages in the wilderness ere they are savage and wild no more.

"'I depart with your blessings. Respectfully, Thomas Payton Ryder.' And here he quotes the Caliph Ali as a postscript: 'Thy lot or portion of life is seeking after thee; therefore be at rest from seeking after it.'"

Lawnce put his hat on his knee and scratched his head. "I heap savvy that part about the huntin' horn," he said. "The rest sounds kind of fuzzy."

"That is perhaps the most important part. The horn represents Professor Ryder's call to come west before the West is tamed by men like you, John."

The ranger shrugged knowingly. "What gave you the notion that your reverend came this way?"

"I lost his trail in the Indian Territory," Nelly said. "Upon leaving Massachusetts, Professor Ryder traveled by rail to Chicago. I spoke to a conductor who remembered him; he is a rather singular character. He traveled northwest into the Sioux Nation from there. He spent some two years among the Sioux and the Village Indians along the Missouri River. Chief Red Cloud spoke very fondly of him.

"Then he moved south to Fort Dodge. According to an outfitter in that settlement, he joined a band of buffalo hunters there who were bound for the Indian Territory. Unfortunately, Professor Ryder's buffalo hunting companions were all massacred by Kiowa Indians, so none of them lived to tell me where he might have gone. An army captain who recovered the mutilated bodies said neither the professor nor his personal effects were among the dead. His trail has vanished for me. But since I last heard of him traveling southward, I decided to search throughout Texas before turning my attentions westward."

"You're on the right trail, Nelly. You just come to a river and you don't know where to ford it."

"What do you mean?"

"An ol' Injun tracker told me once that tracks tell a story that a river makes into secrets. But them tracks cross the water somewhere, and all you have to do is find where. Did you ask the outfitter in Dodge what the reverend carried out of the store?"

"Yes, I asked as many questions as I could think of. He bought a buffalo hunting rifle and a large supply of powder and lead as well as food supplies. He obviously intended to participate in shooting the buffalo."

"Did the feller at the store recognize anything queer about him? Somethin' that would cause a feller to gawk?"

"Yes, the outfitter noticed his fur coat and a wolf-hide knapsack he carried on his back. He said the professor referred to it as his 'medicine bundle.' And of course his great shock of flowing hair drew some attention."

"So you're lookin' for a big bearded feller totin' a buffalo gun and a medicine bundle and wearin' a fur coat and has got long hair. How many head of them critters you reckon could be runnin' loose, anyhow? There ain't no mystery to findin' him. You just have to ask every soul from here to judgment if they seen him—especially the lawmen; they've all got eyeballs used to sizin' men up. If they ain't heard of him, tell 'em where you're headin' next so they can follow you up if they do spot him. Tell 'em to write a letter or tap a message on the talkin' wire to that magazine you work for, an' they can get the word to you."

"That idea hadn't occurred to me. Yes, I shall make sure everyone knows how to contact me from now on. Particularly you, John. However, I'm in no hurry to leave you just yet. I think I shall stay here in Candelilla for some time. I may have trouble with my corset again."

"Gracious!" Lawnce said, angling his hat brim to cover his face. "You are the forwardest woman!"

19

New Mexico began to enchant August north of Santa Fe. The deserts of the south had crumpled and risen into great ranges of mountains. August found the first outriders of his timber at the river's edge. Still, he felt compelled to ride around each successive bend. Exploration appealed to him as much as it must have to the conquistadores who had trekked the same valley centuries ahead of him.

He found the territory completely absent of human activity. The Indian scare had caused everyone to fort up or leave. There were lookouts stationed around Taos, and everyone there eagerly questioned him on movements of the Utes. He told them he had seen nothing and that the Ute scare was nothing but a humbug. They couldn't change his mind about riding out the next morning.

Not far from Taos, the slopes of the winding river valley angled into sheer bluffs along the Rio Grande Gorge. The distance between the escarpment and the water steadily increased. August rode the precipice carefully, in awe of the fissure. A stone kicked from the rimrock fell through voids so abysmal that he couldn't hear it hit bottom.

But the river did not stop speaking to him, even from the depths. He could hear the rapids rumbling in the maw of the canyon hundreds of feet below. Once or twice he saw the river hurl some of his timber toward Candelilla. Entire trees splintered on the rocks like matchsticks and bobbed in the whirlpools like flotsam on the high seas.

On the upstream end of the gorge the claybank mare found grassy slopes where the river skirted the western flanks of Ute Peak, ten thousand feet high. Game sign abounded everywhere. The dung below one turkey roost could have fertilized a hardscrabble section. Bucks and bull elk in velvet skirted every meadow's edge. Black bears ambled about with little caution, and grizzly sign marred the trees.

And there were plenty of trees. Whole garrisons of ponderosa pine seemed to march from the mount to the river's ample loins. Candelilla's hog pen pickets were progeny of their union. Here was the tall timber August had searched for. Here was shelter. The river had guided him, as promised. Here was safety, a fit home for a heart-broken hermit.

August unsaddled and tied the horse given to him by Mel Ferrar. He scattered his tack across a little meadow and leaned his rifle against a tree. A saddle pocket provided a bite of hardtack. He reclined against a trunk and made his plans for the rest of the day. It was time to start hunting, building a shelter, stacking wood. His chores could have made a lengthy list if he had owned a scrap of paper.

As the river gurgled its familiar lullaby, August's secondhand hat began to slide ever farther over his brow. The faint rattle of pine needles and the mere sigh of wind faded as his eyelids drooped. He had almost shut the sounds completely out when an alien strain interrupted.

It lasted only a fraction of a moment, but August seemed to hear it coming for the longest time. It started with a resonant thump and grew louder as it approached—whispering at first, then almost screaming with the voice of death. It reached him before he could get his eyelids open.

A Ute arrowhead slammed into the tree trunk just

above August's head. His body filled with electricity and he sprang without trying. A barrage of projectiles arched toward him with the speed of the shooting stars he had seen over Taos. One of them tore his clothes. A single leap brought his rifle within his grasp. The claybank mare lunged against her rope and pulled free before August could think about mounting.

The Utes were whooping now in a fantastic arrangement that made the traveler's scalp crawl. He worked the Winchester's lever from the hip and saw three Indian dodge the bullets. One of them had a tomahawk ready to throw at fewer than ten paces. The Indians took cover for an instant, giving August a chance to retreat and reload.

The next volley came in the form of lead. Rifled slugs and lead balls from ancient muzzle loaders splintered a fallen pine behind which August had leapt. After shoving more cartridges into his rifle, he rested the barrel across his breastworks and aligned the glimpses of motion within his sights. A pair of Indians shrank from his uncertain aim. He stayed behind the sights even when the screaming voices of doom again left the bowstrings of the warriors and penetrated to the heartwood of his little battlement.

The moment he spent his last cartridge, he sprinted again for higher ground, this time reloading as he ran. Iron arrow tips hammered from barrel hoops and wagon tires rained all around him. Bullets split the timber in his path and ricocheted off the boulders at his feet. The choir of ghoulish voices began whooping again, and August looked over his shoulder to see how near they had drawn. He couldn't believe their speed afoot. They seemed to fly like deer over fallen branches and under living ones. He thought he had killed one and wounded two or three of them, but a dozen seemed to take the place of each fallen one.

The retreat came to an end at the base of a rimrock twenty feet high. August hunkered down behind a small boulder and slid one more cartridge into his rifle. Shards of rock flew everywhere from the bullets that showered his stone backdrop. The enemy swarmed up to take his scalp. The rifle stopped two of them and turned the rest toward cover. August continued to pepper them as they retreated a short distance. He reloaded just in time to meet the next assault. Smoking brass cartridges began to form a pile next to the rifleman's foot, but the number of live rounds in his cartridge belt diminished too quickly. An iron arrowhead raked across his jawbone. Bullets tore his skin every time he rose to shoot.

The faces became distinct with nearness. August could almost count the fringes on their buckskin leggings. He emptied the rifle a third time with no time to reload. Four painted warriors charged in as he dropped the Winchester. He yanked his revolver from the holster, knowing that every little slug would have to hit its mark precisely. He aimed for the wild, rolling eyes of his enemy, eyes that troubled him in their resemblance to Lawnce McCrary's.

The reports of the rat gun sounded like the popping of fatwood after the rifle's thunder. Four Ute braves dropped in succession from left to right with four exacting shots. August fired the last round of his five-shot revolver at a face in the forest. He heard the rapid approach of moccasins across the humus as he concentrated on filling his weapon with shells that had rattled in his pocket since his last night in Candelilla.

Would the river tell Chepita of his death? He thumbed back the hammer of his little shooting iron, aimed at the nearest brave and fired, then fired again, but the warrior continued to charge, carrying a shield of hardened buffalo hide ahead of him, too thick for the pepperbox to penetrate.

August pulled the trigger until the firing pin clicked pitifully against a dead cartridge rim. He hopelessly groped in his pocket for more shells as he saw the curve of a knife blade jutting from behind the scalp-hung buffalo shield. His vision blurred, but he resolved to look into the eyes of his murderer. The gunfire and war whoops became an echo, and the landscape began to whir around the painted shield. He felt dizzy. The buffalo hide lowered and August saw the impossible leering face of Maximo de Guerra rushing at him.

A bowstring thumped and the scream of death whistled through forest air. The victim saw only a blur as the Ute arrow found its mark between his ribs. It jolted him a little and then burned like a running iron where it passed through his body. The image of Maximo rushed to finish him.

In his suspended horror, August sensed a third presence descending from above. He thought the wings of death had come to claim his wicked soul. A shadow dropped down from the rocks above him and then took the form of a great fur heap. It landed between the ghost of Maximo and the wayward son of Candelilla. It caused the echoes to cease reverberating and stopped the surrounding scene from spinning. It transformed the visage of Maximo into the face of a Ute brave who reeled back in terror. Bullets and arrows fell in flight, and the entire force of warriors retreated down the slope. The wings of death had become the arms of salvation.

August collapsed when the furs landed before him. The heap of pelts had arms and legs that shook like the fires of the sun and a voice that roared like a grizzly in a mine shaft. One hand held a rifle, and the other held an odd fur cap, lined on the inside with fine linen cloth. The man in furs was bent forward, away from August, pointing the top of his head at the fleeing Indians.

The bruin voice began to roll with laughter as the Indians disappeared. The fur cap went back on its wearer's head before he stood erect. Then the great cloak of furs turned to reveal a large bearded face reddened by laughter. "Look at them run!" said the mouth in the middle of the beard. "One would think Beelzebub himself had sprung from the earth's very core!"

August stared, mystified by the huge, fur-clad man silhouetted against the sky above him. His wounds began to ache more than he could bear, and a chill blew across his brow. The mountain man stooped to take his hand.

"Allow me the honor of your acquaintance," he said with utmost ceremony. "I am the greatest of mountain men, the last of the Renaissance men, and the finest of gentlemen—the Reverend Professor Thomas Payton Ryder, at your service."

August's sky grew dark around the silhouette.

20

August fought a thousand battles in darkness. Mexican rustlers and painted Indians came in waves to kill him; then giant rats scampered across the rafters to devour him. He managed to fight them back until the last had fallen.

The first sound that came to the wounded Texan was the whisper of the Rio Grande. Then he heard a bird in the trees. He recognized the sound of his claybank mare pulling at grass with her teeth and could hear her chewing it. Gratefully, he listened to the sounds of life for a time without opening his eyes. Then another noise got his curiosity up. It could have been a rat gnawing on a floor plank. It might have been a woodpecker boring for insects. But it sounded more like a knife carving a piece of wood.

The reverend professor looked habitually over his shoulder to check his beneficiary for signs of consciousness and, for the first time in two days, found them. Quickly he jabbed his knife into a stump and propped his carving against it.

"Heaven be praised!" he said as he rushed to the young man's side. "There wasn't much to be done, lad, but to gather the endemic medicinal fauna and apply them to the wounds. The rest came of your own volition and the mercy of God. Huzzah, lad! You're among the living!"

Perplexed, August looked up at the cheerful bearded face with spectacles hooked around the ears and the strange fur cap atop. "Water," he said in a hoarse whisper.

"At your very fingertips, lad," the mountain man said, reaching for a gourd dipper.

August felt a sip trickle down him like the waters of a flash flood across parched desert soil. A fever ran through his chest. Even without moving he could tell that any motion would rack him in pain. Just his shallow breathing hurt enough. He began to recall the events that had brought him here.

"Fortunate," Ryder said, "very fortunate indeed were you, lad, that I happened along when I did. Beyond my usual boundaries of perambulation at that! I was about that region—some seven miles southward, I should say— to rob a colony of perfectly innocent beas of their honey when I heard the war cries of the savages.

"The arrow passed through you quite cleanly. Shattered a rib, punctured a lung, nicked an artery—but rather cleanly nonetheless. I carried you hither on my back. I didn't find your mare until today. You're healing now, but you must lie still awhile. You've beaten the fever while my linseed and cornmeal paste seems to have prevented infection. You no doubt descend from superior stock."

As the professor rambled on, August glanced around. He seemed to be lying on pine boughs covered with blankets. He could feel the ridges of the larger branches and smell the needles beneath his head. Another blanket covered his chest and, he supposed, his feet. The low gable of a small cabin portico shaded him.

Then he noticed something so unexpected that he could only stare in bewilderment. An odd assemblage of sculptures towered above him from his low angle. Leaning randomly against the rough-hewn cabin timbers were wooden planks carved in relief, depicting various scenes odd and familiar, also animals in three dimensions and busts of serious men. August closed his eyes for a second, but when he opened them again the carvings were still

there. He strongly suspected that they belonged to another fitful dream and not to reality.

Ryder noticed him looking around the cabin porch.
"Ah, you admire my artisanship," he said. "I erected this
cabin by the labor of my own hands, like Thoreau on Wal-
den Pond. 'He who lives in another man's house is like
a cowbird,' he said. Wonderful man, Thoreau. I studied
under him at Concord, you see."

August took another sip of water, glanced again at the
carvings, and slipped back into restless darkness as the
professor expounded on the virtues of transcendental-
ism.

When he woke next, the carvings were still there and
he was hungry. Ryder had anticipated this and had prepared a stew with small chunks of venison cooked tender
enough for a toothless crone to chew. After spoon-feeding
August as much as he could stand to swallow, the professor went back to carving on a piece of wood.

When he leaned his burly shoulders into the work,
curls of soft pine spiraled easily before his knife. Chips
and sawdust littered the ground around him like drifts
left by a flurry, and marvelous shapes took form before
August's eyes as he listened to the constant prattle of the
professor.

In the days that followed, August had plenty of time to
study Ryder's works. Carvings lined the cabin porch three
deep. The sculptor's hands had granted the wood suspended glimpses of realism so true that one might have
expected the busts to speak and the animals to leap from
their knotty backgrounds. The stance and attitude of a
miniature wooden horse told August it would kick so certainly that he was glad he wasn't lying behind it.

Among the beasts were busts of great men whose features Ryder had studied with his own eyes: Thoreau,
Channing, Melville, Hawthorne, and, most prominently,

Emerson. August thought often he saw them blow vapor into cold mountain air. The hollowed eyes followed him relentlessly about the cabin grounds and caught eerie shadows from the moonlight.

"How do you remember what they all look like?" he asked one day.

"I served as apprentice to an Italian master who taught me to see that which I look upon—vividly, pointedly, purposefully," the sculptor answered with a thrust of his knife toward his mending student. "For instance, my eyes have noted that the hat you wear is not your own. It has long been worn, but not on a head with the same shape as yours. It fits oddly about your brow and irritates your skin there because of it.

"Your rifle, likewise, is a recent acquisition. When I recovered your mare and the rest of your belongings, I found your saddle provisioned with a coiled lariat to the right of the pommel and the rifle scabbard situated under the left stirrup in a position to take the gun breech downward, muzzle aft. But the previous owner of that weapon, which is, by the way, safe in my domicile there—the weapon, I mean, not the previous owner—that fellow carried it under the right stirrup, breech downward, barrel forward, well nigh opposite to your arrangement. His saddle skirt rubbed a furrow in the stock on the right side.

"But your little revolver! Ah, that is yours of long keeping. Your hand has grown too large for the tiny grip, and so your smallest finger curls under the butt plate and has smoothed it there like the face of a coin in an old miser's pocket. Your palm knows the feel of that stock! And the holster belt fits the structure of your hips as the sling of David drapes o'er his marbled shoulder.

"Shall I pursue it further?"

"No, sir. I get your meanin'," August answered. "You study things with your eyes 'cause you're an artist."

"Not simply for the sake of art, lad, but to avoid missing something essential."

Ryder babbled that way at first, while he carved and chiseled. He seemed to be attempting a compensation for many months spent without uttering a syllable. He admitted that when he jumped from the cliff and yelled to frighten the Indians who would have killed August, he startled himself as much as the braves, so long had he gone without hearing the sound of his own voice.

It still puzzled August how a man's voice, even a voice of the amplitude of Ryder's, could scare away scalp-hunting Indians, even reservation Indians on a tear. There seemed to have been some kind of magic to it, the way he remembered it. But he would soon find out there was more misery than magic in the story of the Indians' terror of the good Reverend T. P. Ryder.

The fugitive and the professor swapped histories and, to each, the other's story sounded as foreign as an ancient fable. The Texan spoke of Candelilla as a microcosm, and he knew horses the way a sculptor would his tools and marble, but he didn't know much of anything else, except grasses and the way they tasted.

The reverend told of foreign kings and queens, university buildings bigger than horse barns that were filled only with books, and statues of men that stood taller than the pines along the river's cleft. But the recent history of the reverend professor had yet to come to the Texan's ears.

The moment August could use his feet, the mountain man prodded him toward the river, a quarter-mile away. Near the rocky bank, a hot spring flowed from the ground. Ryder had fashioned a stone retaining wall to deepen the steaming pool. He had his patient strip and soak there for a half-hour. The hot bath invigorated him, especially when he stepped back into the crispness that the altitude and the season had laced into the air.

One day while taking his exercise toward the hot spring, August spotted a stalk of grass that he wanted to taste but felt too weak to stoop down for. Professor Ryder graciously bent to secure the specimen, and as he did so his fur cap slipped away from his head for a second or two.

When August saw the horribly mangled scalp, he choked a gasp in his throat. Even after returning to his pallet, he thought it impolite to ask, but Ryder heard questions in the young man's silence and entered into his story.

"I suppose you want to know the particulars behind my peculiar injury," he said. "I would fain tell it, lad, as I know it better than the *Odyssey*." He paused to stab his carving knife into the stump where he worked. " 'Tis my own epic.

"The mountains called me hither," Ryder began. "I climbed them to conquer the continent as Hannibal crossed the Alps to conquer Rome. I heard also the cajoling call of the savages. Melville," he said, pointing to a bust on his cabin portico, "Melville had lived among the Typee, cannibals of the South Pacific, and wrote a splendid volume on his experiences there. This before his preoccupation with those irksome novels. *Moby-Dick*, indeed! But the peep Mr. Melville gave me of Polynesian life made me all the more covetous of an adventure of my own to convert, perhaps, into a literary achievement. So, westward I trekked.

"I sojourned two winters with the Sioux, as I have told you. They made me a present of this wolf-skin pack I carry." He lifted the little fur sack he kept nearby at all times. "This is where I keep my herbs and tools and such. The Sioux call it a medicine bundle.

"I say, lad, have I mentioned any of this? Yes, eh? Well, then, I shall get on with it.

"After leaving the Sioux, I resided a brief time among the village tribes, then traveled southward into the Indian Territory with a party of bison hunters. However, in my opinion, they failed to take sufficient precautions against attacks, so I left them. Some time later, I struck a league with four French Canadians bound for the Rockies atrapping. They were fated to fight beside me to their death."

The speaker paused and indicated his surroundings with a theatrical gesture of his arms.

"Upon the shoulders of this very mountain we paused to sup one afternoon, bound for Santa Fe and laden with furs. As we chuckled and passed the gourd, the red hounds of hell crept about us in the forest. Utes, in their last days before submitting to reservation life. Before we could rise to fetch our guns, two among us were dead with arrows through their hearts. The three of us remaining fired and rammed home the wadding and fired again, yet only two of us lived to fire a third. We fought with knives then, and I broke through the ranks and made good use of my legs as my last comrade died. The savages cut the throats of my friends, scalped them, and fought over their trappings like wolves at a carcass.

"I made my escape for the moment, hiding behind yon banian of the forest." Ryder yanked his knife from the stump and pointed the blade at the largest ponderosa pine in view.

August cast a glance toward the actual scene of the struggle. The tree indeed had a girth great enough to shield even Ryder's bulk. The listener could almost visualize the reverend hiding there.

"The savages followed my trail like hounds. I heard them rustle the forest litter. I say without shame, lad, that I heaved in horror and felt my heart would burst within me. My legs trembled and my knees smote each other! At last I bolted from my fastness.

"The rifle ball that struck the nape of my neck was likely one I had molded myself, shot from my own rifle in the hands of my enemy. Then the terror passed. The smarting of my wounds vanished. I fell face forward, limp as if in death. I could no more move than I could move the earth. God had swathed me in his eternal mercy and I knew to fear no more.

"They brandished their knives at my throat, but the ball had torn it open for them, having passed through my neck and under my chin. They rushed for my scalp then, and I saw the cloudless sky jerking as they wrenched at my hair with their greedy fingers. Still, I could not so much as quiver, nor could I feel a twinge. They thought me dead before all their pagan gods.

"I say the sky was cloudless, lad, but thunder rumbled as my scalp peeled away from its skull. They took not one trophy, but seven pieces from my head, that each devil among them might wear a trophy on his belt. I suppose, though, that my shocks were ample enough to satisfy each.

"They stripped me naked, left me to the vultures. I saw them circling before I fell away to rest." Ryder paused and looked sheepishly into August's eyes, as if to apologize for what he would do next. He removed his fur cap and bowed his head to reveal the horrible wound.

The hair of his head grew away from a ragged circle of scar tissue that appeared stretched and waxy. It didn't cover his skull across the crown. The skull, from long exposure, had become exfoliated. At the very top of his head, the bone had died and simply flaked away. A greasy substance covered it, but the hole in the skull was impossible to overlook. August could look into the top of

Ryder's head and see a piece of his brain as big as a silver dollar.

"The wound never closed," Ryder said, raising his eyes to his listener. "My skull and indeed my very brain lie exposed and trouble me terribly. I keep the wound bathed in bear fat, which preserves the skull somewhat, but lends an altogether repulsive aspect." He covered the wound with his cap.

August swallowed hard and panted for a moment. He felt his stomach writhing the way it had after his fight with Maximo. "How did you live like that?" he asked when his color returned.

"Only by the will of our Almighty Father in heaven," Ryder said, rising to his feet. "In my dark sleep, God told me—nay, commanded me!—'Live!' He spake unto me as surely as I speak to you now, lad, and I would obey." The reverend ascended the pulpit of his sylvan tabernacle. "Our Savior extended his hands to me as if to say my time to enter the kingdom of heaven had yet to come. I saw the scars in his palms, lad, as clearly as I see you now before me. He 'breathed into my nostrils the breath of life'!" Ryder looked around as if to remind himself of his surroundings. "Genesis," he said by way of attribution, and then returned to his tale.

"I awoke in anguish. I might have frozen that night, but I found the hot spring where I crawled to the river's edge. I might have starved in the days that followed, but I gleaned sustenance from God's river. I consumed the snails and mollusks along her shore and bits of berry fruit I found floating in an eddy. My swollen throat seized me with pain at every swallow, but I persisted. I gathered cane to fashion a weir for entrapping fish, like the ones the Mandan and Assiniboine manufacture. I ate the flesh without benefit of fire, as the infidels of the Far East are wont to do. I bathed my wounds in the hot spring. The waters healed me more miraculously than the balm of Gilead.

"At length I began to regain my fortitude and had a look around at my situation. The Utes had left nothing but my medicine bundle, having spread its contents over the ground. I was glad to have it, though. I suppose some Indian superstition prevented them from pilfering the contents. Next, I shaped a mace from an oaken bough and honed my throwing skills, taught me during my work in a Portuguese mission on the eastern coast of Africa."

To illustrate, Ryder picked up a rough slab of pinewood and tested its balance in his hand. Then, after pointing at a pinecone clinging to a limb some thirty paces distant, he shattered the target with a deft throw of the misshapen club.

"One day my weapon split the skull of a ground squirrel, which I would prepare for repast," he continued. "I fell upon it with my knife of sharpened bone to remove the raw edibles. Just then I heard the faintest riffle on the wind. I crouched and looked, and there saw the Indians returning to their place of mischief. I watched them proceed slowly toward me and then, with my still-quivering prey within my grasp, I conceived a wonderfully devilish idea."

Ryder began to pace among his wood shavings, rubbing his hands and grinning in anticipation of his narrative.

"I crouched not ten paces from where you lie now, lad, and watched the savages as they indicated to their tribesmen the very ground where my comrades had been slain—the wolves having dragged the corpses away. They veritably recreated the battle! What heroes they made themselves out to be. The entire band had come to see the site of the glorious victory a fortnight removed—squaws and dirty little urchins tagged along. When they filed to-

ward yon forest giant, they might have expected to find
the Reverend Professor Thomas Payton Ryder rotting in
the humus. Instead they found his ghost rising from the
dust!

"I had taken the warm blood of my game and, after applying it to my half-healed wounds, concealed myself behind the tree. When my murderers arrived to recreate my
demise, I sprang from the earth, fresh blood besmearing
my tortured scalp, dripping from my throat and staining
my outstretched hands. I lurched forward like Franken-
stein's monster, filling the air with an idiotic and mania-
cal hooting!" Ryder staggered about his wood chips, arms
groping, eyes rolling, wailing like a peafowl caught in a
steam whistle.

The young Texan rolled on the cabin porch among the
busts of Ryder's mentors and laughed until his arrow
wound ached. He hadn't taken the tonic of laughter since
before his duel with Maximo.

"Ah, but alas, you have caught my act before," Ryder
said, "and you know the savages' reaction. The superstitious curs fled from the haunted ground like fish from an
arrow! They never came near molesting me again and
stay well away from my little domicile in the forest. They
leave their reservation and come this way only occasionally now, to hunt.

"Sometimes I take the busts of Emerson, Thoreau,
Hawthorne, and the others and post them about my territory as sentinels to further frighten the heathens. I have
more than once found offerings of knives and tobacco at
their pedestals. I have them irrevocably terrified! God forgive me for fostering idolatry, but how I do love to see
them flee! I would have you know, lad, that you are safer
here with the ghost of Thomas Payton Ryder than you
would be under guard at Buckingham Palace."

Though Ryder was a big man of tremendous vocal capacity, his voice quivered at the mention of Buckingham Palace the way it did when he spoke of the great cities and the theater. He yearned for them the way August longed to gaze upon Chepita's features.

"Why don't you leave this country now?" August asked. "You're healed up. You could see a doctor about that scalp. You don't aim to stay here forever, do you?"

Ryder had removed his spectacles to wipe tears of laughter away from his eyes. He plopped ponderously down on his log stool and sighed as he replaced his glasses. "I cannot, lad. I am an abomination and will not force myself upon polite society. For all my love of civilized folk, they have their shortcomings, not the least of which is morbid curiosity. Would that I were an oyster and could mend my wounds with pearl." Though it was not a direct quotation, Ryder felt obligated to credit the originator of the idea. "Emerson," he said.

"I have my pinch of civilization in my carvings. Better for the birds of the forest to look upon them with wonder and the savages to gaze at them with terror than for the ghouls of society to look upon my mutilated head with delight."

"I know how you feel, then," August said. "You love your cities and your fancy plays and your books and such the way I love what I have left behind. And neither one of us can go back."

"You mistake me, lad," the professor answered. "No man holds me hither but Thomas Payton Ryder. Are not my legs strong enough to carry me whence I came? Yes! Does my memory cloud so that I forget my path homeward? Of course not! I stay on the mount because I choose it. My destiny is my own."

"But me," August said, "I can't go back. I gave my word to the girl I love that I would never show my face again in Candelilla. I reckon my destiny just ain't mine no more."

"Balderdash, lad. You babble like a blatherskite! No man lives without choices. They are but shards of eternity, these lives of ours. We must choose to live them ere they pass."

"But what choice do I have?" August asked. "I can't break a promise. Especially not to a woman, and never in a million years to the girl I love."

"You vowed never to return, nothing more. You made no other promise—none of which you have told me. That leaves open as many avenues as you care to fathom."

"What would you have me do?" August asked with a roll of his eyeballs. "Send her a lover's letter?"

"There's a course of action already, then!"

August scoffed. "Pardon me, Professor, but I haven't seen no freight wagons pass this way lately. And even if I owned a piece of paper, I still wouldn't have no ink or a pen to dip in it."

"Come with me," Ryder said, offering his hand to help August to his feet. He directed his pupil toward a bluff overlooking the rushing headwaters of the Rio Grande near the hot springs. He carried a knife and a flat plank of pinewood under his belt. For whittling, August supposed.

"Do you like riddles?" Ryder asked as they walked.

"I guess."

"Solve this one if you can: I go up the road, I go down the road, I carry the road home on my back."

"That's it?" August asked, breaking off a stem of grass to chew on.

Ryder nodded.

"Can't figure that one."

"The road is a ladder, of course. Try another: 'My tongue is long, my breath is strong, and yet I breed no strife; my voice you hear both far and near, and yet I have no life.' "

August pondered, then shrugged.

" 'Tis a bell, lad! Now you have the thrust of the game. Solve the following: 'She travels forever, yet stays in her bed; possesses a mouth so far from her head; they'll cross her and damn her; she still shan't be dead.' Who is she, lad?"

"Why, she's the river," August said with little hesitation.

"Bravo! What gave her away?"

"Well, I know you're a reverend and wouldn't cuss a lady like that when you said they'd dam her."

"How very astute, lad! Now, observe *this* river." They had reached the precipice. "Though crossed and dammed, she'll flow forever downstream. Never ceasing, never sleeping, but tossing tirelessly in her bed."

He pulled the knife and wooden slab from his belt. "See this pine plank? Let it serve as your stationery and this knife, your pen. The well of your soul shall furnish the ink. Carve a message to your lover, lad."

"What about the freight wagon?" August asked with a final note of skepticism.

"Freight! Bah!" ejaculated the reverend professor. "Does not your lover launder clothing on the banks of this very stream? Carve a message of your love for her. Toss it in the river. Perchance it will wend its way to her heart. If not, carve another, and another. Fill the riffles and wakes with tidings of your desire for your little lost love. If naught comes of it, at least you will have some exercise for your hands." He tossed the wooden plank to August and offered the knife, handle first.

August took the knife and studied the river. He remembered the driftwood staves of Candelilla's picket fences. "Do you really think it might reach her?"

The reverend professor drew himself upright and

tugged at the sleeves of his great fur frock in preparation to gesture. "My boy," he said with a grandiose sweep of his hand, "you have at your feet the winged heels of Mercury. Call this river Hermes, swiftest messenger of ancient Greeks. Her waters fly down like Gabriel from the presence of God. No mortal steed, no earthly coach or lowly locomotive train shall bear your tidings forth like this ablest of all couriers. Those worldly runners tire, they err, they stop to quench their mortal thirst. But your river runs on, lad. She flows with purpose unceasing, downstream."

Ryder's voice hit the far sides of the canyon and echoed as if beating the stained glass of a great cathedral.

"Offer unto the river your message, lad, and pray the blessed angels of God steer it downstream. Through the canyons, about the hills, across the parched sands of the Painted Desert! Let it ride the current o'er cascade and maelstrom! There lies your destiny, lad! Downstream. Downstream!"

August stepped back several paces from Ryder's vocal cannonade.

The reverend professor stood, arms uplifted, facing the Rio Grande's canyon as the reverberations from his soliloquy resounded among the tall timber. Then he turned to August and spoke with dramatic calm.

"We are so like the river, lad. We travel forever toward our sea of destiny. Yet we differ—*we* choose our *own* course."

August sat down at once on a boulder and began whittling a smooth surface on which to carve.

21

Nelly Blankenship had a way of making her questions sound like passing remarks. People rarely minded answering them that way. "A group of white men came to town a few minutes ago, John," she stated in this way. "Their leader was a large hunched-over man."

"That'll be One-Eyed Butch Gainey," Lawnce said as he unsaddled Little Satan. "Damn. These here barn chores are gonna back up plumb to the rafters. Can't keep the laws and run a livery all at once. I need the kid back." He heard a rat's claws skittering overhead. "And the rats! Never knowed how good the kid was for killin' 'em. A wildcat with a mile-long tapeworm couldn't eat 'em all!"

Nelly had learned to ignore the rodents. Even with them, the livery barn was more accommodating than some places she had slept in since coming west. "The Mexicans," she said. "When they passed Mr. Gainey they made the sign of the cross." She traced the pattern over her bosom. "Perhaps he is a clergyman."

Lawnce dropped his leather and almost swallowed his chaw in the fit of whistling laughter that gripped him. "That cross is for protection," he said when his breath came regular again. "The Mexicans call him El Ojo."

"The eye?" She had learned some Spanish in Candelilla.

"Means 'the evil eye' to them. It sort of means the devil's own hired man, a person that can put evils on you just by shinin' their eyeball at you real hard. Fits Butch like a boot 'cause he ain't got but one eye anyhow."

"Why do the Mexicans fear him so?"

"Well, them folks are sort of spooky. They believe in ghosts and such. That one eye in Butch's ugly ol' face got to spookin' 'em after a while and they made up stories about how he came to lose the other one.

"When ol' Butch first came to this country, he had Mexicans workin' for him. He never did treat 'em good or pay 'em much. Couple years back they got theirselfs too skitterish to work for him anymore on account of them El Ojo stories. The only one to stay was Butch's *cocinero*, Cayetano Pastor."

"Mr. Gainey looks like a rancher."

"Yes, ma'am. Had damn near the biggest spread in the territory before the rustlers took a likin' to his brand."

"Maximo de Guerra's rustlers."

Lawnce looped a thong around his saddle horn and hung the saddle in the tack room. He grabbed a curry comb. "Ain't no proof against Maximo just yet, Nelly."

The journalist calculated her angle for an interview with One-Eyed Butch. "Could you arrange an introduction between Mr. Gainey and me?"

The last thing Lawnce wanted to do with Nelly was put her within Gainey's grasp. But he knew well enough that without his introduction she would make her own plans to meet Butch for the sake of writing one of her magazine stories. The journalism business baffled Lawnce. Before meeting Nelly, a magazine to him was just a handy place to put ammunition.

"I probably ought not to tell you this," he said, "you bein' a newspaper gal huntin' for yarns and all, but I think I can trust you to keep it off the front page for a spell. It looks like ol' Butch is in more than just the ranchin' business. For some time now I've had me a hunch that he's gettin' his boys to rob the stagecoaches on the line to El Paso."

Nelly looked surprised. "But the stage drivers told me Indians had been blamed for the attacks."

"Oh, the robbers scalp the drivers and passengers when they kill 'em, and stick a arrow or two in the dead mules to make it look like Injuns done it, but I think ol' Butch is in back of most of it."

Lawnce had more than a hunch. For a year he had been riding an immense circle around the Doubletree lands, trying to cut the trails of Mexican rustlers. Some trails he crossed, however, led away from Gainey's ranch to the north, instead of in from the south whence rustlers would come. Men riding horses shod by the Doubletree farrier had left at odd intervals for some unknown business in the northern pastures of Gainey's spread. Sometimes Top Dollar's prints, digging low into the sand, showed that Gainey went, too.

That in itself was not unusual. Ranchers and cowboys had herds to look after. But Lawnce began to notice that the departures of these parties were almost always followed by news of stage robberies.

Such circumstantial evidence usually gave a ranger the right to shoot, search, and seize, but Lawnce knew no single lawman could approach the Doubletree headquarters without giving up his guns. Standing unarmed in the presence of cowboys who were probably all wanted in the eastern and southern states for murder or worse didn't fall within his personal view of duty.

Besides, he gave Butch Gainey the same benefit of due process that he allowed Maximo de Guerra, and being absent from home during the time of a crime didn't prove either of them guilty. It just gave him more reason to watch both of them. He could have followed the Doubletree men north, to see what mischief they had been into up there, but the ranger service had restricted him to Presidio County along the border. Other rangers weren't fond of Lawnce because of his friendliness toward Indians and Mexicans. Because he wore a sombrero, some of his fellow rangers were anxious to mistake him for a Mexican bandit.

There was more evidence against Gainey and his men besides the tracks leading north. José Cigarito, the Mescalero chief who had smoked the long pipe with Lawnce McCrary to seal the treaty of Candelilla, hinted that El Ojo's knife had taken the scalps of some stage drivers. Lawnce suspected the chief and his braves had plundered a few stagecoaches, stolen mules, killed drivers, tortured guards to death, and raped women, too, but he had as little proof against the Indians as he did against Maximo or Gainey. Cigarito denied that the Mescaleros had committed any of the robberies or murders, but some of the crimes he denied rabidly, and became upset when questioned about them, sulking and glowering as if insulted. These were the crimes that coincided with Doubletree hoofprints leading north.

"But," the ranger said to Nelly, "I reckon it'd be safe enough for me to bring him over here where you can talk at him, long as I stay in shoutin' distance. But you watch him, Nelly. He's a rounder and a slick talker. Had schoolin' when he was a youngun. He can talk a brood mare out of her colt, and he's probably got his one eye on your flesh already."

"Me?" Nelly said coyly. "Why would he want me?"

"I reckon 'cause he ain't had you yet. Butch Gainey's one of them that has to have everything. You could give him the whole damn Big Bend and he'd still want the moon for a cow pasture. On top of that, he's a mouth-breather, and I never did trust a mouth-breather among men or horses."

"A mouth what?" Nelly asked with a grin of expectation.

"You know. A flop-jawed feller that draws wind out of

his yapper. That's one thing the Injuns have figured out. If they have a youngun that's a mouth-breather, they tie its jawbone up with a strop so it learns to suck air through its nose holes!"

When One-Eyed Butch heard that a litterateur from Boston desired his acquaintance, he let his sense of self-importance swell beyond the size of his stomach. He lumbered with Lawnce, followed by his guard of six men, from the Pitchfork Saloon to McCrary Livery. He didn't like to walk past Las Quince Letras for fear of running into Maximo, but he figured he could risk it with six guards in broad daylight. Lawnce made the guards wait outside as he and Butch went into the barn.

Gainey kissed Nelly's hand as if he had been reared among royalty. "It's a pleasure to make your acquaintance, miss. You must be the writer's secretary."

The rattle in Gainey's voice made Nelly want to cross herself again. "I beg your pardon?" she said.

"Are you hard of hearing? I say you must be the magazine writer's secretary," he yelled.

"Mr. Gainey, I happen to *be* the writer. I have no need for a secretary."

Butch stared out from under his fedora. "A woman writer? I don't know any recipes or quiltin' patterns, Miss Blankenship. What I know is stock-raisin' and money-makin'."

"Those are two subjects I would like to discuss, Mr. Gainey. I have been retained by *Fulton's* magazine of Boston to send regular dispatches from all territories of the West for a period of four years. Economics, agriculture, investment opportunities, and capital are all of vital interest to our readership as are personal histories, character studies, and descriptions of topography, geography, geology, mineralogy, and anthropology—all subjects with which I am well acquainted. Oh, and did I forget to mention criminal activity of the region?"

Lawnce tensed in his tracks.

"Now, if you don't mind, Mr. Gainey, I shall conduct the interview."

Butch bowed his head and touched the brim of his hat. "Why, miss, I have misjudged your abilities. Please get on with it." Though his voice seemed apologetic, his hidden eye glared with malevolence.

Lawnce excused himself and made it known he would be within earshot at Las Quince Letras. He had provided a bench for Gainey to sit on during the interview. Nelly's seat would be on an overturned bucket padded with saddle blankets, just beyond Butch's grasp.

"Now, Mr. Gainey," Nelly said, "I would like you to give me some idea of the capacity of the land in this region for livestock."

"Hell, I don't know, miss. That's one thing the rustlers and Injuns ain't let us figure out yet. But first of all, that's Gainey, G-A-I-N-*E*-Y. Let me make sure you got that right." Butch reached for the reporter's tablet to check her spelling.

"I take notes in my own shorthand," she said as she withdrew from his grasp. "You would never be able to decipher it. But I assure you I shall neither misspell your name nor misrepresent you." She braced herself for a difficult interview.

Gainey first insisted on giving his life story. He began the miserably detailed narrative with his own birth in Mississippi. Nelly wondered what stroke of luck had prevented him from beginning with his ancestry, then quickly concluded it was not luck at all but Gainey's egocentric view of things that had kept him from mentioning his forebears before himself.

Her every attempt to regain control of the interview

failed. Gainey was determined to tell her how his doctors
had sent him to the new Republic of Texas in 1836, at the
age of seventeen, to seek a more healthful climate. He suf-
fered from a persistent cough the doctors had labeled
consumption. They prescribed an outdoor life to improve
his constitution, so young Butch Gainey became a trapper
and predator hunter along the frontier ranches and farms
pushing deeper into Indian country. This he related to
Nelly Blankenship and urged her to get every word.

"By 'forty-five I had collected bounty on over four thousand wolves and probably ten times as many coyotes,"
Butch said. "I had also hunted down almost a hundred
panthers and maybe forty or fifty bear, including the biggest specimens ever killed in the western states. Them
were the days when varmints and Injuns outnumbered
humans. Me and the men that worked for me were in
constant danger from Injuns and Mexicans."

Gainey then narrated several glorious encounters with
Indians and Mexican soldiers or bandits in which his own
role was invariably that of hero, rescuer, or victor. The
gore ran freely throughout his annals.

In 1848, Nelly's shorthand noted, Gainey was mustered
out of distinguished service in the war with Mexico, with
a captain's rank among the Texas volunteers, and soon
followed the rush west to the California gold fields.

"But I had me a reputation by then as a famous Injun
fighter," Butch claimed. "When the governor of Chihuahua heard I was ridin' through west Texas on my way to
California, he sent a special messenger to ask my help in
fightin' the Injuns that were raidin' Mexico—Apaches and
Comanches, mostly.

"Well, I didn't care much for Mexicans, but their
money spent pretty good and I cared even less for Injuns,
so I became sort of a bounty hunter with the Military
Commission of Chihuahua to wipe out the Injuns. And I

swear we gave them hell and made good Injuns out of a
number of them.

"That's when this happened." Butch tipped his hat back
and turned his face to catch a ray of light streaming
through the barn door. Nelly tried not to show her revul-
sion at the sunken eye socket on the left side of Gainey's
head. Almost as horrifying was his right eye, cold with
evil, a mere squint in the rancher's face.

"There was a ranch in the Sierra del Nido where the
damned Mexican ranchers were supplyin' the Injuns with
guns and ammunition. In return, the Injuns left that
ranch and all its stock alone. It sort of reminds me of
Lawnce McCrary's damned treaty here in Candelilla. Do
you know he lets them stinkin' Mescaleros walk the
streets of this town? Makes me sick.

"Anyway, I didn't know about this goin' on at that ranch
in the Sierra del Nidos. I rode in there one day with my
men to check on any troubles the Injuns might have been
givin' them, and the next thing I know there's Apaches
swarmin' out of the house and the barn and a runnin'
fight broke out. I had my horse shot out from under me
and pulled out my old Walker Colt. That gave me just six
shots, and I used them up pretty shortly.

"It was hand-to-hand then as I pulled out my bowie
knife. I was butcherin' the red devils all around till a huge
Apache buck come at me with a knife. He was even bigger
than me and muscled up like a grizzly and gougin' that
shiv of his at me with every step. Next thing I know, he's
on top of me and jabbin' at my throat. I grabbed his arm
and threw off his aim. The knife stuck me right in the eye,
and my eyeball sort of plopped out on the sand. I think
it spooked him, that eye lookin' up at him. Gave me just
enough time to drive my bowie knife between his ribs and
into his heart. That was the nearest fight I was ever in."

Gainey lavished further accounts on Nelly, telling how

the Military Commission of Chihuahua awarded him its highest honors and paid him bonuses for controlling Indian depredations and how he founded his Doubletree Ranch and stocked it with three thousand head of cattle confiscated from the ranch that had been supplying arms to the savages.

"What was the name of that ranch in the Sierra del Nido?" Nelly asked.

"Hell, I don't remember them Mexican names. But I tell you what you ought to put in your story. You ought to write about my trouble with the rustlers—Maximo de Guerra and his gang—and how there ain't no lawman out in this country with guts to stand up to him."

"What evidence have you against Mr. de Guerra?" the reporter asked.

"Hell, Miss Blankenship, everybody knows Maximo is a cow thief."

"But John McCrary has told me he lacks sufficient evidence to arrest Mr. de Guerra."

"Lawnce McCrary is half Mexican. Now, what does that tell you? He's coverin' Maximo's tracks just like every other beaner on the river. Why, not long ago, I had one of Maximo's deadliest gunmen captured down on the river and was about to get a confession out of him with a rope—that's the only way to deal with these people— when Lawnce McCrary himself rode in and rescued the bandito!"

Nelly didn't feel like listening to much more, so she finished her interview with a question that by the tone of her voice, might have been construed as an accusation. "I understand that you can tell me something about the stagecoach robberies that have occurred along the San Antonio–El Paso line."

Butch shrugged coolly. "I know them damned Mescaleros are doin' it with guns they get right here in Can-

delilla under Lawnce McCrary's big ol' mustache. Miss
Blankenship, if I was you, I'd watch out for that character. He drinks like an Irishman, smells like a Mexican,
and thinks like an Injun."

Nelly had heard enough. "Thank you for your time, Mr.
Gainey." She began putting her writing case away in her
carpetbag.

"I want to look over that story before you send it off,"
Butch demanded, grunting as he struggled to rise from
his bench.

"That won't be possible, Mr. Gainey. I have but one editor, and his offices are located in Boston."

"But what if you get somethin' wrong? I want to check
it for you."

"I am a professional, sir. I don't get things wrong. I always double-check my sources. I will go to Chihuahua
and have a look at your distinguished war record."

Gainey turned his head and snorted something out of
one nostril. "Don't go to no trouble. Just make sure I get
a copy of the story when it comes out."

"I shall quite possibly be far from Texas by the time this
story is published, Mr. Gainey. I will give you the address
of the magazine. You may write and request a subscrip-
tion." Nelly searched her bag for a card.

"Never mind. Good day to you, ma'am."

Lawnce saw Gainey gather his guards around him and
plod, grumbling, back to the Pitchfork Saloon. He returned to the livery to check on Nelly.

"What did you learn?"

"That Mr. Gainey is a liar of the first magnitude," she
said, buckling up her carpetbag.

"Hell, I could have told you that."

"And one cannot believe a liar even when he tells the
truth."

He nodded.

"I want to hear these legends of El Ojo, John. The ones you said the Mexicans invented. Who could tell them to me?"

"Maximo tells it best," Lawnce said. "When he tells about hornets, you're liable to get stung."

22

Lawnce arranged a meeting between Maximo and Nelly. After dark the desperado arrived at Las Quince Letras with Chepita on his arm, Apolonio and Guzman walking a step behind. A single coal-oil lantern provided all the light he would need.

Santos served drinks all around—coffee for the ladies and tequila for the men, except Lawnce, who drank whiskey. "Ah, *muy bien,*" Maximo said. He hadn't sipped mescal since getting shot. Chepita had been making him drink the juice of boiled cactus lobes to heal his internal wounds. Lawnce noticed how sad she looked. She had never been as jolly as the other whores in town pretended to be, but she had seemed contented enough before August shot Maximo.

Small talk was exchanged, and then Maximo addressed Nelly's request.

"Doña Lope," he began. The Spanish speakers of Candelilla had encountered difficulty in pronouncing the name Penelope, but they found the last two syllables similar to the Spanish name Lupe, and so the lady with the cinnamon hair had become known as Doña Lope among the Mexicans. "Doña Lope, it is said you wish to hear the legend of El Ojo."

Nelly nodded, her paper and ink before her.

"Be warned, Doña Lope. It is not a pleasant tale."

"I have met the man who is called El Ojo," Nelly said.

"Then you know," the desperado replied. He looked into the eyes of his listeners and removed from his vest pockets the makings for a cigarette. From a silver case he took a corn husk trimmed into a rectangle. From a pouch, he sprinkled tobacco onto the husk and rolled it, his wounded hand giving him little difficulty now. The flame from the lantern animated his eyes with dancing reflections as he lifted the globe to light his *cigarro de hoja.*

"The legend says that El Ojo was once a boy like other boys," Maximo began. "A little bigger and stronger than some, perhaps, but no more evil and no more pure than other boys. But this boy went to sleep in a house each night and had no fresh air. The doctor finally told him that he must live among the creatures in the wild or he would not be able to breathe.

"So this boy, almost a man, traveled beyond the cities and the towns and came to a place where only Indians and wild animals lived. They made him afraid. He was a boy of the town, not of the wild hills and chaparral. At night they made terrible noises—*el lobo, la pantera,* and Señor Coyote. The boy held his gun and trembled like a coward. The wild beasts made him ashamed of his fear."

Maximo tapped the ashes from his *cigarro* and ground them slowly into the floor with his boot. "Every man has evil. Some men have control of it. But El Ojo, as a boy, did not have the strength in his heart to keep evil thoughts from his head. He was strong of body, but not of will.

"One night he built a big fire. When the wild wolves began to sing, he took his gun in his hand. When they came to the fire, El Ojo saw their eyes gleaming. He killed one by shooting it between the eyes, and the others ran away. There was no reason to kill this wolf except that El Ojo was afraid of it, and he felt very strange when it died. He could not say why.

"Wolves—they, too, have evil. The ones with hearts that are weak kill one hundred sheep and eat a single lamb.

"The Indians say a man who kills an enemy takes the courage from the soul of the dead one. So it happened with El Ojo. But he took something besides courage from the soul of his dead wolf. He took the evil. It was not a wolf of great evil, but El Ojo took what there was and it made him feel very peculiar. He thought perhaps this feeling was courage."

The storyteller dropped his cigarette butt and rose from his chair. "He became a *cazador*. His work was to kill the wild animals for the *tejanos*. He killed not only the wolves and *panteras* that slaughtered the cattle and colts. He killed also the pure beasts that hunted only for deer and rabbits to eat and feed their little ones.

"Did you know, Doña Lope," he asked, cupping his hand behind his ear, "that animals have a voice which speaks to them? Yes, Maximo believes it is true. They do not always listen to the voice, but it is there to tempt them. The coyote has a voice that says, 'Kill a new calf while it is still too weak to stand.' The wolf is bigger, so it has a bigger voice that says, 'Kill a good horse tied up, because it is easier to catch than a deer.' But *la pantera* has the most evil voice that says, 'Kill a crying child because it will grow to be a hunter and an enemy.' Sometimes these animals listen to the voices. The ones with hearts that are strong do not listen.

"When El Ojo killed the animals, their evil voices began speaking to him in a language of humans. They told him to kill. And he did. He killed every wild creature that came before him. It made him feel strange to kill them, and still he could not say why. He thought it was courage that he felt.

"He took his knife and cut the ears off and gave them to the rancheros to show how many animals he had killed. The rancheros paid him for each one. And then he could hire men to help him with the killing. With men to go with him, and with the false courage he felt, he was no longer afraid to live with the wild animals and the Indians.

"The legend says that the evil voices of a thousand animals were talking to El Ojo one day when an Indian warrior rode near him. El Ojo had not the strength to disobey the evil voices of the dead animals that tempted him to kill the Indian. He used his rifle to shoot. And when he did this, and he saw the warrior fall to the ground, he felt the strange feeling he knew every time he killed an animal. But this time El Ojo knew what the feeling was. And it was joy."

Nelly stopped scribbling her notes and looked up at Maximo.

"Yes, you are a gentle woman, Doña Lope, and to think of finding joy in killing makes a stone appear in your throat. But this is what the legend says.

"It was then that the evil from the flying soul of the dead Indian leapt into the body of El Ojo." Maximo leapt himself, suddenly, and even Chepita, who had heard the legend a hundred times, flinched when the yarn spinner sprang forward.

"El Ojo did not take the courage of the dead Indian—only the evil that made him take joy in killing. And the evil one now became a *tejano sangriento*—a bloody Texan.

"It was then that the *mexicanos* and the *norteamericanos* went to war. El Ojo went to fight in this war. He had a long rifle, and he knew how to make it shoot straight." Maximo held an imaginary rifle and pointed it at each of his listeners in succession.

"He had soldiers all around him, and this gave him courage to fight. And he collected the evil voices of a hundred men in this war. Now El Ojo thought nothing of killing and loved nothing better. He was even angry when the *mexicanos* got tired of fighting.

"The *americanos* found the gold in California and ran like greedy children to dig it up. El Ojo's evil voices told him to get some of the gold, too. But when he rode through the north of Mexico on the way to the mines, he heard a great cry from the city of Chihuahua. The governor wanted men to fight the Indians. The war had made the *federales* too weak to fight them. The terrible Comanches and Apaches were like butchers, killing the rancheros and stealing their cattle and burning the villages and carrying away the little children. The people could do nothing to stop them. The governor in Chihuahua sent a message to the *tejanos*. He said he would pay one hundred gringo dollars for every Indian warrior killed and fifty dollars for every squaw and twenty-five dollars for every Indian child.

"And the legend says El Ojo heard this call and, because he loved killing more than gold, he told the governor's men he would kill these Indians. It was agreed he would bring their scalps to prove how many he had killed so he might be paid, the same way he had collected the scalps of wolves and coyotes before.

"Doña Lope," Maximo said, pausing. "You cannot understand how evil this made El Ojo. He gathered an army of men to help him kill Indians, and they began killing. They found the camps of the Indians by looking for the tracks in the sky."

"In the sky?" Nelly asked, interrupting for the first time.

"Yes, the vultures follow the camps of the Indians and circle above them. These are the tracks in the sky. El Ojo followed these tracks and rode into the camps when the Indians were sleeping, and he killed everyone who could not ride away—men, women, and even little children. And though it makes the stone rise in your throat to hear of it, Doña Lope, he scalped them all and traded their hair for the governor's money." Maximo made the motions of a man with a scalping knife, as if he had seen the gruesome act accomplished with his own eyes.

"Indians are clever about fighting and hiding, and they became harder for El Ojo to kill. But the one with the evil in his eyes had learned a kind of treacherous wisdom and he thought of many ways to trick the Indians. He turned them against one another—all the different tribes and bands—and he got them to kill one another and bring the scalps to him. He gave them guns in exchange for the scalps of their brothers, and this allowed them to raid more ranches.

"According to the legend, El Ojo became very rich with blood money. He wanted to start a ranch north of the Rio Grande. He decided to kill all the Indians who had been helping him and take their scalps to change for money, too, and he thought up an evil plan to accomplish this."

Maximo took the iron poker from the hearth and scratched the familiar bend of the Rio Grande into the dirt floor. He drilled a dot on the Texas side of the river in a certain place.

"Here is where Señor Ben Leaton had his fort. It was a cantina and trading place on the river. And this is where El Ojo's Indians brought scalps to him and where he gave them their guns and whiskey.

"Well, El Ojo made a plan with Señor Leaton, who had a cannon at this fort. And the two gringos loaded the cannon with pieces of iron and hid it behind a curtain inside the cantina. When the Indian scalp hunters came in to drink their whiskey, El Ojo pulled open the curtain and let the cannon shoot them down and tear them to pieces. It made his evil soul feel extremely joyful to kill so many men at one time. Then he had twenty more scalps to trade for money to the governor of Chihuahua.

"It was then that El Ojo decided to take the last scalps to Chihuahua and start his ranch in Texas. The legend says he was riding toward Chihuahua and was thinking of the governor's man who had the job of counting the scalps and paying the money. And then El Ojo, with a million evil voices singing in his head, thought of the most wicked idea ever conceived by any man."

Nelly looked up from her notes, almost dreading a chapter of the tale more horrible than those she had already heard, yet eager to hear. Maximo's face was sweating and his eyes were wide and glistening. Chepita wore an expression of silent suffering as she watched him tell the story. Lawnce sat by anxiously like a captivated boy.

"The evil one was thinking of the governor's man who counted the scalps. This was no *hombre del campo;* he was a man of the city. El Ojo knew the scalp counter could not know the difference between the hair of an Indian and the hair of a Mexican. He was evil enough to consider this wicked idea, and yes, Doña Lope, even evil enough to test it. He decided to add to his collection of bloody scalps the hair of the Mexican rancheros—the very people he was supposed to protect by killing the Indians. He laughed when he thought of this idea.

"Before riding to the city of Chihuahua, El Ojo and his *tejanos sangrientos* rode through the north of Chihuahua and stopped at all the scattered ranchos to kill the poor Mexican people. It is too terrible to tell about all the many murders El Ojo committed in this way—and the women he defiled before killing them for their scalps. But I will tell the story of a rancho in the Sierra del Nido because it shows how El Ojo came to lose the eye from his horrible face.

"This was El Rancho Rincón. In your language, Doña Lope, *rincón* means 'far away from any civilized place.' It was the time of year when they gathered the cattle near the ranch house to castrate the young bulls, and this they were doing when El Ojo appeared. The ranchero, a brave hombre, saw the evil shining in El Ojo's eyes, and so he put his hand on his gun. But El Ojo shot first, and the ranchero was killed. Then the vaqueros rode to the ranch to protect the women and children, but they were cut down by the guns of El Ojo and the *tejanos sangrientos.*

"The women ran for their lives, except for the ranchera, who was a very brave and beautiful woman. She came out of the cabin with a rifle and she shot at the attackers and killed some of them. El Ojo would not come near her because she had this gun. But when she had used the cartridges, he ran at her with his horse and knocked her down.

"El Ojo was strong like an ox and when he saw the ranchera getting up from the ground, he jumped toward her and put his vile hands upon her, and she could do nothing to get away from him. This most evil of all men tried to tear her clothes away, but in a flash like a shooting star, the brave ranchera had in her hand a knife from the waist of her skirt"—from the red sash tied around his waist, Maximo suddenly brandished his own knife at the listeners, who instinctively drew away—"and with this knife she lunged at his ugly face, stabbing at the evil glare of his eyes. The knife struck him before he could move, and it cut into his left eye. As it sliced the eye from his face, El Ojo struck the ranchera with his fist and she fell. But his eye fell also to the ground, and blood poured from the opening in his face. Now all the evil in his soul shone in just one eye—twice as dark as before.

"El Ojo screamed louder than a tiger, and he fell back on the ground. When he was able to stand, he took his pistol and shot the brave ranchera, then kicked her body and cursed her as she died. He used the same knife that took his eye to cut the scalp from her body. Then he dragged the beautiful hair through the dirt to make it look like the hair of an Indian."

Maximo stabbed his knife into the cantina bar. He backed away from his listeners, panting and sweating, and returned to his chair. To Maximo, telling a story was like living it; he hadn't had so much exercise since the day August shot him.

"The legend says El Ojo took the scalps of *mexicanos* and Indians alike to Chihuahua and collected his bounty from the governor's fools. He received many thousands of dollars. And as he rode back to Texas, he laughed because he knew his *tejanos* were driving the stolen cattle from El Rancho Rincón for him to start his own ranch. But when he thought of the eye that had shriveled to dust on the Chihuahua Desert, he growled like a wolf and swore forever to hate all *mexicanos* and use them up like fodder for his evil plans.

"And that is why the people make the sign of the cross when they pass El Ojo. They are afraid that perhaps he has looked upon them with his evil eye and will cause them to suffer if they do not pray to cleanse their souls."

Silence and stillness fell into the chambers of Las Quince Letras for a long moment. Finally, Maximo shifted his posture and picked up his cup of tequila, and the listeners knew that his story had ended.

"But, Señor de Guerra," Nelly questioned, "how could these things be known if no one witnessed the crimes and murders? What proof can you give of your story?"

Maximo glared at the reporter. He drew a breath to speak, but caught Lawnce McCrary staring before he could say anything. "Doña Lope," he conceded with a shrug, "it is only a legend."

"But ain't it a ear-bender!" Lawnce said. "I swear, Maximo, it gets windier every time you tell it!"

The bandit knew Lawnce put little stock in legend. He

scowled and turned to Nelly. "And there is more to the legend which I will not tell in the presence of Don Lawnce. It is the part about how El Ojo paid a young stable boy to kill a brave desperado."

"Now, hold on, Maximo!" Lawnce came out from behind his table, riled. "That legend don't hurt nobody as long as innocent folks ain't drug in. But when you start talkin' about the kid, it stops bein' legend and starts being just a bald-ass lie!"

Chepita snapped her fingers at Apolonio and Guzman, and they got up from their table. *"Buenas noches,* Doña Lope," she said, curtsying quickly before pulling Maximo toward the door. Maximo unleashed a string of savage threats and accusations in Spanish that could be heard even after Chepita pulled him out into the street. Lawnce just stood there, too mad to speak.

"My, what a scene," Nelly said, more to herself than to Lawnce. "He rather cowed you."

"Now, look here," the ranger blurted, "I don't like the sound of that! There ain't a man alive bull enough to cow Lawnce McCrary!"

23

His first carving looked like a school-boy's work with a penknife on the trunk of a tree. But August dropped the message in the Rio Grande anyway. He watched it bob in the current and thought of its long journey. It probably would never find its way to Chepita's hand. But it didn't matter. He would carve another.

August began taking up the ax to split his own planks. The way the work made his wound ache, he knew the exercise was doing him good. The strength returned to his grasp from guiding the knife blade through wood grain. Before the snows set in, he went with Ryder to fell a dead tree that would become firewood and medium for the sculptors. They spelled each other at the axe handle.

As they worked that frosty morning near a log-dammed rivulet, the professor told tales of history and mythology, facts of nature and anthropology. August never hit a lick with the ax without hearing a word from the professor. It was a still morning and a fog hung over the beaver pond. It rose from the water in general, but its thickest plumes came from the beaver dens.

"The Indians," Ryder said as August chopped, "think of the beaver as a lost race of man fallen into disfavor with the gods and turned into gnawing rodents." He pointed to the conical island of a beaver den. "Notice how the vapor from the heat of the animal's body rises through the ventilation holes of the den. To the savages, the den represents a lodge. You see that it somewhat resembles a wigwam"—August could see no such thing, for he had never laid eyes on a wigwam—"and the vapor that rises through the ventilation hole on cold mornings is like the smoke one would see rising from the smoke hole of a wigwam. That is how the red men developed the conceit that the beaver was once human. And why do you suppose the beaver labors so on his little dams? The savages say he does so in order to please the gods, that he may become human again."

August labored a little harder with the ax. If there was any chance of his work making him feel human again, he wanted to exploit it. He hadn't felt completely human since Chepita stunned him with the back of her hand.

The tree he was chopping began to groan and sway; then it fell with a popping of branches. August handed the ax to Ryder. "How come the gods to turn them into beavers? What did they do to deserve it?"

"I suppose one would have to ask the beavers."

August helped the professor load some of the wood in a sling across the claybank's rump. Her disposition was so gentle that she only looked back once to see what strange load the men were putting on her. August let her smell a piece of wood, which she nibbled momentarily. Then she settled her weight on one back leg and stared blankly ahead without concern. When the sling was full of wood, August jumped across the mare's withers to ride back to the cabin. Halfway there he slid off to walk and offered his place on the horse to the professor.

"No, thank you," Ryder said. "I prefer to walk."

The professor believed in simplicity and independence. He wouldn't any more rely on a horse for his transportation than he would rely on a mule for his thoughts. When he had a long trip to make, such as his annual spring trek to Taos for supplies, he strapped a large pack across his shoulders and made the trip afoot. He could carry more than a hundred pounds of goods as far as thirty miles a day. Native islanders in the Philippines had once shown him how to carry a large part of the load with his neck muscles by strapping a tumpline across his forehead. But he had abandoned that technique after being scalped for fear the line would slip and rub across his wound.

When he needed a tree trunk to carve on, he carried it to his cabin on his back. Even the logs used to build his little house had been dragged and rolled there one by one, with his legs generating the industry to move them.

All of his Concord mentors—Thoreau, Channing, Hawthorne, and Emerson—had been inveterate perambulators. He had walked once with Thoreau and Channing when the two of them decided on an experiment whereby they would hike to a distant elevation without straying from a straight course leading there. Finding a cottage in their path, they knocked at the door, only to find the owners absent. So they entered the front door, walked straight through the house, came out again through the back door, and continued, having maintained the integrity of their course. They had made walking a science, which Ryder had adopted and studied mathematically.

"Don't you ever ride?" August asked.

"Seldom, lad."

"Down where I come from they say a man without a horse ain't no man at all."

"Mark my word, lad. Nothing you put between your legs will make a man of you any more than a gun placed in your hand will. Manhood comes of wisdom and courage, not of stinking beasts and smoking weapons. In addition, walking is faster than riding."

"What?" August said. "I'm sorry, Professor, but that don't make no sense."

"Why, it certainly does, lad, and I shall prove it to you by formula." The professor stopped, removed a plank from the sling, and drew his knife from his belt. "Let us say that we each have a trip of equal distance to make. Your journey will be from your village of Candelilla to whatever place may be near there."

"Presidio," August suggested.

"Presidio it is, then. And how many miles might there be between Candelilla and Presidio?"

"About forty, I reckon."

"Forty miles," Ryder repeated. "That shall serve as a reasonable figure for our formula. Let us say, then, that your journey will take you from Candelilla to Presidio." He was scratching the number forty into the face of the wooden plank with his knife. "As for my part, I would prefer, even in a hypothetical instance, to travel forty Massachusetts miles. Let us say my journey is from Worcester to Boston, roughly forty miles."

August nodded and waited patiently for Ryder to get around to making his point. It sometimes took a deal of waiting.

"I intend to walk," the professor said. "You intend to ride. I leave Worcester at seven o'clock in the morning. Walking at a rate of approximately five miles per hour, which I generally sustain when unencumbered by a pack, I arrive in Boston some eight hours later at about three o'clock, post meridiem." He carved in the appropriate steps and showed his formula to his student.

August allowed himself a laugh over the matter. "Well, Professor, if I jump on a good mustang, I can be at Presidio in half that time without breakin' a gallop!"

"And how much does a mustang cost in your region, lad?"

"What's that got to do with it?"

"Bear with me, lad, and answer the question."

"Well, it depends on how good a horse you're talkin' about, how broke he is and all. Anywhere between five and twenty-five dollars, I reckon. More for a really good mount."

"Shall we strike a median at fifteen dollars, then?"

August shrugged and nodded as the professor carved a notation of the sum agreed upon.

"What wage did you earn in your position with the livery stables?"

August was losing his understanding of the formula, but he answered anyway. "Hard to say. Never came too regular. I guess four, six bits a day on a long haul."

Ryder carved in the daily earnings of seventy-five cents and scratched some quick calculations in the wood. "At that wage, lad, you would have to work twenty days to earn enough money to purchase your horse before starting your trip, making your total traveling time from Candelilla to Presidio some four hundred eighty-four hours while I will have reached Boston in merely eight hours at a cost to myself of no more than a stiver!"

"Buy a horse?" August questioned. "Heck, I never had to buy one. Down where I'm from, Professor, if we want a horse, we just go out and set a loop trap for him on one of his trails. Or get his wind and sneak up on him and rope him. Or build a corral out of brush and get a bunch of Mexicans and Indians to herd a whole stampede of 'em in there. Or you can build a trap around a water hole and when they get thirsty enough, they'll walk in it. That's what me and Lawnce always done. Then he took and herded 'em up to the army and sold 'em, except for the best ones, which we would keep for ourselves."

"Shall I assume, peradventure, that the time spent in catching and training such a horse to the saddle might also take more than eight hours, in which time I might have reached Boston and started on my journey home?"

"I reckon it might, but once we got us a horse, Professor, we can ride him to Presidio every other day if we want to, even though there ain't that much to see there."

Ryder poked his knife blade at his formula again. "I doubt, lad, that you would have time to ride to Presidio every other day. You would be spending most of your time working to earn the money needed to buy the grain to feed your horse!"

"Heck, Professor, you can't even get a mustang to eat grain unless you teach him how by mixing it in with grass and hay for a while. Where there's good grass, you can just stake 'em out. They're wild horses. They eat wild stuff."

Ryder pored over his formula, making scratch marks with his blade. He stopped to rub his forehead once, then took his glasses off to polish them. August thought he looked irritated and didn't bother him while he figured.

"It often occurs," he finally said, putting his knife away inside his fur coat, "that the pupil enlightens his instructor. You have reminded me of a basic precept that had otherwise slipped my mind, lad. That is this: There is a perfect order to mathematics. But there is no perfect order to human reality, and it often defies formularization." He tossed the carved piece of wood over his shoulder and jerked the claybank's horsehair halter toward his cabin.

"Does that mean I got to Presidio before you got to Boston?" August asked.

"From Worcester to Boston, I should arrive afoot before you would on horseback. But from Candelilla to Presidio, lad, I fear I should suffer a humiliating defeat."

August shouldered his rifle and went hunting when the elk began to bugle. He killed a high-antlered bull and a mule deer doe and a black bear all within a week. The bear robe would keep him warm through the winter. The work of stalking, skinning, and butchering sapped his energy, but the thrill of hunting kept him in the field.

Ryder cured the chunks of meat in the mode of the buffalo hunters. First he dug a square hole and lined it with the elk skin by pegging the green hide to the ground around the hole. He salted the pieces of meat and threw them into the hole. He and August put another hide over the meat and piled on rocks to keep wolves from excavating the carnage.

They built a smokehouse nearby. They set four stout pickets upright in the ground as corner posts. They stretched hides between the poles to form the walls and ceiling. August dug a small fire hole in the ground inside the smokehouse.

After eight days of aging in the pit, they removed the meat and hung the cuts in the smokehouse. Green wood smoldered day and night under the elk and venison. The smoker would give them plenty of cured meat for the harshest winter months, when it was too cold to hunt.

When the first snow came, the professor roused August early in the morning for a hike. They walked toward the river with the snow around their ankles and entertained themselves for a while watching snowballs vanish in the hot spring. Then they plodded toward the beaver pond, Ryder lecturing with every step.

There was a marshy area toward the upper end of the pond and, as they got closer to it, Ryder began searching for something in the fresh snow at his feet. Suddenly he stopped and pointed downward. "Look," he said.

August looked but didn't see anything there but snow. The snow in itself was a wonderful thing to him. A few wispy flakes had fallen on Candelilla one winter, but they had all melted upon contact with the ground, like the snowballs thrown into the hot spring. The snow was certainly something to look at, but it seemed strange to him that the professor would suddenly stop to point it out.

"Hetunkala," Ryder said.

"Pardon?"

"The Moon-Nibblers."

August had heard the professor speak of some odd things, but none as strange as Moon-Nibblers. He thought perhaps the cold was getting to Ryder's brain through the hole in his skull.

"Look right there," Ryder said, reading the confusion in August's face. " 'Tis the track of the mice people."

August looked carefully and finally saw the faint imprint of tiny feet. A small rodent had passed lightly over the new snow.

"Come, lad, we shall follow her."

Ryder began tracking the tiny animal. At first her route seemed aimless, but after a while it appeared to be moving with some amount of certainty toward an area of dead grass at the marshy end of the beaver pond.

August felt ridiculous. He had tracked deer and antelope and used to lay for rats on occasion, but he didn't see the least bit of sense in trailing a mouse. "What is it we're huntin'?" he finally asked the professor.

"This is the track of the meadow vole. If we are lucky, we may find her larder."

"What was that about Moon-Nibblers?"

Ryder remained stooped, following the faint trail. " 'Tis a folk legend of the Dakota Nation. The Sioux call these voles Hetunkala, the Moon-Nibblers. They say these little mice people once resided on the moon and were given the task of nibbling the silver sheen away from every full moon." He held his fur cap on to keep it from falling in the snow over which he bent.

"When they had nibbled the shiny covering away to nothing, the gods would restore it for them to feast upon again, and thus another full moon would light the sky. Night after night, the human beings could look up at the amount of the moon's bright surface the Moon-Nibblers had eaten away and know that the great circle of time continued to turn." His finger followed the shallow path left by the vole.

"But some gluttons among the mice people ate more than their share, gnawing great holes deep into the moon. For this the gods shook them down to the earth where, still, they know nothing but nibbling."

"What do they nibble on now?" August asked.

Ryder marked his place along the vole trail by poking a hole in the snow with his finger. He stood aright, grinning at August. "They nibble upon a veritable marketplace of produce—wild beans, wild artichokes, edible roots. And what's more, they hoard them in subterranean storage chambers. The Sioux women showed me how to find the larders and rob them. If we can follow this one's path, perhaps we shall uncover some vegetables for winter!"

August was dumbfounded. He couldn't imagine eating something a rodent had carried in its mouth and buried in the dirt. But, how much food could a tiny mouse possibly put away? Not enough to fret over, he decided. Besides, he was catching Ryder's enthusiasm for the project. "How do we find it?"

"Follow this trail. If we find other trails converging with it, we will find the main thoroughfare of the mice people. It should lead to the storage chamber."

August got to one side of the vole trail, Ryder to the other. Together they followed the barely visible sign of the meadow vole toward the dead grass around the marsh. When they neared the fallen stalks of dried grass, they found other vole trails joining and deepening the one they had followed. Then all the trails disappeared under a mat of dead grass.

Ryder found a stick and lifted the layers of grass from the ground. Under them, pathways had been furrowed into the rich dirt. He continued to uncover and follow the little trenches, getting more excited with every step. Suddenly he stopped and pointed ahead.

A small mound stood there that looked to August like an anthill.

"Tread lightly," Ryder said, "and test every step as we circle the mound. Feel for a soft spot underfoot." He began walking in a circle around the mound, probing the ground with his heels and his stick.

August circled in the opposite direction. He hoped he would be the one to find the soft spot Ryder had spoken of. When he reached the very edge of the mound, he felt the ground give way under his foot. Before he could speak, he heard a faint scampering and looked back to see several mouselike creatures escaping down their uncovered trenches.

"Good work!" Ryder shouted. "You've found it!" He dropped to his knees and pulled the dirt back from the place where August's foot had pushed through.

The chamber was much bigger than August had expected.

"There must be a peck!" the joyful professor shouted. He took the wolf-skin medicine bundle from his back and began filling it. "These are tasty in stew," he said, scooping up a handful of wild beans. "And look here. Roots of the wild lily."

August looked carefully at a few beans. He couldn't find so much as a tooth mark on any one of them. His prejudice against the mice people soon faded, and he reasoned that, boiled, the beans would be as sanitary as any the farmers around Candelilla harvested. He helped

Ryder fill the medicine bundle with stolen produce and began to look forward to eating beans again. He hadn't tasted any in many weeks.

Early winter brought massive cloud banks from the northwest. August liked to walk to the near ridge to watch them roll over. Sometimes they dumped a little rain or snow on him, but often the dry air in the rain shadow of the Great Divide evaporated the showers before they could dampen the ground. He could see the rain falling in sheets halfway from cloud to earth. Then the gray streaks of moisture ended, like a short curtain hung in a tall window. On those days, the rain that never reached earth cooled pockets of air as it evaporated. The invisible pockets plunged through hotter air, hit the ground, and caused little gusts of cool wind from every quarter.

Those were fine days to sit on a ridge cloaked in bearskin. Ryder joined August there one evening when the showers fell short of earth. As they watched, the setting sun made a brief appearance between the clouds and the horizon. Looking across the vast Sangre de Cristo range to the east, the two unwilling fugitives watched the rays of Sol paint the thunderheads in hues of orange and red. Then, just as the sun ducked behind the horizon, it washed the gray curtains of rain in a deep shade of crimson.

"Sangre de Cristo," Ryder said. "Do you know what those words mean, lad?"

"Means 'Blood of Christ.'"

"There's something in that name, Shakespeare notwithstanding," Ryder said. "Imagine the conquistadores trekking this valley three hundred years ago. On an evening like this one they gazed eastward at an unnamed range of mountains, perhaps from this very elevation, and beheld the same spectacle you and I see now. Blood rained from the heavens themselves, yet fell short of staining the lowly planet of mortal man. The Blood of Jesus Christ. A reminder of his sacrifice on the cross for our souls, lad.

"Clever fellows, the Spaniards. They gave proper credit to the Creator in naming the landmarks of this new continent. They cared little for the self-glorification evident in names like Hudson Bay and Pikes Peak. Instead, they christened the Rio de Los Brazos for the Arms of God, the Sierra Madre for the Virgin Mary, and the Sangre de Cristos for the Blood of Christ." He sat silent until the reddish hue faded from the streaks of rain.

"Self-glorification leads to ruin, lad."

"I reckon I know that," August answered.

When the blizzards began to blow, August and Ryder holed up in the cabin, paying little attention to the winds that whistled through the chinks. They sharpened their knives and chisels and carved while they conversed. They used the wood shavings for kindling when the coals lost their flames.

Ryder quoted his mentors. He always assumed the same posture when quoting. He would cast his eyes upward while reciting the quotation, enunciating distinctly with appropriate inflections in his voice. Then, turning to August, he would knowingly give the name of the quotation's author: " 'You can always see a face in the fire.' Thoreau."

He schooled August in styles of lettering to use when carving messages to Chepita. The Texan learned to gouge the serifs of the Romans and the script of Mother England. Each letter he carved improved upon the last. He continued to offer them to the river throughout the winter, knowing each increased the chance that one would find her.

A carved letter sent to Chepita by the river would have

to float five hundred miles. The driftwood on the banks near Candelilla, August recalled, felt smooth as the handle of his old pitchfork at McCrary Livery. The river had polished the wood and would probably erase his lettering unless he carved deeper. At the suggestion of the master, he decided to carve in relief, letting the characters stand out from the wood.

On small chips, he experimented with little designs, which he copied from Ryder's carvings—roses, vines, and leaves. He learned to weave them into a frame around his words of lost desire. His carvings started to rival the works of men who carved for livelihood. At the rate of about one a week, he offered a shingle to the river.

Throughout the winter, the insignificant bits of pine traveled downstream like jetsam before a hurricane. Silt ground away at them in the shallows. The rough stone walls of the Rio Grande Gorge battered and gouged them without sentiment. Rafts of driftwood snagged and held them. Swirls and eddies led them from their course.

Trickles appeared in tiny snow canyons around the cabin toward the end of winter. Reverend Ryder and his companion had work to get at. Provisions had given out. The roof leaked. The annual trek to Taos for supplies was imminent. Time for roasting their shins at the hearth had ended. No more carving would transpire for a while.

August crunched through the snows to the river one morning with a last effort aimed at patching a lost love affair. He flipped an elaborately fashioned plaque into a snow-swollen Rio Grande. The dispatch slipped away amid a roar of mountain river water. It negotiated the bend and rushed beyond surveillance as other thoughts rushed into the young wood-carver's head.

The billet plied the madness of the gorge, tossed in the froth, sometimes shot from the river's surface, glancing off rocks, forever whirling like a plains windmill.

Lazy bends greeted the plank below the gorge. It angled around a raft of debris and avoided the stagnant backwaters. No man or beast took notice of it any more than they would another floating shard of timber. It traveled nicely downstream, but then lodged among rocks in the shallows at a place where horses forded. It stayed there half a day before a harnessed jenny knocked it downstream with her hoof.

Melting snows buoyed August's message just high enough to skim the sandbars toward Albuquerque. Then the effects of a late freeze restricted the flow of the Rio Grande, and a willow branch near a footpath snagged the graven message as the river level fell.

A girl came to fill two tin water buckets and happened upon the message stranded above the waterline. She was a household servant and had learned her letters. She read August's message, enchanted. She was old enough to dream of romance, and this floating letter, with its feeble chance of finding its destination, embraced all the desperation common to matters of love. She waded in and shoved the carved letter into the pull of the channel.

The ancient irrigation canals below Albuquerque sucked the splint in toward the cornfields. It got stuck in a sluice gate above an acre of seed. An illiterate *zanjero* cursed it for blocking the flow, glanced over its carved characters, and hurled it back into the river. Like a swan on a north wind it glided on to the south, past the Caballo Mountains, around Dona Ana where a wading wife tried to pull it in for stove wood, only to slip on a slick rock and soak her skirts.

By the dead of night August's carving slipped under the footbridge at El Paso as Americans and Mexicans walked or staggered across overhead. Now the plank moved between Mexico and Texas, silently navigating the last leg of its journey to Candelilla.

24

Chepita wrung the last of the day's wash water back into the river. Her basket barely held the wash she had to finish now to pay for the things she needed. She thought about happier times when the basket held less work and the river more hope. She remembered a shy boy on a bareback mule who used to visit her there.

There was just enough light left in the sky to guide her home. She had folded the last cotton shirt and was preparing to place the basket atop her head when she heard a squawk from Señora Heron. She looked toward the Mexican side as the graceful bird beat her wings for the roost. A dark dot in the river's orange reflections of sunset caught her eye as it paced the lazy flow of the channel. Just a chunk of wood, she thought. Then a contour on its surface roused her curiosity. It angled toward the Texas side.

She could have reached the object if she had waded. But matters of curiosity no longer beguiled Chepita. Hope had all but deserted her. She had stopped looking for it in her river and the things it carried downstream. She didn't care to get her calves wet again wading for a billet of driftwood, so she lifted her burden onto her head and turned for Candelilla as the floating object drifted by with her hopes.

Events had drained Chepita of the cheery outlook she had once maintained. Maximo hadn't sold any Doubletree cattle or given her any money in a long time. His obsessive desire to find and kill August Dannenberg took all his time and energy. He no longer rode into Mexico with stolen cattle, returned with silver pesos, or spoke of the ranch they would one day return to. He no longer sang ballads in the cantina to the accompaniment of Tristan's guitar. He refused to ride with the bull trains that hauled copper and silver from the mines—afraid some word of August might come in his absence. His sportive disposition had died by the hand of a straight-shooting stable boy. He didn't want to ride unless he thought he might find his would-be murderer. He didn't care to speak unless to learn the boy's whereabouts. He simply paced and sat and brooded. The hatred he had lived with for a lifetime had doubled. He no longer found room in his heart for any other emotion. The debts owed to him began to mount higher than he could figure. He had to collect, and the payments would come in blood. First August Dannenberg, then Butch Gainey.

Chepita prayed God would lead Maximo away from his deviltry, but she did nothing to cheer him. She knew any fire stoked under him would only drive him away to find August. Then more fighting and killing would occur. Maximo or August would die—or both of them. She couldn't stand the thought of either of them dying. Though she had already lost August, she still held on to the hope that he was alive somewhere. It was strange how she had fallen in love with the memory of August in the past months. She had barely known the boy, but the colder Maximo grew, the warmer August's memory became to her. She couldn't decide which of them she loved more. She wondered if it was possible to hate them both and love them both at the same time.

A dozen shiftless rustlers loafed around town, waiting for orders to steal cattle. Jesse Diaz had begun to whisper to his *compadres* about Maximo's fallen courage. The gang had nothing to do but guard Maximo and grumble about the lack of action.

Lawnce McCrary grumbled, too, especially when shoveling manure from his livery stalls. He vowed to give August a substantial raise in pay if he should ever return alive. But that seemed unlikely.

The situation in Candelilla worried him. Maximo's men were in town all the time now, and Butch Gainey's boys seemed to be coming in more often, too. They moved around in little squads, always mindful of the other. They were all bristling for gunplay. A ranger couldn't allow such a thing in his territory.

It was true that Lawnce didn't have much truck with other rangers. He didn't get along with them. He put most of them in the same category as renegades. Some of them could be trusted to hang the right outlaws, but most of them just wanted to hang any Mexican or Indian whose path they cut. Some of them did worse than hanging. It was said that Captain McNelly's men in south Texas would tie a man's neck to a tree and his feet to a saddle horn and jerk his head off by gouging the horse with spurs. That wasn't a bad way to die compared to some of the slow tortures Lawnce had seen the Comanches practice. But it still wasn't a thing for a lawman to do. It didn't sit well with the Revised Statutes, he was sure.

Lawnce didn't worry about what other rangers would think of him if trouble broke out in his town. He was worried more about the town itself. Except for an occasional squabble between drunks, a domestic disturbance of some kind, or Maximo shooting a hired gun, the town had always been quiet. The treaty with the Mescaleros had prevented the bloodletting that could have occurred. And Maximo had kept Gainey too busy to give him time to think about taking over the town.

But since August's bullets had slowed Maximo down,

One-Eyed Butch seemed more determined than ever to run Candelilla. His first chore was to kill Maximo and wipe out his gang. Then Lawnce would have to be dealt with. Lawnce didn't know exactly how Gainey planned to accomplish all the killing, but he knew plans were being formed.

Lawnce had a vast strip of the border to keep the laws in, but he was afraid to leave town to look after other locales. For the first time in his law-enforcement career, he felt the cards being stacked up against him in a game he couldn't control.

Maximo had experienced the same loss of influence in his own realm. He was losing the sway he had always held over his men. They no longer tagged along after him like boys. They had found a new favorite in Jesse Diaz.

Jesse spent too much time unaccounted for, and that worried Maximo. He had noticed that Jesse seemed to cease his conversations with the other bandits every time he approached. It was hard to concentrate on Jesse Diaz while Butch Gainey and August Dannenberg were still alive. Did Jesse have ambitions? Maximo wondered. What would Don Lawnce the ranger do with such suspicions? He would investigate. But there was already too much thinking to do. How would he find August Dannenberg? How could he kill Butch Gainey? Jesse Diaz was not yet a big enough threat to worry about.

Maximo woke before dawn and didn't bother to speak to Chepita. She had cooked the frijoles and eggs she received in trade for laundry chores. He rolled the breakfast victuals in fresh tortillas and ate them sitting on his rolled bed cushion. Then he strapped on his pistol belt and slipped out, leaving his spurs and sombrero inside, as day broke over the Chinati Mountains.

Today Cayetano Pastor, cook at the Doubletree Ranch,

would drive his wagon to Candelilla to buy a month's supplies. Maximo sneaked behind the brush huts and waited
behind a goat pen for Cayetano to show up. The cook's
uncle tended the goats and owned the pen. Cayetano
came to visit his uncle every month while his supplies
were being loaded at the store. He also came to sell Doubletree secrets to Maximo for a silver peso or two.

"Señor de Guerra," he whispered in the deepest gravity
when he arrived, "you must be careful of your life. El Ojo
intends to pay a murderer to kill you."

The grim expression on Maximo's face deepened.
"Who?" he said, rolling tobacco into a cornhusk.

"No se," the old informer answered with a shrug. "El
Ojo did not say the name. But it is someone living in Candelilla."

"How do you know about this killer?"

"I heard El Ojo giving orders to one of his men," Cayetano said. "He ordered five hundred dollars paid to a man
who would ride from Candelilla to a place on the river
to get the money." With a nod of gratitude, the old man
accepted the *cigarro de hoja* rolled by Maximo's hand.

Maximo leaned against the driftwood staves of the goat
pen and stared at the dirt. Jesse Diaz seemed to have more
ambitions by the second. Or was the assassin someone
else? He fingered the fixings for his own cigarette as he
wrestled with the problem.

"There is a way you may know the murderer, Señor de
Guerra," Cayetano said with a grin of self-satisfaction.

Maximo bade him to continue with a gesture of his
head.

"The blood money will be paid in gold, American. Coins
of twenty dollars each. Do you have such a coin, señor?"
The old *cocinero* had the corn-husk cigarette sticking out
of his mouth, unlit.

Maximo licked the edge of his husk and rolled it around

the coarse leaf. He looked at Cayetano, frowned a little, and fished a match and a coin worth eight reales from his pocket. He handed the coin to Cayetano and struck the match on his boot. "Maximo has only this coin."

"Your knife," the cook said, then sucked in with pleasure as Maximo lit his smoke.

Maximo drew a honed weapon from his scabbard and gave it to the cook.

Cayetano held the coin against a rock lying between his huaraches where he squatted. He made a small mark with the point of Maximo's knife in hands accustomed to guiding a blade. "The American coins, like this one, have an eagle depicted on them." He handed the coin to Maximo. "It is not the same kind of eagle, but it has wings like this one, no? *Mira!* Look at the wing of this eagle. He does not fly. Your old spy has clipped his wings."

Maximo looked closely at the scratch Cayetano had made across the wing tip of the snake-fighting eagle on the tails side of the Mexican coin.

"I marked them all in that way—the American coins. I found them in a saddlebag in El Ojo's room—twenty-five coins in all. I clipped the wings on every coin while he was gone. The one who spends such gold is the same who would murder you."

Maximo allowed a broad grin to lift the ends of his mustache. *"Gracias, viejo,"* he said as he flipped the marked coin back to Cayetano. "You are a crafty old informer to think of such a trick."

Cayetano's grin revealed the only three teeth left in his head. He squatted behind the goat pens even after Maximo left, and smoked every sliver of tobacco into ashes, though he scorched his old fingers holding the butt.

When Maximo returned to Chepita's adobe, he asked about Jesse Diaz. The boys said they didn't know his whereabouts, but he had ridden toward the river several minutes earlier. Maximo ordered his horse saddled and brought around. It was done by the time he had put on his spurs and sombrero.

Jesse's trail led to the river, then turned downstream, in the direction of the Doubletree spread. Perhaps the marked coins would change hands this very morning. If so, Jesse was a fool; his tracks were clearly visible in the sand of the river valley. When Maximo rounded a bend, he saw his man holding a secret meeting beneath the shade of the cottonwood boughs.

He saw Jesse clearly, not with Butch Gainey or any of Gainey's men, but with a pretty Mexican girl, a very young girl to be meeting a full-grown man in secret by the river. Maximo backed his horse into cover and watched for a few minutes. They held hands, sat side by side on the bare roots of a big tree, and stared into each other's eyes with whispers on their lips.

Maximo shook his head and smirked. This feuding with gringos was beginning to cloud his judgment and make him suspect everyone, even his allies. No wonder Jesse spent so much time unaccounted for. No wonder the other men had come to admire him so. The beating with the poker must have taught him an appreciation for womanhood. Maximo was relieved. He had too much to worry about without suspecting Jesse. Now he could concentrate on his two enemies again. Maximo reined his mount away from the trysting place.

Jesse knew that such a young girl would be easily charmed. He treated her with the greatest of chivalry, the utmost in gentlemanly courtesy. He epitomized romance. He never pressed her for so much as a kiss. He never fondled anything closer to her heart than her fingers. His young border dove was enchanted. When he asked her to meet him where the river laved the shore, he knew she would come. That way he could sit with her an hour, pretend love of the deepest and most sincere stripe, and anyone who followed—Maximo, especially—would think his mission purely amorous.

In an hour he would send the girl away, and after watching her vanish toward Candelilla, he would ride on to his meeting with the Doubletree men, free from worries about spies on his trail, and collect half of his fee for the murder of Maximo.

Maximo's mood was lighter than any he had experienced since August's bullets hit him. His wounds had healed. He had important intelligence from Cayetano Pastor. Jesse Diaz had proved loyal after all. A word about the stable boy would put him in the highest of spirits.

As he turned away from the river, he detected a film of dust hanging in the air. It looked as if someone had ridden into town fast enough to kick up some dirt. He gouged his horse and rode into town at a lope. Reaching the main street, he turned right and saw several of his men talking to a stranger. Apolonio caught his eye. *"Jefe!"* he shouted, and waved for Maximo to approach.

The stranger was a goat herder from downstream, near Presidio. He had borrowed a horse and ridden hard to see Maximo, but he had not yet said why. That news was for Maximo's ears only.

"He won't tell us anything," Guzman complained.

"Why have you ridden that old horse so fast, my friend?" Maximo asked the goat herder.

The man grinned. "Do you know a woman in this village named Chepita Ybarra?"

"The questions are for Maximo to ask," the desperado said. "What do you know of this woman?"

The herder had an old *morral*—a nose bag used to carry things—tied onto his saddle horn. He began to untie it slowly. "I have never met her," he said. "But I found something in the river that belongs to her."

"What have you found?"

The herder continued to untie the *morral*. "If I must tell the truth, I didn't find it myself. My goat named Yzidro found it first. He was having a drink at the river, and I saw him nibbling on something that was floating." He had removed the *morral* from the horn and was opening its mouth with no particular haste. "I can read," he said proudly, reaching into the bag, "and this thing had the name of Candelilla carved onto it. So I said to Yzidro, 'Isn't that the town where the great Maximo de Guerra lives?' " He handed Maximo an ax-riven slab of ponderosa pine.

Maximo studied the plank for a second, then looked at Abundio. "Give this man a horse," he said. Then he turned to smile at the goat herder. "You must tell your friend Yzidro that Maximo will eat no goats for one week in his honor."

Maximo kicked the door in, startling Chepita so that she scattered dirty clothes all across the flagstone floor. He tossed the piece of wood, still damp from the river, at her feet. "Where is he?" he demanded.

"What are you talking about?" Chepita said, clasping her rosary.

"Where is the boy who sends you messages by the river?"

Chepita looked at the plank on the floor, saw the carved characters, and began to understand. The sight of it both thrilled and terrified her. "I don't know what you are talking about," she insisted.

Maximo stalked toward her. "Then Maximo will ride up the river to find the boy," he said. "Maximo will bring him back to you so you can watch him die!" The desperado's fist rose above his head as he spoke.

Chepita stood quickly, defiantly, to face him. If he

struck her, she would not cower. But he stopped before
lashing out. He trembled to think of what he might have
done. He had never struck a woman in his life, especially
not his pure little angel of the border country. No matter
what the people of Candelilla thought about the way he
treated Chepita, he would rather have shot himself than
hurt her. This madness with gringos had turned him
against those he loved and trusted. Damn all gringos!

He lowered his arm and opened his fist. Then, remem-
bering the inscribed plank on the floor, he turned away
and went outside. The band of restless border thieves
howled for glory when he gave the order to mount and
ride upstream.

As the hoofbeats faded from hearing, Chepita eased toward August's letter. She stirred with anticipation, for she
could read the carved message on it now. She quickly
picked it up and turned it to catch the rays of sun streaming through the broken door. The one side was addressed
like a parcel: "Chepita Ybarra, Rio Grande, Candelilla,
Texas."

She felt weak and strong all at once. She sat absentmindedly on her basket of clothes and turned the carved
document over. She had felt raised letters on the other
side. Water of melted mountain snows highlighted the
rose vines that served as a border. She read with her fingers as well as her eyes the message that had traveled five
hundred miles to reach her:

El rio nos ligamos.
Te amo todavia.

"The river binds us," the message said. "I love you still."

She clutched it against her bodice and worried little
about the moisture that soaked through to her breast. The
slab of pine had buoyed her spirit as surely as it had
floated in the current past mountains and deserts. It

25

Jesse had been told to ride three miles downstream. He had to spur his old stallion constantly to keep him loping. The old stud had made too many hard rides into Mexico.

There was a little draw ahead that branched off the main canyon of the Rio Grande. As he prepared to ride down into it, he saw a man with a rifle looking at him from behind a rock. Jesse raised his hand. The man waved for him to follow.

The rifleman mounted a horse below the rim of the draw and led Jesse down into it. Directly he saw six horses. Then he spotted Butch Gainey and his guards lounging in the shade of the east bank of the draw. Gainey smiled and waved.

"Mornin', Jesse. Me and the boys had a little bet as to whether or not you'd show up. I'm glad you got here. That makes me just a little bit richer."

"I did not come to make you richer," Jesse said. "But to make myself richer."

Gainey laughed. "Light and sit awhile and we'll see if we can't oblige. You know some of the boys. I won't bother with introductions."

Jesse looked at the six men. He recognized most of them from previous meetings. None of them offered any kind of salutation. He dismounted and draped his reins over a branch of a greasewood bush. Then he hooked a stirrup over his saddle horn and loosened the cinch. The old stud was still heaving from his short ride.

"Sid, get that bag off Top Dollar," Gainey ordered.

The guard who had led Jesse into the draw dismounted and retrieved a *morral* from Gainey's saddle pockets. One-Eyed Butch shook it to make the coins inside jingle. Then he grinned and handed it to Jesse.

"Five hundred," he said, as Jesse looked into the nose bag. "Once you kill him you'll get five hundred more. It's worth that to me."

"Why don't you pay with paper money?" Jesse was thinking that bills would be easier to conceal.

"Shit, I ain't a goddamn bank teller!" Butch shouted. "You take whatever I give you. The last stagecoach the boys burnt just happened to be carrying gold." He started laughing. "It tickles me to think about it. That money's payroll for the stage company. That's Lawnce McCrary's salary you're holding on to!"

The thought didn't amuse Jesse the way it did Butch. He put the old sack full of money into his saddlebag.

"Not so fast, Jesse. Let's get a thing or two straight. You've failed me in the past. Told me you'd lead Maximo one place and he ends up stealing my cattle another place."

"Maximo does not like to be led."

"I'll buy that. That's why you're still breathing. But this time you're getting money up front and you'd better come through."

Jesse turned his back as if insulted and started tightening the cinch around his tired old horse. He wanted to get out of the draw at the earliest opportunity. "I will do this thing," he said in an arrogant tone. "And you will have no more need to fear Maximo de Guerra." He heard Gainey laughing, a laugh that grew until it was so loud that Jesse felt compelled to turn and look.

"You still don't get it, do you Jesse?" Butch asked between great hiccuping jolts of laughter. "Do I look like the kind of man to be bullied by a Mexican? Why, you can't see things as clear with your two good eyes as I can with my one!"

Jesse stood wordless beside his horse.

"You think I want Maximo dead so I can sleep nights? What the hell you think I pay these hardheads for?" He pointed at his guards. "You think they're cowboys? You think I'm a rancher? Hell, we're outlaws, Jesse. Ain't you figured that by now? We don't fear no scrawny Mexican. I don't give a damn if Maximo takes every last one of my stinkin' beeves, either. Do me a favor if he would. I want him dead for one reason—because there's money in it for me. Lots of it. Some for you, too."

Jesse didn't follow a word of what Gainey was talking about. The look on his face just made Butch laugh louder.

"You ain't thinkin' the American way, Jesse. This is a business. I invest a thousand dollars to get Maximo killed and I stand to take a hundred thousand or so in profit. When Maximo's dead, you boss his boys. *You* guard the bull trains on the Chihuahua Trail. A big silver shipment comes through and my boys attack, steal half the silver. But your boys put up a hell of a fight, save the other half. You're a hero. You get a cut of what I steal, you keep on guarding the trains and we live high for a while and do the whole damn thing over again. We got us a partnership. We ain't just killin' Maximo. We'll be workin' together a long time, Jesse. A long time."

Jesse felt a sudden wave of panic. "Perhaps," he said, swinging up into the saddle. He didn't like the idea of establishing a partnership with Gainey. He simply avoided accepting the proposal by repeating himself as he reined his horse away: "Perhaps."

"Hell, don't run off," Gainey said. "I want you to meet somebody first." He grunted as he pushed himself up from the rock he had been sitting on, then grunted even louder when he climbed up onto Top Dollar. "Sid, you come with us."

Gainey led the way up the draw. Jesse followed and Sid rode behind him. Jesse was nervous. He was getting in deeper than he wanted to, and Gainey was not about to let him back out now that he knew about the plan to steal from the bull trains. Now he was going to meet someone. He hoped it wouldn't be his Maker.

The draw narrowed as it got farther away from the river. It was a place from which there was no escape. The walls rose sharply on both sides and the draw switched back and forth at such angles that Jesse could never see more than fifty yards ahead.

Butch led him around a bend in the draw and Jesse was instantly startled by the rush of wings. The draw came to an end in a box canyon that widened a bit at the head. Vultures were flying up from a small tree at the head of the draw and filling the air with their black wings. There must have been a hundred of them. An awful stench filled the head of the canyon. Jesse wanted to put his bandanna over his nose, but he was afraid to move.

Then he saw what had attracted the buzzards. A naked corpse was hanging upside down from the tree. It was barely recognizable, but it was human. The vultures had picked out the eyes and torn the most tender pieces of flesh away from the body. Jesse began to feel dizzy, and the canyon seemed to close in on him. He looked back at Sid, who was watching the black wings circle overhead.

Gainey stopped and turned Top Dollar to face Jesse. "Mr. Diaz, meet Mr. Jud Longley. You ought to go over there and thank him, Jesse. Mr. Longley is a former employee of the overland stage coach service. He's the one who told us when that payroll would be coming through."

Jesse was still horrified by the blackened corpse. He

saw a small pile of ashes on the ground, about a foot below the dead man's head.

"Oh, he didn't want to tell us," Butch continued. "But when we lit that fire under him, he started talking quick enough. He told us things we didn't even want to know. Lord, you should have heard him holler. He made sense for about an hour. Then I guess his brains got cooked, because he just screamed about nothing."

Butch tipped his hat back on his head and moved in between Jesse and the mutilated corpse. With his one eye socket shriveled and sunken, he seemed half corpse himself. Jesse felt too weak even to look away. He was locked into the evil stare of Gainey's one good eye. The odor of rotting flesh made breathing almost impossible. The shadows of the buzzards circled in a dizzying swirl.

"I had some Comanches that worked for me once, huntin' scalps," Butch said. "They taught me that trick. And some other tricks, too. I don't guess you'd want to hear about any of them right now, but if you get any ideas of running off with my five hundred without killing Maximo, you'll do more than hear about them. You'll find out firsthand."

When they turned to ride out of the draw, Butch saw that Jesse still looked poorly. He rode up next to the Mexican and slapped him on the back. "Don't take it so hard, Jesse. It's nothing personal. I just have to know that I can trust you. After all, Maximo thinks he can trust you, don't he?"

Jesse felt as if the foul smell of the corpse followed him until he reached the rim of the draw and started riding back toward Candelilla. He had to stop once to get off of his horse and throw up. It wasn't the death of Jud Longley that bothered him; he had seen killing before and had done some of it himself down in Mexico. It was the thought of the fire roasting his own brains that affected

him. Just thinking about it gave him a headache. When
he felt strong enough to mount again, he looked back
over the rimrock toward the head of the draw and saw
a few vultures still circling.

Maximo had ordered Tristan to stay behind. He was to
send Jesse along to catch up with the rest of the border
gang when he returned from his meeting with his señorita. Then Tristan, the best tracker on the Big Bend, was
to watch Lawnce McCrary. The ranger might try to warn
August. Perhaps the lawman already knew the stable
boy's hiding place. Tristan would follow a day behind
Lawnce if the ranger left Candelilla. He got his guitar and
gathered some children around him across the street
from McCrary Livery. He sang ballads of the border to
them as he watched for movement around the stables.

Tristan, whom everyone knew as a half-wit, sang ten
times the words he spoke.

Jesse returned to town about noon. No twenty dollar
pieces jingled in his saddlebags; he had cached them in
a crack between boulders under two particularly thick
guayacan bushes. He carried only a few of the coins with
him, stashed in the fold of the bandolier he wore buckled
crosswise over his chest. The ammunition belt was made
from a strip of pliable pigskin eight inches wide, folded
to four inches, and stitched along the edge. Inside the fold
was room for coins inserted through a slit near the
buckle.

Jesse immediately sensed the absence of his fellow bandits. He found Chepita inside her house coddling a piece
of wood. The door was broken. She refused to speak to
him. He had to hunt up Tristan to learn the astounding
news of the gang riding upriver. He had no idea what it
all meant. Tristan couldn't grasp the complexities—or at
least he couldn't explain them and play his guitar at the

same time, and he wouldn't stop playing. But in the badlands, Jesse thought, he might figure a way to get Maximo apart from the others with his back turned and his hands far away from his pistols. He might have to ride hard to earn his other five hundred. He decided to invest in a new horse before following Maximo.

McCrary Livery kept the best *caballada* of horses in the territory. Jesse decided to purchase a fresh mount there.

Tristan's guitar could be heard inside the livery barn. To its music, Nelly was trying to teach Lawnce to waltz in the darkness when, through a crack between the double doors, the ranger's rolling eyes saw Jesse approaching with his riding gear over his shoulder. It was a relief to Lawnce, who knew how to dance the scalp dance and no other.

Jesse and the ranger haggled and horse-traded awhile, but the Mexican didn't offer much resistance to paying Lawnce's price for a mustang with good bottom.

"Where's Maximo and the boys off to?" Lawnce asked casually, fingering the coin Jesse had given him from the slot in his bandolier.

Jesse shrugged. *"Quién sabe?"*

Lawnce snorted and slid the coin with the clipped wing into his pocket.

By the time Jesse had ridden away on his new horse, Nelly had withdrawn to the tack room to scrawl a story of some kind, so Lawnce took his usual midday station on the porch of Las Quince Letras. She had taken over the tack room, and Lawnce had learned that she did not wish to be disturbed when she was in there. She was a forward woman, Nelly Blankenship.

Everything seemed unusually calm in Candelilla. No Doubletree gunmen were prowling around. No desperados had been seen since Maximo and his men rode out—except for Jesse and Tristan.

The springtime sun felt good on Lawnce's face, and the smell of agarita blossoms mixed with that of cooking frijoles in the desert air. The setting had almost put Lawnce to sleep when he saw Chepita walking deliberately toward him with a piece of wood under her arm.

"Don Lawnce," she said. "I need to speak with you privately." She looked over her shoulder at Tristan.

Lawnce pushed his sombrero back on his head and eyeballed the object Chepita carried. "Well, there's a cantina right here that ain't fancy, but it's handy," he suggested as he rose and gestured toward the swinging doors.

"The stable is better," she said, walking toward McCrary Livery.

Damned if all women weren't getting forward! When Lawnce followed her inside, she placed the wooden panel in his hands. He didn't know what to make of it at first. He turned it one way and then another, admiring the carved rose vines and blossoms around the edge. Then he recognized alphabetical characters. "What in blazes have you brung me here?" the ranger said as he tried to hand the plank back to Chepita.

"Read it," she suggested.

Lawnce squirmed for a second. "A little ol' widow woman told me once that readin' in this dim-lighted barn would make me blinder than a bat, so I give it up. You read it to me, *por favor*, if you don't mind."

Nelly heard the voices and peeked through a crack in the tack room door. She saw Chepita take the carving impatiently and read the brief message.

"August?" Lawnce asked.

"Yes. This letter was meant for me, but Maximo found it in the river. He has taken his men to find August and kill him. *Por favor*, Don Lawnce, try to save him. Try to save them both."

Lawnce admired Chepita for her lack of sniffling and other nonsense. "You sweet on that young feller?"

"I love him," she said.

"What about ol' Maximo?"

"You cannot understand, Don Lawnce, but I love them both. There is no time to explain now. Please, warn August. Tell him to run for his life. Tell him I will come to him when it is safe, and the truth will make everything plain. Can you save him?"

Lawnce took another look at the message August had carved in pine. "I reckon I can beat Maximo to him. But whether or not I can save his mangy pelt is up to hisself."

"Gracias. And tell him *se amo también."* She turned, cradling her piece of wood. "You must go quickly," she said before leaving.

"I reckon I better."

Nelly opened the tack room door to let Lawnce in. He pulled a plank from the floor to reveal his cache of weapons and ammunition wrapped in an old tarp. He took two boxes of cartridges and his Spencer rifle. Each cartridge box held ten metal tubes, and each tube held seven copper rim-fire cartridges. The tubes slid into a loading port at the butt of the rifle, which spring-fed seven rounds in a row to the breech. The two cartridge boxes would give him one hundred forty rounds to fool with. His cartridge belt was already filled with rounds for his old Remington pistol.

"I reckon you heard it all," Lawnce said.

"Yes. Where will you have to go?"

"Somewhere upstream."

"How long will you be?"

"Ain't no tellin'." He threw his saddlebags over his shoulder.

"A week? A month?"

"Is this here how it's fixed for fellers that keep a steady gal around? All these blasted questions?"

"It bothers you, doesn't it?"

"Like a stump-tail bull at fly time. But I reckon you're worth the trouble. You be here when I get back?"

"I've been here too long already."

"That your answer?"

"Well, what do you want me to say?"

"Say you'll be here when I get back."

"I can't promise you that, John. I need to get on with my travels."

Lawnce was loading his pockets with plugs of chewing tobacco. "Damn!" he said. "I don't have time for this."

Nelly put her arms around the ranger. "I can stay another week or two at the most," she said. "If you take longer, I'll leave word where you can find me. You'll not get rid of me so easily." She maneuvered her lips under his mustache.

"I better vamoose," Lawnce said.

Within a minute the cinch strap was tight around Little Satan's barrel, a cream-colored filly trailed from a lead rope, and Lawnce McCrary's back was turned to Candelilla.

Tristan watched the ranger's dust settle back to the Desert of Chihuahua. To others, it might never have risen, but Tristan could find each grain misplaced, and his eyes yearned to follow the trail. He stopped singing, gave his guitar to a Mexican urchin who would return it for him, and walked to the door of McCrary Livery. Nelly watched him, but he didn't seem to notice. The tracker squatted on his heels and memorized the prints Little Satan had left.

After several minutes he walked forward a few paces and squatted by the trail of the cream filly as though he would count the grains of sand in each of her hoofprints, and perhaps he did. By that time Nelly had returned to the tack room to work on her magazine story. Tristan was left alone to study.

A trail to Tristan was like a harlot to a drover, a key to a convict. He longed to forge a chain of hoofprint links. But Maximo had ordered him to wait a day and wait he would. He hunkered down in the street where the shadow of the livery eaves fell on the dirt. He slowly traced a line in the dust, with his finger, around the edge of the shadow's corner. When the shadow filled that same angle tomorrow, he would take up the chase.

But the thought of Lawnce's fresh sign lengthening as he waited made him too anxious to sit still. He had to find a trail to follow. It was a game to him. A game that had taken the place of passion, greed, and almost every other emotion common to ordinary men. And Tristan played the game when he wished, not only when Maximo ordered. He might follow a doe trail among goat tracks until he got close enough to hear the deer snort at him. He often fell away from the other riders at dusk so he could practice trailing them by moonlight.

The first prints Tristan saw as he searched the ground near the barn were Jesse's boot marks. He saw no harm in backtrailing them. He would see where Jesse had been instead of where Lawnce might go.

He went afoot to Chepita's adobe and found Jesse's tired old stud penned with some goats nearby. He backtracked the horse toward the river. He found where Jesse had ridden the horse down from a rocky bluff just out of town. He took his time spotting the places where a hoof had slipped grinding along the stone slope. Here was a broken needle on a cactus. Tristan wagered he could return to Chepita's house and find that needle lodged in the horse's right knee. Here was a rock that had been kicked from sunlight into shade. The darker surface that had been next to the earth was now turned up. Taking the stone in his hand, he felt its warmth compared to those that had been longer in the shadows.

Then the game presented Tristan with boot prints again. Jesse's horse had stood here and stamped several times to ward off flies. Jesse had dismounted and pointed his toes in every direction as if to look carefully around him. The boot prints led in and out of a shallow arroyo. Jesse must have used the arroyo as his private latrine, Tristan thought. To be sure, he followed the boot prints to the place where they doubled back at the bases of two guayacan bushes growing away from a pair of boulders. The tracker saw a dozen tiny guayacan leaves lying on the dust. Someone had dislodged them by reaching into the bushes, so he did the same.

There was a dark crack between the bases of the boulders, hidden by the guayacans. Tristan reached into it and found a *morral*. He shook it twice and heard the jingling of coins. He smiled, returned the sack to its hiding place, and continued to satisfy his passion for the trail.

26

When the livery barn's shadow filled Tristan's scratch mark from the day before, he picked up Lawnce's trail. By that time, the freshest prints were at Fort Quitman. Lawnce looked up the army captain the Mescaleros had seen riding his former gray gelding.

"Yes, I gave the boy a hat and a serape and ten dollars in trade for that gelding," the captain said. "As I recall, he was going up the trail with Mel Ferrar's herd to Granada, Colorado. Seemed like a fine boy. He's not in some kind of trouble is he?"

"Naw!" Lawnce blurted. "That boy is straight as catgut on a fiddle. I have a special message for him from his gal, that's all.

"Say, you reckon you can spare a little cold flour for an ol' Injun fighter?" Lawnce *had* fought Indians. Mostly when he was an Indian. But the captain, not being apprised of the details, provided him with some cold flour to make gruel out of. Bumming grub was a habit Lawnce had gotten good at while living among the Comanche.

"Thank you, Captain," he said. He was about to ride out of the fort when an afterthought struck him. "By the way, have you heard about a big feller name of Ryder with a fur pack and a buffalo gun?"

The captain shook his head.

Lawnce shrugged. "Well, thank you anyhow."

The Ferrar ranch was back toward Candelilla, so Lawnce rode his own backtrail to get there. On the way, he ran into Tristan, howdied, tipped his sombrero, and kept riding. He knew the tracker would hound him to hell and back, but he would have to worry about that later.

Tristan was surprised to see the ranger, but he smiled and returned the courtesies by touching a finger to the rim of his own sombrero. He continued to follow Lawnce's tracks to Fort Quitman and back, as if he had no idea the trail would double on itself.

At this pace, thought the simple-minded tracker, Maximo would have the stable boy long before the ranger would. Maximo's method of search made more sense to a vaquero used to following trails in the dirt. Maximo was riding along the west bank of the Rio Grande with half his troops while Jesse took the other bandits up the east bank. Maximo knew only that August was living somewhere along the river, maybe seven hundred miles upstream. He and his men would ask questions of all the Spanish-speaking races of people in the valley. They would find him if they had to ride clean to the headwaters and run every tributary.

To Tristan this made more sense than McCrary's odd method of riding back and forth between Candelilla and Fort Quitman. But he understood little about the kind of sign Don Lawnce was used to tracking.

"Why, yes, Lawnce," Ferrar said over a glass of brandy. "I remember the boy well. Wish I had a dozen like him. Damnedest buckaroo I ever saw. Oddball youngun, though. Spent all his time broodin'. Loved to go down and look at the *río*. He nighthawked for us all the way up to the Sangre de Cristo country; then he decided to ride on in to Santa Fe. I gave him good wages and a long-legged claybank mare he had his fancy on. That's the last I saw of him."

"Last you're likely to see of him unless I git to him before that ol' fox, Maximo." Lawnce repeated the questions about Thomas Payton Ryder, but Ferrar knew nothing of him. "Thank you for the beefsteak and brandy, Mel. I better cut for Santee Fee."

Lawnce had to avoid Maximo's men along the Rio Grande. He knew they would be combing the riverbanks anywhere August could have dropped the message in. He didn't cherish the thought of drinking brackish water all the way through the badlands, but the Pecos seemed the logical alternative route to Santa Fe. It was said that Pecos cowboys carried salt in their saddle pockets when they went abroad, to make the available water taste like the stuff they were used to drinking. Lawnce had sucked up plenty of it as an Indian and a little as a ranger. He figured he could stand it once more for August's sake. He would have to shake Tristan somewhere along the Pecos.

Tristan didn't know a league from a labor or a mile from a minute. He measured everything in tobacco. Along the Pecos he smoked more *cigarros* between Lawnce's camps and knew the ranger was making good use of his spurs. McCrary was living on hardtack, cold flour mash, and coffee. He was swapping horses, riding mostly on the cream filly. Little Satan's relentless lope on the legs he ran had put him a day and a half ahead of the tracker.

Tristan tried to match the pace on his mustang, following the plainly visible trail along the bends of the sluggish Pecos, but few animals other than pronghorns could run with Little Satan, especially when he had another mount to spell him. Tristan traded horses at a village near Fort Sumner and dogged the trail without sleep as he felt the distance between himself and McCrary lengthening. With a fresh horse, he was gaining again until he reached the territory south of Anton Chico. Then the trails of the two horses began to weave.

The cream filly was good for hard riding, mostly because Lawnce didn't like her much. She was young and strong, green-broke and showing signs of wanting to stay that way. She was ugly, too, with a nose almost too big to fit into a *morral*. But she could run. The Comanche in Lawnce knew how to make a horse run. Tristan found the filly's tracks where the ranger had sought the hardest ground, leaving scant traces. He had run among herds of cattle to obliterate his horses' marks on the land. Fake trails branched toward every nearby rancho and pueblo, but doubled back before calling at any.

The tracker burned hours of daylight untangling the maze of sign. It was still the filly doing the work when the trail led to a mile-wide circle shaped like a wagon wheel, etched by several rounds of riding. Spoke trails angled in and joined at a hub. Other trails led away from the circle, then doubled back in. Sometimes Little Satan's tracks ran with the filly's and sometimes he rested while she circled. When they ran together, the weight they carried changed. Lawnce was switching mounts on the run, confusing the tracker, riding bareback half the time like an Indian.

The wagon wheel had taken a day's riding to make but would require several days for Tristan to unravel, if he could unravel it at all. His eyes could follow the faintest sign, but his mind balked when trying to follow Lawnce's strategy. On the second day he struck a promising trail leading east, but the tracks of the two horses soon split. The weight they carried had switched so often that he didn't know anymore which one the ranger rode. It seemed for a long while that Lawnce had actually ridden them Roman style, with a foot on each mount, continually shifting his weight from one to the other.

Tristan chose to follow the cream filly when the trails split because Lawnce had been riding her more and allowing Little Satan to loaf. He found the filly abandoned, half dead, walking east for the Pecos. Lawnce was somewhere else on Little Satan now. The tracker turned back toward the wheel maze. He didn't feel bad about being tricked. It wasn't that he wanted to catch Lawnce or find August or please Maximo. The trail was the thing he lived for. He would follow it until the wind scattered it to nothing.

"Sorry, mister," said Lawnce's thirteenth Santa Fe trader, "doesn't ring a bell."

"He was straddlin' a claybank, sixteen hands."

"Seen lots of claybanks since last fall," the merchant said, anxious to get back to his customers.

"Toted a little hip iron about the size of a skeleton key. He was probably chawin' on a straw."

The storekeeper stopped suddenly and shuffled through his memories. "Well, yes. I recollect a kid with a pea shooter. I told him I wanted to buy it to shoot shoplifters with, but actually I needed it for a paperweight; it was windy that day, and the doors were open. Anyway, he wouldn't sell. It seems to me there was something else peculiar about him, too, but I don't remember."

"Well, what did he swap you out of? Where was he headin'?"

"He bought the usual traps—a blanket and a Dutch oven, I think. And a lever-action gun with lots of ammunition and . . . Now I remember what impressed me! Said he was ridin' up the river to hunt. I warned him about the damned Utes, but he didn't pay me no mind. He said Injuns didn't scare him none."

"That's the critter!" Lawnce said. "Boy's got a head hard as a pine knot."

The questions about Ryder proved fruitless.

"I sure am obliged," the ranger said. "Now, you reckon you can extend some credit to an officer of the law so I can stock up on some of them coffee beans?"

It amazed Lawnce the way the little Dutch oven tied to August's saddle skirts attracted attention. Pueblo Indians and Mexican farmers by the dozens had seen him riding upstream with it rattling and bouncing along behind him. The fact that he had had the foolhardy intention of hunting the mountains alone with a Ute war festering didn't make him any less memorable.

The scent of August Dannenberg smelled fresher all the time to the hounding ranger. But Maximo's men couldn't be far behind. Maybe a day or two. Lawnce knew he would need a lucky break to locate August soon, or his lead on Maximo wouldn't be enough to give the boy a respectable jump. He predicted it would probably take a day or two of talking to get the boy to stay low any longer, with his sweetheart waiting in Candelilla. Things were going to get close.

Lawnce's break came in Taos. And it was a double-barreled breakthrough in one clean shot. The boy with the pepperbox pistol had been to the pueblo to trade a day earlier in company with the strangest character in the southern Rockies—a big man dressed in fur who preached impromptu sermons on the street corners and challenged any man in Taos to name a word in the English or French languages he could not correctly spell and define—the Reverend Professor Thomas Payton Ryder.

The ranger's head swam in a maelstrom of accomplishment. There were dangerous days just ahead, but once he got through them, he could put August and Chepita together and make up for his neglect of the boy in the past. And when Nelly saw him lope back into Candelilla with the long-lost T. P. Ryder, he could send for the parson to get up a wedding!

"Ryder and a kid camped at the mouth of the gorge last evenin'," said a taciturn fur trapper just arrived in Taos.

"Movin' slow. Claybank packhorse. Probably find their next camp at the head of the canyon."

Lawnce figured he would see August and the reverend professor before another sun rose.

27

Flames from the Ryder and Dannenberg campfire shrank into embers at the head of the Rio Grande Gorge. Potatoes, fresh elk meat, and bacon were stewing in August's little Dutch oven. Bread dough, rolled on sticks, was baking over the coals. The coffee was about to boil, and black molasses lay hard by for sweets.

Ryder's favorite season had arrived, but it wasn't blooms or buds or melting snows that pleased him so much as it was the food. In the spring he had a few extras to eat that he regarded euphemistically as delicacies. He and August had traded some pelts and a carving or two to purchase the goods, and deposited the remaining money in Ryder's account at the adobe building that served as the Bank of Taos. No fortune of his occupied the vault, but his bank account was a treasured extension of civilization.

Ryder had just blessed the repast and was prepared to wade in to the best meal he would know for months when a voice called out from the moonless dark.

"Hallo, the camp!"

August cocked his head sideways at the salutation, as if he recognized the caller.

Ryder rolled his eyes and frowned. "These wretched frontier folk think it nothing to avail themselves of a host's generosity just as he breaks his bread," he said under his breath. "Fie on them! Oh, bother—call them hither." Ryder took a head start on the stew, eating it from a tin cup with a Mandan spoon made of buffalo horn.

"Light and hitch!" August shouted. He crowded three fingers around his pistol grip and squinted into the shadows to see who might appear. Before the flames of the rekindled campfire could cast a flickering beam on Lawnce McCrary's face, August recognized his outline. "Lawnce!" he said, suddenly on his feet.

"What's on the fire, kid?" Lawnce sniffed the smoke.

"What are you doin' here?"

"This must be the good Reverend Ryder I heard so much tell about in Taos. You caused some stir back there, Reverend."

Ryder bounded to his feet and bowed with utmost dignity before clamping his hand in the ranger's. "Yes, it is I, Reverend Professor Thomas Payton Ryder, descended of the Ryders from Concord, Massachusetts Bay, and the neighborhood of Durham, England, by way of—"

Lawnce held his palm toward Ryder and interrupted. "Don't get winded on my account. Where I come from a man's family tree ain't worth sawdust unless he can chop it up and heat a brandin' iron with it."

"Of course," Ryder apologized. "And you, sir, are certainly none other than the esteemed officer of justice so fondly and frequently spoken of by my protégé, Master Dannenberg."

Lawnce looked to August for a translation, but the reverend proceeded.

"I have neglected to question the lad concerning your distinct and singular appellation, my good man. But I would presume it a frontier derivation rendered from the tale of Camelot's round table—'Sir Lawncelot,' as it were."

Again the ranger smirked in August's direction.

"He wants to know what 'Lawnce' means," said the translator.

"Oh. It's short for 'lawnce-um.' On account of I stay off alone so much huntin' rustlers and good-for-nothin's. Lawnce-um John McCrary's my whole put-together handle, but folks just generally call me Lawnce."

"Then we are kindred souls, Sir Lawnce, for what I know of solitude would make Thoreau's chapter on that subject sound like the Mardi Gras of New Orleans by contrast."

Lawnce stepped back and pondered the phraseology for a second. "Wouldn't know about that," he finally said. "Never been to N'Orleans. Never even been to Rackinsack."

The reverend professor flipped through his mental dictionary, but found no reference for Rackinsack.

"Rackinsack means Arkansas," August explained. "Lawnce, what are you doin' here?"

"Them spuds in that stew?" Lawnce asked, pulling his mustache away from his choppers.

"Yes," Ryder said. "Please join us."

The host filled a tin cup with stew and dropped a browned lump of bread on top. Lawnce's hip pockets hit the dirt as he raked in the victuals with his butcher knife. For several minutes August and Ryder kept themselves busy serving coffee and refilling the stew cup.

"You must have been famished," Ryder said.

"Maybe I was and maybe I wasn't," Lawnce said, stirring molasses into his coffee with his knife blade. "Depends on what 'famished' means." Ryder's language reminded him of Nelly, but he was in no hurry to mention her just yet. Bad news first—Maximo. Then the good news.

"It means hungry," August said.

"Oh, that. Yessir. I don't grub too big on a scout. I generally just get up for breakfast, turn around for dinner, and go to sleep for supper."

Ryder chuckled and cataloged the quotation under Frontier Gastronomy in his cerebral encyclopedia.

"Lawnce, what are you doin' up here?" August repeated.

The ranger blew across his coffee cup and decided to spill the unpleasant truth. "I come to warn you."

"Warn me? Is the law after me on account of that shootin'?"

"I am the law, remember? It ain't me, it's Maximo that's after you."

The old ghost rose in August's conscience again. "Maximo's dead."

"Pshaw! It'd take more than a rat pistol to finish that ornery son of a she-badger. I seen him just a few days ago, all humped up and ready to let air into your vitals."

The picture of Maximo lying bloody and motionless in the street came to August as clear as his recent adventures in Taos. "Are you sure it was him?"

"Am I sure it was him? Hell, I'd know his shadow in Afriky. 'Course it was him. He's comin' gunnin' for you. Your sweetheart talked me into bustin' cinch straps and stirrup leathers to give you fair warnin'."

The old ghost flew and carried with it the guilt August had borne with every stride out of Candelilla. He dropped his plate, turned his palms to the sky, and howled louder than a full-voiced loafer wolf.

"What in thunder has locoed you?" barked the ranger. "Ain't you listenin'? I say, Maximo is ridin' up here to kill you!"

"Maximo scares me dead more than he does alive!" His hat had fallen off, and a lost light had found his eyes. "Chepita only made me promise to leave because she thought I'd killed him. But I didn't kill him. And now I guess she wants me instead of him. That's why she sent you after me. You hear, Professor? She'll have me after all. I'm goin' home!" Such a harangue took the wind out of a young man not accustomed to talking much.

"Hold on," Lawnce said as August caught his breath. "You couldn't get one mile back toward Texas. Maximo and his vaqueros will be here in two days—maybe tomorrow."

"He don't even know where I am," August said.

Lawnce began to holler. "You might just as well have drawed him a map the way you floated that carved letter of yours down the *río!* He knew the second he seen it he'd find you holed up in some arroyo along the riverbank."

August imagined his carving floating into Chepita's hands. He looked to Ryder and found the mountain preacher's face lighted up with almost as much surprise as his own.

"Emerson wrote of the value given to wood by carving, lad. What of greater value than love? 'All other pleasures are not worth its pains.'"

"That Emerson feller sounds familiar," Lawnce said. "Emerson who?"

"That's Mr. Emerson," August explained, "an old friend of Professor Ryder's. You wouldn't know him. So Chepita found it in the river, then?"

"Hell, no—pardon me, Reverend—that sorry outfit Maximo found it hisself. All carved up with flowers and fancy alphabets. How'd you learn to whittle thataway, kid?"

"The professor taught me."

Lawnce looked at Ryder. The man preached, spelled words, carved wood, trapped furs, and cooked a pretty fair supper. "By golly, Reverend. Ain't there nothin' you *can't* do?"

Ryder shrugged with modesty.

"Anyhow, August, the idea is for you to git out of the

country and then I'll go back to Texas and tell your sweetheart where to find you. You ought to cut for California or the Oregon territory. Roll your cotton mañana before Maximo catches you."

August shook his head. "It ain't gonna do no good to run now. If Maximo don't catch me here, he'll just get me somewhere else, just like a pack of dogs runs down a panther. I've got to finish it. I wish I had never started it, but now that it's started, I better finish this trouble or I'll be lookin' behind me the rest of my life. Besides, I aim to go see my girl. I'm goin' home."

Ryder remained silent across the fire, but when August looked, he saw the professor nodding.

"I fought Maximo once," August added. "I can do it again if that's what he wants."

"You fought him once when he was half liquored and worn out from me chasin' him all across Chihuahua for two days! Next time you ain't gonna be so lucky!"

"I'm done crawfishin'," August said. "I aim to go get my girl in Candelilla. Besides, maybe I can talk him down."

"Talk? Kid, you *no comprende*. He wants your scalp, not your advice. You shot him up and now you got his woman lovin' you. This ain't the same ol' Maximo. He's meaner than ever before. He struts around town like a Shanghai rooster, growlin' like a muzzle-loadin' bulldog. I tell you, kid, he's bad medicine from the forks of the crick. A rabid wolf. He's ringier than double-distilled chain lightnin'! Meaner than twenty-nine hornets fightin' over a dead grasshopper!"

"The gentleman doth protest too much methinks," said the professor, finally entering the debate. "Shakespeare," he added, turning to August.

"He ain't gonna shake nothin', Reverend. And *me* thinks it's none of your confounded concern, beggin' your pardon and all."

The harsh words didn't ruffle the reverend professor. "The lad must pursue his destiny in order to become resolved into the essence of things, Sir Lawnce."

The ranger twisted his left mustache branch and shifted his eyes toward August. "Kid, how come he don't talk United States like everybody else?"

"He's just sayin' how it's got to be," August replied. "I'm goin' downstream. I'm goin' home. I might get shot at, but that don't scare me none when I'm thinkin' of Chepita just sittin' down there waitin' for me. . . ."

No one spoke for a minute after August's voice trailed off. McCrary tossed his coffee grounds into the fire and massaged his eyebrows with his fingertips. "Well, then, the way I see it," he finally suggested, "we got three choices. We can ride down one bank of the Rio Grande and meet head on with Jesse Diaz and about half a dozen of the second-ugliest desperadoes on either side of the border. Or we can light a shuck down the other bank and butt heads with Maximo and the other half dozen of his vaqueros. Or we can just fort up right here and take our dose."

"I don't expect that of you," August said. "This ain't your fight, Lawnce."

"Well, damn my foolhardy nature and lack of common sense, but I ain't leavin' a rat-shootin' kid here alone to fight a army of cow rustlers with nothin' but a pepperbox and a man of the cloth armed with big words. We'll just have to fort up and hope for a blizzard."

"There is yet another alternative," Ryder said. "A third path wends its way where God pours the fluid of life through a great stone box."

The two Texans sat silent, trying to decipher the professor's riddle.

"My stars, Reverend, drink ain't gonna help none now."

"He's talking about the canyon," August said. "We could

float down between Maximo's boys, and they'd never even look for us down there!"

The professor nodded energetically.

"Ha!" Lawnce injected. "That boilin' mess of whirlpools would bust a log raft to stove kindlin'!"

Ryder was thinking of the elk carcass hanging above the reach of bears in a tall pine away from camp. August had dropped the bull at dusk. The hide had yet to be peeled completely from it. They had just skinned far enough up the hind quarters to get a fresh chunk of back strap. "A log raft, yes," Ryder suggested, "but not a bull boat."

"Bullshit!"

"A worthy vessel," the reverend insisted before Lawnce could apologize for his language, "like the coracle of the ancient Britons. I have seen tons of buffalo meat transported in bull boats by the village tribes of the Missouri River. The Indians construct the boats of bison skins, of course, but an elk hide would serve quite as well. We could build a sturdy bull boat in a half-day and have you off before another sun sets."

"You're a dreamer, Reverend. That canyon is six lariats deep. Once we get in there we'll be trapped like a couple of tumblebugs rollin' a dung ball down a buggy rut."

"Maybe . . ." August said, "maybe we could build the top of the boat like a brush arbor, make it look like a raft of driftwood. That way, even if Maximo's boys did spot us, they'd never know what they seen."

"Bravo, lad! A capital suggestion!"

Lawnce sensed a current of excitement passing between August and Ryder. He started calculating the odds of survival with their scheme. He wished he could convince August that running held the highest prospects for survival, but the boy had cultivated a mind of his own. Besides, the current was starting to pull him in, too.

Lawnce relished a thrill as much as any soul and wouldn't have the kid or the professor mistake him for owning a splinter of cowardice even to keep himself from drowning in a river of snowmelt. He had a great appreciation for resourcefulness, too, and so far a fancy-tongued Yankee preacher and a lovesick stripling had outthought him. And they were looking at him, waiting for him to agree to the plan.

He sighed. "We'll need us a paunch bucket to keep the water out of the boat."

"Paunch?" Ryder said.

"The elk stomach," August explained. "You can dry it and use it for a bucket."

"Excellent! I have known braves of the Kiowa nation to fashion canteens and pails of buffalo stomachs that would never spill a droplet! It would help keep the boat free of water within!"

"She'll float on a heavy dew!" Lawnce shouted as the current of excitement sucked him under. Just then, Little Satan snorted at the claybank mare, and the ranger was struck with an unthinkable notion: if he rode the rapids downriver, his horse would have to stay with T. P. Ryder. "Just one problem," he said, looking at August. "What about Little Satan?"

"Satan!" Ryder blurted. "Think not of Satan! Trust in God, man! 'Though you shall pass through the valley of the shadow of death, you shall fear no evil: for the Lord shall be with thee."

"With the what?"

August broke in. "He's talkin' about his horse, Professor. Little Satan." He pointed toward the two shining eyeballs that were the only indication of the black mustang's presence behind the claybank mare.

"Satan! What a name for a horse!" the professor said, wide-eyed.

"Now, Reverend, don't let Little Satan's name rile you. He's a angel of mercy if ever there was one. I gave him that handle when I caught him off the Bolsón de Mapimí, all swole up with pride and swearin' he'd never be broke. Me and that horse went at it hook and tong for days at a whack. But Little Satan, he finally took religion, and when that roll is called in horse heaven, Saint Pete better let him in, because if he don't, Little Satan will just bust down the pearly gates!"

The reverend professor still regarded the mustang suspiciously.

"The problem is," Lawnce said, "we've got to have mounts when the river spits our carcass out under the canyon."

"I shall purchase your horses from you," Ryder suggested. "You may withdraw any amount from my bank in Taos and acquire good horses there for your journey."

"Says he'll buy 'em," August interpreted.

"I know what 'purchase' means, kid! But Little Satan ain't for sale."

"Then I shall keep him until you return." He glanced once more at the fiery eyeballs in the dark. "I shan't mount him, mind you, but I shall care for him as if he were my own."

August remained silent. He couldn't advise Lawnce in matters involving beloved horseflesh.

Lawnce quietly studied the glow of the embers for a moment. "He's partial to molasses," he finally said without raising his eyes, "but don't spoil him on it."

Reverend Ryder clapped his big paws together and rubbed them vigorously as if trying to warm them. "Then we have our solution! You see, lad, things refuse to be mismanaged long—*Res nolant diu male administrari.* That's Latin, you know."

The ranger felt a little riled at the insensitivity the professor showed when he was about to lose his horse. "You don't say! Well, listen to this here: 'Manuel, gettee your *como-se-llama acá and trabajo pronto!*' That there's cow pen Mexican."

"Then you are a linguist, Sir Lawnce."

"The name's McCrary, I told you. Them Linquists is cabbage eaters. No offense, August."

"Do you know any French?" Ryder asked before August could comment.

"Whores and frog eaters are the only ones I ever knew."

"I am referring to the language, sir. Perhaps you *speak* French. Or Greek."

"Never learned me no Creek, but I can talk a pretty fair Comanch'. And I can parley with any tribe that knows the sign talk." The ranger poked himself in the chest with his right thumb, gestured outward from his heart, tapped the backs of his left fingers, then his right, and motioned as if pulling something from his mouth. "I know sign talk," he had said with his hands.

To indicate where he had learned the signs, Lawnce rubbed the back of his left hand twice then gave the forward serpentine motion with his right index finger. The two signs together meant snake Indian, or Comanche.

"Aha!" Ryder blurted, shaking his finger at the stars. "Then we have a means of communication at last, for I learned the hand symbols from the Sioux!" And as he spoke, he returned Lawnce's exact gesticulations, except to replace the snake sign with that of a knife raking across his throat, meaning cutthroats, or Sioux.

August rose, grinning at the lucky turn of events. He got some of the tin cups together to scrub them out with sand, along with his Dutch oven. He also threw a couple more chunks of wood on the coals.

"Now, then," Ryder said, signing with his hands as he

spoke, "the lad claims you carry a tome of provincial statutes in your saddlebag."

With Ryder's hands adding to his spoken words,
Lawnce understood the reference perfectly and signed
the affirmative with his index finger.

"Might I be allowed to read a few pages, then? My eyes
have yearned to embrace the printed word for many long
months."

"Why, hell, yes, Reverend. Kid, fetch the Revised Statutes out of my saddle pockets. . . . Well, never mind;
you're busy. I'll get 'em myself."

As Lawnce brought the law book, Ryder excitedly
searched the pockets of his cloak for his spectacles. The
search proved fruitless. "Sir Lawnce, I can't seem to find
my spectacles. Please read it to me until they present
themselves."

Lawnce shuffled and stalled for time. "I'd just as soon
not, Reverend."

"It will only take a moment. Please, read a few lines for
me." Ryder was going through the truck in his medicine
bundle.

"August, read for the reverend, will you?" Lawnce held
the law book toward August.

"I got bacon grease and dirt up to my elbows." August
stopped scrubbing his cast-iron pot and looked across the
smoldering firewood at Lawnce. "Why don't you read it?"

"The fire's gone too dark. I can't see the letters."

August blew into the coals and caused flames to leap
onto the fresh firewood as if he had turned up the wick
in a lantern. "How's that?"

"I still can't read it."

Ryder had found his glasses and hooked them around
his ears.

"Why can't you read it?" August asked.

Lawnce ignored the question. He finally handed the book to the professor.

"Never mind, lad. I have my spectacles now." Ryder pretended to bury his nose in deep study.

"Wait a minute, Professor. I want to know why Lawnce wouldn't read for you." August stopped scrubbing the pot.

An uncomfortable silence fell across the camp as the ranger settled onto the dirt. Lying disagreed with him. "Hell, I guess you might as well know it, kid, seein' as how me and you'll probably get drowned like a couple of millin' cow-brutes by tomorrow anyhow: I can't read. Never learned how. I just carry that book to make everything look legal."

The young Texan glared into Lawnce's eyes. "But I've seen you write."

"You seen me scribble my name, more than likely. The only letters I ever learned how to make are the ones that spell John McCrary, and I don't know one of them from the other. I learned how to draw 'em out on paper like a cayuse learns to scratch for grass in the snow."

"You sayin' you don't know nothin' about the laws of Texas?"

Lawnce drew himself up as if insulted. "I don't know the letters of the law, but I know the spirit of it. The letters are in that book, and I don't know how to get 'em out. But the spirit is inside a man's heart. I can grabble on to that."

So Ryder would understand, Lawnce told the same story with his fingers in the sign language the Comanche had taught him—August could almost have done without the spoken words, the way his hands formed the meaning. The explanation satisfied him completely.

Ryder decided to defend the illiterate ranger with a quotation. " 'He who has mastered any law in his private thoughts, is master to that extent of all men whose language he speaks.' Emerson."

"There goes Mr. Emerson again!" Lawnce said.

Ryder continued undaunted, gesturing with one hand to the sky and clutching the other to his breast, not in the sign language, but in the mode of a bad actor. " 'Two things fill the mind with ever-increasing wonder and awe . . . the starry heavens above me and the moral law within me.' Immanuel Kant."

"Can't what?" Lawnce asked.

Ryder explained his quotation to Lawnce with the hand signs and cleared up the matter of Kant's name.

"Your friends have got the damnedest handles," Lawnce said. "But I heard about that feller Emerson before. A friend of yours told me."

The reflections of campfire light danced on the lenses of Ryder's glasses, but his eyebrows perked up inquisitively behind the glare. "Who?"

"Miss Penelope Blankenship."

Ryder's mouth dropped open and created a dark hole in his beard. He removed his spectacles and regarded Lawnce's winks, nods, and grins until he accepted the truth. His line of vision slowly angled toward the stars, and a deep sigh filled his lungs. Remembered images flashed across the dark screen of his night sky.

Suddenly he shook his head as if stung by a hornet and spoke in a nervous rush: "Where is she?"

"She came around Candelilla askin' for me to help find you. I told her I'd oblige her, but I never knew it would come this easy!"

"She knows my location?"

"No, sir, not just yet. But I reckon she'll know soon as me and August get to Candelilla. And, hell, come to think of it, you might just as well come along with us, if you don't mind fightin' Mexicans on the way down!" Lawnce thought he might burst with goodwill.

The Revised Statutes of Texas dropped onto the sand

as Ryder bolted upward. "You must not tell her! Do you hear?" He put his hands on his fur cap and paced in a tight circle as if bewildered.

Lawnce stared up from the ground like a camp dog puzzled by a new scent.

"Professor," August said, "what is it?"

"What? What? My God, think of it, lad. Think of my mutilated body! No civilized woman could bear to look upon me without disgust! To think that Penelope should see me like this—I *cannot* think it!"

"You're not the only man with scars, Professor." August opened the front of his shirt to remind Ryder of his arrow wound.

Lawnce whistled and got on his legs. "What stuck you, kid?"

August ignored him. "Scars don't mean nothin'. Your old friends especially won't let it bother 'em."

"That's right, Reverend," Ryder said, poking at the welt of August's scar. "We got us a gotch-eyed rancher down our way that don't even wear a patch, and nobody funs him." He pulled up his shirttail. "And I've got me a dandy here that Miss Nelly seemed right fond of."

Ryder wheeled, wearing the expression of a madman, and yanked the fur away from his head. "Do your scars bare your skeletons? Do they remain inflamed and festering? Do they ooze with puss and lie open before God every time you tip your bloody hats?" He stood trembling among his own echoes as he glared at the two Texans. "You must never tell another soul of my whereabouts. Promise me!"

No one answered.

"Lad! I must have your word!"

August nodded sadly and reluctantly. His loyalty was with Ryder. He didn't even know a Miss Blankenship.

"Sir Lawnce! Your word as a gentleman!"

"Hold on, now, Reverend. Think of Miss Nelly."

"My Lord, man, don't you see that I *am* thinking of her?"

Lawnce refused to answer.

"If you tell her, she shall never find me. I swear it! I shall vanish in the wilderness! Don't you understand?"

Lawnce looked again at the terrible wound on Ryder's head. He did understand. It was an ugly and bizarre sight in the leaping light of the campfire. He felt a sudden rush of pity so strong that it overwhelmed his own longing to please Nelly. He kicked at a rock and spit into the fire. "Aw, hell. I reckon a man's got a right to stay lost if he wants."

Ryder still looked worried and ashamed. He put the fur cap back on his head. "Your solemn vow, as a gentleman. I must have it."

Lawnce made his trigger finger point out from under his chin and thrust it forward. The sign meant "straight tongue." It was more promise than he could have spoken.

Ryder sank to the stone he had been sitting on. He picked up the book of Texas laws and straightened the pages. He felt so craven he couldn't speak. His eyes turned to Lawnce and, in the language of the hands, said his heart lay on the ground.

August turned quietly away to rinse the sand from his dishes. When he returned, his mentors were still conversing silently, Ryder with the book of laws in his lap.

August looked carefully at Lawnce McCrary. Stripped of his literacy, he was no longer nine feet tall and bullet-proof, but Lawnce hadn't shrunk so much as August had grown. He still loved the man for the things he did have.

They provided quite a contrast—McCrary at home with the seat of his pants in the dirt and Ryder perched piously on a rock, inhibited by his finer sensibilities. Neither man could be all things. No man could. August remembered a fragment from one of Ryder's afternoon lectures. He had mounted his cabin porch as if it were the Concord Lyceum, with the sculpted busts of Emerson and Hawthorne under his arms to illustrate a point.

"Emerson and Hawthorne loved each other as brothers," the professor had said. "Hawthorne read Emerson's essays with ardor, yet never loved his conversation. Emerson thrilled to hear Hawthorne expound, but could not bear to read his novels."

Emersons nor Hawthorne could be all things.

August rested against his saddle and marveled for a long time at the way his camp mates gestured at each other silently. They burst into laughter over some unspoken joke—the professor bellowing and the ranger wheezing.

But then he trained his hopeful eyes on the stars and conjured images of matters downstream. He chose the brightest star at the zenith of the night's dark dome and knew—somehow he just knew—that Chepita's gaze struck the same twinkle of light in space.

28

Plans fell together in the stillness before dawn. Lawnce arranged firewood on top of last night's embers, fanned them with his battered straw sombrero, and had a flame within a minute. August cooked the eats while Ryder explained the process involved in the construction of the bull boat. By the time breakfast was finished, each man knew his responsibilities for the morning.

Professor Ryder would cut stout willow boughs and build the frame of the bull boat. August and Lawnce would skin the elk. Then, while August prepared the hide, Lawnce would strip and split sinews from the elk carcass and twist them together to make a cord for holding the boat frame together.

"I'd just as soon we kept it among ourselfs that Lawnce McCrary ever done squaw's work," the ranger insisted.

With their chores divvied up, the three lingered near the campfire. Dawn came in crisp along the upper Rio Grande.

"At what hour do you estimate your hide and sinew to be prepared?" Ryder asked.

Lawnce bent his fingers into the sun sign and held it directly overhead.

"Come, then, let's along."

Ryder wielded the ax with devastating results. Willow chips flew in clouds until thirteen branches, two inches in diameter and ten feet in length, lay parallel on the ground. He peeled the bark from four of the willow poles and laid the bark strips in an orderly pile.

After lashing two poles end to end with the strips of bark, Ryder bent the far ends around to make a loop. He made sure its diameter exceeded his height by the breadth of his hand, the way the Mandan squaws had taught him. With a rock, he drove four pine stakes into a sandy spot along the river to hold the hoop in shape above the ground at knee level. The hoop fit just around the outside of the stakes.

The diameter of a second hoop came to Ryder's forehead. He put it on the ground inside the four stakes. It fit there perfectly, the stakes serving to hold both hoops to circular form.

Four more pliable willow poles became ribs, running parallel, east to west. The boat builder spaced them across the smaller, lower hoop and lashed them there. Then he bent the ends up and lashed them to the outside of the larger, upper loop. By the same process, five more poles became north-to-south ribs. Where the perpendicular ribs crossed, he lashed them together with more bark. He cut the ends of the ribs off an inch above the upper hoop, except for four ends. These four long uprights were unusual in bull boat construction; Ryder made the modification to support the canopy of brush that would shield the boat's passengers from view.

The sun had just cleared the east canyon rim when Ryder started dragging light brush and driftwood for the canopy into a pile. He used his ax to cut two straight pine poles August and Lawnce would use to keep the boat away from boulders.

Little Satan lunged against his picket rope when August dragged the fresh elk hide down to the river. Lawnce was still stripping sinew from the elk carcass and twisting strips of it into a strong cord.

August paused long enough to judge the spindly boat skeleton that had come together by Ryder's handiwork. It lacked the lines of any seaworthy vessel he had ever seen or heard of. "Are you sure that thing is safe, Professor?"

"Not even by the grace of the Holy Bible, lad. Safety smacks of Eden where neither Eve nor Adam could bear it long enough to let an apple rot. Mortality is fraught with absolute peril for every man of us every moment of each and every passing day, and well it is! Of fear comes courage. Suffer my earthly existence to run rampant with sheer jeopardy! Safety shall be my heavenly reward!"

As he spoke, Ryder wielded one of the pine poles like Moses with his staff. The discourse made August want to fling himself headlong into the river, boat or no.

The professor told August to cut the legs and neck off of the hide. They cut the five pieces into thongs one finger wide by making a spiraling incision around the outside of each until the entire piece became a long strip of rawhide.

With the rawhide thongs prepared, there was nothing more to do until Lawnce arrived with the sinews. Ryder had *The Revised Statutes* out on loan and decided to spend a few minutes perusing the laws of Texas.

August sat against a boulder sculpted by aeons of floodwaters and looked at the professor. Ryder sensed a stare and glanced over the lenses of his spectacles. He raised his hand and shook it laterally from the wrist three times as if waving.

August had picked up enough sign language overnight to recognize the question sign. In Ryder's present context it meant something like "Why are you staring, lad?" On the end of Lawnce's arm the same sign would have meant "What are you gawkin' at, kid?"

August grinned and shrugged. "I didn't want to interrupt your readin'. I guess I was wantin' to thank you for saving me from the Utes and takin' care of me and all. Probably won't get another chance to tell you."

A warm glow crept out of Ryder's beard and covered his face. He grasped his fur cap with his thumbs and index fingers and lifted it up and down a few times to pump some fresh air across his mutilated scalp.

" 'Tis I who am left in your debt, lad. What good is a teacher without students? And never has fate blessed a mentor with a pupil more willing to learn. Another winter in solitude would have finished me with more certainty than a Ute arrow flung with surest aim."

Ryder's shoulders shook the way they did when he didn't want to laugh quite out loud. "And now that I have Sir Lawnce's satanical little mustang in my possession, I know I shall be receiving visitors in days to come.

"It saddens me to see you go, lad. But I know you are like the poet."

"How's that?" August asked.

Ryder turned his head at the angle he used when quoting a source. " 'A farmer, a hunter, a soldier, a reporter, even a philosopher may be daunted; but nothing can deter a poet, for he is actuated by pure love.' "

"Thoreau?"

"Ah, you have developed a keen ear for prose," Ryder said.

"Reverend, we got us enough string to bend half the bows in the Injun Nation!" Lawnce came trotting down the canyon slope with his twisted cord of split sinews.

"Excellent!" Ryder gestured with his right hand, moving it palm down, away from his chest, as if brushing the dust off a tabletop. He put the law book aside and emptied the contents of his medicine bundle onto a flat rock so he could get at the things he needed. He used a buffalo-bone awl to make several small punctures around the bullet hole in the elk hide. Then he used Lawnce's twisted sinew to stitch the hole closed. A little tallow mixed with ashes made a suitable caulk. Meanwhile, August and Ryder used the rest of the sinew to reinforce the strips of bark holding the bull boat frame together.

"Now," Ryder said, "we shall put the skin on the skeleton to produce the body of our river beast. The passengers must provide her with heart and wisdom."

August dragged the hide out of the shade, placed it hair side up on the sand, then set the willow frame on top of it.

"This river beast of yours is gonna be vicey versey and wrong side out," Lawnce declared. "She's gonna have her hair on the inside."

Ryder lifted one edge of the hide to the end of one of the ribs where it jutted an inch above the rim of the frame. He made a hole in the edge of the hide with his knife and simply stuck the end of the rib through the hole. Then he moved around to the opposite side of the boat frame to repeat the operation. The Texans helped him pull the hide tight underneath the boat frame before he punched the hole and hooked the hide over the opposite rib. In this manner they stretched the hide all around the outside of the vessel.

All three men used their knives to trim the edge of the hide an inch or two above the rim of the frame. Ryder punched holes at intervals around the edge. They used the thongs made from the legs and neck of the elk hide to run through the holes and around the willow hoop, lacing the skin to the frame. The green elk skin and rawhide strips would draw tighter as they dried, making the bull boat extremely sound.

" 'Tis pleasant, is it not, to work here to the rush of the river?"

"I like the noise of runnin' water," Lawnce agreed.

"Never heard enough of them wet noises in that country I come from. I like to hear a coyote yowlin' just after sunup. Means rain. And I like it when the rain splatters on a slicker of a hot afternoon. But the wettest noise I ever heard was the sound of one of them stoppers pullin' out of a bottle of kill-devil."

Ryder chuckled. "Worthy strains, all. For my part, I fancy the prattle of students in the university's chambers and the bite of a steel chisel against marble."

August's favorite sounds went unspoken, but the ranger and the reverend knew Chepita's voice would be whispering to him about now.

With the hide stitched fast around the gunwales of the bull boat, the builders prepared to add the bower suggested by August the night before. To the willow members left protruding upright, they lashed a quantity of light brush and driftwood with rawhide thongs. It made a sort of roof over the boat which, from the canyon rim hundreds of feet above, would look like a raft of debris floating down the river. The passengers could look out from under the canopy of brush on all sides. A V-shaped opening on one side allowed for looking out over the top.

The sun had already sunk behind the west canyon rim by the time the bull boat was finished. It looked like a large leather tub with a brush arbor on top. Ryder stood back and admired his handiwork with obvious pride. The green skin had dried some and tightened snugly around the frame, like a piece of wet leather stretched across a saddle tree. August and Lawnce regarded it more cautiously. They decided to pull it to the river's edge to see how it would float.

"I christen thee *Argo*." Ryder sank down on one knee and whispered a prayer for the cumbersome vessel before he and his partners gave it a shove into the river. It floated high and tilted precariously at the end of a rawhide tether, but Ryder said the passengers and cargo would give it ballast.

"What was that you called her?" Lawnce asked.

"Ar-go," Ryder repeated, and he gave the hand symbols for "great," "boat" and "long time ago."

Lawnce nodded.

"I say, do you men fancy a riddle?" the professor said, suddenly thinking of a good one.

"What's that? A puzzler?" Lawnce said, reading Ryder's hands. "I'm partial to 'em. Let's try it."

Ryder recited: "'its shrouds enwrap no lifeless brows; its tacks no timbers burrow; its only tiller never plows; it plows yet leaves no furrow.'"

"Now, hold on, Reverend! Give it to me in the sign talk!"

"It must be a sailing boat!" August said.

"Precisely!"

"Damn it, kid! You give me no chance at it!" Lawnce glared at August, but then turned to Ryder with a grin. "That was right cleversome, Reverend, but see if you can figure this one out: She never stops runnin'; she lays in her bed; she's got her a mouth, but it's far from her head; don't cross her, don't damn hèr; she'll never be dead. Who you reckon she is, Reverend?"

Ryder placed his hand on his chin whiskers and pretended to ponder the riddle. Several times he started to speak, then shook his head. Finally he snapped his fingers and solved the puzzle.

"The answer, I presume, is 'the river.'"

"How did you figure it out, Professor?" August could barely contain his amusement.

"Simple, actually, lad. I know Sir Lawnce would never swear in the presence of clergy, so when he said 'dam her,' I knew he meant the river, not a member of the fairer sex."

"Like hell," Lawnce said, truly disgusted. "You heard it before."

Ryder mounted the claybank mare bareback as August and Lawnce arranged their gear in the bull boat. His burly body looked odd on a horse. He said he would ride to a high spot on the canyon rim where he could see several miles to the south. If he spotted Maximo or his men on either side of the canyon, he would flag the Texans with a blanket. Then they would begin their river journey.

29

When the blanket on the bluff waved, sooner than anyone had expected, Lawnce rose as calmly as if a clock had chimed cocktail hour. He pulled the bull boat to the shore so August could climb in under the camouflage of limbs and brush. August was tying the cargo of saddles and tack to the willow branches inside the boat when Ryder trotted down on the claybank mare.

"We have time to say our farewells. Your bandit friends on the east bank are huddled about a fire brewing coffee as we speak. I have seen no movement on the west canyon rim." He punctuated his speech with Indian hand symbols for Lawnce's benefit, making his fingers wiggle upward like flames to denote the campfire.

Reaching into his fur cloak, he pulled a slab of wood from under his belt and handed it to the ranger. "My check, Sir Lawnce, redeemable for the cost of two horses. I am sure you shall find it all in order."

Lawnce tossed a saddle blanket to August then accepted the carved bank draft. A grin lifted his mustache and crow's-feet creased the corners of his eyes. While standing guard on the ridge, Ryder had carved a rebus that even an illiterate ranger could decipher.

A perfect architectural representation of the adobe Bank of Taos building appeared in the upper left-hand corner. Beside Lawnce McCrary's name on the whittled check there was an encircled star wearing a mustache like the one on his face. Two carved ponies represented the amount owed. They were fine horses, one rearing, one kicking its hooves.

"I'll be derned!" Lawnce said. "Looks like your ol' pard Mr. Emerson knew his stuff when he wrote about the value a piece of wood gets when you whittle on it. This piece has took on the value of two horses!"

Ryder clamped a hand over his mouth to keep his laughter from bouncing off the canyon walls.

"Reverend, you're a learned man. Maybe you can tell me why everybody can't write readin' thataway. Any fool that ain't blind can cipher this."

"Yes, but the alphabet is much simpler. In a pictograph the reader must know a symbol for every word extant—thousands upon thousands of symbols. Even the Indian sign language requires the memorization of several hundred symbols, as you well know. But with the alphabet, the reader must only learn twenty-six symbols. Only twenty-six. That is why learning to read the English language is far simpler than learning to speak it."

A light went on in Lawnce's eyes as if he had seen a map of the Great Mystery painted on a thirteen-skin tepee. "Maybe I can learn it, then," he said. "After all, I ain't never had no tussle with *talkin'* the lingo."

"When you return to fetch your little devil of a mustang, I shall teach you one letter a day, and in twenty-six days you shall read quite as well as you speak," Ryder said, confident of the veracity in his statement.

"I'll wager I *can* learn it! There's just one thing on this check I can't figure, though. What's this meanin' at the bottom? Looks like a Injun lodge with a feller straddlin' it like he was ridin' a horse."

"Let me see," August said. He caught the carving as Lawnce tossed it into the boat. "Don't you get it, Lawnce? It's a man ridin' a tepee. He's a tepee rider. It's the professor's signature—T. P. Ryder!"

"Hell, I knew that, kid," the ranger said, winking at the reverend, "I just didn't want to spoil it for you." He pitched his ten-pound Spencer rifle to August and handed *The Revised Statutes* to Ryder. "You took care of this knot-head," he said, jutting his thumb at August. "I reckon I can trust you to look after my horse and my law book."

Ryder stepped to the bank to shake hands with the two Texans as Lawnce climbed into the boat. His eyes looked a little misty. "It shall be done, Sir Lawnce."

"Cut the hobbles loose, Reverend. We're fixin' to saddle-bust the wild Rio Grande! Me and August has rid bull moose on the prod, gut-shot panthers and long bolts of hot lightnin'. But we ain't never drawed a cinch strap on a ripsnortin' fence-lifter before, and we can't wait to fork her ribs."

The mountain man loosed the rawhide lines and shoved the bull boat toward the channel. As an after-thought, he picked up August's Dutch oven and hurled it toward the boat. August caught it before it splashed into the cold waters. "Take your cooking vessel. You'll likely need it to bail."

Lawnce turned to August. "Hay?" he asked.

"Water," said August, making bailing motions with the pot.

Lawnce nodded. *"Hasta luego, amigo,"* he said, taking up his pole.

"Godspeed, lads." As his friends drifted away, Ryder made a few final gestures taught to him by the Northern Plains tribes.

"What did he say?" August asked as he waved his last to the last of the Renaissance men.

Lawnce didn't know the precise words to translate what Ryder's hands had said, but he caught the gist. "Says he's talkin' big medicine for the Great Spirit to make a sunrise in your heart."

*   *   *

Shadows began to scale the east wall of the canyon. Fully loaded, the *Argo* settled deeper in the water, as Ryder had predicted. The two passengers manned poles six feet in length to keep the hide boat away from rocks. She floated easily down the channel, spinning slowly like a bubble.

The curved, hairy bottom inside the spineless craft made slick boots slide like the hooves of a steer trying to climb a mud bank. The boatmen had to hang their armpits over the gunwales or wedge their knees between their saddles and the bent willow boughs when they used their poles against the river rocks.

Less than a mile downstream of their launch site, the ranger tugged on August's sleeve and motioned for him to squat in the bottom of the bull boat. He had spotted a lone horseman on the east bluff. He recognized the horse as the one he had sold to Jesse Diaz several days earlier. If Jesse had the east bank, Maximo would be riding the west side of the canyon. Jesse's men had finished their coffee, and he was scouting the rim before riding northward.

Through the gaps in the driftwood canopy, the boatmen could catch glimpses of the bandit. He dismounted with a rifle and peered downward for a while. Lawnce moved his hand toward his Spencer when he saw Jesse shoulder his rifle. But Maximo had ordered no unnecessary shooting that might forewarn the stable boy, so the rifleman on the bluff decided not to take any practice shots at driftwood rafts.

Lawnce thought Jesse looked sort of sheepish, even from a distance. Indeed, Jesse had serious worries—more serious than finding a lost stable boy. Gainey had given him half the money for the murder of Maximo, and the desperado was nowhere near half dead yet. Jesse had been riding across the river from Maximo for hundreds of miles, unable to kill him if he had been able to find the nerve. He had started having nightmares about Maximo and El Ojo joining forces to kill him. In his dreams, Maximo would beat him with a poker as Gainey roasted him head-down over a slow fire.

Lawnce and August remained motionless in the shadows until they rounded a bend in the canyon, away from Jesse's line of sight. The last they saw of him, he was mounted and moving north.

Lawnce worried some about the Mexicans cutting Ryder's trail. But that was Ryder's problem to deal with, and worrying about it wouldn't help. Ryder knew a lot of things. Maybe he knew how to avoid Mexicans.

The bull boat had drifted beyond the bend in the channel and into a collection of boulders near the bottom of the west bluff of the canyon. The current carried it against a rocky point at the waterline before August could fend it off with his pine pole. The elk hide bulged inward and the seams around the gunwale creaked, but all held fast.

"Don't fret, kid. Buffalo hides will turn arrows and even bullets when the Comanch' makes shields out of 'em. This here elk skin looks just as thick as a pelt off of any ol' woolly bull. Them rocks won't likely poke through."

"I'm not worried about the hide. But what about that cord we used to tie the frame up with? Don't look all that strong to me."

"Now, that ain't so. Injuns use them sinews to string up their bows and you couldn't bust one if you shot a million arrows off it. And them bows is made out of that springy ol' bodark wood. In fact, that's why they call 'em *bows*, 'cause they're made out of *bow*-dark."

August knew Lawnce had that backwards, but he didn't think it fitting to correct him.

The line of sunlight climbed higher with the bull boat's

progress. The river proved tame for several miles. August had no trouble keeping the *Argo* in midstream and even began to enjoy the trip. The scenery changed around every bend. The perpendicular canyon walls met the river itself in some places, so that a man on the bluff, hundreds of feet above, could have flicked a stone over the edge into the middle of the current. At other turns, ribbons of sandy beach flanked the stream. Above them, old rock slides sloped up the escarpments.

A few ancient ponderosa pines towered from the river's flanks here and there. They had sprouted and grown large between years of high water. Now they could bear several fathoms of ripping snowmelt without losing their toe-holds among the canyon rocks. One had fallen, though, and with the leverage of its lofty trunk had prized a root-tangled boulder from the earth and lifted its tonnage as high as a man on horseback. August amused himself by imagining the moment when the roots would drop the rock.

Lawnce kept his eyes trained on the west rim. He expected Maximo to appear several miles downstream of the east-rim riders because he would be searching more carefully than Jesse. At first sign of the Mexicans, August would have to draw in his pole and let the *Argo* chart her own course down the Rio Grande. The ranger did not intend to get himself or his boat shot full of holes.

"Lawnce, you better duck under and look at this," August warned.

The ranger pulled his head under the canopy and let his gaze follow August's finger downriver. His eyes widened as he spotted froth in a narrow chasm ahead.

"You might want to grab a pole," August suggested.

Lawnce gave a last glance toward the canyon rim before settling in for the rush. A pair of huge monoliths forced the river into a rapid flume a mere quarter-mile downstream. Rooster tails of spume squirted between them. The boatmen could not clearly see what lay beyond the gateway to the rapids. There was no way to stop.

"Just try to hit the hole!" Lawnce shouted over the roar that now filled the canyon. The pine poles clacked against boulders under the surface and guided the bull boat into the vortex at the pit of the gorge.

The smooth pace of the current above the rapids had given no warning of the speed within them. Both men lost their balance when the boat lurched forward into the narrows. They scrambled up again as jets of white water gushed in. The poles couldn't keep the bull boat off the rocks, but they absorbed some of the impact. One submerged boulder caught the bottom of the boat and tipped it precariously forward. August leapt to the high side to keep the boat from capsizing. It wheeled around the boulder and dipped one lip under a few inches of foam, but the gunwales lifted before the river could swamp her.

The current spit the hide boat into calmer straights as the two boatmen looked back at the chute they had run. Water was knee deep in the lowest part of the boat, but she still rode plenty high in the current. August jerked the knot out of a rawhide strap holding his Dutch oven to the frame and began bailing. Lawnce glanced toward the west rim again.

"Looks clear," he said. He had one arm crooked around a willow beam that held the brush canopy above them.

August stopped bailing long enough to look up at him. They both started to chuckle at the look on the other's face. But as soon as Lawnce worked up a grin, a new bend in the river wiped it away. The deep rumble of white water again filled the canyon.

"Looks like shallow riffles," Lawnce said. "Shouldn't be as mean as that last stretch, but she'll catch a few rocks against her hide. Let's dish out a little water and pole her into that fast stretch of blue water." He took his elk-paunch bucket and helped August bail, then grabbed his pine pole.

The *Argo* found the deepest channel and stayed between most of the boulders, with aid from the polers, but a kink in the current brought her hard against a rocky point. Both men heard the crack of the willow frame. The boat pitched and wheeled like a gun-shy mustang and then shot forward about as fast as a lope on a long-legged horse. Lawnce started having such a good time that he risked a half-yell he knew the river's roar would never let out of the canyon. An eddy below the riffles gave August a chance to check the cracked frame.

"It ain't too bad," he said. "I think it will hold together. I bet we've been through the worst part of it, anyway."

"That's plum optimistical, August, but if just sayin' it would make it so, I'd have me a jail in Candelilla." And I'd have me a yellow-haired wife, he thought, but he didn't say it out loud.

A lazy mile in the Rio Grande Gorge seemed to support August's prediction. Then, nearing a bend, he started to feel a rumble so low and strong that it threatened to shake the very walls of the canyon down.

"I hope that's a buffalo stampede," Lawnce said.

As they made the turn, the river's thunder drowned out all sounds of the creaking rawhide boat and shook the atmosphere. Ahead, the river branched into twenty channels that twisted down among fallen pieces of canyon wall like the scaly bodies in a rattlesnake den. Lawnce saw mist rising so high that it reached shafts of sunlight way up near the canyon rim. A deceptive rainbow invited them to cruise under its arch.

"Look, Lawnce! There's a little sand beach. We can pole over there and scout the best channel." August had to shout above the rumble to make himself heard.

Lawnce clamped his fist around August's elbow and pulled him down. "'Fraid not. We got company." He poked his thumb upward toward the west rim. "She's gonna have to hunt her own trail."

Even if there had been another sombrero like the one August saw at the canyon rim, no one could have worn it the way Maximo de Guerra did. No other man could imitate his stance—shoulders pinched back and palms forever level with pistol grips. August and Lawnce retreated into the shadows of the canopy and chose to take their chances with the river's rapids instead of Maximo's guns.

The desperado moved in and out of the mist like an apparition. He had the luck of a charmed catamount to show up on guard at the wickedest stretch of rapids in the gorge, just when his enemies needed to make use of their pine poles.

When the mist blotted out the desperado's outline, the two boatmen risked a peek over the elk hide just in time to see the *Argo* slam against the first in a gauntlet of colossal stepping stones. Then commenced the wildest careening and jolting any cowboy ever survived. For comfort, August latched on to his slick old saddle horn, the handle that had gotten him through many a lesser ride.

The air became white even inside the boat, and the pounding of river on rock came from everywhere. August could feel Lawnce ricocheting around; then he lost him altogether in the chaos. Something hit him sharply in the chin. He bit his tongue, tasted blood. He tried to spit, but the river rushed into his mouth, up his nose. He took a breath, inhaled only water.

The hide boat lurched and wheeled like a thing with life, a beast shaking the devil from its back. Down in the bowels of the beast, August clung to his saddle horn and gasped for air. The rocks battered him around inside like the clapper of a ringing bell.

Half the brush arbor came down, and August began to have grave fears of being trapped in a sinking hide boat with the brush squashed down on him like a lid. Water sprayed everywhere and was already pooling up deep in the bowl of the boat.

He felt as if a colt had kicked him in the back when he flew across the craft, but from the cracking sound of wood barely audible over the din of white water, he knew the willow frame had caved in against a rock. He lost his grip on the pommel, came up choking.

There was Lawnce, thank God, a boot in his stomach. But then, gone again!

Roiling water lacked only a foot or so to fill up the entire boat. Through the rocking and dizziness, August could see that a whole quarter of the boat frame was pushed inward, though the hide was still sound. He braced his shoulder against the good side of the boat and gradually forced the frame back to form with his feet. He had to put his head under to reach across, but he came up for a gulp of misty air every time he thought his lungs would rip. There was a strange sort of peacefulness when he went under. The crash of the current sounded a mile away.

The rapids seemed endless. August thought he would wash up at Candelilla, judging by the number of times he had to come up for air. He lost count. Holding his breath underwater was making him dizzy and confused. A strange recollection came to him. He remembered the summer when he was six years old. Lawnce had made him learn to swim, ordering him to dog-paddle back and forth across the Rio Grande at Candelilla. He got to where he could cross it fifty times without stopping. It had seemed a useless exercise because he could have walked

across the shallow river even at that age. Now he was glad
Lawnce had made him do it. He thought he would surely
have to swim out of the gorge when the bull boat finally
caved in or sank.

August came up for air one last time, and the relative
quietude he had known underwater lingered. He knew
the rapids were behind him, but the bull boat was almost
sunk. The gunwale that was aimed downstream drew
only an inch or two out of the water. To the rear, where
the bower had collapsed, the rim of the boat was actually
level with the river's surface, and water kept trickling in.
In another few seconds, he would have to swim for his
life. He could find no sign of Lawnce McCrary.

Just before August prepared to escape under the open
half of the canopy, a fist splashed through the water between the collapsed brush roof and the sinking rear of
the boat. The fist brought the butt end of Lawnce Mc-
Crary's butcher knife with it. August watched the point
of the knife find the rawhide thongs that held the driftwood canopy to the boat. The blade began sawing blindly
at the thongs. Lawnce was trying to lighten the boat by
discarding the brush top.

August was still holding the frame of the bull boat out
with his feet. Only his nose and eyeballs remained above
water. He took the knife handle in his own hand.
Lawnce's fist released the hilt and slipped back into the
river. August made a few strategic slashes and was soon
able to push the driftwood and brush of the broken canopy away from the *Argo*. Water ceased to stream in.

It seemed like a whole Indian moon passed before the
ranger surfaced in front of the boat. He clung to the gunwale from the outside and, reaching in, began splashing
out water with his cupped hand. Lawnce wheezed the
way a steer coughed until he caught his breath. The boat

was floating a couple of fingers higher and August started feeling around with one foot for his Dutch oven.

A horse tail of a mustache drooped over the leading edge of the bull boat. "That was a right smartish stretch of ripples," gasped Lawnce as August struggled to dump a bucketful of water overboard with one hand. "You see how it done me? It warshed me out of the boat, then blame if it didn't warsh me right back in! Well, I reckon it liked me better on the outside, 'cause then it warshed me plumb out again. It turned me a wildcat underneath the water and damn near pancaked me between the reverend's boat and a hard spot on one of them rocks back yonder. Scattered my wits like they were partridges."

"It worked, though," August said. "I saw Maximo turn back from the ridge at the last minute. He had no idea it was us in this thing. If we can just crawl out of this canyon, I think we can make it back home."

The bailing continued until Lawnce could crawl into the boat and ride. In less than an hour, the *Argo* reached the mouth of the canyon where it met the Taos Trail. The shivering boatmen laughed at nothing in particular when they put their feet on solid ground and began to unload their drenched cargo.

It was dusk when a bull train came groaning down the trail to meet the river on its way south. The wagon master had once been rescued from Comanches by Texas Rangers near Fort Griffin. He helped load the sopping tack without questions when he saw the circled star on Lawnce's shirt. Taos was just a jaunt down the road; Candelilla, a week away.

30

A second after the *Argo* vanished around the bend, Ryder began thinking of his own escape. He knew this fellow Maximo would, in time, figure out that August had slipped by, but he wanted to give the lad as much time as possible.

And there was another consideration. Maximo was from Candelilla. From what August had said of that town, the professor had inferred that it consisted of no more than a few mud huts. Having lived in the village of Concord, in tiny African camps, and aboard even smaller clipper ships, Ryder knew how hard it was for people crowded together to keep their noses out of each other's business.

He knew Penelope was in Candelilla. By now everyone there would know her purpose—to search for him. He remembered her thoroughgoing nature. She would have described him in detail to everyone. Maximo and his men wouldn't have much trouble recognizing a large, bearded man in fur who carried a medicine bundle. And carved. Something had to be done about the wood carvings at the cabin. The prospect of one of Maximo's men returning to Candelilla with news of his whereabouts made the reverend professor shudder.

He could not stand to think of a woman looking at him in his mangled condition. He couldn't even stand to look at himself. He had glanced into a mirror only once since being scalped. The mirror was in the back of an ox cart in a little adobe neighborhood on the north side of Taos.

A year after being scalped, he had gone there on his first annual spring supply run. There were other household effects in the cart with the mirror. Someone was moving into a new house—perhaps newlyweds with the bride's dowry in the cart.

It was siesta hour and no one was stirring in the neighborhood except Thomas Payton Ryder. He was walking, contemplating the ground just in front of him. He walked right up to the cart before seeing himself in the mirror. On impulse, he lifted his hat to check his wound. The memory of the sight gripped him in mental anguish for days as he hiked back to his cabin under Ute Peak.

Since that day, the professor had avoided reflections. There were times, however, when he removed his cap and bent to drink at a still pool of springwater, that he caught sight of the bare skull where his auburn hair had once grown. The permanence of that wound had made him a recluse. No civilized woman—especially one as familiar to him as Penelope Blankenship—would ever see the grisly sight if he could prevent it.

His plan, then, was to lead Maximo astray as long as possible without letting the desperado or his men catch more than a glimpse of his fur coattails. It wouldn't be easy.

Ryder had spent half of the previous night asking Lawnce about the bandits until he knew every one of them by name. Their individual traits were committed to his memory. Maximo, first, of course, with the silver-studded sombrero and the arrogance of royalty. Then Jesse, with the pigskin bandolier, riding a McCrary horse with the Lonesome J brand, if he hadn't ridden it into the ground already. Fermin was young and couldn't stop moving and wore giant rowels for spurs. Cheto had half an ear missing. Abundio carried a machete under his belt like a sword. The others had their identifying characteristics, too. But Tristan was most notable—a half-wit master sign reader.

Ryder had known expert trackers before, among African tribesmen, Sioux Indians, and buffalo hunters. But a half-wit! There could be no better tracker. A man whose mind could grasp only one thing had to hold on to it with every energy. True, Tristan could play the guitar as well as he tracked, but the songs he played were the same every time. Each trail was a new thing.

The first order was to fool the tracker. Tristan would recognize Little Satan's hoofprints, but that could work in the professor's favor. He had estimated Lawnce's weight at about one hundred seventy-five pounds. The packsaddle that the claybank had been carrying was loaded with supplies approximately equal to that weight. While waiting for the professor to wave the blanket on the ridge, August and Lawnce had saddled Little Satan with the pack to make his tracks look as if the ranger had been sitting in the saddle when they were made. Little Satan didn't like wearing the deadweight, but August had snubbed him to a piñon tree, blindfolded him, and gotten the packsaddle situated so that its weight would rest about where Lawnce's did when mounted.

The professor threw scraps of rawhide, pine stakes, and pieces of willow into the river, along with anything else that might give away the building of the bull boat. With his boots, he obliterated the tracks August had made around the camp, especially the ones near the river where the Texans had stepped into the *Argo*. Then he struggled onto the patient claybank mare and rode all around the campsite to further confuse the tracker. Finally, he took Little Satan's lead rope and rode for Ute Peak.

The tangle of tracks south of Anton Chico had long since disappointed Tristan. After he had ridden the giant wheel of sign for two days, a wind came along to ruin it. He then rode for the Rio Grande and caught up with Jesse Diaz and the men who were riding the east side of the river.

North of Taos Tristan picked up Little Satan's tracks again and told Jesse about them. Jesse ordered his boys to gouge their mounts in hope of overtaking Lawnce and maybe the stable boy. He hoped to win Maximo's trust. That might make killing him easier somehow.

Now Tristan followed Little Satan's trail to the campsite above the gorge and got down to read the story written by hooves and boots. Jesse had his men dismount to let their horses blow and drink at the river while Tristan played his game. All the mounts were gaunt from hard riding. There were only two spare horses among the six riders. They were all ready for the chance to sit on something besides leather, except for Fermin who always seemed irritated when idle.

Little Satan's tracks showed where he had been tied up beside a shod horse. Tristan had noticed the same horseshoe prints leading north from Taos, along with two sets of prints left by men on foot—one big man and one of average size. But here the shod horse and the ranger's mustang were standing together for the first time, the tracks of one as fresh as those of the other. The horses had also left together, not long ago, after the mustang had been tied to a piñon tree, which he had mangled badly by pulling on it.

The footprints of the big man had trampled everywhere, making the sign hard to read. It was a poor attempt to hide something, Tristan sensed. It appeared to him that Don Lawnce was still riding Little Satan north, which seemed natural. The shod horse was carrying a heavy load. Tristan decided the big man had mounted the shod horse and departed with Lawnce. That left the third man unaccounted for. Either he was riding double with one of the others or he had fallen into the river and drowned. It didn't bother Tristan that he couldn't figure exactly where the third man had gone. It just made the game more interesting.

There were other amusing things about that camp. Something strange had happened there. There was an elk carcass on the slope above, stripped of its hide but barely butchered. Tracks led from there to the river, and chips of wood lay thick around a willow that had been divested of several branches. He spent two hours trying to wrench secrets from the marked ground. When the tracker had learned all he could, he led Jesse to the elk carcass and the dismembered willow. Jesse shrugged. He was not in a mood to solve mysteries.

"Which way did they ride?" he asked. Tristan pointed. "How many?" Tristan paused and held up two fingers. "Horses?" asked Jesse. Tristan nodded, still showing two fingers. "And two riders, also?" Tristan hesitated, checked the ground once more, and then shrugged. He hadn't decided if the third man had ridden away double or fallen into the river.

Jesse gave the order to make camp. He ordered Fermin to butcher the elk carcass. He had decided to rest until Maximo could arrive, cross the river, and hear the news that the tracks of Don Lawnce had been spotted again, now riding north with company.

"I shall probably suffer riding sores," Ryder muttered to Little Satan as he trotted northward on the claybank. He owned no saddle and was not accustomed to straddling a horse. He drove the mustang in front of him at times so the tracks would not show either horse trailing continuously, as a packhorse would. He reached his cabin before dark and slid gratefully down from the mare. The sweat lather had penetrated his britches and was making him miserable. He felt like soaking in the hot spring, but there was no time.

He took the carvings from his cabin porch and made a pile of them. He looked over each one fondly as he added it to the pile. "Forgive me, gentlemen," he said to a gathering of busts, "but you must be made to suffer for the failings of Thomas Payton Ryder." He stuffed some kindling under the windward side of the pile and set the whole thing ablaze.

Maximo saw the smoke from Jesse's campfire just before dusk. He rode to the head of the gorge where the river valley flattened out a little and saw Jesse waving for him to cross. He went upstream so the current would carry him to Jesse's camp and not beyond. Soaked by the cold river, Maximo stood by the fire while he heard what Tristan had found in the tracks. The desperado ordered food and rest for a few hours. He didn't want to rest but knew his horses needed it. Fermin brought elk steaks down from the slope and started them broiling over the coals.

When he dried out, Maximo made a torch and had Tristan show him where the elk had been skinned and the willow tree dismembered. "What does it mean?" he asked the tracker. Tristan didn't answer. Maximo felt rather ridiculous asking questions of an idiot.

But when they returned to the campfire, Tristan lunged for something on the ground. Something he had overlooked before. He showed it to Maximo, smiling. It was a piece of straw. The stalk had been flattened on one end—almost pulverized. It had been chewed on. August Dannenberg had been at this camp. He had to be riding double on the shod horse that had walked north with Little Satan. And Lawnce was with him, for Lawnce surely would not part with his mustang. Maximo slapped Tristan on the back and rolled a *cigarro* for him.

The horses searched for grass while the men ate elk meat and longed for tortillas and peppers. Some of them slept. The moon, waning a few days from full, rose over the Sangre de Cristos. When it reached the top of its arch, Maximo put Tristan's nose to the trail and pushed his tired men and horses northward behind the tracker.

Ryder had tended the fire by night, turning the carvings to make sure each of them had burned completely to ash. He had unloaded Little Satan's pack and put the goods away in his cabin. Reluctantly he mounted, already stiff from his earlier ride, and led Little Satan up the flanks of Ute Peak to a place where he could look down on his cabin. He expected to see Tristan soon.

At dawn he saw a column of riders winding up the river valley. The first rider leaned from his saddle, with his eyes on the ground. Behind him, Ryder could make out the sliver-studded sombrero, the shoulder-slung bandolier, and the characteristics of each of the other riders. When they saw the cabin with the mound of smoldering ashes in front of it, they loped forward and surrounded the place. Ryder chuckled at them from his vantage. So far, he had predicted their actions perfectly.

Maximo opened the cabin door when no one answered his shouts. He spent a few seconds inside, then told his men to search the surrounding area. He raked through the ashes with a stick in an attempt to see what had burned.

Ryder was pleased to see that, while most of the bandits blundered around, Tristan was still intense for the trail. He followed the path of Little Satan and the shod claybank up the mountain slopes, exactly as Ryder had planned. The only resident of Candelilla he cared to meet was Tristan. An imbecile would never give him away to Penelope.

Tristan followed the fresh trail among the ponderosas, up toward the ridge where Ryder watched. Near the ridge, the ground became rocky and he dismounted to look at the sign more carefully. As he led his horse over the ridge, he saw Ryder standing there with the black mustang and the claybank mare.

They stared at each other for a long time, and Ryder tried to look as pleasant as possible; he didn't want to scare the tracker off just yet. Tristan finally looked back at the ground and, as if to be certain, followed the prints left by Little Satan to the mustang's very heels. Then he put his hand on the horse, patted him, and pointed to the Lonesome J brand on his left shoulder, a question in his eyes.

"Don Lawnce?" asked Ryder.

Tristan nodded.

Ryder pointed southward. "Downstream," he said.

He had given the Texans almost a full day's lead on Maximo. That was more than he had been asked to do for them. He would have done more if Penelope Blankenship hadn't been snooping around Candelilla, but since she had, there was no more he could do to help August and Lawnce.

Tristan looked to the south and smiled. He had been fooled. Little Satan had been mounted with a packsaddle, and Lawnce and August had both fallen into the river, he thought. He wondered why. Then he thought that maybe they hadn't fallen. Maybe they had jumped. Or maybe the big man had pushed them in so he could have the black mustang. He stared at Ryder again, looking at his odd fur cap. He pointed at it. Ryder removed the cap.

Tristan stared blankly for a moment, then grunted and staggered backwards, his eyes growing wider as he reached for his reins. He began to moan as he jumped astride his horse. The big man was a ghost. An evil spirit who drowned men for their horses! He spurred his mount downhill.

That was how Penelope Blankenship would have reacted, Ryder told himself. As soon as Tristan ran his horse down the slope, Ryder checked the loads in his rifle and watched the action around his cabin.

The tracker galloped to the cabin door and called for Maximo. He pointed downriver. "Don Lawnce," he said.

"What are you talking about?" Maximo asked.

Tristan only pointed again.

"How do you know this?"

Tristan pointed to the ridge where he had met Ryder.

"What is up there?" Maximo asked, getting irritated.

"El espectro!"

"What are you talking about, you fool?" Maximo kept Tristan around because of his trailing ability, but the lack of sense the tracker showed often angered him beyond the limit of his short patience. He sometimes thought that a good hound dog would follow a trail just as well and probably tell him more. He leapt into his saddle and rode toward the ridge where Tristan had pointed. He wanted to see the ghost for himself.

When Maximo jumped into the saddle, Ryder climbed astride the mare and rode down a draw for the next ridge. He stopped when he got there, looked around, and saw Maximo just topping the ridge where he had met Tristan. They were several hundred yards apart, but Maximo could see Little Satan and a large man holding a rifle and mounted on a claybank. They looked across the draw at each other for a minute. Ryder was ready to ride clear into the Canadian River valley or trade gunshots to keep from meeting Maximo face-to-face.

The desperado studied the situation. There was

Lawnce's horse and a claybank, but neither Lawnce nor the stable boy was anywhere to be found. He had been tricked. Lawnce had sold his horse to a mountain man. That much was clear. How much the mountain man knew was debatable, but it was obvious he didn't want to be questioned. He didn't fear the mountain man's rifle any more than he feared his own. He could have ridden after him, but the claybank and the black mustang were fresher than his horses, and August Dannenberg was getting farther away by the moment. There was only one place August could be going now.

At last Maximo waved one hand arrogantly and turned back toward the cabin. He whistled as he approached and ordered the men to mount their already exhausted horses and ride south. Tristan led the way.

Ryder stayed on his ridge until he was satisfied that the Mexicans were really leaving. He watched them as long as he could see them. It was a relief to be rid of them. But what lay in store for him gave him no pleasure.

He thought back on the winter he had spent with August and the day with Lawnce McCrary. The memories made him smile. But now the loneliness would start again. He would have to return to his secluded cabin without even the faces of Thoreau and Emerson and the others there to greet him. He had the horse and the law book that ensured Lawnce would return. But when?

Loneliness to a man like Ryder was an immense void in time and space that would kill him if he dwelt on it too much. There was only one way for him to relieve it: start carving. He knew of a seasoned trunk he could carve into a likeness of August Dannenberg, and another for a bust of Lawnce McCrary.

31

It was Friday, and Chepita would not eat meat on Friday. She usually ate armadillo instead. The armadillo had meat under its shell, to be certain. But, through a twist of reasoning, it was considered a substitute for fish in the Desert of Chihuahua.

The early Spanish priests who came to the New World learned that fish for days of abstinence were hard to obtain in some regions. Turtles, because they lived at least part of their lives among the fishes, were declared appropriate enough fare where fish were unavailable. From there, it took only a slight breach of logic to arrive at the conclusion that the armadillo had a shell like the turtle and therefore was fishy enough to satisfy the Friday rule. This interpretation was especially popular in South America, and the priest at Presidio had come to Texas from a mission there.

Fish could be caught at times in the Rio Grande, but hardly enough of them to feed even the devout portion of the valley's Catholic population one night out of seven. Armadillos seemed more plentiful than fish and were easier to catch. Candelilla stood along the western extremity of the nine-banded armadillo's natural range. This little relative of the South American anteater did not see well, nor was it gifted with a keen sense of hearing or smell. The armadillo's protection was the hard skin that had given it its name—"the armored one." The animal's shell and its burrowing trait protected it from most predators.

Its worst enemy in the border country was a Mexican with a grubbing hoe.

Chepita borrowed a grubbing hoe from a field laborer and, propping the heavy digging tool against her shoulder, marched back toward the river after her laundry chores were done. Every evening that week she had seen an armadillo in the prickly pear flats, raking grass together to line its burrow.

When Chepita saw the mail hack approaching on the Presidio road, she fixed her eyes on the ground so she wouldn't have to look at the driver when he made the lascivious suggestions he was bound to make to any known border whore. When the hack came nearer, however, she could see Doña Lope sitting beside the driver. When the paths of the armadillo hunter and the mail hack came together, Nelly ordered the driver to stop.

"Señorita Ybarra," she said, "has there been any news from Maximo or Don Lawnce?"

Chepita shook her head and felt like apologizing. She knew Nelly had a stake almost as big as hers in whatever was happening up the river.

"Where are you going with that immense tool?" Nelly asked.

"To kill an armadillo for my Friday meal," she answered. By tradition of the frontier, she was then obligated to invite Doña Lope to dinner. "If you wish, you may join me in eating it."

The invitation was a courtesy she did not think Nelly would accept. Chepita had no female friends—no friends at all, really. No one but August Dannenberg had ever tried to cultivate an acquaintance with her, and he only in his awkward and bashful way. Given her reputation, Chepita didn't think that Doña Lope would care to dine with her.

"I wouldn't think of it," Nelly said, "unless you allow

me to kill the beast with you. I insist on doing my fair share."

Chepita had never seen a white woman chase an armadillo. There might be some fun in it, she thought, so she nodded and curtsied as gracefully as she could with a grubbing hoe on her shoulder.

"Mr. Sawyer, kindly leave my bag in the livery barn," Nelly said in a commanding tone. "Thank you."

The driver rolled his eyes and spit between his mules as Nelly jumped down from the hack. He didn't like men bossing him, much less women.

Nelly and Chepita talked about armadillo hunting as they walked briskly toward the cactus flats where Chepita expected to find her Friday dinner. The hunt was a rather simple matter, she explained. You simply approached the armadillo slowly, preferably from downwind, and broke its skull with the hoe. If you missed, or just wounded the armored mammal, you could try to catch it by the tail before it dived into one of its burrows.

The hunters found the armadillo by the side of a goat trail that led through the cactus flats. Chepita stalked to within twenty paces and then looked around quickly for a burrow. She found its entrance under a rock that slanted out of the ground.

"Doña Lope," she whispered, "you stand in front of that hole and if the armadillo runs there, do not let it in. Grab it by the tail."

Nelly looked nervously at the armored beast and saw that it apparently didn't have a mouth big enough to bite with. It had claws, though, and was using them to excavate for bugs or worms or something at a terrifying rate through the rocky soil. Nelly almost flagged, but gathered her resolve and nodded.

Quietly the hunter crept toward the snuffling beast as it rooted in the dirt like a pig. When she got close enough, she raised the grubbing hoe above her head to strike. The motion must have alerted the armadillo. It jumped about a foot straight up, and the hoe merely brushed its nose on the downstroke. Grumbling as it ran, the animal made straight for Nelly's ankles.

She screamed as it charged, but valiantly held her post. The armadillo rammed into her shins, bounced back, and then prepared for another assault.

"The tail!" shouted Chepita.

Nelly latched on to the armored tail when the armadillo made its second lunge, but when she lifted the animal it squirmed so violently that it slipped from her grasp and landed on its head with a grunt. The armadillo then decided to try another burrow.

"Catch it again!" yelled Chepita. She spotted the second burrow and ran to cut the armadillo off.

Nelly ran as fast as she could bent over and grabbing for the armor-encrusted tail as she dodged cactus lobes covered with needles.

Chepita beat the armadillo to the reserve burrow entrance, but couldn't chance a swing of her weapon with Nelly so close to the prey, so she sent it rolling with her foot. Recoiling from Chepita's kick, the crazed beast jumped about halfway up Nelly's skirt and struck out across the desert for another burrow somewhere. Nelly followed a few paces, then dived headlong for the tail. Grabbing it, she managed to hang on as Chepita ran around in front of the armadillo with the hoe. The digging blade caught the animal right behind the head, and a definite crunch—like that of a tortoise shell under a wagon wheel—let Nelly know her Friday meal had been bagged.

Nelly's cinnamon hair stood in snarls like the limbs of an ocotillo plant. She struggled to her feet and began dusting herself off as she watched the dying quivers of the smitten beast. She suddenly became aware that Chepita had been laughing at her for some time. In fact, she was laughing so hard she couldn't hold her hoe up and was leaning on it instead.

"Perdóneme, Doña Lope," Chepita said. "You are a good armadillo hunter, but it is a lucky thing you are not a Catholic. You do not have enough dresses in your little suitcase to go hunting every Friday."

Nelly looked at the mess she had made of her clothing. The cactus needles had caused several rips, and a fabric-covered button was missing from one of her cuffs. "I have gone fishing with other Catholics and prefer it," Nelly said, maintaining her dignity. "But one does what one must for her religion."

Chepita picked up the armadillo by the tail and handed the hoe to Nelly to carry. "Come. After we eat this animal, I will mend those tears for you."

Chepita basted the armadillo meat and put it over some coals in the corner fireplace of her adobe. The machete-harvested hearts of two sotol plants had been roasting there under the coals for hours. Nelly had gone to Las Quince Letras to fetch a cup of ground coffee beans to go with the Friday meal. When she returned, Chepita was just finishing her prayers. Nelly had never known a con-cubine to carry a rosary or recite Hail Marys or hunt ar-madillos to eat on days of abstinence. It seemed odd to her that such a girl had come to Candelilla to live with a desperado.

The reporter tried hard to enjoy her meal of armadillo meat, gnawing it from the bones as she would a roasted chicken, but she didn't eat very much of it. It had a rich, gamy taste that must have resulted from the beast's own diet of too many ants. She found the roasted sotol heart more palatable. The coffee, however, was by far the best part of the meal, with a little brown sugar and goat milk mixed in with it.

To Chepita it was a unique occurrence to have a female guest in her little house. Maximo was not much for small talk, and she enjoyed making conversation with Nelly. She found a patch of material inside the hem of Nelly's dress that was big enough to make into a button. She clipped it out and used it to cover a circular piece of gourd the same size as the other buttons on Nelly's cuff.

As she sewed the button on at Nelly's wrist, the guest all but forgot Chepita's reputation. She seemed too young and beautiful and too exceedingly angelic to be a whore. "You will make a good wife for some lucky man one day," she said before she realized what she was saying.

Chepita looked suddenly at her with an expression of bewilderment, then put her concentration back into the mending job to stave off embarrassment. No one in Candelilla had ever spoken to her as if she had any prospect of a family life. *"Gracias,"* she said.

"Have you thought about becoming a wife?" the reporter prodded.

"Yes."

"Maximo's wife?"

"Oh, no."

"August Dannenberg's?"

"Yes, I have thought of it."

Nelly sat silent as long as she could. "Forgive me if I intrude, Chepita, and tell me if it's none of my business. But I overheard when you spoke to Don Lawnce several days ago, when you told him you loved both men. I have loved, or thought I loved, more than one man, but never two at the same time, equally. How can that be?"

"Equally, yes. But for different reasons. I can say no more."

"But you want to marry Mr. Dannenberg?"

Chepita paused to think. She had never heard August referred to as Mister, or even as Señor. "Yes," she answered.

"Then what about Maximo? Won't he fight to keep you? Might there be a killing?"

"God willing, it can be prevented."

Nelly sipped her coffee. "It must be exciting to have men fighting for you."

Chepita pulled the last stitch into Nelly's new button, sighed, and became sullen. "It is not me they fight for. They fight for their ridiculous pride."

"Perhaps. But there isn't much left to a man when you take away the pride." She now regretted forcing the issue, ruining her hostess's evening. "I haven't met Mr. Dannenberg," she said, hoping to improve Chepita's mood. "Tell me about him."

Chepita was putting her needle and thread away in a battered cabinet which, other than her table, was her home's only piece of furniture. It served to divide the dining half of her adobe from the sleeping half. Because it stood between the two areas, it held her clothes as well as her cooking vessels and utensils, a few containers of medicinal herbs, a washbasin, some colorful feathers she had collected from her flying friends, a comb, and her other meager possessions—including the carved plank found in the river.

She smiled when the memory of August on his bareback mule came to her. "He is very shy," she said. "But he is tall and strong. He works very hard." She became somewhat irritated that she could not say more about him. But after thinking for a second or two, she remembered his other qualities.

"He is not fearless like Maximo and Don Lawnce, but he risked his life for me. I was a fool to make him think it was necessary. He would have died for me. He thought Maximo would hurt me."

"Others think the same," Nelly said. "In fact, it is common knowledge that Maximo is a rough man."

"He is gentle with me. He only pretends to be rough."

That didn't make sense to Nelly. Why would a man pretend to be a woman-beater? What reputation could be less respectable? "Why would he pretend?"

Chepita looked suddenly flustered. She had said too much. "I cannot explain." To change the subject, she quickly picked up the carved letter and gave it to Nelly. "August carved this for me and sent it floating down the river."

"My, this is quite a nice bit of sculpture. These rose vines are classic in design. And this lettering. It is very similar to Latin uncial. Who taught him to carve this way?"

Chepita shrugged. *"Quién sabe?"*

Someone had, Nelly thought. Frontier stable boys weren't born with a knowledge of such things. Someone schooled in art history had shown him how to carve those characters. Who could it have been? She didn't think there were many educated men in the West, but there must have been a few. August's handiwork proved it.

"It looks as if he loves you very much indeed. But how will he feel when you tell him you love Maximo as much as you love him?"

"He will understand. And Maximo, too, will understand. I can say no more."

"You know Maximo much better than I, Chepita. But he does not impress me as one capable of a great deal of understanding."

"I can say no more," Chepita repeated.

Nelly's instinct for investigation made her want to press the issue further. But she had an instinct for friendship as well. After sitting quietly for a moment, she thought to examine the button Chepita had sewn onto her sleeve. "Which one is it?" she asked. "They all look perfectly identical."

32

Nelly Blankenship's duty to *Fulton's* magazine prevented any protracted stay at Candelilla. As roving reporter she felt bound to travel. While she quartered at McCrary Livery, she accomplished several jaunts in search of stories.

She rode to Chihuahua with copper freighters into Mexico's anarchy, then back through Presidio and up to Fort Stockton. She took the stage westward to El Paso, then eastward to San Antonio, riding only in coaches that took cavalrymen as escorts. A running scrape with Comanches at Castle Gap confirmed the prudence in her precaution.

She interviewed anyone who might supplement the information she had obtained about border conditions and relations with the savages. She queried the commander of Ranger Company D, questioned United States marshals and U.S. Army officers, spoke to incarcerated outlaws, and conversed with ordinary citizens.

Several minor incidents made interesting reading for the subscribers of *Fulton's* magazine. She recorded a horse race between Indians and soldiers at Fort Concho, a lynching from a telegraph pole at El Paso. But Nelly had for some time been planning a major feature article. A comprehensive character study. A tribute to John McCrary. For this reason she returned to Candelilla to write. By the time the agarita blossoms filled the air with a fragrance almost thick enough to make her swoon, her article was penned and stuffed into a heavy envelope scrawled with a Boston address. She intended it to justify her prolonged stay in western Texas and her preoccupation with Candelilla and its people.

The John McCrary story rode in the mail hack downstream to Presidio where it turned northward for Fort Stockton. The main line of the overland mail picked it up at that post and carried it across the Pecos, through Indian haunts like Castle Gap, and on toward Fort Concho.

Just west of the fort, a small band of Comanches gave chase in the hope of capturing some mules and taking some scalps. But the team was fresh and managed to keep the coach ahead of the Indians while the guards fired to the rear. One brave came close enough to fling an arrow at the driver. His aim was low, however, and the arrowhead slammed harmlessly into the mailbag locked onto the back of the coach.

At Fort Concho, the postmaster found the arrow embedded in Nelly's magazine article. He felt he couldn't extract it without tearing up the contents. He was forbidden to open the package, so he simply broke off the arrow shaft and left the point in the manuscript.

From Fort Concho the dispatch went through Fort McKavett, down the San Saba River, through the German settlements of Mason, Loyal Valley, Fredericksburg, Comfort, and Boerne, and into the old Spanish outpost of San Antonio. The daily stage northward carried Nelly's article to Austin and the railheads.

The International and Great Northern Rail Road transported the dispatch on to St. Louis and thence to Boston. When the battered packet arrived, the editors of *Fulton's* magazine gathered around Mr. Fulton's desk to hear the further adventures of their wayfaring female reporter.

When the envelope was opened, the men gasped at the arrow point they found embedded in the manuscript. It had about an inch of the arrow shaft attached to it with sinew stripped from a deer carcass. They argued over the artifact like boys until Mr. Fulton slammed his fist on his desk and proclaimed it his own property with which he would never part. The arrow point seemed to presage a particularly important piece.

They read the John McCrary story through once, made a few minor editorial changes, proclaimed it publishable, and ordered a copyboy to deliver it to the pressroom. The boy found a deserted corner and eagerly absorbed the story before delivering it.

A typesetter who read more sentences in mirror image than most citizens perused aright set the story letter by letter in lead characters. An illustrator produced a fanciful likeness of John McCrary with lines carved in relief on a block of wood. The woodcut and the lead type were clamped tight into a printing plate, inked, stamped onto some thirty thousand sheets of newsprint, and collated into position on page three of *Fulton's* magazine. The story ran under a banner headline: "Texas Ranger Parleys Peace to Savages."

Here, full across the face of page three, *Fulton's* magazine compounded Penelope Blankenship's greatest shame thirty thousand times over as each of its readers saw the author's byline—Perceval Blanc. The masculine pseudonym was one point on which the editors of *Fulton's* magazine had remained adamant. Mr. Fulton deemed his readers unable to accept a female reporter, especially one who dared penetrate wild country most male readers would think of approaching only in their heroic fantasies.

Perceval Blanc, a nonperson, would take credit for Nelly's articles, her research, her interviews, the miles she crossed on stagecoaches and mule back, the nights she slept under wagon beds and open skies, and the sagacity that poured from her pen. She was expected to write in a male voice. This she finally had agreed to do, no matter how deceitful. She would deny in writing the one overwhelming aspect of her character: womanhood. This to accomplish her search for the long-lost Thomas Payton Ryder.

Perceval Blanc, however, as he evolved through Nelly Blankenship, was a rather readable fellow, unencumbered by vainglorious bravado or masculine conceit. He readily admitted timidity—even outright fear—and a host of other human responses regarded by some as unmanly. His literary pieces had earned third-page status by virtue of their popularity with *Fulton's* public. Letters praising his energy and style, his wit and thoroughgoing correspondence, swamped the editor's desk. During the first week in April, most *Fulton's* readers thumbed impatiently past pages one and two and found Perceval back in Candelilla, Texas.

"There is a pass at Candelilla," he began, "and a shallow ford in the Rio Grande. . . ."

33

". . . and to this circumstantial feature of topography, the village owes its origin. A trail leads from Chihuahua, Mexico, through the pass, across the river, and into Candelilla, Texas. Speculators envision the day when the village will rival Presidio and El Paso for the rich trade with Chihuahua. A wagon road has been cleared to Fort Davis, and huge trains of freight wagons bearing copper, silver, leather, rope, and salt are expected to start passing through Candelilla soon. American merchants have located their enterprises here to profit by the coming prosperity.

The peacefulness of this border hamlet, however, results from the work of but one man Texas knows little of yet owes more than she realizes. The state should lionize him before all its citizens as a paragon of the statesman, the frontiersman, the diplomat, and the law officer. Instead, it has exiled him to this collection of squalid huts with the lilting name of Candelilla.

I refer to Texas Ranger John McCrary. Were it not for his knowledge of Indian society and warfare, his devotion to justice and order, and his tireless pursuit of honor for all races on this border, the mud buildings of Candelilla would long ago have crumbled under the flaming arrows of savages, the guns of Mexican bandits, and the treachery of American fugitives.

All other settlements west of the Pecos River, and a

good many east of it, lie in constant preparedness for Indian attacks. But in Candelilla, there is no fear of the Apache lance or of the Comanche knife. The people of this village go about their business unafraid, for there is a treaty with the Mescalero Apaches here which makes them friends and allies of the villagers, the Mexican goatherds and farmers, the hay cutters and mule drovers, and the American merchants. The author of this treaty is John McCrary. By the circumstances of his parentage and subsequent captivity among the savage Indians of western Texas, he is one half Mexican, the other Irish, with an overall inclination toward adoptive Indian habits.

Atop his head sits the straw sombrero, headwear of his maternal ancestry. At his heels are found the rowels of Mexican spurs. The rest of his accoutrements are American of origin and style, including high boots, buckskin or denim breeches, and woolen overshirt. This outfit suits his needs and, when laundered, afflicts no appreciable consternation on those downwind. An encircled star, emblem of the Texas Ranger, appears on his shirt, fashioned by Mr. McCrary's own hand from a silver Mexican coin. His revolver reposes on the hip as usual. His mustache rivals a brace of bottle brushes. His swarthy face betrays the Spanish blood in his veins, and his eyes roll constantly about like those of a Comanche warrior. All in all, Mr. McCrary represents a finer physical specimen of manhood than your humble correspondent might ever hope to embody.

Mr. McCrary's idiom is another matter altogether. He speaks English, Spanish, and various Indian dialects, but none with precision. His phraseology is both corrupt and picturesque. He confuses tenses with positive propensity, mixes words of various languages in a single utterance, and conjugates verbs with frightful inaccuracy. Yet any yarn spun by Mr. McCrary is invariably among the most amusing and lively heard anywhere on the Texas frontier. . . .

Perceval Blanc then related John McCrary's past, telling how his father, an Irish immigrant, had married a Spanish beauty in San Antonio who brought John into the world on April 21, 1836—the day Texas won its independence from Mexico at the Battle of San Jacinto. The legend of McCrary's birth maintained that he came into the world just as his father shouted "Remember the Alamo!" on the San Jacinto battleground:

And so our subject was born a true son of Texas. His father received a league and labor for his service in the Texas Army and located his land on the Colorado River in the vicinity of the Marble Falls. John McCrary believes he was ten years old when captured by savages who attacked and killed his parents. The Indians tied him across the back of a mule when he was first captured, and thus he rode every time the tribe moved its camp. The Indians tied him to the mule because he was wont to attempt escape if allowed to ride astraddle. . . .

Perceval told his readers how a successful treaty between the Comanche Indians and the German founders of Fredericksburg gave young John McCrary, Indian captive, the notion that a broader treaty could bring peace between whites and Indians across the entire Texas frontier.

He also included the tales of how the Indians abandoned McCrary after eight years of captivity when he contracted smallpox; of how he studied law in San Antonio by attending court; of how a lawyer gave him an old book of Texas statutes.

The readers of *Fulton's* learned, too, of the epidemic in San Antonio that killed the German immigrant parents of an infant named August Dannenberg. Then they read of McCrary's employment by the overland stage company; his establishment of Candelilla at the canyon pass where a few Mexicans had set up a camp to boil wax from the candelilla plant; his treaty with the Mescalero Apaches:

> Your humble author has complete faith in Mr. Mc-Crary's ability to bring peace by treaty to this entire region if allowed to pursue it, having witnessed the influence he has over the Mescalero Nation. When your author first arrived in this village, Mr. McCrary visited the camp of his Mescalero friends to ask that the safety of your correspondent be ensured. He then gave the Indians a description of your correspondent—a task for which he was well qualified, having become as familiar with this writer's personal physiognomy as any man in the country. Suffice it to say that your reporter has not been molested in the least by any full-blooded Indians in the region of Candelilla.

> But your correspondent has lost the chronology of the narrative and must regress to delineate our subject's entry into the theaters of the military and law enforcement. . . .

And Perceval told at length of McCrary's adventures as a scout in the Frontier Regiment of the Confederate Army, of his later acceptance into the Frontier Battalion of the Texas Rangers, and of how he was forced out of two ranger companies for insisting that Indian and Mexican suspects should be tried in court instead of summarily shot or hanged:

> The Ranger Service ordered him to patrol the region around Candelilla, knowing of his popularity here. He is the only officer of law in a titanic swath of uncharted frontier. Yet he holds firmly to the laws so precious to him in spite of the dangers and the unreliable remittance from the Ranger Service.
>
> And thus the situation of John McCrary now stands. He is a living human paradox. An armed pacifist. A reluctant warrior. In his own words: "I ain't a violent man, but I can fight as good as any. . . ."

Perceval purposefully styled his subject "John" McCrary throughout most the profile. He saved the nickname for the conclusion:

> Thus far, your correspondent has failed to mention Mr. McCrary's sobriquet, though it is something more than an incidental facet of the man, as every soul on the border calls him by this handle. Forgive your author for thus far concealing the nickname, as it is intended to sum up the man as well as this account.
>
> Recall, as you have read in the paragraphs above, the solitary existence of our subject since the tender days of his boyhood; consider his ostracism from the ranks of red men and white; think of his singular duty to enforce the laws in a vast land; gather all these conceits before you and wonder little that our subject is known as "Lonesome" John McCrary.
>
> Mind me, readers, the mere appearance of our subject's appellation on the cluttered pages of this journal spells nothing of the solitude experienced when the title

is heard rolling from the tongues of lonely people in a lonely land. It drawls about direfully in their mouths and comes to be pronounced, as nearly as your author can phonetically represent it, "Lawnce-um" John Mc-Crary. Perhaps in a benevolent attempt to abbreviate the desolate sound of the thing, the border folks refer to our subject endearingly as "Lawnce," though the Spanish speakers are wont to prefix the epithet with a respectful "Don."

This illustrative sobriquet represents our subject more accurately than any history your humble correspondent has herein submitted. A maundering "Lawnce" so perfectly tells of his privations and sufferings that your author can but little bear to refer to him thus. By the nature of his own noble character and chivalric ideals, John McCrary's destiny follows a trail marked only by his own footsteps. His fate is loneliness. Yet so endeared has he become to your reporter that if ever a reasonable course of action should arise that will to any degree alter that destiny, trust, dear readers, that it shall be accomplished without hesitation.

34

The mail hack and two cavalrymen had waited half an hour for Nelly Blankenship. Though quite capable of punctuality, she was stalling for time. She hoped any minute to see Lawnce McCrary and, for Chepita's sake, August Dannenberg trotting in from the northwest. She finally realized the futility of her tactic and tossed her carpetbag into the hack.

Sawyer, the driver, preferred to use mules on his route. They had sure feet on the canyon-rim road to Presidio and tempted Indians and rustlers less than horses did. When the two mules took the slack out of the trace chains, Nelly chanced a last look upstream. To her astonishment, she saw a narrow column of dust rising from the desert and spotted two riders coming fast. One of them, by the way he flapped his elbows birdlike when he rode, Nelly recognized as Lawnce. The other had to be August Dannenberg.

She virtually jerked the reins from Sawyer's hands and stopped the mules. She apologized and jumped down, unloading her carpetbag as she lit. Sawyer and the horse soldiers were relieved to get rid of her; they wanted to reach Presidio before midnight. Sawyer cussed the mules so pointedly that they lurched in the rigging.

By the time Nelly had sprinted back to McCrary Livery she could hear the riders hooting. The ranger's boots hit the ground squarely in front of the barn. He tipped his sombrero and winked at Nelly. She grabbed him by the ears and kissed him on the face as he lifted her by the waist. The whole scene made August's eyes bug out.

"August and me stood guard for one another just up the *río* so we could warsh up and shave," Lawnce said.

"I can tell," Nelly answered. She looked at August.

He tipped his hat. "Ma'am," he said.

"I've heard so much about you, Mr. Dannenberg, from Lawnce and from Chepita. You'll find her at home, I believe. I said good-bye to her just a while ago."

August wiggled his feet in the stirrups.

"I would go to her immediately if I were you."

"Yes, ma'am," August said. He trotted his New Mexico horse around the corner and down the side street.

The first glimpse he got of Chepita through her open doorway showed that the trouble she had seen in the past months had exacted a toll. An expression of tired suffering had replaced her childlike exuberance, but when she recognized August, her eyes brightened. Recognizing him took some looking, though. He wore a new pair of jeans, a linen shirt, and a buckskin jacket lined with red flannel, which Ryder had bought for him in Taos. She glanced both ways down the street and pulled August into her adobe house.

"Howdy," he said bashfully. Standing in the dark adobe with only the cracks in the door to cast a dim light on his sweetheart, it took all of August's courage to reach for her hand. When he did, Chepita pressed her body against him and turned her face up toward his. He thought he'd better kiss her quick before he lost his nerve.

Chepita pushed herself away from him after their lips had been together only a brief and wonderful moment. "Maximo," she said in a half-question.

"He's on my trail somewhere." August was puzzled when Chepita breathed a sigh of relief.

"Then you must leave immediately. Tell me where you will go, and I will follow soon."

"No, ma'am," August insisted. "I ain't leavin' you behind for that bully to pick on you. I came here to get you once and for all, and I ain't runnin' from Maximo or anybody else another step."

"Don't be foolish," Chepita said. She had worked out all the arguments in her head. "Perhaps you can beat Maximo with guns again. But if you don't—if he wins—I will be here with him alone. Do you wish to protect me or not?" She didn't fear Maximo any more than she feared her feathered friends along the river, but she wanted to use August's presumptions about Maximo to save both of them.

August thought about his options. "Then you've got to leave. If we hurry, we can still catch the mail hack and put you on it. We'll decide right now where you'll go and nobody will know but me and you. Then I'll wait for Maximo. I'll catch up to you soon enough if I kill him. If I don't, you'll know he got me."

She had anticipated this argument, too. "No," she said. She wanted to explain how she loved both men, but she knew that would only confuse and maybe even anger him. The truth would have to wait for a more appropriate moment. The present situation called for a different strategy. "I cannot live another day away from you," she said, throwing herself against him. "I will not leave unless you come with me. That is the only way. We must both leave Candelilla before Maximo returns."

August felt as if he could whip a dozen Maximos when Chepita wrapped her arms around him. But when she said they would never be parted again, he liked the sound of it. He decided to do the thing her way. But one question bothered him. "You sure it's proper?" he asked. "Me and you on the run together? We ain't married, and I ain't got but one set of blankets."

The suggestion charmed Chepita more than any she could have anticipated. This argument she had not counted on, but she thought of a quick solution. "Do you like birds?" she asked.

"Naw," August replied. "Too many bones and not enough meat."

The señorita laughed. "No, I mean birds when they fly. When they sing. When they court in the air. Do you like birds then?"

August smirked quizzically. "I reckon I do at that. I like to hear an old tom gobble of a mornin' in the spring."

"Then the birds will marry us."

August cocked his head at a questioning angle.

"I am sorry," Chepita said. "Perhaps I assume too much. I mean if you want to marry me."

"Of course. Why, I rode a river of white water down a box canyon to get here and make you my wife. But I don't *sabe* about the birds marryin' us up."

Chepita touched his hand. "Our love is something of nature, like a dove singing or a hawk flying. I know the birds. I know what they say. I know what they mean when they chatter and flutter in the branches. They will see us together and they will sing for us. It is all I need to become your wife."

The months August had spent under the influence of Thomas Payton Ryder had opened his mind to things he would have scoffed at before. If a padre could join man and wife, why couldn't a bird of some kind do the same? They were both creatures of God, were they not?

"Then it'll do for me, too," he said.

The birds were singing even before they saw the bride and groom. August and Chepita rode double on the New

Mexico horse to the timber along the river. He jumped off and helped his bride down. They strolled into the trees to hear the birdsong as dusk approached.

The mockingbirds held their raspy squawks and whistled suggestively instead. Scissortails chased flying bugs, cavorting in the air as if dancing for the wedding ceremony. A vermilion flycatcher sputtered like a flutist. He made periodic dashes after insects flying low over the water surface. His flaming reddish orange breast reflected as a bright blur in the river. Chepita pointed them out to August. Except for the mockingbird, they were all new to him, though he had lived among them forever.

"What are they sayin'?" he asked.

"El sinsonte," Chepita said, pointing at the mockingbird, "asks if the caballero will honor and protect and love the señorita until death takes one to heaven."

"I will. And after that, too."

"La cola-de-tijeras," Chepita continued, indicating a scissortail, "asks if the señorita will love, honor, and obey the caballero."

"Will you?"

"I will."

"What does Señor Red Vest say?"

"El chaleco rojo says, 'Before God, you are man and wife.' You must kiss the bride."

It was as sensible a ceremony as any. There were no stained panes or adobe belfries to stand between God and the couple. There were no fees to pay to priests, no licenses to purchase, no guests to usher, no forgotten invitations to offend neglected friends, no food or flowers or gifts to be arranged. There was only a man and a woman and the love between them to unite them for life.

When they kissed, a flutter in the low branches made them look to the trees. A red and black oriole courted his yellow and brown mate. They chased each other among the cottonwood leaves, singing and swooping gracefully from branch to bough. Their colors made them look as if they came from different races, but none could deny they belonged together.

The newlyweds watched them until the sun set; then they spread their blankets under the cluster of cottonwoods lining the shore.

Back at the livery stables, Lawnce was drumming his callused fingers against a bottle of tanglefoot in the loft. "Where you reckon they are?" he asked.

"Oh, mind your own affairs," Nelly answered. "Tell me more about what went on upriver."

"Plenty of hard ridin' mostly," Lawnce said. He avoided the details because he didn't want to have to start lying about the Reverend Professor Ryder. He threw one leg over Nelly and tickled her neck with his mustache to divert her interest.

The birds sang again at dawn. August listened to them with his eyes closed, half asleep. When he remembered, he sat upright. "Mornin'," he said.

Chepita had already dressed and tied her hair back. "We must leave soon," she said.

As August tightened the cinch on the New Mexico horse, he heard the rumble of hooves coming from Candelilla. It was Lawnce, hollering as he came. "Run for your life, kid! Maximo just blew in." He galloped into the cottonwoods, ducking the branches. "That wildcat is always a day up on the game. Roll your cotton and cut for Presidio. I'll try to tangle him up."

August tied on the bedroll, mounted, and helped Chepita up behind him. But by the time he got ready to run, the war cloud was coming down on him.

"Slap leather!" Lawnce ordered.

Chepita also urged him on.

But August wouldn't move. "It's no use. He's on us now. We can't beat him ridin' double." He swung his right leg over the saddle horn and hit the ground. Then he helped Chepita down. "I'd rather him shoot me standing' than on the run."

"Damn it, August, how many chances you think you'll git?"

"I just want one more," August said. "He must've been ridin' all night. That'll give me an edge."

Lawnce cussed and put himself between the couple and the gang of bandits.

August was checking the loads in his little revolver as Chepita pleaded with him not to shoot Maximo. She said it as if she feared Maximo dying more than the man she had slept with the night before. It was odd that she didn't want Maximo dead, he thought. A man who would beat her. Why did she care at all what happened to him? Maybe before, Maximo was all she had. But now she had a husband. A better man than Maximo. He figured it was still the desperate air of the bandit that attracted her. August had yet to prove how desperate he could be.

Maximo raised his hand, halting his troops. "Chepita!" he yelled. *"Venga!"* He got down from his horse and walked forward as his men stayed back. They looked as if their horses had been riding them. Maximo's lust for August's blood had given them little in the way of sleep or food for the past couple of weeks. They were ready to see the stable boy stretched out across the sand so they could do their own stretching out in their jacales. Jesse wore the most bedraggled expression of the lot, and his mind was wearier than his body. Two weeks had passed, and Maximo was still living. He knew he had to get his killing done quick or Butch Gainey would want a refund in blood.

"Come here, Chepita," Maximo repeated.

"That's my wife you're talkin' to," August said. "She don't have to do what you say no more!"

Lawnce shot a puzzle smirk at August.

"It's true," August said. "We married ourselves last night. With some birds to help us."

Maximo burst into cruel laughter. "You are a liar and a coward, muchacho."

"You're a coward and a bully, Maximo."

Trouble was a hair trigger away. Lawnce yanked his Remington from its holster. "I aim to arrest both of you for tryin' to shoot each other. It's against the Revised Statutes to duel in Texas." Habitually, he slapped the saddlebag that usually carried the book. It felt flat and languid.

Maximo turned his attention to the ranger. "Your book of laws does not go across the *río*. Muchacho! If you are not afraid, we will fight with guns in Mexico, across the *río*."

August did not answer, but he swung into the saddle and reined his horse toward the river. Maximo backtracked to get his own mount so he wouldn't have to wade across on foot.

Lawnce cussed and spit on the ground. "Go on and kill each other, then," he shouted. "Shoot yourselfs colder than cartwheels. I don't give a damn anymore. You're both more trouble than a blind lead horse, and you're both goin' farther down than a wedge can drop in twenty years!" He twirled his revolver by the trigger guard and, holding it by the barrel, rode up next to August. "Here. Use a man-size iron. If you're lucky enough to kill him again, this time kill him to death!"

Chepita suddenly knew she would have to tell all the secrets she knew to save the two men she loved. Maximo wouldn't like it, but it was time she told the truth. It felt good to her, being on the verge of revealing the lies she had lived with since she came to Candelilla. It was like

cleansing her soul at confession. She ran toward Maximo
as Lawnce tried to get August to take the Remington. August refused the weapon and turned to watch out for her.

"Oiga, Maximo!" she said. "It is true what he says about
the birds. Don't kill him. I love him!" She had her hands
clasped, begging.

Maximo was cold and incredulous. "A gringo?" he said.
"The one who would kill Maximo?"

"It was only because of your lies that he shot you," she
shouted. "You made everyone think of me as your whore!
You made them think you did not treat me well and everyone believed it, and only one man had the courage to
defend me." She pointed at August. "He thought you
would hurt me. That is why he shot you."

"You are talking too much," Maximo warned.

"And I'll shoot again to keep you from hurtin' her any
more," August said.

"No!" Chepita ran toward August. "Maximo has never
harmed me. He has protected me."

"Hush, Chepita, and get out of the way. Everybody
knows he's a hard man. I seen him knock you down with
his horse. I seen that with my own eyes."

"That was an accident. The horse jumped. You cannot
kill a man for the things his horse does! Don't shoot him,
August. I love him."

To August the words felt like a knife turning in his vitals. It wasn't possible for her to love two men. "You can't
have it like that, Chepita. If you won't pick one of us, then
we'll decide ourselves. Me and Maximo. The one left
standin' gets you."

Maximo nodded once, arrogantly.

"I don't have to choose!" Chepita insisted. "I can love
you both."

"Cállate!" Maximo said.

"No! I will not stay silent longer." Turning to August,

she said, "I can love you both because Maximo is not my lover. He is my brother!"

August's eyes squinted. Lawnce gasped so hard that he almost inhaled his mustache. Maximo threw his hands into the air and uttered a string of Spanish expletives. A low mumble passed among the ranks of the bandito gang, and Jesse Diaz perked up like a startled buck.

"What do you mean?" August asked.

"I mean brother. Brother and sister. The same mother, the same father. Maximo is my brother." She came closer, put her hand on August's knee as he looked down from the saddle, and spoke so that no one else could hear. "I am not a whore. I thought you would know. Last night. I didn't know how . . ." She finished the sentence by gesturing vaguely with her hands.

August flushed around the ears. "Didn't know the difference myself," he admitted.

"Now, hold on," Lawnce said. "This don't figure. How come you to keep this brother and sister thing a secret all this time?"

"Maximo made me. Because of his enemies. If they knew about me, they would use me against him. The lies were supposed to protect me. It was not a good idea."

August wondered why he hadn't thought of it before. Maximo and Chepita even bore some family resemblance to each other, now that he looked for it. It was said that Maximo was rough with her, but she had never been bloodied or bruised; she had never complained. The threats he made on her in public were all for show. That was suddenly so obvious that August didn't know how he had missed it. Maximo had wanted everyone to believe he didn't care about her. If he had openly honored and adored her, as a brother should, Butch Gainey would have kidnapped her to bait Maximo into an ambush. Gainey would do anything to see Maximo dead.

But Chepita was right. It was a bad idea. Maximo hadn't counted on anyone defending Chepita. He was too arrogant to think that any man would risk facing his guns to stand up for her. He hadn't reckoned with the conviction of a young man's love.

There was another flaw in the plan. It had heaped undeserved guilt on Chepita's shoulders. She had been a virgin made to feel like a common prostitute. It was peculiar that the ruse had even worked, because she didn't look the part. Yet no one had doubted Maximo when he claimed her as his woman. Her beauty made women jealous enough to look for fault and men desirous enough to indulge their wicked fantasies.

It had all been a curse to Chepita. It was a sin to bear false witness before God. She had drawn some solace from the killdeer, who pretended to have a broken wing in order to lure her enemies away from her chicks. Chepita had lied to save a loved one, too, but her lies had made her feel like a border whore. She would have given anything to trade deceptions with the killdeer. But now that the lies were told, she felt as free as Señora Heron, stroking the sky with her wings.

Maximo approached, holding his hands in front of him, away from his guns, so August would know he did not mean to shoot. "Your mouth is too big," he said to Chepita. "Now nothing is safe for you here."

He scowled at August. "Maximo does not like you, muchacho." He aimed down his knuckle joints like gun sights. "Your damned little pistol almost killed the great Maximo de Guerra. But one thing is true: you have the courage to fight for Chepita—even to fight against the greatest *pistolero* in the north of Mexico and the west of Texas. This is more courage than any man has under the sun. And so Maximo gives you permission to marry his sister. You will both leave tomorrow for Mexico."

August thought for a moment that he would tell Maximo he didn't need permission. He was still in the frame of mind to fight. Then he realized in one avalanche of relief that all the chases and the fights were over. He was thankful he had chanced the return to Candelilla. He was glad the professor had talked him into carving messages to throw into the river.

"Tomorrow you will leave for Mexico. But today . . ." Maximo turned to his band of thieves and raised his hands like a bishop blessing the masses. "Fiesta!"

The band bolted like a covey of quail. Pistol shots and wild yelps pierced the silence.

Lawnce contributed the deafening blasts of his old Remington to the celebration. "We'll send a fast rider to Presidio and haul the padre back. Birds ain't duly vested authorities accordin' to the Revised Statutes—at least they ain't as far as I know." He rode in circles, shooting his old pistol in the air.

Maximo turned back to the newlyweds. He was grinning until he looked at August. "That first shot was not a good one," he said, showing where the bullet had entered his right hand. "Always aim for the heart or the head. You need a bigger gun."

35

Chepita had spent most of her life at the convent in Chihuahua where Maximo had come to visit her once or twice a year. But after Comanches attacked the city, some of them gaining the convent walls, he had moved her to Candelilla where the treaty would keep her safe from Indians. However, he had to force her to play the unseemly role of his mistress to protect her from Butch Gainey. Maximo knew Butch would happily kidnap her to use as bait, and the suffering she was likely to experience in his sordid hands would make acting like a border tramp seem like a mere inconvenience by comparison. Maximo always considered the act a temporary necessity, for he intended to exact his revenge against El Ojo at the first opportunity and return with his sister to Mexico, where she would no longer have to pretend.

August's assumption of responsibility for Chepita's safety came as a relief to Maximo. And he also felt less burdened now that he didn't have to kill the boy. But he still had worries. Foremost was the existence of an unknown assassin who might try to kill him at any moment. It could be anybody—perhaps even one of his own men. He had taken little sleep on his recent ride up and down the Rio Grande, even though he had craftily found ways to check most of his men for double eagles with clipped wings. He had found none so far, but every glint of specie caught his eye.

Maximo started giving orders as soon as his men and Lawnce had emptied their pistols into the air. He sent

Fermin and Apolonio to Presidio for the priest. He instructed Tristan to round up enough musicians to entertain dancers. He gave Jesse Diaz and some other bandits the task of killing and butchering goats, pigs, and chickens to be barbecued for the wedding fiesta. Jesse didn't look forward to wringing necks and gutting livestock all morning and afternoon. It reminded him too much of what might happen to his own corresponding body parts if he didn't come up with a plan to murder Maximo within a day.

Maximo didn't demand anything of Lawnce, but he suggested that Doña Lope might organize some women into a work force that would decorate the street outside Las Quince Letras for the feast and *baile*. He sent the rest of his men to assist the women with the heavy work.

"Candelilla ain't knowed a fandangle for a many a moon!" Lawnce said, jabbing his horse with spurs.

The Mescaleros could tell a fiesta was brewing in the village. The gunshots and the smoke from the barbecue fires tipped them off. About noon they began filtering into town in small parties, carrying turkey, antelope, and deer carcasses for the feast. They sat in the shade of the livery barn and spoke with Lawnce in sign language and some Spanish as they watched the women prepare the fiesta grounds in front of Las Quince Letras. One of them walked up behind Nelly Blankenship, touched her blond hair, grunted, and returned to the barn.

After siesta, the work commenced again. Nelly and her work force collected sheets of canvas and spread them out in the dirt street to serve as a dance floor. She had Maximo's men sink posts around the canvas flooring where lanterns could be hung. An odd collection of tables and chairs was secured and arranged for the feast. A party of women had been patting cornmeal dough into tortillas for hours.

Mr. Grimes drove to the river in a wagon from the Candelilla General Mercantile Store and chopped down a bee tree he had spotted some time before. Actually, he watched while some Mexicans he had hired did the chopping for him. He even secured the honeycomb and took it to a mule driver with a penchant for whittling who carved it into a model of Mexico's Pyramid of the Sun. The beeswax sculpture would become the centerpiece on a long serving table made of unhinged doors.

The street in front of the cantina would serve as the site for the wedding as well as the fiesta. To spruce the place up, Santos decided to go ahead with a long-procrastinated plastering project. He had kept a pile of limestone rocks behind the cantina for months. Now he baked them in an outdoor oven half the day until they became soft enough to break apart with a hammer. He steeped the crumbled limestone in a copper cauldron, stirring it in the hot water until it reached a viscosity perfect for plastering. Santos's wife, her two sisters, and their combined eleven daughters spread the wet lime on the cantina with sheepskins.

A large band of Indians gathered and erected a few tepees behind the corrals of McCrary Livery. Most of them slept, saving their energy for the feast, though a few of them ran horse races, gambled with cards, or had shooting contests. August watched them from the barn loft where he had been told to wait until the priest arrived. He looked out on the same mountains he used to dream of crossing. He had seen so much, and yet, compared to adventurers like T. P. Ryder, he had seen almost nothing. That didn't matter to him much anymore. He wanted to see Chepita and that was all.

Finally, toward sundown, the shouts of Fermin and Apolonio were heard as they escorted a harried priest into town. The clergyman, who was driving a spring buggy, looked relieved to reach his destination. He was a fat, balding little man known affectionately as Father Gordo.

The bride and groom were summoned. August wore his new suit of clothes and had a fresh coat of saddle soap on his boots. Chepita wore a white dress of new-made cotton cloth someone in the village had recently woven. As she carried a bouquet of Indian paintbrush to the makeshift altar, the citizens of Candelilla hung their heads in shame for the things they had thought and said about the bride in the past.

Father Gordo abbreviated the mass as much as possible, as if he knew he was merely reaffirming the bond Chepita's birds had forged the night before. When the groom kissed his bride, pistol shots again rang throughout the valley. The lanterns were lit as the sunset faded, and the Mescaleros began to stir. Only a few of them had been curious enough to attend the ceremony, but now they sensed the feast pending and began to crowd the long table of horizontal doors.

Chief José Cigarito arrived and headed the grub line. He was grizzled, and the whites of his eyes were not white at all, but muddy. Lawnce used his redskin diplomacy to thank the chief for bringing game to contribute to the feast. Otherwise, he said, the Indians would not have been allowed to eat.

Father Gordo was an honored guest and was served behind the bride and groom. Lawnce caught his arm before he could poke his fork into the victuals. The priest carried his own silverware with him everywhere he went for just such a lucky encounter with food. Nelly was standing beside Lawnce, and Maximo was approaching.

"Say, Padre," Lawnce said, searching in his pockets for money. "I reckon you ought to git paid more than just grub for makin' the ride up here on short notice. Here's a new roof for your chapel."

He flipped a coin at the fat priest, but Maximo's snake-quick hand caught it in flight.

"Don Lawnce," he said testily, "Maximo is able to pay for the wedding of his own sister." Turning to the priest, he said, "Padre Gordo, you will be paid well for your blessings on my sister and her husband."

He held the coin out to Lawnce, but the ranger refused to take it back.

"Look here, Maximo. Some ol' lawnce-um skunk like me ain't liable to have another youngun to stand up for. What squaw would have one with me?"

Maximo argued his side by shifting his eyes to Nelly.

"Mr. de Guerra," Nelly said nervously, "John only intended this money as a contribution to Father Gordo's parish. It was not meant to pay for the services."

Maximo seemed to deliberate. *"Pues,"* he said, "if that is the case, Maximo will allow it." He held the coin in his hand, turning it between his deadly fingers. Father Gordo's soft palm waited eagerly for it. Maximo had only to hand it over, but—purely out of a habit developed in recent days—he glanced first at the eagle side of the coin. What he saw jolted him with disbelief. The wing had been clipped by Cayetano's carving knife. Lawnce carried the marked coinage of the assassin. Maximo tensed as he slapped the coin into Father Gordo's hand and glared malice at the ranger.

"I swear, it's just for the padre's church roof," Lawnce said, misinterpreting the angry eyes of the desperado. Then he pretended to be serving Father Gordo just so he could get in line behind him and get a crack at some fresh chuck.

Maximo felt like a fool for having trusted Lawnce Mc-Crary—a ranger and a half-gringo. He felt ashamed, too, for he had always relied on his ability to judge a man's character and yet he had misjudged Lawnce McCrary. Only Cayetano's marked coin had saved him from the big Remington revolver. Had Lawnce been on Gainey's side all along, he wondered, or had he just recently been bought?

Baked chickens and barbecued goats were kept coming by the cooks to flank the waxen pyramid centerpiece. The wild game also went as fast as it arrived. There were stacks of corn tortillas and pots of beans stewed with pork and laced with peppers. Jars of fresh honey, with just a few dead bees embalmed within, stood at the far end of the horizontal doors. José Cigarito stacked as much meat as he could carry on a tortilla and then wedged a turkey leg under his arm.

Santos had removed his entire stock of liquor from Las Quince Letras and was doling it out in minuscule portions to make it last through the night. Even with Santos's thumb acting as a governor over the spouts of the tequila bottles, the spirits were flowing at a frightening rate. And the Indians weren't even drinking because it went against the treaty for them to do so. Lawnce made it up to them in tobacco, however.

For once, Santos was happy to see his competitor, Jigger Shanks, proprietor of the Pitchfork Saloon. He came down the street with a wheelbarrow loaded up with about half his stock of whiskey. He didn't really compete with Santos because each barkeeper served a different segment of the population. But there was a natural rivalry between them nonetheless.

"Sure is good to see that load of popskull," Lawnce said to Jigger Shanks, helping unload.

"Slow down, Lawnce. Put these bottles up first. Them other ones are for later—watered down, you know."

"By gum, Jigger. Smart thinkin'. Hell, this will half clean your doggery out for a piece, won't it?"

"Yeah, but I'll just up the price. Business is slow anyway. Most of the outfits are roundin' up."

"That so?" Lawnce said. "Which ones?"

"Doubletree is, if that's what you're after. I don't expect you'll see any trouble from One-Eyed Butch tonight. He's been tryin' to get his boys to start a herd up the trail while Maximo's been gone." Shanks started to laugh. "Them boys of his, though. They couldn't turn a stampede with a wagon tongue!"

Barkeepers knew everything that went on, and Shanks had merely affirmed what Lawnce had already heard from José Cigarito. The Mescaleros had been watching the Doubletree outfit. Cigarito didn't say exactly why, but Lawnce figured they were watching for easy stock to steal, and for the pleasure of seeing the maverick brutes stomp a few cowhands.

When Tristan finished gorging himself, he picked up his guitar and started to play a ballad under the light of a coal-oil lantern at the corner of the canvas dance floor. Grimes played a decent fiddle and had learned how to make it go with Mexican music. It didn't take long for half-drunk mule drovers to start whirling the señoritas. A couple of other *guitarristas* joined the band, and one of the storekeepers kept the rhythm with a washboard.

"I wish this town had a piano," Nelly mentioned to Lawnce. "I might join the boys playing. Or at least tune them up."

"Pianer?" Lawnce said. "No gottee."

After midnight, when the fiesta was loudest and the *baile* most lively, Jesse Diaz took advantage of the commotion and sneaked away. He mounted a fresh horse from the bandito *caballada* and rode fast along the road that led to the Doubletree Ranch.

Only one guard was stationed atop the ranch house when Jesse galloped in. The rest of the Doubletree boys were over the hill, sleeping on the ground around the chuck wagon or riding night herd on the five hundred beeves bedded there. Butch Gainey hadn't slept on the ground in years. His four-poster feather bed had spoiled him. He would sooner let a Mexican ride Top Dollar than sleep on the unyielding dirt like a common cow waddie.

The guard on the roof had a half-moon above him to spread ragged shadows around the buildings and scrub brush. He could see anything moving across the bare ground surrounding the ranch house for a half-mile. A chorus of yipping coyotes goaded themselves into a frenzy of singing canine voices to the south. To the northeast the wooden barn and pole corrals stood empty, except for Top Dollar and a few other mounts. The roof guard strained to hear the songs of the night herders to the east, but they sang too low and far away.

Standing in heeled boots on a dirt roof all night made the rifleman long to prop his Winchester against a parapet and guard the inside of his hat instead of the yellow-gray desert floor. But when One-Eye Butch caught a guard who slept on his post, the kangaroo court would convene. A jury of slovenly cowpunchers who knew as much as they cared about due process would convict the accused without benefit of counsel and, holding him face-down to the dirt by the four limbs, would wet a pair of leather leggings and beat the offender with them until he was too weak to holler.

Respect for the leggings kept Gainey's night guard alert when Jesse's hoofbeats first reached the ranch house roof. The guard looked for a moving shadow to cross the barren circle around Gainey's fort. When the shadow appeared and approached, the guard fired a warning shot. "Who are you?" he demanded.

"I have news for Señor Gainey," Jesse hollered.

Gainey was out of bed and on the gallery before his guard could shoot again. "Let him in," the boss yelled.

"Jefe," Jesse said. "There is big news in Candelilla." He trotted his heaving pony to the hitching rail and loosened the cinch.

"Must be big enough for you to risk gettin' gut-shot. Did you come to collect your other five hundred? Is Maximo dead? Did you get him?"

"No, señor. There was no chance. But we will have him soon. Maximo has a sister."

"The hell! Where at?"

"In Candelilla." Jesse hitched his mount and ducked under the rail. "Chepita Ybarra, the washing woman. She is no *puta,* she is Maximo's *hermana."*

Gainey went back into his fortified bedroom and returned with his clothes and his guns. "How do you know?" he asked as he got dressed on the moonlit porch.

By the time Gainey had pulled on his boots, buckled his gun belt, and heard Jesse's explanation, hoofbeats were coming from the roundup. The four night herders had heard the rifle shot and wakened the sleeping cowboys. They had jumped on their night horses and come to investigate.

"Boys," Gainey said, "this here is Jesse Diaz. Most of y'all know he's on our side. He says Maximo's got a sister gettin' married tonight in Candelilla. Me and Jesse have got her a little wedding present planned out.

"Dood, you ride back to the herd and tell the boys to let 'em drift. Tell them to come back here and fort up. Get ready for a fight. The rest of you boys come with me and I'll tell you the plan on the way to town. We're gonna clean all the damn Mexican rustlers out of the country come mornin'. And maybe that worthless ranger, too."

From his bedroll under the chuck wagon, Cayetano Pastor heard Doodlebug Tatum tell the night herders to prepare for war at the ranch. He also heard who had brought the news of Maximo's sister—Jesse Diaz. He figured Jesse was the carrier of eagles with clipped wings. He was ordered to stay with his chuck wagon, but as soon as the herders rode out of sight, Cayetano threw a saddle blanket over the lead mule of his wagon team and cut a new trail to town to warn Maximo.

36

It was two hours before dawn when Jesse rolled a husk cigarette and stepped casually back into the lamplight of the fiesta. The mariachis were still playing, as he suspected they would until sunup. No one had missed him. Maximo's eyes had been on Lawnce McCrary all night. Knowing Lawnce for his assassin actually gave the desperado a sense of comfort. Now he had just one gun to watch.

Maximo had grown especially festive as the party wore on. He seemed to have made a project of dancing with everyone who wore a skirt. When he asked Nelly Blankenship to dance with him, Jesse saw a perfect opportunity to take his turn dancing with the bride. He waited until August and Lawnce were rapt in telling the story of the Rio Grande Gorge to Jigger Shanks; then he approached Chepita.

"I wish you much happiness," Jesse said, with a warm smile and all the charm he could fake. "May you give your husband many children."

"Gracias," Chepita replied.

"May I have a dance?" he asked, extending his hand.

Chepita regarded him suspiciously for a moment, then curtsied and stepped toward the canvas-covered street where the dancing took place. The mariachis were strumming a lively tune, Tristan reading the stars like sheet music and watching moths circle the hot lantern globes. Jesse whirled Chepita, dancing at a proper distance so not to alarm her, staying on the outside ring of dancers, opposite Maximo and Nelly. As they danced the circle, Jesse led his partner closer to the shadows. Checking against watchful eyes, he suddenly forced her beyond the circle of light.

"Jesse!" Chepita complained. Just when she began to struggle to get away, a palm pressed hard against her mouth and she was carried away kicking by two cowboys who took liberties with their hands. Butch Gainey waved at Jesse from behind a corner.

"Turn around and take your sombrero off," he said.

Jesse did so and gritted his teeth hard.

"I'll just hit you hard enough to make you bleed a little," Gainey said. He raised the barrel of his pistol and brought it down smartly on the back of Jesse's head.

The spy stumbled forward onto his knees, but uttered not so much as a grunt.

"That'll make it look good, Jesse. Lay down there until they find you. You know what to do after that. Get Maximo to take cover in the barn at the Doubletree. When you lead him out the south side, we'll be waitin'."

Chepita was gagged, thrown on a horse across the lap of a cowboy, and rushed through the side streets toward Gainey's fortified ranch. The fiesta music drowned out her muffled screams and the hoofbeats that carried her away. A mile from town, Gainey and his men topped a rise and ran into Cayetano on his mule.

"Where you goin'?" yelled One-Eyed Butch.

Cayetano saw Chepita with them and kicked his mule harder. Gainey pulled at his pearl handle and shot the cook in the back. Cayetano held the mule's mane and lay flat, but he knew he was hit hard by the bullet and was already feeling numb.

"You want me to go after him, boss?"

Gainey lashed the cowboy with the ends of his bridle

reins. "You think I miss? He's dead. Besides, we got all we need."

Cayetano's old lead mule knew the path to the Candelilla General Mercantile Store, and it led directly through the fiesta grounds. The mule trotted blindly in among the dancers, and the cook slid off and collapsed amid the screams of the ladies. Blood covered the entire front of his shirt where the bullet had ripped through.

Maximo knew his old spy had been discovered and rushed to the dying man. "*Viejo,*" he said, "what has happened?"

"You have a sister?"

"*Sí.*"

August and Lawnce approached Cayetano to listen.

"El Ojo. He has taken your sister to his rancho. Be careful. A trap . . ."

Screams from the women interrupted Cayetano's dying words as Jesse Diaz stumbled convincingly into the lantern lit fiesta site. August looked everywhere for Chepita, but couldn't see her.

"*Gracias,* Señor Pastor," Maximo said. "You have great courage."

But the old man was already dead.

Jesse covered his face as if in shame and told how the Doubletree men had sneaked into the fiesta grounds wearing Mexican clothes and grabbed Chepita when he danced with her. He said they had used a gun barrel on his head, and he showed them where.

Maximo gave the war yell, and his men scattered to get their horses.

"Saddle the horses, kid," Lawnce said. But August had already disappeared into McCrary Livery. The ranger caught Maximo before he could run for his mount. "Bring your boys around here when you git 'em in the middle of their horses. This is ranger business, and I'm countin' on you to keep your boys in the law."

Maximo swiveled his dark eyes in their sockets and studied the ranger hard. "Do you think, Don Lawnce, that Maximo will trust a tejano rinche?"

Lawnce was staggered and insulted all at once to think a judge of men like Maximo would doubt him. He stood silent for a moment, not knowing what to say or why he was being questioned. "Trust me? I'll go to the bluff and look over with you," he finally declared.

The desperado turned without comment, but he brought his men around to the fiesta grounds as Lawnce had asked. August was there with two fresh horses from McCrary's remuda. He had also opened the secret floor plank in the tack room where the ranger kept his rifles and ammunition. He had his pockets full of .44 shells for his Winchester and had dumped a supply of the tin cartridge tubes for the Spencer into Lawnce's saddlebags.

Maximo's instincts were trying to tell him to trust Lawnce, but the marked coin made him doubt. He would have to make up his mind about Lawnce by sunup, for that's when the shooting would start.

Just as Lawnce gave the yell to ride, another party of horsemen showed up. José Cigarito had the toes of his moccasins hooked under the belly of a spotted mustang. Thirteen grim warriors rode behind him. They were all armed. This was what Lawnce had wanted for a long time. A party of men big enough to take on Gainey's army and a damn good reason to shoot.

As they thundered out of town, Nelly Blankenship was struggling to saddle a horse inside McCrary Livery. If there was going to be a fight, she didn't want to miss it.

Five men led the unlikely band of riders to Gainey's fort. August was one of them. Cigarito was another. Maximo purposefully rode between Jesse and Lawnce. He thought about Lawnce's gold coin with the clipped wings. He could have gotten it from Gainey or from someone else who had gotten it from Gainey. That was the flaw in Cayetano's plan. Money circulated freely. Lately, all of his old plans were proving unsound. There was no evidence against Lawnce other than the one coin, and the ranger was now riding ahead with a purposeful set to his jaw and an eye trained for danger.

Then there was Jesse Diaz. He rode alongside Maximo like a loyal *compañero.* His face was stained with blood from a wound inflicted by El Ojo. He had scouted Gainey's territory many times and come back with bullet holes through his shirtsleeves, yet he was never caught or killed. He knew how to shoot; he owned a fine brace of pistols. He knew how to ride; he always straddled a good horse, like the one that had carried him up the Rio Grande and back. The one that had worn the Lonesome J brand. The one he must have acquired some time earlier from Lawnce McCrary. The one he could have bought with double eagles with clipped wings.

Before the riders reached Gainey's fort, August dropped back and cut in between Jesse and Maximo. "Maybe it don't mean nothin'," he said, leaning toward Maximo and speaking just loud enough for him to hear, "but when we left town a while ago, I smelled horse lather before we ever started runnin'. It was Jesse's horse."

A slate gray had washed away the twinkle of morning stars when the rescuers saw Gainey's fort, half a mile away across the open flats. The Doubletree gunmen had left a trail of dust still hanging in the air. They were taking their stations behind the adobe breastworks on the roof. Lawnce raised his hand to stop the party. He slid from the saddle and skinned his Spencer on the way down.

"What are you doing?" August asked.

"Don Lawnce, we must ride quickly. Into the barn," Jesse suggested.

"Keep your britches on, boys. We'll charge directly. Just give me half a dozen shots to stir 'em up first. I believe in drawin' first blood."

"How do you expect to draw any from here?" August asked. He was pulling a stalk of straw out of his hatband. Chewing on it would calm him some.

Lawnce shaved some thorny twigs from a low mesquite limb with his butcher knife. "With ten pounds of Spencer fifty-two-caliber army model rifle. It'll shoot today and kill tomorrow." The rifleman slid his legs under the limb he had whittled for a gun rest and put the big piece in position. "It's your wife in the house, August. When them skunks on the roof duck their heads, take Cigarito's boys chargin' and get inside somehow. Me and Maximo and his boys will get to the barn and make it hot for 'em on that side."

Only Jesse protested. "*Jefe,*" he said to Maximo, "the barn is empty. Let us all begin our fight there. The sun will rise behind us."

Maximo ignored him.

The Spencer roared and a split second later a puff of shattered adobe sprayed near the top of Gainey's ranch house wall.

"A little shy," Lawnce said to himself, adjusting the sliding rear sight on his rifle.

The next shot hit a man peeking over the corner of the house. The heads ducked under for a second, then set up a barrage that fell well short of the rescuers. The Spencer fired again.

"Go, kid."

August gouged his mount, and the warriors followed with a chilling war whoop that made his horse lurch forward. Lawnce fired three more shots to keep the Double-

tree men down as August and his warriors rode in close
to the house. The adobe stronghold had no windows on
the outside walls, but it had loopholes and two rifles
began shooting from them. One of Cigarito's men
dropped from the saddle.

Jesse looked uneasy. He spurred his horse without orders and rode for Gainey's barn. Maximo followed some
distance behind, and then Lawnce mounted and came
with the rest of the Mexican rescuers.

"That's Jesse," One-eyed Butch said, squatting with four
men behind an overturned buckboard at the northeast
corner of the fort. "Shoot all about him and make it look
close."

When they began firing, Jesse put one pistol through
the loop of his reins and fired twelve slugs into the buckboard. Gainey and his men ran, as if flushed, along the
adobe wall and into the eastern gateway to the courtyard.
Jesse pulled his rifle and fired toward a man on the roof,
missing him, but not by much. He waved for Maximo,
Lawnce, and the others to follow him in through the
north doors of the barn.

Maximo didn't care to charge into the barn, but Lawnce
suspected nothing. He rode in before Maximo could warn
him. But no ambush waited inside as Maximo had feared.
Things were getting close, and he still didn't know for
sure who his enemies were as he galloped through the
open barn door and dismounted.

Jesse reloaded his pistols, and Lawnce removed a box
of tin tubes from his saddlebags and shoved it into the
front of his pants. The Spencer had killed two men on the
roof. The Mexican scout had missed seven men behind
the wagon. Maximo had all but figured his betrayer. A
fight was the finest test of a man's loyalty.

August and his men had reached the north wall of the
fortified house. His aim now was to get on the roof and

then drop down inside the courtyard to gain entry to the house and rescue Chepita. The Mescaleros were riding along the north and west sides of the fort as if they were bulletproof, keeping the Doubletree bunch confused and dispersed along the scaffold inside the courtyard.

Before dismounting, August had taken his coil of rope from his saddle horn. The Doubletree men shooting through the loopholes withdrew when Cigarito and his braves began firing in through them. August figured they would move to the roof. He wanted to get there before they did.

Some of Maximo's men were firing blindly through knotholes in the barn wall. Jesse went to the south barn door. He put his sombrero on his pistol barrel and held it out in the open air. Not a single shot pierced it. Waving his pistol for Maximo and Lawnce to follow, Jesse put his sombrero back on his head and stepped from the protection of the barn with both pistols ready. No bullets flew his way. The path seemed clear.

Lawnce started to follow Jesse into the open, to try the east wall of the courtyard, but Maximo held him back by the arm. The ranger knew Maximo feared nothing under the sun of Texas or Mexico, so he figured some other motive caused the bandit's caution.

Maximo ordered Jesse to come back into the barn. *"Necesito cartuchos,"* he said, indicating the empty chambers of his revolver.

Jesse frowned and returned to the barn to supply the cartridges. How could Maximo have run out of ammunition at such a time? He took his bandolier from his shoulder and handed it to Maximo.

Maximo instantly holstered his guns and probed the slot behind the buckle where Jesse kept his money. Two coins came out. The eagles had scratches across the wingtips. Maximo threw them down.

Jesse was baffled. Why had Maximo asked for cartridges but taken money instead? The desperado leader
removed the silver-studded sombrero from his head.
With the back of his hand, he slapped Jesse's smaller
brown sombrero away and put his own hat on Jesse's
head. "Maximo's sombrero looks good on you today," he
said above the sound of gunfire and war whoops. He gave
Jesse a sudden push through the south barn doors into
the open.

Within a second Gainey and his ambushers recognized
Maximo's headgear and rifled a dozen shots into the
wearer.

Lawnce watched Jesse's blood ooze into the trampled
sand outside the barn. A stray bullet glanced off a metal
wagon tire somewhere outside and flew singing into the
sky. "Ain't bullets got a lawnce-um sound out in this here
country?" he asked. He motioned toward the loft, and
Maximo nodded.

August was standing at the northwest corner of the fort,
shaking a loop into his lariat. A warrior stood beside him,
covering him while he prepared the rope. August saw that
the warrior was Blood, his hunting guide. In Spanish he
told Blood what he wanted to do. A big man on the corner
of the roof jumped up every few seconds to shoot down
on the attackers. August had his rope swinging the next
time the big man stood up and he settled a wide loop over
him from the blind side. Blood shot the big man as August
jerked the noose tight. The man fell back inside the
breastworks of the roof giving August a counterweight on
the other end his rope. He would have to climb quick before somebody cut the line.

Lawnce peeked through a knothole in the loft just in
time to see Gainey and his men duck inside the courtyard
and close the thick wooden gate behind them. Then he
saw the taut lariat around a fallen man's shoulders lead-

ing over the roof parapets and knew August or one of Cigarito's bucks was fixing to climb in. When a Doubletree gunman rushed across the roof with a knife to cut the rope, Lawnce used the butt of his ten-pound Spencer like a sledgehammer to splinter a piece of board on the barn wall. Then he aimed at the knife wielder, who died on the roof with a fifty-two caliber ball through him.

Maximo kicked a board down and used his lever-action rifle to drop the one remaining man from the roof. August climbed the rope with Blood boosting him from below and hauled himself over the parapets. Blood then tossed his rifle up. He was inside the walls now, waving to Lawnce and Maximo across the way in the barn loft. He heard a wheezing sound and realized it was coming from the big man he had roped around the shoulders. He put his rifle against the man's chest, but decided to spare the ammunition.

The guns went silent for a moment. Butch Gainey's voice was heard booming in the courtyard, ordering every man to the roof. He didn't know it had already been captured by the rescuers. Blood and some other Mescaleros had climbed the rope and were on top behind August.

"Fermin," Lawnce said, using his rifle butt to knock the loft ladder loose, "gettee *esta cosa allá* and get on the roof!" Fermin and three others ran toward the adobe wall and propped the ladder against it.

Maximo and Lawnce watched from the loft like a pair of generals viewing the battle from afar. As his eyes took in the scene, Lawnce happened to see a horse standing a quarter-mile off back toward Candelilla. Nelly sat in the saddle. He could make out her carpetbag hooked around the saddle horn. She was taking notes.

August knew Chepita's rescue depended on his own actions now. Gainey's men would charge up the narrow steps to the roof any second. When they found their roof occupied, they would turn into the house and put a gun to Chepita's head. He had to get to her first. He reloaded his rifle and checked the grip on his revolver in the holster. Glancing back at the Indians, he saw Blood taking the scalp of the big man he had roped. For a moment he thought of Professor Ryder.

The first of One-Eyed Butch's men reached the top of the steps as Fermin reached the top of the ladder. The shooting erupted again like fireworks, and young Fermin fell dead from the ladder with his pistol in his hand.

August jumped from the adobe roof onto the wooden beams over the gallery and dropped into the courtyard. The horses stood at the hitching rail between him and the Doubletree men. He leapt for the kitchen door of the ranch house, but it was barred on the inside. One of Gainey's men fired at him and August felt something like a hornet's sting across his left collarbone and another through his right thigh. He returned the fire with his rifle and scattered the Doubletree boys, sprawling one of them dead at the bottom of the adobe stairs.

One of the horses was hit by a wild shot, and Gainey was screaming like a treed panther for his men to kill Chepita, but most of them were trying to get on their horses. Gainey shot Dood Tatum through the neck in an attempt to get control of his gang, but his men continued to move toward the courtyard gate to the south.

August coiled himself, closed his eyes, and jumped through the dirty window beside the door, not knowing what stood on the inside. He landed on a wooden table, rolled among a handful of butcher knives, and dropped to the floor. He was in Cayetano's kitchen. He struggled to his feet, wondering why his right leg refused to work up to snuff. The house was unfamiliar to him, but he shuffled through the first bunk room and into the second.

There he found Chepita standing beside the fireplace holding a piece of cordwood like a club.

"Drop it!" August ordered.

One of the Doubletree boys had come through Gainey's bedroom holding a pistol.

"It's over," August said, aiming his rat pistol at the cowboy. The gunman threw his pistol on the floor. August spit something out of his mouth. It was the straw he had been chewing on. He had bitten the end of it clean off.

The Doubletree men had thrown the bar off the south gate of Gainey's courtyard and galloped for the river. The Mescaleros would catch them before they crossed. When Lawnce scaled the loft ladder leaning against the adobe parapets, he saw One-Eyed Butch chasing Top Dollar toward the gate. Maximo saw, too. He jumped from the ladder and ran around the outside of the courtyard wall to level his irons once and for all on El Ojo. Lawnce dodged into the house to look after August and his wife.

Fat Butch Gainey labored piteously through the gate in Top Dollar's dust, yelling after his men for a rescue that wouldn't come. He glanced to his left and found Maximo's glare. Any move would kill him quick.

"Aw, hell," Gainey said, raising his hands. "I'm licked. No need to shoot, Maximo."

Maximo grinned and chuckled in a devious tone. "There is much need to shoot, El Ojo. You will not leave your tracks without dying. It is time for Maximo's revenge."

Gainey lowered his hands slowly. On the way down, his right hand stopped to push his big hat back on his head. His single eye glared at Maximo, but without effect. "Damn you, Maximo. The whole Big Bend was mine before you came here. You and your boys have pestered me like a swarm of damnable mosquitoes. Just who the hell are you, anyway, and what's this revenge for? If you aim to shoot me, you ought to tell me that much."

"I was ten years old," Maximo said. "I was watching. Hiding in the woodpile with my baby sister in my arms. I almost had to choke her to keep her from crying. I was watching when my mother plucked your eye from your ugly head."

A sudden nightmare loomed in Butch Gainey's mind. A sickening conclave of guilt, fear, and rage twisted his senses.

Maximo's hand moved like a snake to the handle of his nickel-plated Colt.

Lawnce had the captured Doubletree cowboy at gunpoint and was supporting August on his shoulder when he stepped onto the gallery. He saw One-Eyed Butch standing beyond the gateway, facing left. Gainey never moved, but a bullet struck him high in the stomach and staggered him two steps back. He reached for his pearl-handled pistol but barely had the strength to pull it from the holster. He dropped the gun and fell face forward on top of it, limp like a sack of feed.

The ranger let August down on a bench beside the door and told him to guard the captured man. Chepita appeared in the doorway, realizing where the lone gunshot had come from. She reached for her rosary beads, but they were long since lost somewhere toward Candelilla. She knelt in the doorway and prayed silently for her brother.

"Maximo!" yelled the ranger before he stepped through the courtyard gate. There was going to be trouble, so he drew his Remington revolver before he stepped into the open. He peeked around the corner and saw the desperado letting his weapon settle back into the holster. He glanced at Gainey's corpulent body lying spread-eagled, his hands empty.

"What in thunder did you do that for? We had him hog-tied with the piggin' string on plum taut, Maximo. We damn near had the hangin' rope around his neck for murderin' Cayetano Pastor and kidnappin' your sister." Lawnce turned his back on Gainey's body and walked cautiously toward the desperado, his Remington in his hand, pointed downward.

"In half a day's time we could have had him in Presidio, locked so far back in the hoosegow they'd have had to shoot beans at him with a musket. And you shot him down in cold blood, Maximo. He didn't make nary a grab for his pistol. I told you when we was leavin' Candelilla to stay in the law. Now I've got to arrest you to stand trial for murderin' a one-eyed skunk. I hate to do it, Maximo, but that's what the Revised Statutes say. Now, *por favor*, drop them thumb-busters."

Maximo made no move for his buckle. "Don Lawnce," he said, "is it not possible that in your book of laws there is a page unwritten for Maximo de Guerra?"

The ranger didn't answer.

"Turn your eyes, Don Lawnce. Maximo will vanish and never again come north of the Rio Grande. There are no more cattle for Maximo to steal. No more demons for Maximo to kill. *Por favor*, Don Lawnce. Make one exception to your book of laws. Only one. It is best."

How could Maximo ask for such a thing? Forget about the laws of Texas? Yet as foreign as the idea seemed to Lawnce, as insulting as the suggestion was, he considered it. What was the harm? Who would know? He stared blankly beyond the desperado, across the rims of the Chinati Mountains and into the rays of the rising sun, hesitating in indecision.

Maximo's hand snatched at his pistol butt, and the surprised ranger feared he was beaten even with his Remington already in his hand. He could only hope to get off a wild shot as Maximo's bullet hit him. When the report came, the desperado was lost in a sudden swirl of dust and black powder smoke. Lawnce returned the shot with his eyes closed and his teeth clenched.

The ranger heard Chepita scream inside the courtyard, sounding almost as shrill as the ringing in his ears. He checked his body for wounds but felt none. How could the desperado have missed at that range? He looked up. The Remington had knocked Maximo onto his back. Lawnce turned around. The top of Gainey's head was blown off, and his pearl-handled pistol was in his hand. Only Maximo's aim had prevented Gainey from firing.

Chepita Dannenberg ran through the gate, saw her brother on the ground, and went to him. She put her hand under his head. "Maximo," she whispered.

"No. Maximo has taken his revenge. He is dead. I am Juan Ybarra . . . your brother." He smiled, all the hateful fight gone from his eyes, and died.

37

"**D**eseo," Gavino Carranza said, "I wish I were a sailor." He sopped his dirty cotton sleeve across his brow.

"How come you to wish a thing like that?" Lawnce asked.

"Because the grave of a sailor does not need digging. The sea swallows up the corpse when you just push it in, like that." He rolled the body of Doodlebug Tatum into a shallow trench. "Have you ever seen a ship to carry a shovel, Don Lawnce?"

"I ain't never seen a ship."

When Gavino's work was done, the mounds of a dozen fresh graves looked damp and dark against the bleached surface of the desert. Blank wooden crosses stood over the corpses of seven fugitives from the eastern states, lately employed by Butch Gainey and known only by aliases. Lawnce thought it a shame he couldn't collect the bounties those men surely carried on their heads. The surviving Doubletree outlaws had been taken to Presidio to stand trial.

The crosses over the graves of Butch Gainey and Jesse Diaz had their names and the date of their death scratched in the wood with a butcher knife. Neither had any known kin to notify.

In the opposite corner of Candelilla's hilltop cemetery, the resting places of Juan Ybarra, Cayetano Pastor, and Fermin Rodriguez were lined neatly with stones. Their grave markers were extravagantly carved from scraps of lumber. The one at the head of Juan Ybarra's grave bore intertwined vines around its border and was lettered in relief. The cypress planks had been bought to build a new water trough, but they served equally as well to mark the tombs of fallen heroes.

The Mescaleros had carried their own dead away.

Two wagons waited in the street outside McCrary Livery. The buckboard appropriated from the abandoned Doubletree Ranch carried the meager belongings of the newlywed couple. The harnesses held Cayetano's two mules. A saddle horse would trail behind on a lead rope.

The mail hack had a seat reserved for Nelly Blankenship and room in back for her carpetbag. Sawyer was ready to move, but Nelly was helping August and Chepita pack their things in the bed of the buckboard.

"Where will you go?" she asked them.

"Chepita owns a ranch down in Mexico. Been in her family for a long time. What's the name of them mountains, darlin'?"

"Sierra del Nido," Chepita said with a polite smile.

"It's stocked half full with longhorns of the Doubletree brand. That won't make up for all that's happened, but it will give us a start at a ranch." August had a crutch under his right arm and a sling on his left. The wound to his thigh involved only flesh. But his left collarbone had been shattered and would mend oddly, causing his shoulder to draw slightly inward. He would bear the effects of the Doubletree scrape for the rest of his life.

"I have wanted to ask you," Nelly said. "Where did you learn to carve so beautifully? I admired the rose vines you carved as a border around the letter you sent to Chepita by the river, and the grave marker you carved for her brother."

August look a little nervous. Nelly took it for modesty.

"I copied them designs off another carving I saw somewhere."

"Where?" the reporter asked.

August shrugged. "Can't say."

Lawnce threw another bag of oats into the bed of the wagon. "The damn rats will get this if y'all don't take it. Won't be nobody here to scare 'em off no more."

"Well," Nelly said. She extended her best wishes and excused herself as August helped his bride climb to the wagon seat.

"Señora Dannenberg," Lawnce said, "I want you to know that I'm gonna put a new rock on Maximo's . . . Juan's grave every time I ride past."

Chepita extended her hand toward the ranger. *"Gracias,"* she said.

August climbed in as Lawnce touched the forgiving hand. "What about you, Lawnce? What do you aim to do now that all the outlaws are run out of the territory?"

"Well, kid. Ol' Lawnce-um John McCrary is just too dad-gum lawnce-um without his horse. I reckon I'll ride back up in the Sangre de Cristo country to get Little Satan."

"How long do you figure on stayin' up there?"

"Aw, I don't know. I reckon . . . twenty-six days or so. Maybe catch up on some readin'." He winked.

August grinned. "Have you thought about askin' Miss Nelly to ride up there with you?"

Lawnce kicked the hub of the wagon wheel. "I've thought on that. In fact, I ain't thought on nothin' else since we put Chepita's brother in the ground. I want her to go with me. That would work dandy for me, but some other parties might not approve. I just don't know if it's proper. I might decide to ask her just the same, though. Can't make up my mind."

August was gathering the reins in his hand. "Well, you write us a letter and let us know what becomes of it."

"I promise I'll try it." He clamped August's hand in his own and noticed how big it had grown since the first day he had held the orphaned German boy. "Adios, Mr. Dannenberg."

August shook the reins, and the buckboard rolled toward the river.

"Esperan!" an unfamiliar voice shouted. August tightened the reins. It was Tristan. The voice was unfamiliar because he rarely used it. He approached the wagon with a dirty *morral* in his hands. *"Un regalo,"* he said, placing his wedding gift in the wagon bed and turning quickly away.

"Gracias," August said. He shrugged at Chepita and shook the reins again. They suspected a bag of pearapples or jerked meat or some other such offering from the simple tracker, and they didn't see the need to get down right away and look, since Tristan had already disappeared. They didn't hear the coins clinking in the *morral* over the rattle of the running gear as they headed for Mexico.

Sawyer sat on his mail hack and twitched his buggy whip impatiently while the escort of two cavalrymen sat in the shade of their horses on the ground.

Lawnce found Nelly inside the livery barn sliding hairpins through her straw-colored tresses.

"Nelly," he said, bundling her hand in his own, "the trouble's done around here. Why don't you stay on?" He knew already what her answer would be. She felt honor bound on two fronts—fulfilling her contract with *Fulton's* magazine and finding the Reverend Professor Ryder. Lawnce knew she wouldn't stay even if she wanted to.

They were as different as east and west, Nelly and Lawnce, in background and upbringing. But they were much alike when it came to principles. In fact, Lawnce suddenly realized they were too much alike in that way. Both of them would keep putting their ideals ahead of all other considerations, even their personal desires. If they both stayed at it that way, they would never find the time for each other. Somebody had to let up.

Lawnce decided right then that when she declined his invitation to stay in Candelilla, as he knew she would, he would tell her the truth about Reverend Ryder. That would put an end to her searching the continent, and the reverend would surely get over a small broken promise. It would do the old mountain man good to see her again, anyway. Lawnce would take her up there himself. Then it would be a simple matter for her to finish up the contract with the magazine and devote herself to being a wife. That's what he decided to do. Yes, sir, it was high time Lawnce McCrary did something for his own benefit.

"I'd like that, John," she said. "But I have my job to do with the magazine. I want to get to the telegraph office in Fort Stockton and send the rest of the story to Boston. My readers will want to know the truth about Juan Ybarra . . . and Butch Gainey. It's a tragic story, except for the part about August and Chepita.

"I wrote a story about you, too. Some time ago. Did you know that?"

Lawnce shook his head. "What all did you find to say?"

She stepped nearer. "I simply related the things I most admire about you. Your dedication to duty. Your honesty. Your ability to stick to your word."

Way down in his throat, Lawnce choked back the words he had planned. He shook his head, gathered his mustache whiskers, and spit into the dust. "Stick? Hell, I reckon I'll stick. I'll stick like glue boiled out of the devil's own hooves. I'll be damned if I ever *comprende* that job of yours with that blasted magazine, but I damn sure savvy that other stuff you're talkin' about. Things like stickin' by what you know is right whatever it costs you. If you don't remember nothin' else about John McCrary, Nelly, I want you to remember that."

Nelly halfway scoffed. "Don't get sentimental, John. You talk as if we shall never see one another again. When I fulfill my obligation with the magazine and find the professor, I'll come to see you again."

"Hope you'll still want to."

"Come closer," she said.

"I ain't warshed lately."

"I don't care what you smell like."

Nelly lavished a repertoire of kisses on Lawnce calculated to make him indefinitely desirous of her company. Her other charms had already worked that effect on him, but her parting kisses didn't hurt any. His senses felt dulled when he finally walked with her back out into daylight.

She said good-bye and climbed up to the spring seat of the mail hack. Sawyer cracked the whip over the backs of his mules, and Nelly trundled away toward Presidio.

Lonesome John McCrary waved and watched her disappear, then stood in the street alone. He put his hands in his pockets and shuffled back into his livery barn. He settled onto a stack of burlap bags and took stock of what he had. He had never felt so destitute, and there had been times when he owned little more than a breechcloth.

His best prospect for marriage had just rolled off to search for another man.

His boy was grown and heading for Old Mexico.

The cantina hadn't had a drop of whiskey since the wedding, and Jigger had sure raised the price of his wares beyond the reach of a ranger who hadn't seen a payday in almost a year.

That was another thing he didn't have, come to think

of it—his status as a vested lawman. He had realized some months back that the Ranger Service had let his name slip from the rosters.

The best horse he had ever straddled was getting fat in northern New Mexico Territory.

He didn't even have his book of laws, which perhaps should not have seemed incredibly disheartening, seeing as how Lawnce couldn't read the thing anyway. But that old book was a symbol of everything honorable to him, and he missed feeling the weight of it when he slung his saddlebags over the rump of a horse.

He had his livery barn and his job as a mule buyer for the overland mail. But the railroads were building farther west across Texas every day. They would soon replace the overland stagecoach service which, of course, would no longer need mules or mule buyers. Unneeded things tended to get brushed away from the landscape, and Lawnce felt unneeded.

He still had Candelilla. It was his town and a good town. It wasn't pretty, but it was peaceful, overall. Lawnce had almost made something of Candelilla. He had brought in the mule trade, attracted merchants, and pacified the Indians. If he had had another decade, maybe he could have gotten the silver and copper wagons of the Chihuahua Trail to come through and provide more work for more people. But the old wagon trade with Chihuahua would peter out after the railroads reached Mexico. Without the mules and without the wagon trade, Candelilla would die. She was doomed. Soon there would be nothing left of her but crumbling walls and a graveyard.

The unwritten treaty of Candelilla represented Lawnce's greatest accomplishment, but in it he felt the deepest sense of failure. It was not one-tenth the treaty he had envisioned. He had wanted to tame every Indian on the Texas frontier and preserve for them something of the way of life he had once lived with them. In this he had utterly failed, despite his meager successes in Candelilla.

"How?" he thought. How did a fool who could neither read nor write expect to draft a treaty between Texas and her Indians? He had trimmed his sights high, but his shot had fallen far short of the mark.

It became suddenly apparent to Lawnce that everything he had worth salvaging was up near the Colorado line with the good Reverend Ryder. It galled him to think he would have to leave Texas to find his dignity. The Texas his daddy had fought for at San Jacinto. The Texas whose dirt he had slept on and bled into. Lawnce had worked hard for Texas. But she rewarded only those who worked hard for themselves.

The Revised Statutes of Texas. Lawnce had used them as a foundation on which to build his life. They were printed bold on real paper and bound solid in leather. They were absolute. They allowed for no vagaries. Lawnce had always followed them without question, and they had never left him regretful.

But now Maximo was dead because Lawnce had refused to bend his precious statutes. Maximo had only carried out a sentence any honest jury would have handed down, for if ever a man deserved killing it was Butch Gainey. If Lawnce had even gone so far as to dog-ear a page for Maximo's sake, he might be riding to Mexico as Juan Ybarra right now. The foundation of his life had been shaken, and Lawnce had begun to wonder for the first time if justice was a sure enough thing to be set down on the pages of a book, if honesty was so steadfast that a promise, once made, should never be broken.

"I should have told her," he said aloud to himself. He had hated keeping secrets from Nelly. Secrets had killed Cayetano Pastor and Jesse Diaz. The secrets Chepita had held from August had almost gotten him killed. "I should have told her," he repeated as he sat alone in the barn.

Lawnce suddenly felt an overwhelming need to talk to Thomas Payton Ryder, to be with him on the cool slopes of Ute Peak. Maybe the reverend professor had gotten used to the idea of seeing Nelly by now. Maybe he even wanted to see her. Maybe he would bring Lawnce and Nelly together now, instead of holding them apart.

That cinched it. He would ride up to the Sangre de Cristos. Get his horse and his law book. Learn his letters. Persuade Ryder to see Nelly. Then he would prove a thing or two to Texas.

Just then Lawnce's ever-rolling eyeballs spotted a rat sniffing its way across a rafter. He eased his hand over to the butt of the old Remington and pulled it out of the holster. He latched the hammer back and took a slow, sure aim. But instead of splattering the pest across half of the barn ceiling, he started laughing and put his gun away.

"Hell, y'all damn roodents can have the place!"

He wrapped everything he might need in a tarp and made a pack of it on the back of old Quatro. Then he let his remuda of five horses walk out of the corral. There wasn't anybody he wanted to say adios to. He mounted a piebald Indian pony and herded his stock slowly upstream.

About the Author

Mike Blakely lives with his wife and son on a 1,500-acre ranch in the Hill Country of Central Texas. The author of numerous articles on the history of the American Frontier, he also writes a monthly column on Texas folklore.

≝ HarperPaperbacks *By Mail*

To complete your Zane Grey collection, check off the titles you're missing and order today!

❏ Arizona Ames (0-06-100171-6).............................. $3.99
❏ The Arizona Clan (0-06-100457-X)....................... $3.99
❏ Betty Zane (0-06-100523-1)................................. $3.99
❏ Black Mesa (0-06-100291-7)................................. $3.99
❏ Blue Feather and Other Stories (0-06-100581-9)....... $3.99
❏ The Border Legion (0-06-100083-3)...................... $3.95
❏ Boulder Dam (0-06-100111-2)............................... $3.99
❏ The Call of the Canyon (0-06-100342-5).............. $3.99
❏ Captives of the Desert (0-06-100292-5)............... $3.99
❏ Code of the West (0-06-1001173-2)...................... $3.99
❏ The Deer Stalker (0-06-100147-3)........................ $3.99
❏ Desert Gold (0-06-100454-5)................................ $3.99
❏ The Drift Fence (0-06-100455-3).......................... $3.99
❏ The Dude Ranger (0-06-100055-8)................... $3.99
❏ Fighting Caravans (0-06-100456-1).............. $3.99
❏ Forlorn River (0-06-100391-3)........................ $3.99
❏ The Fugitive Trail (0-06-100442-1)................. $3.99
❏ The Hash Knife Outfit (0-06-100452-9)........... $3.99
❏ The Heritage of the Desert (0-06-100451-0)....... $3.99
❏ Knights of the Range (0-06-100436-7)................. $3.99
❏ The Last Trail (0-06-100583-5)............................ $3.99
❏ The Light of Western Stars (0-06-100339-5)........ $3.99
❏ The Lone Star Ranger (0-06-100450-2)................. $3.99
❏ The Lost Wagon Train (0-06-100064-7)............... $3.99
❏ Majesty's Rancho (0-06-100341-7)....................... $3.99
❏ The Maverick Queen (0-06-100392-1)................. $3.99
❏ The Mysterious Rider (0-06-100132-5)................. $3.99
❏ Raiders of Spanish Peaks (0-06-100393-X)......... $3.99
❏ The Ranger and Other Stories (0-06-100587-8)... $3.99
❏ The Reef Girl (0-06-100498-7)............................ $3.99
❏ Riders of the Purple Sage (0-06-100469-3).......... $3.99

- ❏ Robbers' Roost (0-06-100280-1)............................. $3.99
- ❏ Shadow on the Trail (0-06-100443-X)................... $3.99
- ❏ The Shepherd of Guadaloupe (0-06-100500-2)..... $3.99
- ❏ The Spirit of the Border (0-06-100293-3)............... $3.99
- ❏ Stairs of Sand (0-06-100468-5).............................. $3.99
- ❏ Stranger From the Tonto (0-06-100174-0)............ $3.99
- ❏ Sunset Pass (0-06-100084-1)................................. $3.99
- ❏ Tappan's Burro (0-06-100588-6)............................ $3.99
- ❏ 30,000 on the Hoof (0-06-100085-X)..................... $3.99
- ❏ Thunder Mountain (0-06-100216-X)....................... $3.99
- ❏ The Thundering Herd (0-06-100217-8)................... $3.99
- ❏ The Trail Driver (0-06-100154-6)............................ $3.99
- ❏ Twin Sombreros (0-06-100101-5)............................ $3.99
- ❏ Under the Tonto Rim (0-06-100294-1)................... $3.99
- ❏ The Vanishing American (0-06-100295-X)............. $3.99
- ❏ Wanderer of the Wasteland (0-06-100092-2)........ $3.99
- ❏ West of the Pecos (0-06-100467-7)....................... $3.99
- ❏ Wilderness Trek (0-06-100260-7)........................... $3.99
- ❏ Wild Horse Mesa (0-06-100338-7)......................... $3.99
- ❏ Wildfire (0-06-100081-7)....................................... $3.99
- ❏ Wyoming (0-06-100340-9)..................................... $3.99